The Woman He Loved

A novel by Solange DewBerry

Published in the United States by Spilled Ink Press
Newington, CT

Copyright © 2022 Tina Kane
The Woman He Loved
First Edition, April 2022

ISBN: 978-1-7342276-5-9

Dedicated to the memory of the writers, cast and crew of Singin' in the Rain, the best movie ever made. And to all the Jeromes and Isabels out in the world: those who dreamt of fame, those who found it, and those who walked away.

Appreciations

Special thanks as always to Liane of Edit Expert for keeping all those commas in control and preventing me for defaulting to British spellings (I blame all the hours I spent reading Agatha Christie, Ngaio Marsh, and Dorothy L. Sayers); to Jasper McCord Means for the wonderful cover art; and special, heartfelt thanks to the Connecticut Writers Circle for their patient advice, unflinching criticism, laughter, tears, and plans to save the world from itself. You were the ones who made me believe I could publish, and so I have.

Hard to believe a youngster like yourself is interested in an old relic like me.

Well, sir, you're what my grandma calls a curiosity, that's for sure. I mean, I first heard of you in a crossword puzzle clue. She had to help me solve it.

Jerome smoothed his mustache to hide his grimace. *Mind if I ask what was the clue?*

Sure. I mean, I don't remember all of it, but it was something like, 'A second banana from silents to talkies.'

Jerome smiled, making sure to show all his teeth. *So that's what I've become, eh? A sprightly old chap they trot out from time to time. Well, sure, let's get this interview over with. What paper did you say you were with?*

Hollywood High Times. Hey. Hey, mister, Wait. What about our interview? Watch where you're going, that there's a busy road. Hey, mister!

Chapter One

Ten Years Ago

"Not interesting enough," Clark Conrad muttered as he left his faculty advisor's office. "Boring!"

He shoved his way through the double wooden doors. They slammed against the cinderblock walls, not hard enough to shatter the reinforced glass. What was it with institutions of higher learning that they embedded chicken wire in the windows fifty years ago? Or was it a hundred? What did it matter? Clark's advisor, the venerable Dr. Pompolsos, just rejected his master's thesis proposal—wouldn't even send it to the Film Studies faculty review board. He said it had been done a thousand times before. There was nothing new to be said about the transition of film from

1

silent to talkies. Worse, he wouldn't give Clark the time to defend it, didn't look at his detailed proposal—nothing. Clark sighed for the umpteenth time about the dismissal of his original thesis advisor. They'd been working on his proposal for months before the man ran off with the chairman's wife a week ago. Fired. And now he was stuck with this guy who hated everything and everyone. "Impress me," he'd said to Clark the first time they met. Yeah, right. The guy was infamous for not being impressed by anyone but himself.

Clark shouldered his way through clumps of students and ran down the steps into the late afternoon sunshine. What the hell was he supposed to do now? His professor gave him twenty-four hours to come up with a new proposal and submit a ten-page outline, or he'd have to start over next semester. A delay like that was going to blow his savings, not to mention damage his chances for the doctoral program he'd had his eyes on.

Clark tore his fingers through his hair. It had taken him six months to work up the rejected proposal. How could he come up with a replacement in one day—he glanced at his watch—twenty-three and a half hours? He would have moaned out loud, but he was already getting stares. He hurried across campus to the film library, managing to trip on half the sidewalk slabs. He needed to immerse himself in period films for inspiration. Maybe watching one or two or ten would do the trick. Maybe pigs would fly. No, wait. That was flying monkeys. Or was it? Had there ever been a film where pigs grew wings?

Hours later, Clark emerged, bleary-eyed, into the dark of late evening, no closer to his goal. Every film he wanted to check out was unavailable, so he'd settled for watching a long reel of snippets from the film career of a second-string actor, Jerome Percy. He'd been stuck in one of the small viewing rooms, having to load the projector himself. Why the man hadn't become a bigger star was a mystery. He'd had plenty of talent and on-screen

2

charisma, not to mention staying power. The guy had appeared in silent films, playing everything from European aristocracy to a slum rat, then graduated to the talkies, gradually taking roles in romantic and screwball comedies, westerns, and serious dramas. In his last appearance, probably in his late seventies, he'd played a retired, debonair mob boss on TV. The guy had screen cred, no doubt about it, but only one starring role, in his entire career.

Clark couldn't recall a specific thing about the man's life, other than something tragic, or more likely scandalous, had derailed him. Once upon a time, he'd been an up-and-coming actor. But there was no thesis material there. Hell, Clark could probably spend the rest of his life searching for enough source material for an idea. It was unlikely there was anyone left in Hollywood who'd known the man, let alone cared.

Hands in pockets, Clark wandered off-campus. Before he knew it, he'd entered a sketchy neighborhood that bordered the university. As this was probably his last day as a grad student, he figured he might as well drown his sorrows in a pity party of one. Next week he'd be flipping burgers to pay his rent and slurping ramen for dinner.

For a moment, he worried he was being followed. Warily, he looked over his shoulder but saw only shadows. Actually, only one. And it looked like it was wearing a fedora at a jaunty angle. Given Clark had just seen clips of a murder mystery, and he knew he'd always been impressionable, it made sense his imagination was running rampant. Maybe he should write screenplays since he'd clearly never become a professor of film history.

Clark pulled open the door of the first bar he came to.

"What'll you have?" the bartender asked as he dried a beer glass behind the battered wooden bar. The guy could have been featured in any one of a hundred old westerns, except he wore a yellowed wifebeater instead of a leather vest and bolo tie, and the apron tied around his bulging middle looked like it hadn't been washed in a decade.

3

"Whisky, neat," Clark said as he bellied up to the bar the same way film cowboys once did. "Bottom shelf. I don't have a lot of cash."

The man grunted and reached behind himself, grabbing a bottle with an off-label. He poured a shot and slid it across the bar. "Tough day?"

Clark didn't say a word as he tossed it back, gritting his teeth at the burn. "Another," he rasped as he slammed the glass down. He treated it the same way. "One more," he demanded as if he were Tom Mix.

The bartender's eyebrows rose. He poured again but held back passing Clark the drink. "Just a word, sonny. It may not be good booze, but you treat this one like that, I'll be calling the authorities to haul your ass outta here. No way your day's been so bad that ending up in the slammer's gonna improve it any."

"Duly noted," Clark said as he slid his last twenty across the scarred wooden bar top.

The bartender rang up the sale and pushed the shot glass and a bowl of pretzels toward him. "Take this and your sorrows to a table in the back. I don't want anyone comin' in here to turn right around if they get a look at you."

Clark blinked once. The booze had hit his gut, then made a U-turn straight for his brain. "Yeah, yeah, sure." He balanced the bowl on his laptop case, took his drink, and made his way to the back. He set his things down, then carefully opened the computer. There was no wi-fi to speak of, but that didn't matter. He was going to start writing crap in the hopes something would come of it. It wouldn't be of any use. He'd never send anything to his professor at this rate.

Ten minutes later, he stared morosely at the blank screen when he heard someone clear their throat. "I haven't touched my third drink yet," he said without looking up.

"I, er, am not the proprietor of this fine establishment," came a wry, elegant baritone. "Though I have played one in several films. Not my best work, but then beggars cannot always be choosers. And yes, sonny, that's a direct quote from more than one movie classic."

Clark looked up. He blinked and blinked again, then rubbed his eyes. "I beg your pardon?" he said to the dapper man standing at his table. The guy wore a double-breasted suit, crisp white shirt, and wide, muted tie. It was impossible to see his face in the shadow of his wide hat brim. "I don't want to be rude, but I've got a deadline, and I'm running out of—"

"I don't mind if I do," the man said as he removed his hat and tossed it on the table before sliding into the booth.

In the blueish light of the laptop screen, the man looked like a cross between David Niven, Douglas Fairbanks, and Paul Muni. And someone else, someone at the tip of Clark's tongue. "Uh—"

"Young man, I believe I may be able to assist you."

Clark looked at his untouched drink, at his unexpected companion, and back at the bored bartender. He blinked again. Something in his cranium was struggling to make sense of this, but the pieces weren't connecting. "Sorry, what? Who are you?"

The man looked chagrinned. "I was hoping you'd recognize me. Alas, time has not been kind to my reputation." He closed his eyes and sighed. "I suppose I shouldn't be disappointed."

Clark wanted nothing so much as to send his third drink the way of his first two. His hand reached for it, but he recoiled as the other man covered it in his well-manicured hand. Funny though, despite the dim light, it seemed as if he could see right through those long fingers to the amber liquid in the scratched shot glass. His gaze met his companion's, and suddenly synapsis began firing in unexpected corners of his brain. "What the hell—" he mouthed.

The other man smiled under his clipped, grey mustache. "Ah," he said with delight. "You do recognize me. You are perhaps the only one who might, this fine evening."

Clark reared against the cracked Naugahyde bench. There was no chance of falling out of the booth as his legs had turned to jelly. "You are *not* Jerome Percy. He's—I mean you're—"

"Technically—" The man looked upward before he continued in his Transatlantic-affected vowels, just like William Powell used to talk. "Yes, and no. I wasn't born Jerome Percy, though I played him most of my life. But I suspect you know that or will shortly. And that *is* the name on my gravestone." He gave an enigmatic smile. "The rules were looser back then. A man, or a woman for that matter, after living some ignoble scene in their life, could wake up one morning and decide to become someone other than who they were. In fact, lots of folks did that any number of times. Didn't like how life was treating you? Walk away and become someone else. Hell, you could change your stride and start to strut. If that new persona wasn't working out so well, try again. Move somewhere. Take on a new name, new career, new locale, look or personality—" He released the glass and folded his ghostly hands on the table. "You get the idea."

"I couldn't—" Clark swallowed against a suddenly dry throat. "It's not that easy these days. A man can't just become someone new. There's things that track him. Social security numbers. Bank accounts. Fingerprints. Social media—"

Jerome's shade—if that's what he really was—leaned forward with a conspiratorial wink. "Those are all piddling details, m'boy. If a man really wants to change, then nothing and no one can stop him. It's not your name, location, or the cut of your clothes. It's attitude. Confidence mostly. Or acting confident despite how you feel."

He nodded at the drink on the table. "Better take a sip of that, sonny. It looks like you saw a ghost." He laughed until he wiped his eyes with a snowy, translucent handkerchief. "Sorry about the joke. It's been a while since I spoke to anyone other than my own kind. There's not many of us out there I care to associate with.

Most have, you know, crossed over, so one must amuse oneself as one can."

"But why—" Clark grabbed the whisky and swallowed half of it, choking at the burn. "This must be really crappy booze if I'm hallucinating."

There was a harrumph from the bartender, and Clark darted his gaze there and back at the man sitting across from him. Jerome Freaking Percy. He blinked again, suddenly aware that his thick glasses were slipping down his nose. He pushed them up and prayed the cracked nosepiece would hold.

The ghost put his fingers to his lips. "Keep it down. I made sure the barkeep could see me, but he doesn't like customers who don't buy drinks. And he's not stupid, actually a rather an open-minded chap. I've found mixologists tend to be."

"Should I buy you a drink?" Clark asked.

"A fine idea, given my money's no good around here." Jerome grinned, his teeth shining. "That also was a line from some movie or another. Or perhaps more than one."

Clark laughed in spite of himself. "Whisky okay? Rotgut grade."

Jerome sighed and flicked at his hat. "I was a martini man back in the day, but I know your pockets won't support my habit. And since I won't be able to drink it anyway—you might as well get another of whatever you're having. It's going to be a long night. You and I have a lot of work to do." He nodded Clark out of the booth. "You get along there, so the barkeep will stop sending dirty looks our way. Maybe order a hamburger instead. You're going to need your strength."

Clark made it to his feet and walked a few unsteady steps before he turned to look back to make sure he wasn't asleep at the table. But no. His side of the booth was empty, and the well-dressed ghost was still sitting there, making a shooing motion. "I can't believe—"

7

Jerome shook his head. "I suppose you haven't had nearly enough to drink, or perhaps too much. We've but met, so I can't really tell." He squinted. "No. You're not the drinking type. Better get a glass of milk with that burger. Tell the barkeep I'll drink the rest of yours."

"I mean, I can't believe I'm actually talking to you."

Jerome splayed his hand at his chest and adopted a humble look. "I've forgotten what the adulation of my fans was like. You flatter me."

"That's not what I meant—oh, never mind. I need food. And maybe after I've eaten, I'll discover you are a figment of my imagination."

Jerome bowed his head. "And now you wound me, boy, but never mind. Now hurry—your deadline's fast approaching. I have a lot to tell you. In return, you are going to do something for me."

"What—"

"I'm going to give you a proposal that's going to knock your advisor's socks off. It's going to be so good, you're going to go straight on to a Ph.D. Why, universities across the land—across the world—will be clamoring to hire you."

"That's imposs—"

"Entirely possible. And that's not my ego, which is considerable, talking. Now git. Because once we're done, I'm going to tell you exactly what the cost is going to be."

"I don't have any money," Clark said.

"As if I have use for it," Jerome scoffed. "I can't pick up a dime in your world. No, what you're going to do is use that sizable brain of yours to solve me a mystery."

Clark rubbed his face once more. "Right. No problem."

Jerome nodded. "Exactly. And as a rather colorful character I once played said, 'time's a wastin' so git a move on.'"

Clark looked at his watch. "Sixteen hours to write a ten-page proposal, citing verifiable references." He looked at the ghost with a smile. "I don't think my quoting a ghost I met in a dive bar is going to be acceptable proof."

Jerome's mouth firmed. "I may not have had a fancy education, but I've been hanging around that dag-blamed library for decades, and I've learned a thing or two. I know you're the right guy as you're the one who sprung me from that joint. Never have been able to follow anyone else out of there, and not for lack of trying.

"You'll have your citations. Bonafide hard evidence. Don't you know I left all my worldly goods to that university? The danged curator mislabeled the boxes when he checked them in, and I've been waiting for the right person to set that error straight. I alone know the call letters. And I'm giving you the keys to my kingdom to set matters aright. Restore my good name, and maybe a little posthumous fame.

"Boy, between you and me, I'll have you write a dissertation so amazing it'll be flying off the bookshelves. I'm thinking you can write a boring one full of footnotes for the professors and a popular version for public consumption at the same time." He leveled a look at Clark that had him shivering. "And then, once you've achieved your fame and fortune via *my* life story, you're going to solve that mystery for me or die trying. Capiche?"

Clark looked at Jerome, at his computer, and back at his companion when he threw up his hands. "Why the hell not? I've got nothing left to lose."

Burger consumed, they talked for hours. Clark asked questions, and Jerome replied, often at length, meandering from memory to memory before collecting himself and returning to the salient points. Sometime after midnight, they left the bar and walked to campus, talking all the way. Those few they passed gave them a wide berth, making Clark laugh. To passersby, it must have seemed he was having a spirited conversation with himself.

Back at the campus library, open all night, Clark typed in the call numbers for the first box of materials. It was a treasure trove,

9

more than enough to satisfy the most demanding thesis advisor. He photocopied several critical pieces of information, including a photograph of Jerome in a tuxedo. The image was torn, but there was a bit of skirt visible at the bottom, indicating Jerome hadn't been the only one in the picture. Jerome wouldn't say who it was or why it was torn. In fact, he became downright grim at the question. Running out of time, Clark then began to write.

They remained in the carrel for hours. Jerome whispered in his ear as Clark's fingers flew over the keyboard, correcting a fact here, adding a tidbit there, until twelve pages of outline were completed.

At a quarter to four the next afternoon, not having slept, eaten, or washed, barely daring to breathe, Clark was done.

He pushed away from the desk, suddenly aware of his aching back, numb legs, and growling belly. He glanced up to see the faint outline of Jerome, leaning against a book stack, casually smoking a cigarette. Seeing Clark's interest, he tossed it away. Clark cringed until he realized the ghostly embers couldn't start a fire.

"Done?" Jerome asked.

Clark nodded, too tired to speak.

"Run through it for me. Damned fingers can't make one of those infernal machines work. Don't think I didn't try. I was the proverbial ghost in the machine back when I first came to the library along with my stuff. Never been so scared in my life. Worse than when I used to shoot cliffhangers, and that time they had me doing stunts, and I was stuck hanging off a genuine cliff for hours. A thunderstorm came up. Couldn't wait to get off the darned thing. Almost put me off westerns for good."

Clark let out a bark of a laugh, startling himself. "Yeah, sure. I've got a few minutes to go."

Jerome drifted over. With the light coming in the windows, it was hard to see if his legs truly moved. Clark was so tired, if the box of Jerome's life work wasn't right there beside him, he would have sworn he was dreaming.

"Down," Jerome ordered, and Clark slowly scrolled through his proposal. When he was done, the ghost nodded. "Never was much of a student. Can't tell if the commas are in the right places, but it looks damned good to me."

Clark saved his document once more and downloaded a copy to a thumb drive for safety. "Okay. This is as good as it's gonna get," he said. With a few keystrokes, he opened an email and attached the file. "Here goes nothin'," he said and pressed the send button on the screen.

"Good job, m'boy." Jerome raised his hand to pat Clark on the back but pulled back at the last minute, his features wreathed in a flash of distress that quickly evaporated. "Well done. And time for you to go home. God willing, I can follow you out of here again. When d'you think you'll hear back from the rotter?"

"My professor? An hour or more. He needs to read it once he's done with office hours." Clark checked to make sure the email was sent before he powered down the laptop and shoved it in his bag.

Jerome stood and stretched, then tsked at Clark. "I suggest you eat and get some sleep. I know the ruffian look is in for your set, but to my eyes, it's an offense to good grooming, and I imagine you reek by now. I'll have you dressing like a gentleman before too long." He turned his hat in his hands before settling it on his head and flicked it to a jaunty angle. "I'll even have you sporting a snappy chapeau before we're done."

Clark laughed, then looked around to see if any prying eyes were staring. There was no one around. "Not on my income."

"Well then, I'll acquaint you with a good secondhand store, an iron, and scissors to trim that—that—" he gestured to his own chin, "—growth, since obviously razors are too costly for your budget."

With a shaking hand, Clark smoothed his beard. "Yeah. I guess I've gotten kind of scruffy. But if this proposal isn't accepted, I'll be flipping burgers next week. Don't think I'll be able to afford even cheap booze for a while."

They walked out into the sunshine. Jerome all but disappeared as he sighed in pleasure. "I never want to see the inside of another library. If it's all the same to you, I'll follow you home. No need to talk at the moment. Awkward and all that." He stretched and turned his face to the sun. "Oh, but it's good to be out of that building after all these years."

Twenty minutes later, they stepped into the gloomy foyer of Clark's apartment building. Jerome seemed to solidify as they rode up the rickety elevator to the seventh floor. Clark got off and waved Jerome ahead of him. "Home, sweet home." He unlocked his door, and they made their way into the efficiency. "Not much to it, not until that fame and fortune you promised kick in," Clark said.

He made his way to the tiny bathroom. "If you don't mind—"

Jerome waved him away as he lit another cigarette and settled into the lone chair in the room.

"Watch out, there's a spring poking out of that thing," Clark warned.

Jerome laughed and appeared to make himself comfortable. "One of the advantages of having a body like mine. No pain. No blood, sweat, or tears, for that matter. So, have at it, boy. Just set up that contraption. I'll monitor it for you and let you know when Professor Dumbass responds."

Ten minutes later, Clark emerged cleaner but exhausted, wearing only his shorts. "Anything?"

Jerome shook his head. "Maybe I ought to head over there and haunt him into checking—" His face was a study of worry. "Ahem, not sure I can get there on my own. Not sure how this whole business works, seeing as I was stuck in that library for so long." He gave a sad laugh. "It's not like they handed me an instruction book when I took this form."

Clark shook his head with a yawn. "He's a busy man. I've got the volume on high, so I'll hear it ping when I have incoming mail." He swept several DVD cases off the sheets before he crawled onto the mattress in the corner of the messy room. He yawned again. "One last question."

"Shoot," Jerome said as he made himself comfortable in the threadbare chair.

"Why are you still here and not— not wherever it is dead movie stars go when they—?"

Jerome chuckled. "Wondered when you'd get around to asking. You read a good many press releases about my wicked life. What makes you think heaven would have me?"

"Oh, well, figures," Clark said and closed his eyes. He was asleep within minutes.

Moments later, the computer dinged. Clark dragged himself out of bed. Aware of Jerome hovering behind him, he clicked open the email.

> *Not sure how you did it, Conrad. Brilliant coup.*
> *Congratulations. Call the office for an appointment.*

Jerome sat back in the ruined chair and took a long drag off another ghostly cigarette. "What did I tell you, m'boy? Yes, this is the start of a beautiful relationship."

Mama, don't worry. I'll be fine. I'll be gone and back before you know it.

Lilly, I can't bear the thought of you going off on your own. California! It's so far away. Your father is furious. He doesn't want you shaming the family. And to think you want to be in moving pictures? I never— Those actors out there want nothing more than to ruin a beautiful, innocent girl like you...

Mama, it's a lark. What are the chances I'll ever get an audition? I'll be back before you know it. I'll even change my name, so no one knows me. And I'll write home every week. I'll even send you any money I earn so you can keep it safe for me, okay?

Chapter Two, Nine Years and Ten Months later

Leigh

There were days when nothing went as planned. For Leigh Mason, Memorial Day was one of them.

It started the moment she'd woken to find Gram hovering over her bed, staring. Before Leigh was fully awake, Gram demanded to know if she really intended to see 'that man' again.

"Of course, I am. Gram, we're dating. Exclusively. He's the first guy I've been seeing in forever. I want to see if something can come of this."

Gram scowled, then sighed. "I suppose every woman has to suffer one foolish love affair in her life. I'd hoped you'd be spared." She left the room shaking her head.

Flustered, Leigh had lain in bed, wanting to bite her fingernails the way she had as a child, but she'd splurged on a manicure the day before and didn't want to ruin it. Rocky was very particular about how he looked. And by default, how she did, too.

When she went down for breakfast, she discovered the milk was sour when it curdled in her coffee, and then she'd had to make another cup, only to drink it black. There was only enough jam to cover half a piece of toast. When she tried to catch up on work emails as she waited for her date to pick her up, she discovered she'd left her power cord at work. Her battery ran out, and she lost the long email she was writing. Gram was still sulking in her room and wouldn't speak to Leigh. To top it off, Rocky was late and wouldn't answer her calls. That made her want to bite her nails even more.

Rocky Samuels wasn't her usual type, but he had been charming when they'd first met, flirtatious and complimentary. Then he'd swept her off her feet—an achievement she never thought would happen. He'd given every impression was he was smitten. Even her mother had noticed—had in fact introduced them the first time Rocky came for a business meeting to talk about a merger with the conglomerate for which he worked.

"You'll like him," Miranda had gushed. "He's very nice. Dresses well and is so handsome." Her mother bit her lip. "He's a bit older than you, but that shouldn't matter." When Leigh demurred, her mother laughed. "Okay, call him seasoned—that touch of grey at the temples makes him very distinguished. And he's so well-spoken. I'm sure you'll like him."

"Fine," Leigh had replied. It had been months since she'd dated, and she was bored and ready to go out again, if only to prove her mother wrong. But when they met, Rocky seemed to be the whole package: solicitous, handsome, generous, and urbane. He took her to fancy restaurants, the symphony, and a sunset river cruise. He'd done all the right things, complimented her appearance and intellect, and sent her flowers. Her lonely heart wanted him to be the one, and she found herself daydreaming about the future. In the first two months they were dating, they talked about everything, except he never mentioned his family until the time they'd run into his sister at an art show opening.

Berry Samuels Conrad was the opposite of her brother: warm, down to earth, and full of laughter and good cheer. Despite Rocky's uncomfortable relationship with his sister, the two women hit it off. They met for lunch a few times, and as far as Leigh was concerned, Berry was one of the best things about dating Rocky. But as the friends grew closer, the more distant Rocky became, rarely calling to talk other than to make plans for the following weekend. But he always called, and Leigh began to grow suspicious. A man like him could have his pick of gorgeous women, and she was not beautiful, slender, or even that sociable. They hadn't slept together often, and when they did, it wasn't followed by cuddling or even warmth. He always had an excuse to push her out the door before she was ready to go. Then he was busy, and she was reticent. Their few encounters were more awkward than satisfying.

She knew she was smart and successful. She also happened to be the daughter of a woman looking to sell her highly rated software company. Before long, her suspicions became doubts about Rocky's motives despite him having told her that wasn't the reason he wanted to see her. Then he'd kiss her, and she'd try to forget about her worries and feel guilty when the shadow of distrust crossed her mind. Rocky was different from other men she'd known. She wanted to love him. It would be so easy if she did. But there was always doubt.

The more in love Leigh wanted to be with Rocky, the more disdainful her grandmother became. It had been several months, and things were not improving.

Several days before Memorial Day, Berry called to see if she and Rocky would come to her cookout. Surprised, Leigh'd sputtered a response. When she called him to ask, Rocky had sighed. "Yeah, I suppose we could." He'd hung up shortly after that.

They hadn't spoken again until he arrived that calamitous morning.

He arrived an hour late, then sat in his black sportscar and blared his horn rather than ringing the doorbell or calling her. When she came out holding a bowl of fruit salad, he lifted his glasses to stare at her.

"Babe, you're not planning on wearing that, are you?"

Leigh looked down at her comfortable sundress and flat sandals. "What's wrong with it?"

"I don't know. It makes you look dumpy. At least put on some high heels to make your gorgeous legs look better."

"Really?" she asked.

He gave her his best smile. "Come on, sugar. You're making me feel like a dick for saying anything. It's not like I ask you for a lot. I want you to look your best."

A thousand thoughts crossed her mind. "Fine." Leigh cursed under her breath when she went inside to change her shoes. When she opened the car door, one of her fingernails broke down to the quick.

"Why were you so late? I tried calling a half dozen times," she asked after a mile of tense silence. She picked up her phone. "I'm telling Berry we're on our way."

He took it from her and set it on the console. "She'll figure it out when we get there."

"Rocky, what's with you today? You're not acting like yourself." She sniffed, but with the open convertible, she couldn't be sure she smelled alcohol on him. Surely Rocky wouldn't be so foolish as to come to her drunk. He sped down the street, but then he always drove fast.

He turned to her, a grimace on his face. "You know, you could put out for me a little more often. Don't you think it's time for a little more payback?"

Leigh's body went still. She took a deep breath, considering her words. "Really? That's how you ask? Maybe you ought to bring me home."

"No. Forget I said anything." His jaw ticked, and his fingers tapped erratically on the steering wheel for the remaining miles, when they weren't gripping it until his knuckles turned white.

When they arrived at Berry's restored Victorian, Rocky swerved the car to the curb and stopped it with a neck jolting jerk. He turned to her, his face growing crimson. "You know, what I really want is your ball-busting mother's god-damned company, but it doesn't look like I'm gonna get that any more than I'm gonna get in your pants today."

"This is hardly the time or place—" Leigh sputtered when she saw Berry walk up to the car.

"Forget it," he said through clenched teeth, then cursed under his breath as he ripped the keys from the dash.

"Leigh, Rocky, I'd given up on you," Berry said.

He got out of the car and slammed the door, walked across the sidewalk and past his sister without a nod. "The beer better be cold."

"Hello to you too," Berry said before turning to Leigh.

She got out of the low-slung car. It was a challenge to do so gracefully on any given day and even more difficult when she was wearing high-heeled sandals. If he thought she was going to 'put out' as a reward for his being a jerk, he had another think coming—or not.

Berry took the bowl from Leigh and stood aside. "What's wrong with him this time, or do I not want to know?" she asked under her breath.

Leigh shrugged as she straightened her skirt and closed the door. "His latest business deal isn't going well."

Berry rolled her eyes. "Figures. When I worked with him, he was always in a piss poor mood when things didn't go his way. That's been his MO all his life," she said with a laugh. They walked slowly to the Conrad backyard, where the cookout was in full swing. Leigh's narrow heels sunk into the grass as she walked.

"Any guesses what it is this time?" Berry asked. "Oops. I probably shouldn't say that to you since you're dating him."

Leigh stopped and slipped off her shoes. "It must be the deal with my mother's company. She didn't like his offer. She didn't share the details in case it would hurt our relationship. I'm trying to stay out of it."

"That can't be easy," Berry said as they made their way to the house. "But forget that. I hope you'll have a good time today. You know everyone except Moe's cousin, Clark. He arrived a week ago from California. He's going to teach at the University. He doesn't know many people yet. Nice guy."

Leigh glanced around to see Rocky sprawled in a lawn chair between his elderly parents, a beer bottle tipped back and his Adams apple working overtime. Her glance flowed over the small crowd to a tall, bearded man standing with Berry's husband Moe, and his brothers. The man looked like his Conrad cousins, perhaps a little more refined with his neatly trimmed brown beard, his glasses, and khakis.

She took her time to apprise Clark. The man looked intelligent and interesting, and his smile caught her attention. There was an unexpected plink in her heart when they caught each other's eyes. *Hmmm. What would Gram have to say about that?* She wondered. "I'll be happy to meet him," she told Berry. *Rocky be damned.*

Clark

He pushed his glasses up his nose as he watched the woman walk across the grass. She'd immediately taken off her high-heeled sandals, then shook back her hair. As he watched, she and Berry leaned in closer to talk, and her eyes landed on him. She was of average height, with brown curls, bright, dark eyes, and had a lush figure she held with confidence. But she'd clearly come with another man, though they seemed to be on the outs. She smiled when their gazes met across the yard, and he experienced a particular kind of zing he hadn't felt in a long while.

Clark glanced at her as often as he could without feeling like a creep as she went around and greeted the other guests. The man she'd come with sucked down beer after beer and sat in his little enclave, looking more ornery as the minutes passed.

Berry introduced them moments later. "Leigh Mason, this is Clark Conrad, Moe's cousin. Clark, this is my dear friend Leigh. And don't be put off by the fact she's dating my brother." Berry leaned in closer. "She can do better than him, so if you can convince her to ditch him and date you instead, I'd be eternally grateful."

Leigh had laughed and blushed, and he took her hand. "I'm not the type to steal another man's woman, but I'm willing to make an exception in your case."

Leigh grinned. "I can rescue myself if it comes to that, but if things go haywire, I'll keep your offer in mind."

From the corner of his eye, Clark saw Rocky glower at Leigh, and positively sneer at him when he got up for another beer.

Berry left to check on her children, leaving Clark and Leigh together.

"Berry says you're a professor?" she asked.

He pushed his glasses up his nose once more out of habit. "Yes. Film history. I love all film, but my concentration was in early American film and the transition to talkies."

Leigh nodded at him. "I love old movies. I haven't seen many, but I enjoy them."

"Preservation is one of my passions. The University has one of the best libraries in the states but it needs restoration. I'm hoping to get a grant to oversee that."

She grinned. "My work is in computers. We've done some restoration for companies in California. We might be able to work together. Not that I do much coding anymore." She glanced

20

nervously over her shoulder at Rocky, who scowled at his newly empty beer bottle, then glared at Leigh.

"What do you do?" he asked.

She gave a tentative smile. "I'm the chief systems architect at MirandaTech. I won't bore you with the details, but essentially I have to stay on top of the latest trends in technology to ensure my company stays up to date."

"That sounds challenging."

She nodded and turned again to the man sitting across the yard. "It is, she replied. "I like it. Lots of travel. No two days are alike."

He rolled out his best small talk, trying to win a smile from her. Every few minutes, she'd glance over his shoulder at Rocky, then turned her attention back to Clark with a smile—but it seemed forced until they moved on to other topics where she grew animated, and then he made her laugh. But that was enough. With a certainty unlike any he'd ever felt, Clark knew Leigh Mason was exactly the kind of woman he wanted: smart, attractive, lush, and seemingly confident about everything, other than the man she'd arrived with. It was the oddest, most engrossing sensation. It wasn't that he wanted to save her—he believed she was more than capable of dealing with any man by herself. It was that he felt he could spend a lifetime looking at her, laughing with her, sharing his secrets. And oh, what secrets they were. Jerome would probably like Leigh—at least Clark wanted to believe he would. When one shared one's apartment with a ghost, it was the best one could hope for. A cold shiver ran down his back. He only hoped Jerome was back at the apartment and not lurking about, ready to gossip later that night. But he was getting ahead of himself.

Clark's phone rang—it appeared to be a call from his parents, but when he tried to answer, the phone went dead. She looked at him curiously. "Old technology," he said with an embarrassed laugh. "I need another paycheck or two and time to do some research, before I get a new one."

"You're not a Luddite, are you?" she asked.

21

"No. Just a film professor who hasn't been paid yet. Rent and food before technology, I'm afraid. I promised myself a new phone as soon as my checkbook stops crying."

They ate together, still talking as other guests came and went. The sun was dropping into the western sky, and they'd just gotten dessert when Rocky staggered over and snapped his fingers at Leigh.

"You. Woman. Time to go."

Beside him, her body became rigid in an instant.

"Rocky, I just got my dessert. And you haven't met Clark yet…"

"The last thing you need is dessert," Rocky said with a sneer. "Come on. I'm taking you home, and then we're going to—"

Leigh's mouth dropped open.

Clark got to his feet. "I think the lady said she isn't ready to leave. I wouldn't let her get in a car with you, the way you've been drinking." He looked down at Leigh. "I can take you home later if you'd like."

"You're not doing anything with my woman," Rocky slurred with his hands fisted on his hips.

She put a gentle hand on Clark's arm. "Thank you, but I've got this." Leigh stood and turned to the other man. "Rocky, I don't want to go, and you're not in any condition to drive. Give me your keys. I'll call you a cab and drop your car off later."

"I'm not letting you drive my car," he said, barely keeping to his feet. "You wouldn't even fit behind the wheel."

Leigh's cheeks grew red. Clark could see her jaw clench. "That's enough about my weight."

"No, it's not. Do you have any idea how much crap I've had to put up with from my friends for dating a fatty? And you don't put out enough to make up for it."

She swallowed hard and firmed her shoulders. "Rocky, that's no one's business—"

22

"Oh yeah? You think this guy'll go out with you unless you suck his—?"

Clark moved into Rocky's space. "You're out of line, buddy," Clark said, bumping chests, when their host, Moe, rushed over and slung an arm around Rocky's neck, turning him away from the center of the party.

Leigh crossed her arms. "You're drunk and making a fool of yourself."

Rocky shook off Moe's arm and stood, wobbling in the fading sunlight. "I don't give a fuck. You've been leading me on, and I've put up with it because I'm supposed to get a big payday because of it. Hell, I'd marry you if I had to, to get that merger signed off. But you're nothing but a cold, fat, controlling bitch. Learned it from your mother."

Clark saw the shock in Leigh's eyes. He stepped closer, but she held up a hand, and he stopped, waiting to see what she'd do.

"Rocky, you're not just drunk, you're also a jerk. If you think I'm going to sleep with you tonight, you're delusional." She stepped closer. "And if you think I'm going to help you take over my mother's company, the one she built with her own two hands, and fought for, for years, then you're out of your effing mind. You can go to hell."

"Hey, that's cold," Rocky sputtered. "You go to hell, you fat cow."

Leigh's eyes narrowed as she faced the livid man. "That's enough. You'd better leave. I can't believe I cared about you. Do not contact me again. Ever. Don't call tomorrow, saying you're sorry because you said things when you were drunk that you didn't mean. I think the only time you tell the truth is when you've had too much to drink, and that's way too often. I may be overweight, but I'm done being stupid. So, you can take your car, your fancy apartment, your expensive suits and go eff yourself. And if you think you still have a chance to get your smarmy hands on

MirandaTech, you better think again. And as for sleeping with a goddess like me, only in your dreams."

Rocky threw out his chest. "Yeah? Well, I've fucked my share of women since I started seeing you. I've had a hard time getting it up with a dumpy broad. Why the hell do you think I was late? Because I was getting a manicure?" He laughed harshly. "More like a blow job so I could tolerate being with you."

Even the crickets went silent. In a flash, her arm struck out and smacked Rocky so hard he stumbled.

"Hey, what the hell's that for? What's wrong with you, bitch? Think you could do better'n me?"

"I should have listened to my Gram from the start. You're nothing but a sorry, sleazy excuse of a man. If you think you're the best the world has to offer, then I'm swearing off men. All men." She whirled and walked to the house as the stunned silence continued. Clark wanted to applaud, but the whispers started with twelve sets of stony eyes lasered at Rocky.

"Oh yeah? Well, we'll see about that, you bitch. I know people in this town. I have influence. You'll be begging me to take you back. Just wait. You'll see." When she didn't respond, Rocky looked around and found himself surrounded by angry stares. "Fine. Fine. I'm leaving. And don't expect to see me again." He stumbled as he tried to dig his keys from his pocket. "Thinks she's gonna best me? Like anyone would listen to an ugly broad like that. Thinks she's so great…"

Moe stopped him. "I want your keys."

"Like you care if I wreck my car," Rocky shouted as he twisted away. "You only wish you could afford a fine piece of machinery like that. You—you blue-collar hack."

Clark moved quickly and held the man's arms behind his back.

"You can crash it on your own time," Moe replied as he patted Rocky down. "I won't be responsible for your wrecking anyone else's. Or killing someone. Your sister would never forgive me." He found the keys, removed the house key and stuffed it in

24

Rocky's shorts, then tossed the rest to one of his brothers. "Go home, you jackass. Sleep it off. I'll be sure to call and yell at you tomorrow for using that foul language in front of the kids."

"Fuck you. Fuck all of you," Rocky shouted.

"Son, language," his mother said from behind him.

"And fuck you too, Mom, and that bitch in the house. Screw her. Screw all of you losers," Rocky hollered as he shook free from Clark's hold and fell to his knees. "One of you fuckers call me a goddamned cab."

Leaning on the balcony of a Hollywood mansion, Jerome nudged his friend in the ribs. *Hey, Mack, who's that hot little number by the door?*

Her? She's fresh off the train. Says she wants to be in pictures. Ain't she somethin'? You ain't the only one who's noticed her, Jer. Can't remember her name. Don't matter. You know the studio heads'll change it on her anyway. But she won't look at you. Not as long as that wedding ring's on your finger. She told Sidney off when he tried to pick her up yesterday.

This old thing? It's coming off in a few days once my papers are set. I'll be free as a bird this time next week.

Not sure that cutie will still be available then.

Chapter Three, Four Months Later

Berry

Hi. It's your narrator speaking to you, Berry Conrad. I also go by Solange DewBerry, the pen name I use for my romance novels. I'll pop up every now and then as I tell you this story. I promise to try to keep these interruptions short. I know it's awkward, but I need to explain some things, and this is the best way I know how.

Here's the thing. I'm not only a writer, but a bit of an amateur matchmaker—I won't go into my history or tout my success here, but so you know, I've had plenty with Moe's four brothers, and I also have to tell you there's been something, er, extra about every one of those romances. I'll get to that in a moment.

When Moe and I first met Clark, I knew I had the perfect woman for him—my brother's girlfriend, Leigh Mason. Complicated story there. Let me say my brother and I are not close. Our mutual animosity started years ago, but it bloomed anew this past spring when Rocky was dating Leigh. I know he was horrible—used their relationship to get leverage in a hostile takeover attempt and never really cared about her. She gave him the benefit of the doubt as long as she could, but being the strong woman she is, she let him have it when she broke up with him. I know she felt horrible that she was taken in by him, but like many psychopaths, Rocky can turn on the charm when he wants something. Anyway, Leigh and I are friends, and I kind of felt I owed her something. Because of my brother.

You see, to my horrified embarrassment, Rocky was even worse after the breakup. From what I heard, his badmouthing her to their common acquaintances was the least of it. She never said a word to anyone to defend herself or retaliate against him but kept her silent dignity. I think she came out of it okay, but she's been overly cautious around men since. I don't think she'd gone out with anyone for some time, which is a shame because she's smart, beautiful, and pretty darned funny when she wants to be. Not that I blame her, but Leigh won't talk to me about this, given Rocky is my brother, so I'll leave it there for now.

Because she's a friend, and a family member hurt her so badly, and because Clark was the perfect antidote to my jerk of a brother, I felt maybe it would be a good thing to re-introduce them. And I can't resist the temptation to get two good people together.

Anyway, before you read any further, I want to fill in a few blanks. Clark wrote his dissertation about that actor, Jeffrey Perkins or something like that. A publisher got a hold of it and asked Clark to write it as a biography for the general public. Clark did and got some great notoriety from it. But he's an academic first and foremost, so he needs to continue his research and publish again. The subject of his new story is the mystery of what happened to Jeffrey—no, Jerry's lover. It's been unsolved for about a hundred years. The reason Clark came to the east coast was to follow up on some leads, and start a film studies program at the local university. He's on a tenure track, so being able to publish is more important to him than ever.

This then is his story. And Leigh's. I'll do my best to fade into the background unless I simply can't help myself. But I promise I'll be brief, okay? And this is all completely true, except for the parts I had to make up because I wasn't there.

Clark

He rolled his shoulders and then sat back and scrolled to the top of his newly typed document and began to read.

It would seem the only happy endings Hollywood produces are in the movies.

Example: the venerable actor and one-time Hollywood playboy extraordinaire, Jerome Percy, ~~the subject of my doctoral dissertation,~~ romanced countless women in his long life but never found happiness.

He married five times, buried one wife, and divorced the other four. He fathered one child, a boy, whom he gave to the child's maternal grandparents after his wife's death, fearing the boy had been fathered by his wife's lover. He later admitted to friends he considered himself unfit to raise a child but always regretted it.

Percy died alone, the last of his kind, in a city that had forgotten ~~him~~ its roots.

The one verifiably true love of his life, silent-film actress Isabel Standish, disappeared without a trace. Rumors were rampant that she'd been murdered by Percy in ~~the proverbial~~ a jealous rage, though the man was never inclined to physical violence.

Although the whispers have grown softer with the passage of time, the rumors have not died despite the fact he spent the rest of his life alternatively mourning, searching for, and trying to forget ~~her~~ Isabel. The scandal kept him from ~~achieving~~ the stardom he deserved. Multiple critics then and now agree he would have achieved greater fame had Isabel not allegedly boarded that east-bound locomotive at 9:17 AM on July 19th, 1921, never to be seen again.

For over 100 years, moviegoers, and now film historians, wondered what happened to the young, vibrant Isabel. By all accounts, she was a beauty: impish, photogenic, and clever—she was poised to give Mary Pickford a run for her money. Where did she go and why, and more importantly, what would have happened to her, to Hollywood and the film industry, and to Jerome Percy, had she stayed?

All anyone knew was that Isabel vanished without a trace, and Jerome— well, Jerome was thought to be the reason if not the actual perpetrator.

In the weeks and months following her disappearance, there was no hint or sighting of Isabel. No one traveling across the country came forward with reports of seeing the Hollywood sensation. Of course, part of Isabel's talent was her chameleon-like ability to appear differently in every film, and yet remain her inimitable self. It was whispered that if she wanted to remain hidden, no one would ever find her.

~~To the best of our knowledge, no word was heard from Isabel Standish ever again.~~ In the following years, Jerome went on to marry his second, third, fourth, and last wife, not to mention taking a multitude of lovers (male and female according to rumors) in between, ~~racking up the scandals~~ and provided juicy fodder for fan magazines. The studios wouldn't release him given his popularity but also didn't dare feature him for fear of bringing the wrath of the film morality boards upon them.

He died in 1980, alone, his fortune depleted as the bulk of his funds were tied to the reward he'd created for whoever discovered Isabel's fate. At the time of his death, there were rumors the remaining funds were bequeathed to a home for unwed mothers, once again sparking rumors that the radiant Isabel had left Hollywood to bear Jerome's love child and died in childbirth, her baby along with her.

The reward remains locked in a trust until such time as someone can prove what happened to the woman he loved.

Until this day, no one knew what caused Isabel to discard a promising career. If she lived, why didn't she come forward in later years? If she had fallen onto hard times and needed the money, all she had to do was go to her local police department and declare herself. What we know is that Jerome himself never intimated to his friends or acquaintances what had transpired on that fateful July morning, and with his death, we were likely never to know. Until now.

What was it about Isabel Standish that left Jerome Percy heartbroken for the remaining 55 years of his life, and if rumors are true, in the decades of afterlife to follow? Following clues found among his personal papers, as well as using modern forensics, the answer to this famous mystery has now been solved...

Clark stared at what he'd written. "'Write from your heart,' they say. Well, my heart's full of dribbling, moronic melodrama."

Jerome quietly surged into the room and peered over Clark's shoulder. In the years since they'd met, he'd gained meager control over his physical environment and was able to scroll to the top of the page and read down. "Ahem," he commented quietly. "Not quite what I had in mind."

Clark groaned as he pushed the laptop across his desk and took a sip of tepid coffee before he glared at the screen. It was impossible to write anything with any authority when he didn't know the ending or if he'd ever solve the mystery. And his last typed words were the worst sort of melodrama.

"I need to approach this systematically. And you promised to leave me alone, so I could work this afternoon." He glanced over his shoulder. "So, get out of here, old man."

Clark opened a blank document and set his hands on the keyboard without looking back. Over the years of their acquaintance, Clark learned that words were not always effective in getting Jerome to do as asked. Ignoring the spirit was far more effective on the ghost's obstinate ego. Clark thought a moment and then began a list of to-dos.

31

1. See if I can get a DNA test from Jerome's purported son.

"Why do you need to do that?" Jerome asked.

Clark kept typing.

2. See if there is enough DNA left on the hairbrush from Jerome's effects to do a DNA test on it to confirm parentage.

"They can do that?" Jerome asked.

3. Revisit theories of what happened to Isabel and refute them one by one.
    a. Review the police report.
    b. Reexamine the PI reports in Jerry's effects.
     i.   Are all of them accounted for? Any gaps?
    c. Ask for modern-day detective's opinion of both?
    d. Suspects and Theories:
 i.   Mary Pickford: discounted as the two never met and weren't true rivals.
ii.   Verify Jerome's story about what happened during the last confrontation at his home.
    1. What he said. What Isabel said, according to Jerry.

"I've already told you everything," the ghost said peevishly.

"We need to go over everything again," Clark said, not breaking stride. "I can't ignore the fact you might be holding back on me, deliberately or something I haven't pried out of you yet."

"I haven't held back," the ghost said, sounding offended.

Clark looked at him over the rim of his glasses, his brow creased. "Come on, Jer. There's got to be something—maybe it was embarrassing or humiliating so you've blocked it out."

Jerome stuck is nose in the air. "My life is an open book. You should know. You wrote it."

Clark shook his head and returned his focus to his computer screen. "If we're going to solve this, we can't afford to overlook anything.

```
2. What Blanche LaFleur said. And figure out
how to verify any of it.
```

"That— that woman," Jerome sputtered. "She was a pain in my ass— er, side. Never trusted her. Never. A liar and a very bad actress."

"And yet you married her," Clark said under his breath.

```
3. Check police reports on BL's various alibis
and her own history.
4. Look for anecdotal stories about her
ambitions.
5. Check to see if anyone ever accused her of
doing Isabel in.
```

"Oh, well—" Jerome stopped talking. "Do you really think something horrible happened to my Izzy? I mean, I always assumed she went on with her life. And Blanche was a chatterbox. If she'd done something, there's no way she could have kept it a secret. A drunk and chinwagger if ever there was one."

Clark shrugged and focused on his work.

```
iii.    Check Jerry's diaries about his
   relationship with Isabel and if she really set
   him free from the relationship while she was
   on location.
```

"I hate when you read that drivel." Jerome floated away. "It's humiliating. It was never meant for any eyes other than my own. My writing was atrocious."

Clark shrugged. "We've been over this before. If this is going to be taken seriously and for my sake, accepted for peer review, I need to be able to cite documentation. Since I can't officially interview you and have it be credible, I have to go to the original sources."

Jerome harrumphed and muttered under his breath. Clark forged on.

1. How many times did they break up and resume their relationship before the last time?

"It was only the once," Jerome said, sounding miserable. "She was it for me."

2. Ask him how he felt about that even though that can't be used directly, I may be able to substantiate it in other ways.
3. Reverify Jerry's alibi: what did he say vs. what the studio said.
4. Review his cooperation with the police at the time.
5. Review his continued search for Isabel: PI reports and how much of his fortune went to pay them. When did the search end? Make a chart of all known payments. Will bank statements be available after all this time?
    iv.   Former boyfriends or lovers of Isabel? Were any interviewed? Inconsistencies or clues?

"There were none. At least no important ones." Jerome cleared his throat. "I was, er, her first, ah, lover."

    v.   Her other leading man: 'Latin Lover' Juan Antonio Ferriera. Did they have an affair, or was he devoted to his pregnant, jealous wife as the papers said at the time. What happened to them?
    vi.   What about her roommate, Juliet Jones? What happened to her later in life? Motive? Jealousy?
        1.   She had Isabel's car. What happened to it?

     2.   What about the apartment they shared?
Did she find another roommate, or did she
move?
     3.   Did they rent or own the furnishings?
What was common at that time?

"Juliet was a fine woman. Very beautiful. She had no reason
to do Isabel in. You know she changed her name. Married a studio
exec and had a bunch of kids. We exchanged Christmas cards until
my death."

vii.   Reexamine alibi of her last costar.
     4.   Revisit the studio's biography of
Isabel. Any missing clues?
       a. Check other bios they put out about
       their other stars? Any inconsistencies or
       clues for similar fabrications?
     5.   Check train schedules. Did they run
on time? Any engine breakdowns, and if so,
where?
     6.   Were there alternatives for her to get
home if she didn't travel by train the whole
time?
     7.   Did anyone ever check into the affairs
of Jerry's other wives or their papers for
clues? Did one or more of them discover
something and hide it from him?

"What? They'd never—" Jerome sputtered.

Clark gave him a skeptical eye. "Really, Jer? Weren't they the
least bit jealous that you spent your married life searching for
another woman? And the money…"

"Well, I suppose if you put it that way—"

a. What about financials? Was Isabel in
trouble with money?

"Izzy was very careful about money. She used to send it home
to her mother. Not sure why. Said her old man was loaded. Maybe

he was stingy. Remember, that's why we came to this god-forsaken town in the first place."

Clark turned. "Do you recall the address on the envelope? Names?"

Jerome shook his head. "She wired the money. And I didn't snoop in her things. We didn't spend much time at her place—roommate and all. When we were together, it was at restaurants, or clubs, parties—" His eyes drifted off to look at nothing. "—my place."

    b. What happened to the money she had?
  8.   Follow Pinnacle Studio's history,
founding, key players, financial history.
        a.   Did Isabel have any enemies
    there?

"Enemies? Everyone loved Izzy. Everyone—"

Clark turned to look at Jerome once more, effectively silencing him.

        b.   Was it true the studio head was
        sleeping with multiple stars and
        paying blackmail to keep it out of the
        news? Is that why they never invested
        in sound equipment? What about his
        divorce settlement? Did he have it in
        for Isabel, or did his ex-wife?
        c.   Did he have Pinnacle's publicity
        department put out all the rumors
        about Isabel's grisly end? What about
        the other rumors? Did they profit from
        them?

Jerome gasped. "What? Why, that's preposterous."

Clark kept typing.

9. How much money did Jerome put in the reward for information about Isabel? Is the reward still extant?

"Damned if I know," Jerome mused. "I spent a pretty penny on those private investigators. If they were taking me for a ride—" He did his best impression of stomping around the room. "I have no idea what happened to the money. I was locked in that library for decades — couldn't read the papers other than what someone left open on a table. I suppose the money's still there, waiting." He looked at Clark. "You planning on collecting it?"

Clark looked up. "I hadn't thought about it. I suppose so. I have no idea how much is left if anything. You know how untended money can be pilfered. But I have student loans to pay. The royalties from your biography didn't cover everything. And I still want to get a new phone."

"If you crack this mystery, the money's yours, m'boy. Can't quibble with you on that."

Clark laughed. "Not sure anyone will believe me when I say you want them to pay me."

10. Review what critics were saying at the time about Isabel's chances for stardom. Rumors were that they were magic together on screen. Did the critics and the public really think so, or is it all a lot of hooey stirred up by the studio?

    a. His divorce wasn't an impediment (Mary Pickford and Douglas Fairbanks paved the way for that), but would the public have accepted her, an ingénue in the role of homewrecker?

11. Find out if there are any copies left of Jerome's scenes in his ill-fated final starring role, the one where they recast and reshot it after Isabel went missing. Blanche

```
LaFleur was in that. See if any versions of
the final film remain.
   12.   What am I missing?
```

Clark sat back and stretched his arms over his head.

"Oh, there's plenty more I can tell you. Bent an elbow or two with those critics," Jerome said.

Clark scrolled to the top of his list and reread it. "I've got to cite everything I write," he mused aloud. "Your papers are all available, and the material I collected while I was still in California. It was all scanned and cataloged. But how the hell do I cite what you tell me if there's no supporting material? I can't exactly write a scholarly paper and quote a spirit, even if it's THE spirit in the center of this or stage left. I can't tell them it's all from my gut. I'd be laughed out of the profession if I even hinted at it. And then, if anyone ever bought another one of my books, I'd have to go and find another ghost to talk to." He sighed. "If only Isabel was still around. Or if she were a ghost who'd talk to me..."

Jerome was unusually quiet as he floated up near the ceiling. "Tell me about it, m'boy. If she were a ghost, I wouldn't need you to find her for me."

"She'd be really old now, were she still alive. Like the oldest person on the planet."

"I mean, if— or when she, er, departed this earth. I can't imagine she'd have lingered. I'd have known. I would have known," Jerome chided.

Clark rested his chin on his fist, feeling defeated. "Maybe I should write popular crime stories instead. It might pay better. My reputation be damned." He looked around his small apartment, hoping a bottle of bourbon would suddenly appear. But there was none and no one to go get it. "That, and the fact that now I need to go and solve the damned mystery."

"You promised," Jerome reminded him. "Condition of my helping you in the first place."

Clark sighed. "I know. And I'll keep at it." He looked at his watch. "Crap. I need to get moving. I have to be at the university auditorium in an hour."

Leigh

As she walked out of her bedroom, she glanced down at her jeans and thick wool sweater. They weren't stylish, but it was a cold October night, and she'd be out in the wind. It didn't matter what she dressed like. She wasn't planning on meeting anyone, just having a night out for herself to see a classic, old movie.

She stopped at her grandmother's suite and rapped her knuckles on the carved oak. "Gram, I'm heading out. Don't wait up," she called through the door. "And I have an early morning, so I won't see you until tomorrow night."

"Come in for a moment, darling," her grandmother called in her wavering voice.

Leigh pressed the door open and peeked inside. She peered across the small sitting room into her grandmother's bedroom to see the grand dame sitting up in bed. The lights were dim, but her grandmother appeared to be holding a letter. She saw Leigh and smiled.

"Have a splendid time, my Lei-Lei," her thin voice curlicued through the rooms on the second floor of the majestic house they shared. "Wear the Indigo cashmere scarf I bought you online. Goodness, but that was an effort to learn how to use the computer. It's cold out there. And for goodness sakes, put on some makeup. You never know when you're going to meet Mister Right."

"Really, Gram? Don't you think I'm a bit old to fall for that?"

The old woman nodded emphatically. "Yes, really, my girl. And don't roll your eyes at me. It's terribly unbecoming. There's never an excuse for not looking your best. And it's high time you met someone new. You need to put that horrible man and his shenanigans behind you. I'm still angry that he led you on the way

39

he did and made you feel so badly about yourself. Why, in the past few months, you've become absolutely cynical. And a recluse."

"Gram, don't start. I'm still kicking myself for letting him fool me for as long as he did. I thought I was a better judge of character. It's made me want to give up on the whole idea of finding someone."

"Lei-Lei, the time for bitterness has come and gone. It wasn't your fault. You're not the first woman to be fooled by a stinking, rotten, handsome scoundrel, and you won't be the last. You've been done wrong, as the old song says. But no need to let it spoil the rest of your life. Now, go, make up your face. Start by putting a smile on it."

"Really, Gram. No need for makeup. I'm simply going out for a few hours by myself."

The old woman laughed gaily. "You know I'm right, my darling. Just a swipe of eyeliner. A hint of color in your cheeks, that's all you need. Your lips are a beautiful, natural pink."

"Okay, fine," Leigh huffed, then her shoulders softened. "What would I do without you?" she said with a laugh and blew her grandmother a kiss.

The old woman pretended to catch it and held it to her cheek before sending one back. "Have a splendid time. And don't forget that scarf."

"I love you too," Leigh said as she backed out of the room and into the hall.

Once out of sight, Leigh did roll her eyes as she dutifully made a quick trip to her bathroom to apply the suggested makeup and only then wrapped the soft scarf around her neck. She made her way to the detached garage—a converted carriage house—for her car. It was all part of the estate on which she lived, seven sprawling park-like acres on the outskirts of the city. It had once been farm country but was now surrounded by housing developments and strip malls.

Leigh headed across town to the local university. There'd been notices advertising a new film series that featured silent and early talking films. She was indulging in a rare night off, so wanted to go treat herself, despite the nippy early October air.

Once on campus, she found a parking spot and hurried to the theater through the blowing leaves that crunched underfoot. Somewhere in the distance came the unmistakable scent of fresh popcorn.

Following a couple with linked arms and a few lone students, Leigh made her way into the lobby. Her glasses fogged up at the sudden warmth, and she took them off with one hand as she unwound her scarf with the other.

"Hello!" The warm tones of a baritone came from one side, and she turned as she slipped her glasses on. Her mouth dropped open in surprise.

"Oh, hi," she said. "You're—uh—"

"Clark Conrad." He smiled and held out his hand. She took it without thinking. "If I'm not mistaken, we met at my cousin's last summer. Moe and Berry?"

She remembered him but hadn't made the connection to the film series. Clark resembled Berry's husband, Moe, with his height, breadth, and light brown hair. But he was dressed in professorial tweed with a crooked bow tie. A grey cashmere scarf was draped around his neck and shoulders. His black, horn-rimmed glasses sparkled in the light and echoed the dark tone of his closely cropped beard. His eyes were a warm brown through his lenses and crinkled up at the edges. She'd been intrigued when they first met, finding the tall, dark professor more than a little handsome and quite charming. Especially compared to Rocky. The thought of him still set her teeth on edge.

She smiled back, albeit cautiously. "Yes, of course. I remember. Leigh Mason. How are you?"

Leigh had enjoyed talking to Clark. It was a refreshing change from Rocky, who'd talked about his latest professional conquest, or money, or what he was going to buy with his next bonus check, and Clark had seemed interested in her as well.

Clark looked around, clearly nonplussed at the number of people in the lobby and more coming in every moment. "Good. Good," he said with a nervous laugh. He pushed his glasses up his nose, a curious gesture that belied his sophisticated appearance. "Opening night of the film series. I think I expected ten people to show up. The sheer number is terrifying."

"This is your program?" Leigh asked.

He smiled, and his chest puffed out. "It was part of the agreement for my getting the research and teaching position. I promised to start a film series open to the public. Who'd've thought the public had such an appetite for it?"

"I've been looking forward to it since I heard about it," she said.

He looked over her shoulder. "So, your boyfriend—Berry's brother—is he parking the car?"

Leigh shook her head, barely resisting the urge to grimace. "Rocky. No. We broke up. Permanently."

Clark's eyebrows rose. "Oh, right. I'm sorry to hear that—"

"Don't be," she said with a laugh she didn't know she was capable of. "I'm not." She squinted at him. "In fact, I think you were one of the witnesses to my humiliation that day."

He blustered a bit. "I— yes, I was there. He really made an ass of himself. Very unfortunate. You, on the other hand... I didn't exactly see it that way." He cleared his throat. "Well then, since you're alone tonight, maybe you and I could— wow, that sounded awfully opportunistic of me." Clark paused as he spotted someone over her shoulder. "If you'll excuse me, my department head arrived, and I need a word with him, but I'd like to chat with you later. Maybe after?"

"Oh, ah, sure," Leigh replied automatically.

"I hope you enjoy the film. It's one of Jerome Percy's first. Not the star, but he makes a good showing..." Clark said as he made his way through the crowd. She turned to watch him walk away, noting how he turned back twice to smile at her.

Well. What was that all about? She made her way to the old-fashioned grill-fronted ticket booth. She glanced over her shoulder to find Clark's eyes flicker in her direction as he spoke with a shorter, bald man. He smiled one final time and then returned to his conversation.

"Okay then," she murmured to herself and made her way into the crowded, dimly lit theater. *He's more handsome than I remember. And nice. Polite. Too good to be true.* She felt her heart speed up at the thought he might be interested. Maybe Gram was right, and it was time she started to think about dating again. Rocky had spent enough time rolling around in her head. It was time to evict him and the way he'd made her feel. But she'd go slow this time. Make sure the guy wasn't using her. She wouldn't be fooled again.

The theater was packed. Leigh carefully picked her way across multiple sets of knees until she came to an empty seat next to an elderly gentleman. "Is this one taken?"

"I've been saving it for you," he said and tipped his hat with a smile.

She hesitated and gave a quick shiver as if the cold had followed her in.

"Don't mind me. I'm a harmless old flirt. Perfectly benign. I do love these old films. It's been ages since I had the chance to see one in a fine old theater like this."

Leigh made up her mind and sat. She set her coat and scarf in her lap. "It is beautiful. I haven't been here in years."

He removed his hat and held it in his lap as he leaned nearer. "I don't want anyone behind me to complain about not seeing the screen. Why, back when I was a young man, I recall it was quite a problem, gentlemen with their fedoras, ladies with their pinwheel hats and the like, not like in the olden days when one went to the

43

theater to be seen, rather than to see and no one could see the stage."

Leigh laughed. "I never thought of that. Being short, it's always been a problem. When I was a kid, I used to sit on my coat. I can't quite get away with that anymore."

He smiled at her. "Back in my day, the women were all petite and lovely—"

He stopped as the lights dimmed and turned his focus forward. Clark strode onto the small stage, microphone in hand.

"Enjoy the show," her companion whispered as Clark began to speak about the film series and the movies they'd see that night. Leigh watched his eyes scan the audience as he spoke, until, it seemed, he found her. His brows rose, and he frowned, then smiled as if enjoying a private joke but never broke his concentration.

Leigh felt herself tingle. Gram might just have been right after all.

Did you see the papers this morning? Juliet asked Isabel across their tiny breakfast table. *That handsome Jerome Percy got his divorce.*

Isabel pretended to think about it before she asked, *Now, which one was he again?*

You don't fool me; you know as well as I do, he was giving you the eye at the party last weekend. I wouldn't be the least bit surprised if he shows up at your door.

Let me see that paper. Isabel grabbed it from her roommate. *This says his divorce is final one week from today. His wife was found with another man, but he's being generous with her.* She set the paper down, her eyes dreamy. *Wow, what a guy.*

Chapter Four

Leigh

The silent films were surprisingly engrossing. The first was a Keystone Kop comedy short, and Leigh laughed along with the rest of the audience. There'd been little plot, but the action was hilarious.

The second film took a more serious tone. Clark's opening remarks about the studio and action had helped. After the first few minutes, Leigh found she could easily follow the actors' pantomime and the few storyboards that appeared between scenes. This was the film Clark mentioned that summer afternoon when they'd chatted about his thesis about Jerome Percy. Leigh had anxiously awaited that actor's appearances.

During the film, she heard the man next to her muttering. He had clearly seen it before and was critiquing the performances. When it was over, she turned to ask his opinion, but he was gone. She didn't recall his getting up. Being in the middle of the row, she'd have known if he'd gone by, but it would be odd to ask the man on the other side of the empty seat. It was all very strange, but she shrugged and went to find Clark.

There was a mob in the lobby. Clark's tall form was in the center of it, surrounded by theatergoers with questions about the film, the series, and the academic program he was running. It seemed everyone wanted to talk to him. His face was earnest as he answered questions left and right. Catching her eye, he gave a shy smile and a wink before he refocused on the elderly woman giving him her opinion of the film.

Leigh waited at the edge of the ornate lobby. She had her own questions and had enough time to wait for the others to filter out into the cold night.

She watched as Clark shook the last hand offered to him and looked around. His warm gaze met hers as he approached her. "I'm glad you came tonight. And waited. Sorry to keep you."

She reached out one hand and had it gripped in both of his large, warm hands before he let go. "I don't mind. I'm glad this series is off to such a great start."

His smile lit up his face. "I can hardly believe it. I've had a dozen folks ask if I can show the films again tomorrow. They want to come back and bring friends." He ran his hand through his hair. "What did you think?"

"I enjoyed them. I liked the contrast between the silliness of the first and the drama of the second. I didn't expect to be so moved."

"Both were filmed using the best technology available at the time. I know most people think the special effects can't compare to today's computer-generated stuff, but those early filmmakers put so much heart into their work, not to mention ingenuity." He rubbed his hands together and gave a shy smile. "There I go again. I'm afraid I get a little carried away."

"Nothing wrong with loving your subject," Leigh assured him. "Your enthusiasm is contagious."

46

He shot her a grin that had her catching her breath. "Thanks. Most of the time people tell me to dial it back."

"Oh, well, don't get me started on the latest graph technology my team is working with," she said with a laugh. "Another one of my teams works on computer graphics. We have an odd assortment of things we do, based on whomever my mother met and wanted to hire. She's always been good at attracting interested and talented staff and letting them follow their technological bliss. We've always been able to find customers to match their abilities." She felt her cheeks heat. "See, now you've got me going on and on."

Clark took her elbow and smiled. "I'm glad you came tonight. I've thought of you so many times since we met. Even after all these months, I hardly know anyone other than through the school, so seeing a friendly face in the crowd, my students and faculty aside, was great. I hope you can come again. We're running every other week at this point. I have to share the screen with another film group that's been here for years."

She wanted to grin. He spoke quickly as if she made him nervous, but he wanted to plow through it. "I will if you promise to give more background information before each of the films. You speak very passionately about your subject."

It was his turn to blush. "I... uh... well, sure. I don't want to bore anyone," he stammered.

"Not at all. I like hearing how glamorous their lives were back then. My grandmother used to tell me stories she read in the fan magazines—" She pressed her lips together. "Anyway, I wanted to congratulate you again on your successful launch."

His fingers gently squeezed her arm. "I'm glad you came. Listen, if you don't mind—"

Someone nearby cleared their throat, and they turned to see the man Clark had talked to earlier. "Conrad, sorry to butt in, but I need to speak with you." He turned to Leigh. "You don't mind if I steal him away, do you?"

47

She looked at Clark, whose expression was hard to read, perhaps a mix of disappointment, annoyance, and resignation. "Is that your boss?" she asked in a low voice. At his nod, she shrugged. "I'll be back in two weeks for the next showing, okay?" She stepped back and wrapped her scarf around her neck. "I'll see you then."

"Promise?" Clark asked. "I'm asking as the director of the series, of course," he said with a wink.

"And I'm answering as a member of your adoring public," she replied with a nod, said good night, and left the auditorium, aware of Clark's gaze following her.

She stopped on the theater steps to button her coat. As the lights started to wink out, she glanced around to see several couples standing around chatting, others hurrying through the chilly wind to other parts of campus. In the shadows on the other side of the marquee, a lone, hatted figure stood. The glow of a cigarette outlined his arm' s arc before he flicked it away.

Leigh walked quickly to her car and started the engine. As she drove away, she passed the same solitary figure who saluted her as she passed. Before her very eyes, he seemed to vanish into the dark, starless night.

Clark

He strode into his apartment to find Jerome on the sofa in a dignified sprawl. All thoughts of the beautiful woman Clark had spoken to earlier flew from his brain.

"You did well, m'boy. I particularly appreciated your remarks about my performance," Jerome drawled with a regal nod.

"Thanks. Everyone seemed to like it. Just about every faculty member I know was there." Clark took off his glasses and rubbed the bridge of his nose.

"And that's not all," the ghost added with a waggle of his brow. "I seem to have noticed a particularly adorable little dish—"

Clark groaned. "Tell me you don't mean Leigh. You promised to stay out of my—"

"Leigh?" Jerome's brows ceased wiggling and rose to his hairline. "What a lovely name for a lovely woman. And no, I did not agree to stay out of your love life, but as far as I can tell, there's nothing between the two of you except some heated air." He laughed as he rolled to his back and crossed his legs, then folded his arms behind his head. Looking at him, Clark could almost imagine he was real, except the cushions didn't sag under his weight.

"Maybe not—yet. But I'm hoping." Clark hung his scarf and overcoat in the closet and threw himself into the antediluvian easy chair that had followed him across country, shifting to avoid the broken spring that perpetually tried to poke his kidney.

Clark had come up in the world since his grad school days. He now had a genuine bed and bureau and shelves for his considerable collection of DVDs. Most were of films made before 1940, but there were a few of more modern vintage, including the entire collection of movies and television shows in which Jerome Percy appeared.

"You could do worse," Jerome mused. "She looks like she could be Isabel's great, great, great-granddaughter. Not that they look alike, other than the luminous skin and big eyes. There was something about the way she turned her head," he mused. "My Izzy was a blond. I used to call her Buttercup to tease her, while your Leigh—"

"She's not my Leigh." Clark sighed. "Not by a long shot. I wanted to get her number, but my department head had an urgent discussion he had to have with me, and she got away." He sighed again. "She said she'd come to the next screening in two weeks." He sank further into the chair. "I suppose I could find her online."

"Isn't she the same dame you met this past summer? I seem to recall you coming home depressed at having met a beautiful, smart woman with a stinker of a boyfriend."

Clark's eyes popped open. "You're a genius…"

Jerome straightened his tie. "I don't like to flatter myself, but if you say so, my dear boy."

"She's a friend of Berry and Moe." Clark sat up and looked at his phone for the time, shaking it first, to get the screen to light up. "It's too late to call now, but I can tomorrow morning, before class." He lay back and closed his eyes as he loosened his bow tie. "You really thought she was beautiful?"

Jerome rumbled his laugh. "I wouldn't say that. Alluring perhaps. And charming, if cautious. I did like the look in her eye. Always was attracted to intelligent women. I might have been a playboy in my time, but when I took a woman to bed, I wasn't opposed to having a little pillow talk about something other than the pillows. Never could abide those dumb ones who only thought about their career and being in the spotlight. Why, my Izzy—" He closed his eyes. "Nothing I haven't told you a hundred times before." The ghost sat up and looked across the room at Clark. "Speaking of which, I helped you with that fancy degree of yours. But we had an agreement. You're supposed to be looking for my lost love. I haven't seen you do more than make a list of questions."

Clark rubbed his tired eyes. "I'll be in the city library before I go to Moe's Saturday afternoon. I plan to make some calls after class tomorrow. They have electronic copies of the local papers going back a hundred years. If my hunch is right, I might be able to find traces of your Izzy right there."

Jerome harrumphed. "Not even sure we're in the right city. She could have gone anywhere."

"Yup, she could have. But the best sources we have led us east, and by luck, this job was also here, so I'm going to make the most of both. For all we know, by this time next year, we could be

50

somewhere else, searching archives long distance. You know I'm going to spend plenty of hours traveling to all the local libraries, looking at their microfiche."

"You going to get sidetracked by that little chickadee you met? She was awfully cute."

Clark rubbed his eyes again. "Nothing saying I can't date and do research. You know it's important that I make a good impression. Continue to build my reputation. That'll open more doors than being brash and demanding things. That might have worked in your day—"

Jerome laughed. "Only in the movies. Real life was entirely different from what you see up on the silver screen."

"Even so, I have to be methodical. This is nothing like the research I did on your book. I'd hate to miss something because I was rushing. And I don't mind being on the tenure track here. It's a nice small city. Not California, but I don't want to go back there, even if I do miss the sunshine. Too many distractions. And I'm hardly in a position to seriously romance anyone. I don't know if I'll be here next year, and I still have a mountain of student debt."

Jerome frowned. "But if you get stuck here, and you don't find any trace of Izzy, if you have to move on—"

"Then I keep searching but keep this as home base. I was lucky to land a job at the best university in the state and one of the best in a two-hundred-mile radius, but there are others. It's easy to travel just about anywhere from here. Just a few hours to New York, Boston, Providence, Washington, Baltimore, even the Midwest is a half day's travel by plane."

The ghost shuddered at that. "Can't stand those contraptions. Never could. Can't imagine why anyone would want to travel through the air in a tin can when you could have a powerful locomotive taking you across country."

Clark laughed. Jerome seemed to have forgotten he was nothing more than thin air himself—if that. They didn't exactly

51

know what he was, other than he'd learned to manipulate light objects, though the cost to him was inevitably heavy.

"What I don't understand is why you want to settle down to teach here. If you spent your time writing biographies of my pals in the business, you'd make your fortune. Just say the word and..." He snapped his translucent fingers, "—I'd have my chum Mack here in a jiffy talking your ear off. And Andy after that. I've got a dozen pals. You wouldn't have to spend your time trying to teach snot-nosed kids to appreciate a lost art form."

Clark shook his head. "Not that I don't like you, Jerry, but living with one ghost is enough. Living with a bunch of them—" He shuddered. "At least now you warn me when you invite them over. And I like teaching. Come on, Jer, if people like me didn't keep your art form in the public eye, the public would forget all about it, and you. Is that what you want? And you know I'll keep my promise to find Izzy for you."

The ghost didn't answer.

"And why the sudden rush? You've been hanging around me for ten years now and barely mentioned this mystery since we first met."

"Never you mind," Jerome snapped.

Clark ignored that. "Maybe you need to plan another card game. And this time, could you and your buddies keep it down? I need to sleep if I'm going to lecture in the morning. Or better yet, wait until I'm at work since you guys don't care what time of day it is. I'll keep the shades down so you can see each other."

Jerome remained silent for a long moment. "We lost another one," he said softly.

"Huh?"

"Louis. He, er, gave up the ghost a few days back. Said he was tired of waiting around. The world wasn't interesting to him anymore. Nothing to look forward to. So, he left. Seems all the guys have a set period of time they can abide here, but we never know how long it'll be. We need someone new to take his seat at the poker table."

"Ah, man. I'm sorry." Clark sat pondering that for a while. A pit of dread formed at the thought of losing his ghostly companion. A long moment later, he asked, "You ever think about it? Leaving. Seeing what comes next?"

Jerome seemed to be staring at nothing. "Sure. I think about it. But the thought of crossing over without my Izzy—losing her forever—I'm not ready. I can't."

"There's nothing to say she hasn't already—"

"Don't say it, boy. Don't even think it," Jerome said, anguish clear in his voice. "I've been waiting too many years, and I'm not ready to give up hope. Not tonight, I'm not."

Clark rose and went to stand before Jerome. "I'll find her for you. I promised I would, and I'm doing my best to keep that promise. I've got the best lead we've had since we started."

Jerome looked up at him. Damned if there weren't tears in his eyes. "I know you will, Clark. It always seemed like I had all the time in the world, but for the first time since I left the mortal coil, I've been getting the feeling time is running out. I may have died old and alone, not quite penniless, but certainly seeming a fool. The last thing I want to do is to head out into the great beyond to be confirmed one. I mean, what if we do find her, or what remains of her, only to learn she never cared about me?"

Clark stopped what he was doing and turned to his friend. If he were anyone else, he'd give him a bro-hug, but they never, ever touched. Not from the first night. "Jer, don't think like that. From everything you said, she adored you."

Jerome shook himself, and then a mischievous smile formed beneath his trim mustache. "On the other hand, I have it in mind I want to see you settled before I hit the road of no return."

"Jerome, you know I'm not in a position to woo or win a woman. My job—my student loans. Hell, I told you I don't know if I'll be here a year from now."

The ghost cast him a pitying look. "You worry too much."

"So you've told me. About a thousand times. Maybe you never learned to worry enough."

Jerome ignored Clark's comment. "Leigh—charming young woman. I like her. I think you should see more of her. Despite your protestations. So, what if you have to leave? Who's to say she wouldn't come with you?"

"We're not going to talk about Leigh tonight."

Jerome threw back his head and laughed. "Right. So, you can dream of her, unsullied by my observations. She's not like those other women you've dated, all angular. I mean, Katie Hepburn had her charms, but give me a soft woman over a bony one any day. Just mentioning it, old chap." He winked before he rose, plucked his hat out of nothing, and jammed it on his head. "As pleasant as this has been, if you don't mind, I think I'll go out after all. No need to wait up for me."

Clark smiled. "I'll keep the lights on if you want."

Jerome gave a hint of a smile in return. "I'd appreciate that, m'boy. I do so hate the dark. Even the great movie palaces have lit exit signs, you know."

He vanished, not even a pop or plink to mark his going.

"I hate when he does that," Clark muttered as he made his way to the bedroom. "I hate when he's right." Because, of course, he was going to fall asleep thinking about Leigh, her soft cheeks, her sultry voice, the sweep of dark hair against her forehead, and the sparkle in her eyes. And her smile. Oh yeah, he was going to think a whole hell of a lot about that hesitant smile and how it made him feel inside. And how he might get to see more of her in the weeks and months to come.

Why hello there. Jerome's hat was in his hands. He turned it about, pinching the crease in the crown with his long, square fingers.

How do you do? Isabel feigned disinterest in the man standing at her elbow. It was the most difficult role she'd played to date, pretending her heart wasn't all aflutter. She blinked slowly, aware of his gaze upon her.

He gave her a brilliant smile in return. *My name's Jerome Percy. That's what they're calling me this week. And who might you be?* He nodded at her empty wineglass and renewed his blinding smile. *May I get you another?*

She gave him the mysterious smile she'd begun practicing in her mirror when she was fifteen. *My name is Isabel Standish. At least it is for now. And no, thank you. I only allow myself one drink per party. I don't want to end up in the newspaper headlines.*

There're worse things than a little free press. But since you're not drinking, mind keeping me company? I've gotten bored with the conversation of these same old people.

Suit yourself. But if you must know, I'm otherwise engaged. I'm keeping company with a nice boy back home.

He gave her another look that set her heart to pounding. *A nice boy, is he? And why do you want a boy when you could have a man?*

Chapter Five

Clark

He drove to his cousin's house Saturday afternoon. Berry had said something about his keeping Moe company at a local kid's costume birthday party, but he wasn't certain what to expect. All he knew was he'd left a pile of research notes, his warm apartment, and a grumpy ghost behind.

Clark pulled into the driveway and shut off the car. The heater wasn't working, something he'd never had to worry about before. Maybe Moe could help fix it or direct him to a good mechanic. Despite having lived in town for months, Clark had few contacts to ask. His students were little better situated than he, as their cars were held together with spit and duct tape. And his department head drove a late-model Mercedes and wasn't much help when it came to fifteen-year-old American cars.

Moe sauntered out the kitchen door with a ready smile. "Ready to party? Where's your costume?"

"Uh—"

Moe laughed. "No worries. We'll give you a tool belt and a gimme cap, and you can masquerade as one of the Conrad brothers." He eyed his cousin with greater scrutiny. "The tweed jacket and fancy scarf won't work." He sighed audibly. "Maybe you'll have to pretend to be a college professor."

Clark smiled. "That'll work. I still feel like an imposter most days."

They walked into the kitchen, where Berry was putting the final touches on the kid's costumes. "Hey, Clark." She kissed his cheek. "If you don't want to go out with the kids, you can stay here and watch me write for the next hour and a half."

Behind her, Moe shook his head, pointing to the two thermos bottles on the counter and his back pocket.

"No, thanks. I'm looking forward to scoring some birthday cake," Clark said.

Berry smirked. "Suit yourself." She checked the kids' costumes once more. "You guys ready to go?"

"Yes!" they shouted.

Moe shrugged into a jacket and held the door open. "Come on, you two. That party's not gonna wait for man nor donkey." He kissed his wife before he picked up a travel mug and handed it to Clark, taking the other one. "Cocoa," he said with a wink.

As his kids ran down the driveway, Moe pulled a small whiskey bottle from his back pocket and poured some into each thermos. "Hot chocolate will only go so far keeping a man warm on a night like this. Besides, I have to tell you something, and I need to be slightly snookered before I do. And you need to be even drunker before you believe me."

"What?"

"Trust me," Moe said with a wink. "You'll thank me later."

Clark kept his eyes on his feet as they walked a few blocks to another house, where they could hear the happy shrieks coming from the back. Maddie and Max were old enough to ring the doorbell on their own while the men stayed on the sidewalk. Moe waved to the parents and shouted that he'd be along in a little bit to watch the kids in the bouncy house set up in the backyard.

"So, you were saying?" Clark asked as he took a sip of his drink. "I'm curious. How drunk do you need me to be?"

"It's nothing bad, exactly," Moe said in a hushed voice.

"You mean you're not going to confess to a crime?"

"No, but I think you'll find that we have a criminal in the family a lot easier to believe. Or accept."

"Now I'm really intrigued."

Moe took a long drink from his thermos and followed it with a sip from the glass bottle. "First thing you need to know is that if she finds out I've told you this, Berry'll kill me. Or worse, lock me out of the bedroom."

Clark laughed. "I'm a single guy without a partner, so you won't get much sympathy from me," he said.

"Oh, well, that's part of what I wanted to tell you. See my wife, for all her wonderful qualities, is an unrepentant, unrestrained matchmaker. If you like being single, you may want to steer clear of her."

The whiskey was having a warming effect. Clark pushed his glasses up his nose and unbuttoned his jacket. "Speaking as a single guy who doesn't like the bar scene but does like women very much, I'm not sure if I should take that as a warning or a promise." He leaned closer. "Is she good at it?"

Moe chuckled. "She made sure my brothers were all happily married off, if that's what you mean. So far, she's four for four. Five if you count her and me."

"Are you implying I'm her next project?"

Moe nodded cautiously.

"As long as she can introduce me to a nice woman, I'm not sure I mind." Clark stroked his beard. "The problem is, there's someone I met that I like."

Moe's face lost its smile. "Well, hey, that's great, and Ber can help you out if you run into the same trouble my brothers and I did. But here's the thing… and maybe you need to drink some more before I tell you the rest—"

Clark upended his thermos. "Not going to get much drunker than I am right now."

Moe looked at the small bottle, now empty, and frowned. "What I'm gonna tell you—you gotta promise not to tell Berry I told you this."

"I can keep a secret." Clark schooled his face into a serious mien. "You have no idea of the secrets I'm keeping right now."

Moe slung his arm around Clark's shoulders as they walked to the backyard. "Not just Ber. You gotta promise not to tell anyone. It's only me and my brothers who know this stuff. And their wives. And my mom, but none of them will tell anyone."

"Moe, you're starting to scare me."

"Aw, hell, I probably shouldn't have said anything."

"Well, you can't not tell me now," Clark reasoned. "What?"

"It's this—" Moe looked around. None of the other parents were within hearing range. "See, Berry's got these magical powers."

Clark stopped while Moe walked on a step or two. "You got me out here on this cold night to bullshit me?"

Moe walked back with his finger to his lips. "Not in front of the kids. And I'm not bullshitting. It's not that she's got superpowers like in the movies. She can't fly or anything. I didn't want to tell you, but since you're family, and you're going to be around, and she's probably gonna try to fix you up, I thought I should let you know."

Clark folded his arms. "What sort of magic are we talking about here?"

Moe glanced around again and then leaned in close. "She can make her story characters come to life," he whispered.

Clark laughed. "Now I know you're shitting me."

Moe rubbed his forehead. "I only wish. It's not like I want to give you a demo or anything. The first time it happened, there was hell to pay afterward. So, she keeps it under wraps. Most of the time. But if you ever come over and meet someone who's a little— let's say 'off'," he said with air quotes, "I can almost guarantee it's one of her heroes or heroines that she's let out into the world to teach them how to behave."

Clark took in a deep breath, his mind whirling. "You do know this is impossible to believe," he said slowly. Except he talked to ghosts daily. Well, one ghost. But no way was he going to confess that to Moe. Or Berry. No matter how much he'd had to drink.

"Yeah," Moe replied. "I do. But that's not the only thing."

Clark shuddered as a cold wind cut through his tweed jacket. "Okay, better tell me all of it."

"See, Berry seems to attract people with other, er proclivities of a supernatural nature."

Despite the cold evening, Clark felt a bead of sweat drizzle down his nape. "What?"

Moe's shoulders slumped. "My brothers—all four of 'em are married to women with some sort of weird powers of their own. And Ber and I got together due to the fact that my wife had characters loose in the world that were so life-like they fooled everyone." He pulled the bottle from his pocket once more, but it was still empty. "I mean, don't be surprised if when we get home, Berry's got some good-looking guy with her, or some babe too beautiful to be real. And then they'll leave like that." He snapped his fingers. "But you won't see a car, they'll just sort of fade into the dusk."

Clark forced himself to laugh. "Moe, that's quite some story you're telling me. I get it. Gullible cousin you're trying to fool."

Moe shook his head. "Don't say I didn't warn you. And what I said stays between us." He patted Clark's chest. "Got it? Trust me. If I didn't love her as much as I do, there's no way I'd put up with that stuff. But that's my life. So, if you value your bachelor status or your sanity, think twice before you let Berry start to fix you up. I can guarantee you once you do, the woo-woo stuff is gonna start to come out of the woodwork."

Clark stared at his cousin. The man seemed perfectly sane, and there wasn't a hint that he wasn't sincere. It was only the fact that there was a ghost waiting for him back at his apartment that kept Clark from bolting. "Right," he said at last. "Good one. I'll keep that in mind."

Moe nodded and slapped him on the back. "See that you do. And don't say I didn't warn you," Moe added before turning around and started talking to another parent who'd stayed for the party.

When the cake and ice cream were history, the presents all opened, and dusk had settled deeply into dark, they headed back to the Victorian home Moe had restored for his wife. While walking up the front steps, Clark saw Berry speaking with a tall, striking couple at her front door.

Clark looked at the three of them backlit on the front porch. The two kids ran up the steps and hugged their mother as they pushed into the house between the other couple, barely giving them any notice. Moe looked meaningfully at Clark, then shrugged as he jogged up the steps, kissed his wife, and nodded to the two strangers.

"Hey, Berry," Clark said as he came up last. He smiled at the couple. They looked to Berry before turning back to him and nodding in return. "Have a good night writing?" he asked her.

"Clark." She looked back at her companions with a frown. "Nice seeing you two. We'll talk again soon," and she pushed them, literally, out the door and down the steps. "New neighbors," she said breathlessly. "Don't know the first thing about when to end a social call." She rushed Clark into the house and shut off the outside lights. Clark peered through the sidelight to see the neighbors walk off, but there was no one there. He had no sense of them whatsoever, no ghostly presence, no soul, or wisp of sentience. He shivered.

Well, perhaps Moe wasn't pulling his leg after all. Or he'd had more to drink than he thought.

Thank you for taking me to see the Pacific coastline, Jerome. It's so beautiful. Not at all what I pictured. She turned to look at him as she removed a chiffon scarf from her hair. Jerome had removed the top of the car for their drive. Now that they'd stopped, she wanted to feel the sea air. *If we're going to get to know one another, I'd prefer to call you by your real name. What is it?* she asked.

Tom. Tommy Judson. It's been a lot of years since anyone's called me that. But if you're going to call me Tommy, Isabel, may I call you by your real name?

She laughed, and the sound stole his heart away. *Oh, I can't. I'm still getting used to the new one. Maybe when we know each other better. If I let you call me anything else, I'm likely to forget who I'm supposed to be. Oh, look. Are those whales? It's all so lovely. And to think the sun sets over the ocean instead of rises like it does back home. It will take me forever to get used to that.*

He grinned, his smile more dazzling than it appeared on celluloid. *If you won't tell me your name, perhaps I'll have to call you Buttercup. No, Izzy. My Darling Izzy.*

Chapter Six

Leigh

"Lei-Lei, you never told me about your evening. Did you meet someone?"

Leigh looked up to see Gram's eyes twinkle despite the pale October sunlight shining behind her. "G'morning, Gram. I didn't hear you come in." Gram's companion must have left. She was more silent than her employer, to the point Leigh often forgot about her. Leigh took another bite of toast and turned back to her tablet to read the news.

"You did meet someone," Gram continued, a laugh sneaking out of her voice. "You don't normally avoid answering questions unless you're hiding something."

"I didn't meet anyone new," Leigh said with a smile that matched the older woman's.

"That's a trick statement if ever I heard one," Gram said, shaking a pale finger. Her bright smile faded. "Don't tell me you met up with your old boyfriend."

Her hands shaking, Leigh set down the device before she dropped it. She felt the blood rush to her face. "I didn't meet Rocky. I'd never go out with him again. I can't believe you'd even think that. You know how he treated me, called me horrible things in front of the board after we broke up, badmouthed me behind my back to potential clients, used me. I can't believe he comes from the same family as my friend…"

"Calm down, my darling. You relieve my mind. If not that terrible excuse for a human being, then who put that sparkle in your eye?"

Leigh could not help the smile on her lips. "Remember this past summer I went to Berry's? It was the day I told Rocky to take a hike."

Gram nodded.

"Her husband's cousin was there. Really nice guy," Leigh offered.

"Handsome?"

"Yes, not to mention smart and nice," Leigh affirmed. "He's the one who's running the film program I went to."

Her grandmother sat up straight, her smile fading. "Films. You know I don't approve."

"Gram, it was harmless. I went. I sat. I watched, and then I came home and fell asleep. Same as always. Nothing happened."

"Oh, fine," Gram snapped. "This young man, he makes movies?"

"He's a professor at the university. He has his Ph.D. in film studies. We talked about it when we met, but I don't recall much. He didn't ask for my number, and I didn't ask for his. I'm not sure I'll see him again. I have an evening appointment the next time there's a showing." *But I'm going to see if I can reschedule it*, she thought.

There was silence in the room as Gram sipped from her translucent teacup.

Leigh picked up her tablet once more. "He was a really nice guy. But it probably won't amount to anything. I'm not cut out for a relationship. Rocky's really soured me on men. I can't help but wonder about their motives. Every one of them."

Gram's gaze met hers. "I'm sorry you've become so touchy about that. I know things have changed since I was a young woman," she said. "And you really should try to trust again."

Leigh lifted a shoulder in a silent rebuke. She finished her meal in silence as Gram gazed out at the greying sky.

"I'm going to call Berry," Leigh said as she balled up her napkin. "She left a message yesterday, but I was too busy to return it. Also, I noticed a gutter is detached on the east side of the house. I'll ask if Moe can fix it. I want to be sure the water hasn't started to rot that window next to your bedroom. I'll let you know when he'll be here."

"I appreciate that, darling." Gram waved to her companion, who appeared silently in the corner. The tall woman gripped the handle of the wheelchair and turned her out of the room on silent wheels.

Leigh frowned to herself. Gram's quirkiness was getting worse. Leigh knew Gram didn't need the chair. Well, it was the old woman's prerogative to keep her companion employed. And Leigh would do as she pleased, provided she didn't put herself or Gram in danger. Asking a friend's husband to do some work around the old house was certainly easy enough.

Berry

Hey, it's Berry, again, and as it's hard to talk about myself in the third person, you'll have to indulge me and my commentary.

Leigh returned my call, but before I could mention Clark, she asked if Moe would be able to come by to fix something. I put him on the phone, and he agreed to swing by after he dropped the kids at soccer and basketball practice.

Leigh lives in a beautiful mansion on the other side of town. For the past year, she's contracted with my husband's business, Conrad Brothers Building, to take care of maintenance she can't do herself. When I took back the phone, I told her about my call from Clark Friday morning and our later visit.

I didn't tell her how nervous he was, or apologetic, or how he was trying to play it cool when he asked about Leigh. As if the slightest question wouldn't stir my curiosity and get my match-making juices flowing. Ha! He didn't know me very well back then.

No, I didn't tell her all that. What I did tell Leigh was that Clark mentioned he'd met her. She confirmed she'd welcome my giving Clark her number. We hung up after I promised if she could free up the following Thursday night, I'd meet her at the movie theater for Clark's next film.

Moe was sitting next to me, listening to my half of the conversation with a funny smile on his face. My husband is a big, strong softy, and despite the fact he's discouraged me from aiding and abetting his brothers' relationships, he has a romantic heart underneath his gruff exterior.

"What are you thinking?" I asked when I ended the call.

He smiled again and reached for my hand. "I'm thinking that if I'm about to go climb a two-story ladder, I need someone to hold it for me. Sammy took Priya and the baby to visit her parents for the weekend. I wonder if Clark's free this afternoon?"

"You devil, you," I said with a smile. "Caught the match-making bug, have you?"

He squeezed my hand before reaching out and stretching his long arms and broad chest beneath his thermal shirt. He gave me a wink and leaned over for a kiss. "Naw, you know me better than that."

Okay, tidbit delivered. Berry out.

Leigh

She glanced out the window of her home office when she heard a truck pull up. She waved through the glass and returned to catching up on emails. She could hear Moe unload the ladder and set it outside the house.

She poked her head out the door to call up the stairs to alert her grandmother, then went back to staring at her monitor.

She heard the ladder treads creak as Moe began to climb, but when she glanced out the window again, she saw another man holding the foot of the ladder, looking up. She had a small shiver of appreciation.

She opened her window despite the cold air. "Hey, Clark. I wasn't expecting you."

He gave her his shy smile and pushed his glasses back up his nose. "Moe needed someone to spot him."

"Oh. Well, great." She grinned. "When you're done, come on in, and I'll make you guys something hot to drink."

He adjusted his cap. "Sounds good. My California bones aren't used to this kind of cold."

Leigh made a commiserating sound. "You poor thing. This is nothing. Just wait until February."

"Better close your window, or you'll lose all your heat."

She nodded and looked up to see Moe wrenching the aluminum gutter in place. "I'll meet you in the kitchen. Moe's got a key and knows the way."

She shut the window and went back to her desk to log off, then walked to the main foyer and called up the stairs, "Gram, Moe, and Clark are coming in for coffee." She thought a moment, remembering Gram teasing her about Clark. No sense in getting the old woman's hopes up that wedding bells were in her future. Overweight women didn't attract a good-looking man unless said man was looking to profit from the relationship. Hadn't she learned that the hard way? She looked back up the stairs. "Don't make anything out of it."

There was no reply. There often wasn't when Gram was involved in whatever it was she did all day. Leigh made her way into the large kitchen to heat water and discover what sort of snacks she had in the pantry.

Half an hour later, the two men came into the kitchen, laughing and rubbing their hands. Moe gave Leigh a kiss on the cheek, and she held out her hands to Clark. His hands were freezing, and she rubbed them. "You guys all done out there?"

"Yeah. The ladder was more work than the gutter," Moe said. "I didn't see any damage. Is that coffee I smell?"

"Coffee and hot chocolate. Take your pick."

Moe helped himself to a mug of coffee while Clark opted for the hot chocolate. She caught him gazing at her, but he looked away shyly.

"I'm glad it wasn't anything serious. Would you mind taking a look at the room upstairs? I want to be sure no water seeped in."

Moe took a sip of his coffee and set it down. "Sure." He glanced at Clark. "This here's a one-man job. Sit tight and warm up." He looked at Leigh. "Which room?"

"Second on the right. Next to my grandmother's. The door's open."

"You live with your grandmother?" Clark asked as they heard Moe's boots trod down the hall.

She nodded and bit her lip. "She's kind of a recluse these days, doesn't like to meet new people. I'm told she was once a great hostess." She gave him her practiced professional smile. "So, you're adding home repairs to your impressive resume?"

Clark grinned. "I would if I thought holding a ladder would enhance my professional credentials. I know which is the working end of a hammer, but that's about it. I'm afraid all the handyman skills stayed with my Conrad cousins. My brothers and I are mostly on academic tracks."

He looked around at the kitchen, a blend of antique cabinetry and modern appliances. "This is some house."

She lifted a shoulder. "I used to be embarrassed about living in this relic. But I've come to accept it."

"You grew up here?"

"Oh no. My parents had a small place a few towns over. This is more like the American version of our Ancestral home." She stopped and rubbed her nose. "My er, my great-grandfather was a pretty big deal back in the day. He built it for his first wife. What remains of his fortune is wrapped up in the trust that preserves the house and grounds."

"I guess that's good. It's a beautiful house. It must cost a fortune to live here. Not something a junior professor like me could afford."

Leigh cringed. Since Rocky, any mention of money made her uncomfortable. "As a descendant, I live here for a reasonable rent as long as I act as the caretaker. I also sit on the board that oversees it. The trust takes care of the major household bills otherwise, I couldn't afford it. We rent it out from time to time for weddings or other big parties. Moe helped me install locks to keep people out of the family rooms. There's a cleaning service that comes in, caterers, that sort of thing." She looked around. "It is pretty grand, but don't get me started on the heating bills."

He whistled. "Must be astronomical."

She nodded. "I had the heating system modified a few years ago so I can close rooms off. The only public room I make sure

68

stays warm is the music room. We have an old harp and a gorgeous grand piano. I'd hate to ruin them with too much cold."

"So, your folks are still in their house?"

"My mom. My father died when I was little. She started the company I work for as a way to make a living. It was her and one other developer at the time. There are now about a hundred full-time staff and about the same number scattered around the world. We'll be celebrating the twenty-fifth anniversary of the founding in a few weeks."

She rubbed her nose. In the back of her mind, she considered asking him to accompany her, if only to ward off questions about her single status that came up despite living in the twenty-first century. Why was her marital status anybody's business? She was a successful woman, established in her field. It shouldn't matter if she arrived alone. But it seemed people always had expectations, and those made it awkward.

"Anyway, I've lived here since I was a grad student. I had some roommates at the time, but they've all moved on. So, it's Gram and me now. Where are you living?"

He laughed, his eyes crinkling at the corners. "Nothing nearly as nice as this. Just a one-bedroom apartment about a mile from the university. I didn't think too hard before I rented it sight unseen. Lots of grad students living there, so I'm housing with some folks in my classes. It's a little awkward, but it's only for a year."

They chatted more about his work and class schedule until Moe returned. "No water damage I can see. You caught it early."

"That's good." She turned to Clark. "About five years ago, I heard some dripping. I didn't want to be bothered and ended up with a mess. Had to have the whole basement emptied and cleaned because of black mold. Now, first thing when I even suspect something's wrong, I call this guy." She pointed at Moe.

"I thought you did mostly rehabs and new construction," Clark said.

Moe looked up at the kitchen's patterned tin ceiling. "Mostly, yeah. But when I can get my hands on one of these grand old houses, nothing's going to stop me. It's like going to a museum. I admire the hell out of the craftsmanship that went into a place like this." He grinned at the two of them. "Berry'll never gripe about my head being turned by another woman, but she can't say the same when I see a house as amazing as this. I've been known to lose track of time when I start exploring."

"And that right there is exactly why I hired Moe," Leigh laughed. "What about you, Clark, what's your passion?" It wasn't until the words were out of her mouth that she worried he might take her question the wrong way.

His cheeks, already red from the cold, deepened their color. "Oh, you know. Old movies. The stories. The plots. The actors and actresses and their history. I've always had my head stuck in a library or a screening room. Some people read a book every day. I'm more likely to watch a film when I'm not writing about them. Speaking of which, I need to get back to the library. I promised a... er... friend, I'd do some research, and I have a few hours of work ahead of me."

Leigh's smile drooped. "Oh, sure. Well, Moe, thanks as always for coming out. Send the bill to the foundation. Clark, I hope to see you soon."

She watched him blink, his eyes looking into hers. "Ah, well, yeah." He looked at Moe, who indulgently looked away. "I was, uh, thinking maybe we could get together some time?"

Leigh's heart began to hammer. Damn, but she hated the hope that sprang up despite her efforts to tamp it down. "Sure. Maybe sometime. You want to meet for lunch or coffee?"

"Or drinks? Or dinner?" he asked.

She paused. Oh, what the hell. He probably wouldn't call. Why not let him have his moment. "Why don't you give me your phone, and I'll put my numbers in it," Leigh suggested.

Clark pulled it from his pocket, but his fingers fumbled, and it dropped onto the slate floor. Leigh picked it up to see a crack on the screen. "Oh, I'm so sorry. I wanted to replace this floor. It's so darned hard, but Gram won't let me."

"No. The screen was already cracked. I've been too busy to get it repaired," Clark assured her. "I'm afraid I can be a bit absent-minded despite missing calls and texts all the time."

"He's a klutz," Moe said affectionately. "Especially when he's nervous."

"Moe!" Leigh exclaimed.

"Hey, I'm only telling the truth."

"He's right," Clark agreed with a smile. "And if you hadn't already agreed to meet me sometime, I'd be too embarrassed to ask you now. But I'm not letting you off the hook."

Leigh laughed. "Well played." She keyed in her numbers and handed the phone back. "There. I'll wait for your call."

He grinned at her. "I'll call tonight to make plans?"

"Yeah, sure."

"And you'll come to the next film?" he asked, hope evident in his voice.

"I'm trying to rearrange my travel schedule so I can. Berry said she and Moe were going if she could get someone to watch the kids." Leigh couldn't help but grin. "I'll be out of town most of the week at a conference. I'm speaking about women in technology to high schoolers and their parents."

Clark pocketed his phone and held out his hand. She put hers in his without thinking, and he covered it with his other. The warmth infused her with a reckless sort of hope she hadn't felt in years.

"I'll be counting the hours until we see each other again," Clark said in a low voice.

Moe whistled and rolled his eyes. "Smooth move, Romeo," he said with a grin. "Let's pack it up. I need to secure the ladder, then go get the kids."

71

Leigh felt herself grinning like an idiot, damn it. "I'll see you."

Clark pressed her hand once more and then turned to the door. "Goodbye." He leaned in to gently kiss her cheek, and her heart started beating so erratically, she feared he would hear it. That seemed to be all she could hear. "I hope we'll see each other sooner rather than later."

"Bye."

Clark left the room. Moe stood there until Leigh stopped looking at the closed door and turned to him. "What?"

He shook his head with a smirk. "Kids."

She laughed self-consciously. "Was I really that transparent?"

He cracked a grin. "I was thinking of Clark. He's got quite a crush on you."

Without thinking, she gasped as her hands clasped together at her chest. "A crush? Really?" *So not cool,* she thought. *I'm a glutton for punishment.* She laughed. "Geeze. I sound like I'm fifteen again."

Moe grinned. "Yes, really. Now, I'd better get going. Shall I give your regards to my most despised— I mean esteemed brother-in-law, Rocky?"

It was Leigh's turn to laugh. "You can flip him the bird for all I care. And yes, you can tell him I said so."

"Then it's one bird from you and another from my wife. I've got no hands left for me." Moe laughed again, set down his empty coffee cup, and left her kitchen, whistling.

Leigh gathered up the cups and put them in the dishwasher as she heard the truck drive off. When she turned, Gram was in the doorway, smiling. "So, that's your young man."

Leigh's cheeks heated. "I wouldn't say that."

"Not yet," Gram said. "I must say, I'm impressed. Polite. Kind. Rather shy. And very good looking. Of course, in my day, no one wore beards except old men. And a gentleman intending to court a woman would never show up in anything other than his best suit."

Leigh rolled her eyes. "Gram. He was helping Moe work on the house. He's not going to wear a suit for that. Besides, I thought that black and white flannel suited him."

Gram's eyes gleamed mischievously. "I would agree. And as much as I liked the look of loose trousers on a man back in my day, there's something about those tight-fitting jeans that's attractive. So, the question is, what are you going to do to encourage him, my dear granddaughter? And what can I do to help? Don't forget you have that fancy dinner to celebrate your mother's achievement. You definitely need a date for that, and I happen to think young Clark would be perfect." Her fingers formed a loose rectangle. "Can't you picture him in a tuxedo? I know I can."

Izzy, I know you don't fool around with married men, but my divorce has been final for months. And Juliet told me you sent that boy back home a letter telling him you're breaking it off with him. Will you come away with me? Please?

Tommy— I can't. Not overnight. Unless we have separate rooms.

Why, my darling Buttercup? We're not committing adultery.

If we— oh, I know how silly this sounds, but I can't help but think if we spend the entire night together, it's a sin.

Chapter Seven

Clark

"You've been gone a while," Jerome complained as Clark came in the apartment bearing a bag of Chinese take-out and his computer case. "Progress?"

Clark set his things on the table and shrugged off his coat. He looked up at the ceiling where Jerome gravitated most days. It was an odd choice, but after living with the ghost for so many years, Clark chose what to question and what to accept without comment. "It depends on how you define progress."

"Being deliberately obtuse is not flattering for man or woman," Jerome said petulantly as he walked down the wall and came face to face with Clark. "I've been stuck in here all day, not knowing where you were or what you were about—"

Clark laughed. "Come on, Jer. You're free to come and go however you'd like. And half the time, I don't know you've tagged along with me until you want me to. What's going on? Did you miss me?"

"Don't be ridiculous," the ghost huffed and turned only to drift away. "I simply wanted to know if you've got any more leads on finding my Izzy."

"I didn't crack the mystery if that's what you're asking," Clark said as he hung up his coat.

Jerome lit one of his phantom cigarettes and slouched against the wall. "Oh."

Clark pressed his lips in a stubborn line. "Listen, Jer, this means as much to me as it does to you. You ever hear the phrase Publish or Perish?"

The ghost rolled his eyes. "Only about a thousand times since we met."

"Well, I need to crack this mystery for my career every bit as much as you want me to so you can move on, move over, or go wherever the hell it is you're going to go, once I do."

Jerome straightened. "It almost sounds as if you're going to miss me when I go."

"If you ever go," Clark corrected. "It sometimes seems like I'm stuck with you for eternity."

"Ha, that's a good one. Almost make a decent film name."

Clark felt his good mood returning. "Yeah, it would. Or book title. Think I could get away with it?" He paused. "Hell no. I'd be laughed out of conferences."

"Oh, my boy, don't think I won't miss you too," Jerome said as he drifted closer. "Why, if I had a real body, I'd— I'd—"

"You'd never hug me," Clark said wryly. "You've told me a hundred times it wasn't done in your day."

"Certainly not. Except behind closed doors, of course. No, if I could, I'd— well, I'd shake your hand."

Clark laughed. "Feeling that strongly, are you?"

"I'd shake it heartily," Jerome amended. "And considering you're my only hope, yes. Yes, I am."

"You flatter me. Now, if you don't mind, I've put in a hard day's work, and I'm hungry. I'll fill you in on what I found when I'm done. Deal?"

"Deal. Providing, of course, you also fill me in on your interaction with the delectable Miss Mason this morning."

Clark stopped reaching for a dinner plate and turned to his ghost. "How do you know I saw her today?"

"My dear boy. Just because you couldn't see me doesn't mean I'm not privy to your phone conversations— not that I intended to overhear your call this morning." He cleared his phantom throat as he drifted to the small table where Clark sat. "Well, not precisely. I— I feel somewhat responsible for you. Seeing as I didn't have the raising of my own son, you might say I feel somewhat paternal toward you."

Clark snorted. "Not even my father eavesdropped on me," he said. "And at thirty-two, I'm past the age when I need a parent hovering. And I mean that literally." He looked up. "Stop looming while I'm eating. Aren't you the one who's been teaching me table manners for the past ten years?"

"Ah. Right you are. If you'll kindly push the other chair out for me? I fear my power over large objects is lacking."

Clark kicked it out, and Jerome righted himself before he did a fair approximation of sliding into the chair. "So, you saw the fair Miss Leigh today?"

"Hey, no changing the subject so fast. And if you've done all that eavesdropping, you better tell me right now you never hung around when I had a girlfriend over. You said you wouldn't. You promised."

Jerome smoothed his already tidy mustache. "I— I have always been discrete."

Clark set down his loaded fork and glared at Jerome. "Discrete as in, you left the apartment?"

Jerome smoothed his pencil mustache. "Ah, not always."

Clark rolled his eyes. "How about left the room?"

76

"My boy, my dear boy, it's only recently that you have more than one room."

"I always had a bathroom door," Clark said between gritted teeth. "Not to mention a door to the hall of whatever building I was living in."

"Yes, well, let us say I have always been a gentleman and never told anyone what I saw."

Elbows on the table, Clark pushed away his dinner and hid his face in his hands. "Should I be happy that you never told your phantom cronies what you saw go on in my bedroom?"

"Your bed, to be specific," Jerome corrected. "I notice you tend to business under the sheets. I've wanted to speak to you about that. I mean, until this year, you've lived in Southern California. It's not as if the weather forced you to cover up."

Clark made a strangled sound, so Jerome pivoted. "Speaking of my cronies— trust me, they wanted to know. Just because we're no longer corporeal doesn't mean we've lost interest. None of us are angels right now for a reason."

Clark shook his head. "I've got about a million thoughts going on in my head, and I can't formulate a question. Or statement. Or outrage. Maybe I shouldn't want to know."

"Take your time, son."

Peeking between his fingers, Clark saw Jerome was wearing his serious mien, not that he trusted it. The man had been an actor for decades and could easily mask his feelings.

"You can't— I mean, can you— I mean, can your kind—"

"Make whoopie?" Jerome shrugged. "To be honest, I haven't tried. Not that we can't approximate a rise when suitably inspired. But as far as I know, none of my companions has had any such experiences. The fact is, we seem to have a dearth of females of our persuasion round about these parts." He looked up at the ceiling. "To tell the truth, in all these years, and there have been a lot of them, it never occurred to me to question why." He pondered a moment more. "Perhaps not. Maybe this stage of my existence deliberately forced celibacy upon me for a reason. Conceivably it's punishment or to encourage us to move along to the next plane? I'm sure none of us were supposed to hang around at this, er, stage for very long." He rubbed his chin. "There was a distinct lack of information shared about my state when I…" His hands swept down his body, "…made the transition."

"All the more reason for me to get on with my research." Clark pulled his plate closer and picked up his fork. "So, to answer your first question, no, I did not find Isabel today. What I found is an archive of the weekly newspapers from the years she would have returned home, mostly social news. It tells who threw parties, and who attended, where they were from, who wore what, marriages, engagements, all that sort of thing. From the few articles I read, if anyone was the least bit interesting, famous, infamous, or noteworthy, there was a full write up of who they were, what they were doing in town, what their dresses or suits looked like, or who made them, who they danced, argued, or flirted with. The time frame is right. I'll go back to look at that paper the next time I get a chance and look some more. You can be sure if a movie star waltzed into town, it would have been covered."

Jerome rubbed his hands together soundlessly. "A promising start. And while we're on the topic—"

Clark looked up sharply. "What topic?"

"You. And women. Perhaps I should say, style and aptitude."

Clark covered his ears. "I don't want to hear this."

Jerome tsked, which Clark could hear as loudly as if his ears weren't covered.

"But, my boy, I was going to pay you a compliment. Your style has certainly improved over time. I haven't always approved of your choice of partner, of course—"

"Jerome!"

"—but your stamina is to be admired. Not to mention technique. Very impressive. And way more generous than I ever claimed to be, even with my darling Izzy. Made me quite ashamed, let me tell you—"

Clark lay his head on the table and covered it with his arms. "Please. You're killing me here."

Jerome had the gall to look affronted. "In my day, all men wanted to know about this. It's not something we specifically *asked* about back when I was... you know, alive, but when someone was talking, we listened. And it's not that I didn't attend an orgy or two in my day. Great opportunity to check out some new moves and all that."

"Please, Jer. Stop."

"Why, when I was talking with the chaps about what I observed—"

Clark reared to his feet. "You said you didn't talk about it with them."

Jerome looked chagrinned, but it was every bit as fake a look as the rest. "That might have been a bit of a prevarication. And it's not like you were serious about any of those women."

"That doesn't matter, you Neanderthal. I might have been if you'd butted out. I still can't believe you spooked Heather like that. She's probably still freaked out about it."

Jerome stared at the table as he straightened his tie and shot his cuffs. "I have to say, she frightened me every bit as much as I frightened her. Why her scream, it curdled my blood for sure. Or would've if I had any."

"She ran off without her stuff," Clark mused. "I had to pack it all up and take a bus across town to give it back. And then she made me leave it on her parent's doorstep. She wouldn't open the door and talk to me. Trust me, that did wonders for my ego."

"Are you being sarcastic with me?" Jerome demanded. "I happen to despise sarcasm."

"So, sue me," Clark said and tried to eat another bite. He pushed his plate away once more. "And another thing, and I can't believe I even need to say this but let me make it very clear, the next time I'm with a woman, be it here or anywhere else, to use your own phrase, you are going to absent yourself. Understand? You will not be hovering anywhere near the bed, be in the room, in the apartment, or in the building. I'd be happy if you left the city, no, the state, for the duration. You will not know if we are on the sheets or under them, who's on top, what moves I make or how long I last, or how generous I am. Nothing. And you will not ask me when you return, a discrete and very long period of time later, once the woman in question has vacated the premises. Got it?"

Jerome looked meek. It was all an act, but Clark knew it was the best he would get. "I have one question."

"What?" Clark snapped.

"Er, as a matter of discretion, how exactly will I know the lady in question has vacated the premises unless I'm sitting on the roof, watching her quit the place? Not to mention you and I both know I can't travel far from you in this realm or stray from my earthly belongings. You, and they, are a rather inconvenient anchor, as we've learned."

Clark's forehead hit the table once more, his hands too slow to cushion it. "I'm never going to have a life. I'll never get tenure. Or another girlfriend, let alone a wife. No wonder I'm on a first name basis with every take-out joint in the area. You are going to drive me mad." He lifted his head and stared at Jerome. "One of these days, you're going to talk to me one too many times when I'm in the middle of a lecture, and I'm going to answer instead of ignoring you. I'm going to get fired for being a lunatic and have to move back into my parent's house. No school, prestigious or otherwise, will ever hire me again. I'll live in the basement and drool on myself as I watch old movies hour after hour. I'm going to die an old maid. Or whatever." He dropped his head again. "I'm doomed."

Jerome maintained his place across the table, open-mouthed at Clark's dramatics. The O closed into a smile, and he began to applaud. "Well done, my boy, well done. I can see my tutelage has paid off. That performance was worthy of a screen test. Alas, if only you were comfortable in front of the camera, I could make an actor of you."

Clark stood and took a bow in his small kitchen. "Thank you. But I mean it. If I bring Leigh here, I don't want you anywhere near us. And if you're not sure if you should come back, wait twenty-four hours before you do. Make it forty-eight if it's a weekend. On the roof. Not across the street. I don't want you peeking in the window."

"For you, son, if you can get her, I'll do it. Providing you tell me the juicy details upon my return." Jerome rose and sketched an elegant bow. "Besides, you know I can't go that far from you, or my 'stuff' such as it is. We've tested that. Just like I couldn't leave that library until you came along. Don't ask me to explain it. I don't understand the dynamics of it any better than you."

Clark hung his head. "Fine. In the event it becomes pertinent, make yourself scarce, okay?

"Of course, m'boy. Say no more."

Leigh

She'd no more than taken off her coat and booted up her laptop when her mother, the founder of MirandaTech, burst into her office. "The party is a few weeks away," she said breathlessly.

"I'm aware," Leigh replied, her eyes on the screen as her fingers keyed in her password. "You and Sarah remind me daily." She looked up with a smile. "If not hourly."

Her mother threw herself into one of the chairs in Leigh's office and covered her face with her hands. Her salt and pepper hair spilled over the back of the chair. "I know. I'm being terrible to you that way. It's that this is so— so—"

"Monumental?" Leigh supplied.

"Astonishing is more like it. When I started out, I never thought I'd survive the first month, let alone years," Miranda replied.

Leigh came to sit beside her mother. She gently pried one hand from her mother's face and held it. "You are amazing. You know that, right?"

Miranda's smile lit her face. "Do you have any idea what it means to me that you say that?"

"I'm not just saying it. I mean every word. You *are* amazing. You raised Sarah and me, you started this company, and it took off despite the extra stress of being a woman in the man's world of IT. And the company continues to grow and grow and grow."

"You mean you've forgiven me for not staying home and baking cookies? I still have guilt flashes that I had to leave you and your sister alone so much."

Leigh let out a strangled laugh. "I forgave that years ago. It made us both strong and self-reliant. I'm sorry I ever said anything. I mean, I was the only kid whose mom was a CEO, and who came into my class to tell the kids all about computer programming, and insisted it was something everyone could do, not just boys like that awful Andrew Peters said."

Her mother peeked at her from between her fingers. "I did do that, didn't I. Wow. I guess I am remarkable."

They laughed together. "Please, don't get mad at me for saying this. I know it's old-fashioned," Miranda continued. "But I want you to have a date for the party. It's not so much that I won't think you're a successful, accomplished woman without one. But these things are a lot more fun if you're with someone. I know how you love to dance, and there won't be a lot of singles to dance with. And I don't care how it sounds, but I want you to have someone in your life because it will make you happy, and I want you to be happy. Like your dad and I were happy."

"Oh, Mom, I know. I've been racking my brain thinking of who I could ask."

Her mother winced. "Anyone other than that Rocky, please."

It was Leigh's turn to groan. "I wish everyone would stop reminding me of that lapse in judgment."

"Well, he's very good-looking," her mother said. "And he *was* charming at first, the sneaky devil. You weren't the only one he fooled."

"I was totally taken in by him, painful as it is to say."

"Well, that's history. And you are over him. So, have you come up with anyone?"

Leigh thought for a moment. Was she over Rocky? He'd made her doubt herself over the past few months, and she'd turned down almost every opportunity to socialize since. In fact, she'd about given up on the idea of meeting someone when Clark came back into her life, and it scared the stuffing out of her to take another chance. "I met... well, met someone. I met him for the second time. He's a professor at the university. Nice guy. But I'm not sure. It's kind of weird for me to ask him to go when we haven't even gone out for coffee yet."

"But you will, right?"

Leigh weighed the option of telling her mother everything or enough to appease her. "I'm going to see him next week. I'll see how that goes. If not, I can always ask Darren."

"But sweetheart, isn't he in a relationship?"

"Yes. But he and Stu always said I could ask him any time if I needed a plus-one. I did it for them before they came out to their families. They always said they'd return the favor."

"I'd hate for you to have to. Let's see how this other fellow works out." Her mother leaned closer. "Does he have a name? Oh, I can't believe I asked that. Of course, he does. I'm turning into my mother! I meant, do you mind sharing his name?"

Leigh smiled. "You're not going to call him or anything, are you?"

Miranda reared back. "Of course not. What does he teach?"

"Film studies. And his name is Clark Conrad. You remember Berry? Clark is her husband's cousin."

"Film?" Miranda asked doubtfully.

Leigh tensed. "Yes, film. Why is everyone so put out by that?"

"Who's everyone? And I'm not. It's, oh, I don't know. You know how my mother was, and my grandmother."

"I do know," Leigh replied. "I just don't get it."

"I don't either, considering we do so much CGI development," Miranda said as she stood and smoothed her skirt. "I never said it made sense. It was what I heard all my life. You know how overbearing my mother was about everything, especially things she didn't approve of. But about your date, let me know. My admin is nagging me every hour since he's working on the seating charts and needs to know even more than I do. You know how he likes everything to be just so."

"Tell him I'll have a date and will give him the name sometime before the event. Tell him to reserve the chair next to mine."

"Sounds good." Miranda leaned over to kiss her daughter's cheek. "And wouldn't it be nice if this guy turned out to be the one."

"Mom!" Leigh exclaimed. "Why are you suddenly turning into a normal mother at this point in my life? Now I've got a ton of work to do before I fly out this afternoon. I should be back tomorrow night. I'll talk to Darren later, from my hotel."

"But I thought you were going to ask Clark—"

"I'll ask Darren to be on standby. And you know what? I'm too busy for a relationship at this point. Between all the travel and the late meetings and early meetings, I'm not sure anyone would want to put up with me."

"Most of that is self-imposed, and don't think I don't know it," her mother fretted from the doorway. "That sounds more like an excuse. Now, no more backtalk. I'm still your mom and your boss, and both of us are telling you to get to work." She blew a kiss, and with a smile, took off down the hall to her own office.

Leigh shook her head. It wasn't lost on her that the last time she'd walked into her mother's office unexpectedly, Miranda had been on the phone with a friend and bemoaning her lack of grandchildren. So why was she getting the pressure instead of Sarah, who was older and married? It was also surprising, given Miranda had never coaxed her daughters into expecting an ordinary life when they were younger.

What would any child of hers and Clark's look like anyway? She was petite and dark while he was tall and sandy. It wasn't as if she didn't want a child or two, but the prospect wasn't something that had kept her up nights. Though knowing the way her mind worked, there was every chance that lying in a strange hotel bed that night, it very well might.

Tommy, I saw the way you were looking at that actress—like you wanted her. After our weekend... I thought you swore you'd be faithful to me.

They stood side by side, looking out over the ocean. He ached to take her in his arms, but she had to learn to trust him. *My darling Izzy, if you will recall, the camera was rolling at the time. That is called acting. And if you must know, the only way I could get that look on my face was to imagine she was you.*

He heard her draw in a startled breath. *Really, Tommy?* Her hand crept over the balcony until her little finger touched his. A moment later, she curled it over and squeezed. In a heartbeat, she was in his arms.

Izzy my sweet, darling girl, you have my heart like no other. Really and truly.

Chapter Eight

Clark

Living with a ghost was challenging. For example, one couldn't look at one's roommate in the mirror while conversing in the bathroom while tying a bowtie.

And then there were the convenient lapses of memory. And lack of gravity, or any other law of physics he could cite, where Jerome was concerned.

Clark stood before the scratched vanity in his bathroom and battled with his bowtie. It was a new one, and the silk was stiff and uncooperative. Jerome was bobbing along the ceiling, cross-legged. He'd done so bemoaning what it would do to the wrinkles in his trousers until Clark reminded him that, unlike the living, all Jerome needed was think a simple thought, and the sharp crease would reappear as the other wrinkles dropped out of sight. Unlike the one in Clark's trousers, not to mention the furrow on his brow.

"Think that little doll will show tonight?"

Clark flicked his gaze over to Jerome and back again. He'd long known his house ghost cast neither reflection nor shadow. His appearance was sometimes like a silhouette. Only once had Clark taken a picture of Jerome that resulted in an image, but it was more blur than likeness.

"I hope so," Clark replied as he checked his teeth to make sure nothing of his dinner remained. He flicked his gaze back at Jerome. "You like Leigh."

"I do," the ghost replied as he gently rose and fell in the air above the tub as if riding swells at the beach. "I always did like smart women."

"Was Isabel smart?"

"Too smart," Jerome mused as he lay back on nothing, smoking yet another cigarette. "Smart enough to disappear without a trace." He rolled over laterally, then dipped and went head over heels before settling back into his original pose. "Are you sure those newspapers said nothing about her?"

Clark shrugged as he combed his hair. "I looked them over pretty carefully. There was a big to-do about some woman returning to town, but the description and name were wrong, and they made it sound as if she'd been overseas, and that's ridiculous given that Europe was recovering from the first world war at the time she was gone. It was all pretty muddled. I'm going back to the weekly papers. They had a lot more gossip. I've got my work-study student, Bonnie, checking as well. I gave her a list of names to look for, including Isabel's stage name, plus every named character she ever played in a film that I could find. If you think of any others she might have used, let me know. I'm having Bonnie recheck the railroad rosters with the new list."

Jerome sighed. "Her character names. That was inspired, m'boy. I never would have thought of it. I do wish I remembered what name she was born under. She must have told me, but for the life of me, I can't recall."

Not for the first time, Clark wondered if Jerome were deliberately withholding information. Did the old man really want to find his lost love, or was there something that held him back? It was impossible to tell. Jerome could be aggravatingly evasive.

"Keep thinking, Jer. It would make this search a lot easier. Anyway, next weekend I'll head over to some other town libraries that have different local newspapers. It's possible you mistook the name of her hometown. She could have gone elsewhere."

Jerome shook his head. "That's the one thing I'm sure of. But that doesn't mean she returned here. I know she had a good childhood, so since she was upset, she'd want to return to her roots, but you never know. Not like me."

Satisfied with his bowtie, Clark turned and looked at Jerome. Jerome didn't often mention his early life. While Clark had been researching his dissertation, he'd had to be the most patient when pulling information out of the ghost about his childhood.

Clark recalled the time early in their relationship when he'd finally been able to pry the information out of the ghost. They'd been companions for about six months at that point. Jerome had been more than happy to wax rhapsodic over his career in film at any time, night or day. Still, he was strangely hesitant to provide Clark with anything other than the origin story Pinnacle Studios made for him. It finally required Clark taking Jerome back to the bar where they'd first met and plied him with imaginary liquor to get him to open up.

The two of them had sat in the same booth where it had all begun. Jerome had seemed solid enough that night to fool the bartender. Instead of the same rotgut he'd had the first time, Clark had ordered a beer along with a burger and fries. He set Jerome up with a dry martini and placed it in front of the ghost, who looked simultaneously grateful, thirsty, and rueful. "You'd best drink that and describe how it tastes," he said wistfully. "I'll conjure up my own."

"I can't get drunk," Clark replied. "I need to type up my notes since a tape recorder won't work."

"Humor me, m'boy. Take a sip."

Clark did and nearly choked. "It's quite… an acquired taste…" he managed to wheeze.

Jerome chuckled. "I suppose it's too much to ask that you acquire that taste on my behalf."

Clark swallowed hard and shook himself. "It'll have to wait until I can afford your taste." He pushed his plate aside and opened his laptop. "So, at the risk of sounding like a cliché, tell me about your childhood."

Jerome cast a sardonic stare. "Are you sure you want to know about my formative years? It's not a pretty story, m'boy."

Clark nodded. "Anything and everything you can remember. Don't try to pass that garbage the studios dreamed up by me, and don't tell me you can't remember. You reportedly had the best memory in the business in your day."

"Absolute necessity, son. Never could read very well. All those numbers and letters liked to dance around before my eyes. When I was between wives, and this is after I started in talkies, mind you, I had to hire someone to read the scripts to me. I didn't want to waste my money having them go over them too many times."

"You were dyslexic?"

"They called me stupid back then when they weren't calling me stubborn." He tapped the side of his head. "Got my ears boxed a time or two when I was a kid. Learned to hide it."

Clark typed that in. "Don't worry. I'll make it sympathetic. No way you were stupid." He looked up. "So, tell me about where you were born. Your family. How you got your start."

Jerome frowned. "I truly don't remember much of my early years. As best I can recall, I was the youngest of twelve or thirteen children, a pile of boys and two girls. Can't recall all their names though. I think there was a John, a Wilber, Clarence, George, and Mary. None of them paid me much mind—the newest and least interesting of the lot. The rest are a blur. I'm told my father died when I was three. The story, told in whispers in the dark, was that he was shot in the back after fleeing from a bank robbery gone wrong. He'd lost his job as a farmhand and couldn't support the family other than through theft."

"Wow," Clark breathed, typing furiously. "What was his name?"

Jerome stared longingly at the martini glass before he conjured his own and tossed it back. When he set it back on the table, it was once again full. "Not sure. Maybe John. Or Jack. Or Herbert. Don't know if I ever knew."

"I can Google it. What else can you tell me? Maybe about your mom."

Jerome took a sip of his conjured drink and closed his eyes. "Mother was destitute. I think she hired the older children out to work as farmhands, or maids in our small town."

"Where was it?"

"Damned if I can recall," Jerome mused. "Somewhere in the center of the country. I remember fields of wheat or corn as far as the eye could see. Flat. Grey and dismal. The house was little more than a shack and was always cold when we weren't blasted by the heat or thrown around by the wind. Lots of wind back on the prairie, you know."

"Got it," Clark said under his breath. "What was your mom like?"

Jerome clenched his hands together. "Not a warm, kindly soul, that much I recall. Mostly worn out, I would guess. I don't recall many conversations with her. Or hugs."

"What became of all of your brothers and sisters?"

Jerome sighed. "They scattered. I recall my mother crying, for, despite my tender years, I understood that my eldest sister had turned to prostitution and took off for Chicago, later taking our other sister with her. The brothers went wherever. Given our father's poor reputation and the lack of work in our small town, they would have had to leave. I seem to recall that I was the only one left with mother. She'd taken to drinking hard by the time I have stronger memories. Hell, m'boy, for all I know, she could have been the town whore, and there never was a Mr. Judson." Jerome upended his drink and chewed the olive before filling the glass again with the blink of his eye.

Clark stopped. "Jerome, I'm sorry. Do you want to take a break?"

The ghost shook his head. "May as well get it all out while I'm on a roll." He tossed back a third phantom drink and replenished it once more. "When I was six or seven, I was already getting into trouble, running wild. Never went to school regularly as I didn't have the clothes or a pair of shoes, and not enough to eat. Not that I learned much when I did go. A traveling show came through town, and my mother sold me to the thespians for a pittance." He paused, and Clark's fingers stopped typing, waiting for the next word. "Best thing that could have happened to me.

"I think her final words to me were to the effect I could do better with strangers than with her. Chances were, they'd give me food, teach me to read and write. I'd see something of the world and forget all about her and the heartache of the prairie before too long. Told me not to bother running away and finding home again."

"You remember that?" Clark asked.

Jerome nodded his eyes misty. "Clear as day. We rode off. Wagons, mind you, not automobiles. I was homesick for about five minutes before I took to my new life. Who would blame me for I was fed on a regular basis and had a blanket to call my own?

"I was small for my age, so I was given to one of the older actresses to be cared for. Molly was her name. A fine figure of a woman, not that I noticed at the time. She wasn't exactly maternal,

91

but she taught me to launder, do her hair and makeup, and to stay out of the way when she entertained. I got the occasional hug and pat on the head more often than a fist to the kidneys. More affection than I was used to. Made me not want to run away.

"Whenever the troupe needed a child for a production, I was taught a few lines, a dance step or two, and thrust onto the makeshift stage, wearing a wig and dress if I needed to play a girl. It didn't take me long to realize doing well meant coins were tossed my way. The more laughs I got or sighs, the better I was treated. And paid.

"We were on the move constantly but never returned to my hometown. If we did, I didn't recognize it. I never again saw my mother or siblings." Jerome looked Clark in the eye. "It wasn't an easy life, but it was exciting."

"Do you recall what plays you did?"

Jerome laughed. "No Shakespeare if that's what you mean. It was mostly a bunch of hooey that the director threw together. Morality plays. Melodramas and comedies. Some songs and some dance, and most of the players made themselves available for individual performances after the show, if you know what I mean."

"Were you—"

Jerome sat very still. Clark thought he detected a slight shiver. "No. It was a close thing, but I knew how to hide when I needed to. I made sure I earned enough coins from my performances that no one forced me in more nefarious ways. Suppose I was lucky. Folks back then didn't talk about such things the way they do now."

Clark nodded and kept typing.

"So, how did you get to Hollywood?"

Jerome grinned. "You might say luck struck one year when I was nearing puberty. I wasn't able to play the juvenile any longer seeing as how I was growing. And my voice took its time stabilizing, so I couldn't take on adult roles. I couldn't sing for beans, so I mostly handled the props at that point. Our troupe happened to pick up an English actor at one of our stops. The man was a drunkard who'd been abandoned by his theater company in the middle of nowhere, but he stayed sober long enough to teach me, an impressionable child, the basic elements of fine theater: diction and projection, not to mention a variety of accents and curse words. He also dubbed me Jerome, though the last name Percy didn't come until later."

"So, that's how you learned to speak so well. And your vocabulary."

Jerome nodded regally.

"I'll bet that's why you were able to make the transition from silent to talking pictures," Clark blurted. "I can make that the crux of my thesis. I'll start searching for any information I can find about your troupe and that actor."

It had taken several more trips to the bar and countless faux martinis before Jerome confessed why he'd been left behind in California.

Jerome smiled at the memory. "Well, now, it was about the time when my voice became reliable. I'd done a fair amount of growing, you see, and all that work on the sets made me as strong as a laborer. We were in Los Angeles—still a small, upstart town. There was this—this young woman—we'd picked up along the way. Wanted to be an actress, she said. Made out that she was sweet on me. I found her to be tolerably pretty, and we started spending time together."

"Your first lover?" Clark asked.

"Heavens, no." Jerome grinned at the memory. "That happened some years before with one of the other actresses who found me handsome one night and a bother the next when I wanted to learn more. No, it so happened this sweet young thing was an innocent, and I didn't want to be the one to ruin her. Unfortunately, our manager didn't have the same honorable compunction. He wanted her, and I got in between them."

Clark looked up from his laptop, mouth agog. "You got into a fight?"

Jerome rubbed his chin. "In a manner of speaking. He got in one punch, I got in another. And then the young lady got between us, looked at me, then at him, and made up her mind. Don't let anyone tell you good looks will win over power and prestige, such as it is."

"That must have smarted," Clark said.

The ghost shrugged. "It's not like I was in love with the girl, and she'd been with us long enough to know what she was getting herself into. I realized then and there I was thenceforth a *persona non grata*, so I packed my bag and hit the streets. Luckily, we were only a few streets away from a fledgling movie studio—the great and terrible Pinnacle. I knocked on the gate. They took one look at my impressive black eye, my musculature, and that was that. I was hired as a stunt man."

Clark laughed. "Quite different from the PR they put out."

Jerome dipped his chin in acknowledgment. "Can you imagine anyone believing I was the illegitimate son of a foreign duke? Familiar with European courts?"

Clark grinned. "It was one of the more outlandish stories they created, but you did good, Jerry. You did good."

In the months that followed those conversations, Clark had scoured libraries and town records in the Midwest looking for traces of the troupe, specific performances, any piece of information that would tie Jerome back to documentable history. There were some, few and far between, but enough to validate Clark's thesis. He managed to find traces of the British actor's sojourn in the States, and even a few pieces of information about him back in London. There was a single photo Clark found, scanned into a forlorn little library, grainy and torn. The English actor stood on stage in profile with the young Jerome peeking out from behind the scenery. Clark ultimately used it on the cover of the commercial biography of Jerome.

And now, years later, Clark was trying to retrace the steps of Jerome's lost love, the beautiful and elusive Isabel Standish. Only without having her ghost to talk to, an actual name to trace, or any physical clues.

Clark sighed again and returned to his stubborn bowtie. Clark's musings on the past fell away, and he felt his heart break for his friend. "Don't worry, Jer. I'll find her. It's going to take time. It's not like we don't have some leads."

The ghost nodded as he sank below the rim of the clawfoot tub. "I know you're doing your best. I can't fault you. But something has changed. Don't ask me what, and I can't help feeling my days are limited. I can't stand the thought of not knowing what became of her. All I ever wanted was for her to be happy. Happy with me. I always expected she'd return someday. And then we would be together. Happy forever after." He sat up. "Did you know every single time I married—well, after the first, it was because I was tricked into it?"

Clark nodded. "You've mentioned. It's in the book."

"Right. And each time I said, I will never marry again. Because I wanted to be a free man if my Izzy returned to me. So, I could snatch her up and marry her right away. I would have, too. Up until the end, when I was a decrepit old man, tottering around on my cane."

Clark laughed. "You never tottered, Jer. You danced around that cane. It was a prop, and you know it. It was the car that jumped the sidewalk that did you in. I think you'd still be hanging on to life otherwise."

Jerome grinned. "True, but I fooled some of the people some of the time." He floated up with a joyful spin. "I must say, I'm glad that car hit as hard as it did. Never felt a thing."

Clark shook his head. "You were a damned fine actor, Jer. You still are. I only wish others could see you as I do."

Suddenly in top hat and tails, Jerome struck a pose with his cane tucked under one arm as he stood on the edge of the tub, one foot up on the toilet. "I did cut a dash, didn't I? Can you imagine if my mother had kept me? What a bore my life would have been. I was not cut out to be a farmer."

"You would have found your way to Hollywood one way or another. On the back of a turnip wagon if you'd had to," Clark agreed.

Jerome's look turned wistful as he presented Clark with his chiseled profile. "I do wonder, though, what happened to my people—"

"You specifically asked me not to track them down," Clark reminded him. "You didn't want to know, and since they weren't part of your life, they wouldn't have made a difference to the outcome of your story. And no one's come forward to claim kinship. My publisher said she'd let me know if she got any inquiries."

"Yes, yes, yes," Jerome waved away Clark's words as he popped back into his regular suit and tie. "You've made me reflective. And when I get reflective, I get melancholy. And when I get melancholy, I get morose. I don't suppose it's too much to ask if you change your mind and let me come along tonight."

"We talked about this," Clark said as he made his way to his front door. He wrapped his scarf around his neck and slid his arms into his overcoat. "I think it's dangerous to have too many people see you. You know you have trouble for days after maintaining your form after you have to work so hard at looking solid. And I don't want you to spook anyone who might figure out what you are. Or who. I'm showing one of your later films tonight, and in it, you look like the form you take these days. That's when you first grew the mustache. Anyone who sees you would make the connection. And then there'd be all sorts of questions."

"But Clark—"

"We agreed, Jer. Come on, be a sport and stay home. I've got the DVD of the film. I can leave it running if you want."

"One of these days, Clark, you're going to listen to me. Life's not worth living unless you take a few chances. Live a little. Get your heart racing. You know it's called thrill seeking because of the thrill, don't you?"

"Not tonight," Clark said as he buttoned his coat and reached for his keys. "I expect I'll be out late. Do you want that film, or don't you? And don't wait up."

"Fine. Leave the damned film running so I can watch myself and cringe."

Clark walked over to the DVD player and pressed a few buttons, then turned on the TV. "You can give me your critique over breakfast."

He walked out the door, locking it behind himself.

Jerome

He had never been a man who examined his motivations too carefully, nor was he given to self-reflection. Most of the characters he'd played on stage, and later on screen, contained a bit of himself, and it had never been much of a struggle to find that bit and bring it to the surface. He'd been a man who'd craved his comforts and sought affection, if not downright adoration, and had acted accordingly. If he saw something he wanted, he took it. If it proved too much of a struggle to attain, he quickly shifted his focus to something easier. There was never any point in self-reflection—it could only lead to unhappiness, which is why he was a bit surprised for suddenly having a goal in his, well, his life such as it was.

The ghost had determined that his protégé finally found the perfect woman to woo and win, and Jerome would be damned if he were going to stay home and not put his transparent finger in when help was needed, as well as abetting the boy's research, of course. Just as long as he never had to step foot in another library, of course. Those places still gave him the heebie-jeebies.

He listened at the door, pressing his ghostly ear to the panel. With a sneaky smile, he spun around until he was wearing a camelhair overcoat, and his trusty fedora. At the last moment, he snatched his cane out of thin air and gave it a twirl. With a dash, he flung his invisible, incorporeal self through the glass window and into the backseat of Clark's car as it pulled away.

Clark

He was uneasy as he drove to the university. It was another cold night, and the old car's heater wasn't doing what it was designed to do. No surprise—it had spent most of its existence in California and had rarely been expected to do more than clear a foggy windshield. But it was more than the cold that had Clark shivering.

It had been some time since he'd asked a woman out. He'd had relationships while in college and later, grad school, but none since he'd arrived on the east coast. The women here were different. He was different. Gone were the days of casual hook ups. He was older now, and the women he was interested in were as well. Sexual attraction had suddenly gone from being easy to something complex, and Clark wasn't certain how that change had come about. One thing was clear: when he looked at or spoke to Leigh, there was something in the mix far more than an immediate impulse to grab her and head for the nearest horizontal surface. The urge was there, but it was more a desire to go slow, to get to know her, to build something lasting and meaningful. And that scared the heck out of him. Oh, he wanted her. Had from the first time they'd met, and he found out she was with that jackass boyfriend.

The thought scared him almost as much as the thought that Leigh might discover that not only did Clark believe in ghosts but was convinced he was living with one. He shuddered to think how well that would go over, seeing as she was a logical, sensible, intelligent woman. Bad enough he was too tall, still gangly, and tripped over his feet from time to time. What did he have to offer a woman like Leigh?

But what if he were able to solve Isabel's mystery before Leigh found out about Jerome? He'd always assumed once he found her, Jerome would depart for... well, he'd depart. That way, Leigh would never have to know, and he could keep his secret forever. Except there was no guarantee Jerome would leave once Isabel's fate was discovered. For all Clark knew, he'd be stuck with the ghost forever. Exactly how could he keep that a secret if he married Leigh or some other woman, and they were living in the same house. And what if they had children? Would they be able to see Jerome? How would the phantom interact with them? He groaned out loud in the car.

What was he going to do? Tell the old guy to take a hike? Where would he go? As best they could fathom, Jerome was tied to him. There wasn't any way he could ditch the ghost. Then again, he wasn't sure he wanted to. He'd gotten accustomed to his phantom roommate, not to mention fond of him.

Clark considered he was feeling guilty because he'd lain down the law to Jerome about not interfering this time. But Jerome's too easy capitulation to stay out of Clark's love life worried him. The ghost had never yielded easily. In fact, Jerome was the primary reason Clark's recent history with women lacked depth and duration. He'd never had any trouble meeting them or asking them out. Yes, he was the shy, bumbling type, but he'd been lucky enough that some women found that endearing in a Jimmy Stewartish sort of way, along with his good looks and strong body, both of which still confounded him at times after an awkward adolescence. No, Jerome had definitely had an influence on Clark's love life, be it simply giving his opinion about this one or that, to making Clark's life an unlivable hell until he broke up with the other one or, in one instance, haunting an extremely sexy, but (in Jerome's opinion) unsuitable woman away one dark and stormy night. When confronted, Jerome's excuse was Clark could do better, or this one was using him to get a better grade, or that one to make an old flame jealous, or worse, another was using Clark for sex and had no interest in him as a person.

The damned thing was, Jerome was usually right. No matter how Clark might have felt about the woman in his life, not one of them was what he wanted in a partner. His last flame wouldn't consider leaving sunny southern California with him as he found his niche in academia. Hell, none of them was ready to commit to an exclusive relationship.

It was maddening to think about. Clark had learned that making comparisons between his life and the ghost's was pointless. For all Jerome had been a playboy back in the day, he'd never cheated on a woman in his life. When he was done with a relationship, he'd always laid his cards out on the table. There'd occasionally been hurt feelings from his lovers or his wives, but more often, a fondness for the memories and a willingness to move on. Isabel Standish had been the one tragic exception, and as far as Clark was concerned, it was all a big misunderstanding that could have been prevented had Izzy stayed to talk to Jerome that fateful morning. To the detriment of Jerome's career, and Izzy's, and to the dismay of the movie-going public, she'd hadn't.

But Jerome knew Clark wasn't like him. He'd teased and despaired but ultimately understood that the two were quite different. But what was it about Leigh that was different from all the others? She had an established career she wasn't about to leave. She was independent. And she didn't need anything from Clark. So, what exactly did Jerome see in her that he hadn't in any of the others? And what's more, why did Leigh seem to be interested in him one moment and then hold him at arm's length the next? It didn't make sense. But he wanted to find out.

Clark was still wondering when he pulled into the faculty parking lot. He was pondering it still as he walked through covered campus archways and into the theater lobby, where the first person he saw was Leigh. She stood staring into the distance beneath the lobby chandelier where crystals cast bright lights and rainbows down upon her, making his heart stop in his throat. "What the hell?" he whispered to no one in particular. "My god, but I want her." He didn't have time to wonder how he could have fallen so far and so fast. All he knew was that he needed to follow her as fast as he could, for as he watched, she disappeared into the theater, leaving him more anxious than before.

Only Jerome, floating along unseen behind him, heard. And he mentally rubbed his hands together in delight.

Come, Izzy. The picture's a wrap. Let's go away for the weekend. We'll put on rings along with our disguises, so everyone thinks we're an old married couple.

I can't, Tommy. It's one thing for me to sleep with you. It's another to lie before others.

But, Izzy, I love you. You know I do. I want to marry you. He looked down at his shoes, rubbing the dust from the toe of one on the back of his pant leg. *Darn it all. You ruined the surprise. I was going to propose to you this weekend.*

Chapter Nine

Leigh

Aware that everyone around her seemed to be walking in pairs, Leigh entered the theater lobby alone. She quickly caught sight of Moe as he stood half a head above most. His arm was around his petite wife. Leigh stopped a moment to watch them. Moe was gazing down at Berry with such affection that Leigh was almost jealous. No man had ever looked at her that way, and in that instant, she wanted the same sort of connection, wanted it so badly it almost hurt. From old photos, she knew her mother and father had shared that brand of abiding love, which might have been why Miranda never pursued another relationship after her husband died. That, or she was too busy founding a company and raising her two daughters.

But now. Leigh wanted it and wanted it with someone like Clark. She knew with a pang she wanted someone smart, funny, and sensitive, not to mention good-looking. Exactly like him. Who was she fooling? It was Clark she wanted, despite the fact they hardly knew one another. She wanted him and hadn't a clue how to get him. It scared her to death. She once thought she wanted

Rocky, and look how dreadfully that turned out. But Clark wasn't Rocky, and as far as she could tell, nothing she had or was connected to was worth anything to Clark. But there was no way she was going to approach a new relationship with anything but the utmost caution.

She felt someone looking at her. Leigh turned and saw another tall man at the doors, gazing at her with a look that made her so dizzy she couldn't quite name it, but whatever it was, it made her heart speed up.

She and Clark approached one another, mindless of the crowd between them. They were like magnets of opposite poles, circling nearer and nearer until— until the same professor from last week grabbed Clark's elbow and neatly steered him away from the orbit of Leigh.

She felt wrenched from a dream. She gulped and looked wildly about, only to find Berry approaching with a big smile and bag of popcorn at the ready, her tall husband in tow.

"Hi." Berry wrapped Leigh in a butter-infused hug, her gaze following the line Leigh's had already taken. "Er—"

"Hi," Leigh said, forcing herself to look at Berry. "I'm glad you came. I didn't mind too much last time, but I hate sitting alone at the movies."

"You don't think Clark will—" Berry began.

Leigh shook her head. "We're not exactly together. And technically, he's working."

"Babe, I'm going to go save our seats," Moe said softly. "Here're your tickets."

Berry gave Moe a quick kiss before he made his way into the theater. She turned back to Leigh. "I know, but the way Clark was looking at you, and you at him, I mean the two of you looking at one another." Berry stopped and wrinkled her nose. "You do realize it, right? This isn't simply 'Solange Dewberry, Romance Writer' talking," she said using air quotes. "The two of you are attracted to one another. I could practically see sparks flying."

"I, uh, well, I wasn't sure." Leigh shook her head. "This feels so high school-ish, but I don't want to get my hopes up. Right now, I don't consider myself a great judge of character after what happened with your brother." She pressed her lips together. "I promised myself I wouldn't fool myself that I'll ever find the right one."

"Oh, Rocky is such a jackass," Berry said dismissively as she linked arms with Leigh. "That wasn't your fault, and guess what, you ended up with me out of the debacle, so it wasn't all bad, right? And even if Clark wasn't interested, which he is, you need to get back in the game. Don't let the cretin I share DNA with stop you from living your life. If you do, it means the bastard won. And we can't have that."

Leigh laughed despite herself. "You're right. But do you really think—" She turned to find Clark looking at her as he spoke to the older man. She leaned closer to Berry. "You're sure he's interested?" she asked softly. "You're not being nice? He's not feeling sorry for me because of— or out to use me?"

Berry grinned. "He called me to get your number. And he was adorably nervous about it too. I'd say that means he's interested." The lobby lights flickered. "Let's go in. Moe's saving us seats, including one for Clark. And I've got your ticket. We arranged it ahead of time."

Berry tightened her arm around Leigh's, and the two of them walked into the theater.

"You're sure? He's working and needs to—"

"Stop worrying," Berry said with a little shake of her head. "I know what I'm doing. I know what I've seen and heard. He's interested. You're interested. You're both a little gun-shy, which means you both need someone like me to pave the way. Fortunately for both of you, I happen to love matchmaking."

They reached the end of a row where Moe sat, his long legs stretching into the aisle. He had his coat draped over two seats on the opposite side. "Ber, get in here next to me. You took off with my popcorn. Hey, Leigh. Toss me my coat, will ya? I told Clark I'd save him an aisle seat so he could stretch out, too."

She did as he asked. "I meant to get here sooner, but I was delayed. Family issues."

Berry frowned. "Huh?"

"My, ah, grandmother. She kept finding excuses to keep me home."

"I didn't know you lived with your grandmother," Berry said. "All Rocky said was he never got inside your house." She sent Leigh a smile full of wicked humor. "He said you were secretive, and that's not all he said he didn't get inside," she added with a snicker. "Can't say I wasn't delighted about that. It's not often he's foiled. So, you're a grandma's girl, are you?"

Leigh grinned. "I don't advertise it. Gram's very private these days. She's uh, elderly, and I've gotten overly protective. The only people she sees are her companion and me." Leigh bit her lip. "I don't really like to—"

The lights went down, and Clark walked on stage. Moe tugged Berry into her seat, and Leigh sat as Clark began to speak. Leigh felt the small hairs on the back of her neck prickle. She looked around and found the older gentleman she'd sat next to the last time, sitting three rows back. He took his hat off and saluted her with a big grin. She returned his smile and sat back to listen to Clark's introduction to the film.

"Persons, ladies, and gentlemen, boys and girls, I'd like to thank you for coming out on a cold October night to enjoy the land of make-believe. Tonight's two films are among my favorites, though that's not really saying much as I'm hard-pressed to find a film that survived a hundred years that I don't immediately love."

There was laughter from the audience, and Leigh found herself chuckling along.

"These early films were surprisingly complicated. Many were morality tales. As you'll see in both the short—made to be funny—as well as the full-length film, filmmakers played with the stratified layers of society. The heroes and heroines are all archetypes you'll recognize, but I think you'll find that you most identify with the spunky underdog, as audiences did back then. Look at Mary Pickford's career. She wasn't America's sweetheart because she always portrayed an angel. Most of the time, she played a plucky kid down on her luck who somehow made it past her poverty and troubles to succeed. She was more than just a pretty face, given she was able to play an ageless street urchin until she was in her forties.

"Other ingenues were the same. Life was tough back then. We tend to forget how hard it was for the average American. Long hours in factories or on the farm, for pennies a day. Child mortality was still high, and the average life expectancy for a male adult was mid to late forties. A female, should she survive childbirth, maybe her early fifties.

"Audiences came to the theater with their hard-earned nickels and dimes to escape. They wanted stories where the hero or heroine was smart enough or lucky enough to catch a break to succeed despite the gritty reality of life. They cheered for the one who was spunky and clever enough to succeed. Audiences wanted to laugh as much as they wanted to cry. They wanted an escape. I think more than anything, that's what this film series is about. That is why I've made the preservation and appreciation of these films my life's work.

"Not to give away too much of our future showings—but as time went on, films became grander, a little surer of themselves, with greater melodrama. The filmmakers learned what the audiences wanted and were able to play with their emotions. In the mid to late twenties, when talkies were introduced, there was a huge shift in film culture. The silent acting, such as you'll see tonight was no longer needed once there were actual words coming from the mouths on the screen. The film sets and stories grew more lavish. There were few actors who were able to make the transition. One of my favorites, Jerome Percy, is—I beg your pardon, was such an actor. He has a secondary role in this film, and in the weeks to come, you'll see how his career took off at the same time some of the world's favorite actors faded from view.

"One more thing—Jerome Percy was one of the few actors who were not directly impacted by what was then a huge problem in Hollywood—booze and drugs. Yes, he partied, but he was careful not to let them get the better of him. While there are scandals galore associated with his name, not one of them involves a verifiable unwanted pregnancy, lost weekend, murder, or the like. Instead, it seemed every time he got drunk, he found himself married. The worst that befell him—and it was the great tragedy of his life—was a mysterious disappearance that still confounds us today." He smiled in a self-conscious way. "Or I should say, confounds me, as I'm researching it in my spare time."

He paused and looked around the theater. "If any of you happen to know anything about that—and I speak about the disappearance of Isabel Standish—feel free to contact me. My name is in the campus directory."

There was muted laughter.

"But enough about that. Here, I present to you tonight's short and full-length presentation. I hope you enjoy them."

There was applause as Clark climbed down from the stage and walked up the aisle. Leigh bit her lip as she watched him. With a grin, he sat next to her, leaned over, and whispered, "I hope you don't mind."

Without thinking, she placed her hand on his arm, and a pleasant tingle ran up her arm. "Not at all."

He looked at her hand and then up to her eyes and smiled warmly. "Still on for coffee later? I'll need to talk to a few folks first, but I won't be as long as last time."

She nodded. He covered her hand with his and gave it a light squeeze, and settled in to watch the short comedy that came before the feature.

Leigh relaxed into the seat and watched the film credits. Something felt funny, so she turned to see the older man grinning at her, giving her the thumbs up. She smiled, and turned back to look at Clark's profile, then focused on the screen.

Clark

When the ending credits began to roll, Clark bounded up the aisle and onto the small stage. "I hope you all enjoyed tonight's films. I'll be in the lobby for a short while to answer questions. Our next showing is in two weeks. It's the one where Jerome Percy first got his screen credits at the start of the film, a career boost. Many thought it would be a turning point for him, but if I tell you too much now, you won't come back to see it next time."

The audience laughed and applauded.

"Good night, and thank you again for coming."

As the spotlight faded, Clark stepped back and looked for Leigh. She was petite enough that she was easily lost in the crowd making its way back to the lobby. He jumped down and used his tall, lanky frame to wend his way to the front of the theater to try to head her off. After sitting silently next to her for the last ninety minutes, there was no way he wanted to lose her now.

His department head met him, full of bonhomie at the enthusiastic crowd. "Professor Conrad, well done. I don't mind admitting I was skeptical at first, but so far, this film series has been an excellent success. I hope you can keep the crowds coming back."

"Thank you, Dean Davis. I'm certainly doing my best to see that we can. I've been fielding some inquiries from the local paper, but I wanted to speak with you before agreeing to an interview."

"By all means, Professor. And give them my name as well. The university always welcomes good press about our programs."

From the corner of his eye, he saw Leigh chatting with Berry. So far, so good.

"So, perhaps you and I could chat a little about that tonight. Maybe prepare a game plan on how to steer the interview?"

Clark's heart sank. "Oh, well, I'm meeting friends for coffee at the café around the corner—"

"Surely they won't mind if I tag along."

How could he get out of this? He was dependent on the man to recommend him for tenure. "Uh, well, of course not. Let me let my friends know there'll be five of us. If you'll excuse me?"

"Excellent," the man said.

Leigh

"So, you mentioned you live with your grandmother," Berry asked.

It took everything Leigh had to keep from squirming. "Yes." She bit her lip. "She's quite frail, but her mind's still sharp."

"I didn't think anyone still lived in multi-generational homes," Berry wondered.

"I suppose that's why I don't like to talk about it much. She's been pretty much my best friend my whole life. I can tell her anything." Leigh smiled. "And if I leave anything out, she gives me hell, but I have no idea how she ever would know."

"How long have you lived with her?"

"Since grad school." Leigh closed her eyes and, when she opened them, leaned closer to Berry. "I don't know what I'd do without her. She's been such a huge influence on me. The tales she's told, the adventures she had— I don't know what I'll do when she finally leaves me." A familiar pang hit her at the thought.

"I'd love to meet her sometime. I hardly get to talk to anyone that age. Think of all the stories she'd have to tell—fodder for my romances..."

"Oh." Leigh wrapped her arms around herself. "She's very private. She'd be mad to know I was even talking to you about her."

"Could you ask? Berry pressed. "I mean, I'll take no for an answer, of course, but I'd love the chance." She leaned closer with a twinkle in her eye. "And since she knows everything, she'll know if you don't ask her and tell me you did."

Leigh gave a startled burst of laughter. "Trying to trick me?"

"Just being my ever-loving, tenacious self," Berry admitted with a grin.

"I'll ask," Leigh conceded. That's when she caught sight of the elderly man over in the shadows. "Hey, Berry, can I ask you a question? And please act naturally. Don't stare, okay?"

"Don't stare at what?" Berry whispered as she spun around.

"No! Don't turn around. There's a man over there. He sat next to me last time, and he keeps smiling at me. He's too old to be threatening, but it's a little unsettling."

"How can I look at him if you don't want me to look at him?" Berry asked.

"Turn like you're looking for Moe. The guy's over by the wall, near the exit sign. Wearing a hat."

Berry did as Leigh asked, turning quickly and searchingly before looking the other way as if trying to find someone. She stood on her tiptoes and looked again, then turned back to Leigh. "The old guy? With the mustache?"

Leigh nodded.

"Very debonair. Looks like he stepped out of a 1940s movie."

Leigh clutched Berry's arm. "That's what I thought. Slightly out of place, right?"

"Kind of. But also intriguing to see someone that well dressed in a place like this," Berry agreed.

"Oh shoot."

"What?" Berry spun around before Leigh could stop her.

Leigh frowned. "He's gone. It's like he vanished. But of course, I wasn't trying to look at him."

Berry turned again. "Look. Here comes Clark. And he's got someone with him. Act natural."

Leigh turned to Clark with a smile she hoped was neither too eager, nor too strained. Why, oh why was it so hard? "Hi."

He nodded, his returning smile looking forced. "Leigh Mason, and Berry Conrad, I'd like to introduce my department head, Dr. Davis. I've asked him to join us for coffee."

Leigh's smile froze as she held out her hand. "Doctor. A pleasure."

"Mason, Mason," the professor muttered. "Are you by any chance related to Miranda Mason?"

She nodded. "My mother."

The older man smoothed his mustache and brushed his coat's lapels. "How fortuitous. I've known Miranda for years. She's provided technical expertise to the university from time to time with preservation issues and collection recommendations for our film library, not to mention the occasional small gift to the program." He turned to Clark and patted him hard on the back. "I had no idea you two were acquainted. I was planning on introducing you to this young lady's mother and her company sooner or later. I had no idea you already sought them out. Well done, well done of you."

Something clicked, and Leigh was suddenly wary. So, there was something Clark wanted from her. But on the other hand, he hadn't sought her out, so perhaps it was a coincidence. Did she dare give him the benefit of the doubt?

"Oh, er, well, I wasn't aware of the connection," Clark said quickly. "It seems my cousin and his wife—Berry here, know Leigh and introduced us shortly after I arrived. We haven't er, exchanged professional courtesies."

"Well, no time like the present," the man insisted. "We can talk over tea and crumpets. My treat, of course. Or given the hour, perhaps something a tad stronger, heh?"

He propelled Clark forward and was about to do the same with Leigh when Moe stepped up. "What are we waiting for?" he asked Berry.

"Clark's department head's going to join us," Berry said as she gripped her husband's arm.

From Leigh's perspective, it looked like one of those silent signals couples who'd been together for a long time seemed to share.

"Oh, I thought we were—ouch." He rubbed his elbow, his brows arched. "Oh. Well, sure. The more, the merrier," he said, his tone belying his words.

The lights in the lobby dimmed, and Leigh looked around to see they were the last, other than the students running the program.

"Well, if we're all here, why don't we get going?" the dean said gleefully.

Leigh wasn't certain how he managed it, but as they stepped into the cold wind, Clark was suddenly on her right and had gently taken her elbow while leading the way out the door. Moe and Berry were behind, chatting with the other man.

Before she knew it, she and Clark had outpaced the others. He wrapped an arm around her shoulders as he leaned closer. "I'm really sorry about this. I was hoping you and I—" He hesitated before seeming to take a deep breath. "Well, that we could finally have a chance to talk, the two of us. But I couldn't say no. I can explain later—"

She looked up at him in the dim light of the covered arcade they walked down. He seemed sincere, but then so had Rocky, once upon a time. "Maybe we can cover whatever it is he wants to talk about, and he'll leave? I know Moe and Berry can't stay too late."

He smiled in relief and squeezed her elbow before releasing her. "Thanks. I think we'll still have some time to ourselves."

She nodded, adrenalin coursing through her. Was Berry right—was Clark really interested in her? *Play it cool,* she scolded herself. *Don't appear anxious.*

They slowed their pace as they approached a café. It was busy, but they found a table in the corner, away from the noisiest part of the room.

Clark took her coat as she slid into her chair. "I hope you'll still be understanding if Dr. Davis asks for a donation. The few times we've been out together, I've noticed he can be subtly relentless."

Leigh laughed as the others joined them. "I'm forewarned. I can be amazingly stubborn when I want to be."

Clark smiled, and at the warmth she saw in his eyes, something inside her started to blossom. She was going to do what she needed to, to see if a relationship could blossom. A real one.

"And now I'm forewarned too. And I'm up for the challenge."

Izzy, please put me out of my misery. You know how much I want to marry you. I'll hire a car. We'll run away to Nevada tonight—

Oh, Tommy, I want to, so much. But the studio says no.

Drat that morality board. They want to portray you as the sweet innocent that you are. And I'm the older, divorced man. How I wish—

What do you wish, Tommy?

I wish I'd met you years ago. I'd never have married that other woman. I'd have waited for you. I'd have waited forever. I will wait forever. But please don't make me.

Chapter Ten

Clark

He leaned back and looked at the woman across from him. They sat at a low table. She was posed elegantly, one arm over the back of her chair, and her legs crossed at the ankle. Her smile was relaxed as she sipped her cocoa slowly, her eyes meeting his, then flickering away.

Clark leaned forward, his elbows on his knees. "I can't tell you again how sorry I am the professor tagged along. And sorrier he dominated the conversation."

He caught a whiff of chocolate as Leigh leaned forward to set her cup on the table. "It's not a problem. He had some interesting things to say. Who knew he'd back off and leave once Moe promised to take a look at his leaking windows?"

Clark groaned. "At least he didn't ask you for anything."

"Not when he and my mother know each other so very well," she said wryly. "I don't recall her ever mentioning him, but I'm not involved in the charitable giving her company does."

She smiled slowly. "So, now that we're alone—" She looked around and waved a hand at the few students loitering in the café. She stopped for a moment as if she caught sight of someone. Clark turned and wanted to groan at the sight of Jerome hanging around, reading a paper in a dark corner. Why didn't anyone question that? There was no way an elderly man would be able to read in the dim light. Leigh was watching him steadily when he turned back to her. "What did you want to talk about?" she asked.

Clark fumbled with his coffee mug before setting it down. "Would you think me a moron if I told you that you make me nervous?"

The look on her face started as surprise and grew into delight. "I thought I left my resting bitch face at the office."

He laughed and took a deep breath. "I mean, because you're so beautiful and smart, and I don't mind admitting I'm very attracted to you. The thought that you think me a bumbling, absent-minded, easily-cowed professor is rather demoralizing."

"Well, you'd be wrong," Leigh replied as she leaned closer.

"About the easily-cowed part? Or the bumbling?"

"All of it. I find you intriguing. I don't get to meet many people outside my profession, and I suppose I do have to be intimidating to hold my own in a room full of men who can be easily offended when a woman—particularly a young woman—knows more than they about a particular subject."

"Really?"

"IT professionals have a notorious gender bias against women. It's a highly competitive field, and despite all the early female superstars in the profession, it remains very male-dominated."

"And I thought academia was bad."

Leigh gave a small laugh. "Look under the covers of any profession, and I think you'll probably find the same sort of misogyny, no matter how far we've come." She looked at him through her lowered lashes. "So, you think I'm pretty?" she batted her lashes to hide the twinkle in her eyes before she sobered. "I hate asking because I hate sounding so needy or vain. Contrary to what I just said, maybe I need an ego boost."

He shook his head. "I didn't say that. I said beautiful." He watched her blush lightly. "You are. As well as being so smart, I'm afraid you'll leave me in the dust intellectually."

Leigh leaned forward on the low table and rested her chin on her fisted hand. "Keep talking," she said, batting her eyelashes exaggeratedly. He laughed.

"I noticed the first time we met, but of course, you were with that—"

She groaned and sat back as she covered her face with her hands. Clearly, her coquettish game was over. "Awkward. Rocky. The one big mistake in my life, and you had to witness it." Leigh shook her head. "I swear, my having dated him is going to dog me the rest of my life. The fact that I dated him is like a ghost that won't go away."

Clark acted on impulse and tapped her knee to get her attention. "I also witnessed your coming to your senses about him," he said. "You were brilliant. What I didn't know was if you and he were having a moment or if it was permanent. I, uh, couldn't quite ask my cousin since I didn't know Moe or Berry that well."

Leigh closed her eyes and, with her hands still framing her face, took a deep breath. When she opened them again, she said, "I'll be happy if I never have to see or talk about that man again. Ever."

Clark moved to the seat next to her.

She lowered her hands and shook her head. "It took me a while to recover from him, emotionally. Far too long. I swear I'm still in recovery. I haven't gone out with anyone since. And it would help if he left me alone…"

"Would you consider—" His voice broke like a fifteen-year-old Mickey Rooney, and he choked back his nerves. He swallowed to regain his composure. "I mean, I'm not seeing anyone either, and, well, maybe you and I—"

She smiled. "If I did, you need to promise to keep telling me how beautiful and smart I am."

Clark's nerves eased. "I promise I'll continue to remind you how smart and beautiful you are because it's the truth, and everyone needs to hear the truth about themselves, no matter how awkward it might be. And trust me, beneath this suave, sophisticated shell, I'm the reigning Mr. Awkward champion."

Leigh bit her lip as if thinking hard before she reached out a hand. It seemed the coquette had returned. "And if we were to start dating, and I'm not saying yes, would you let me tell you how intelligent and handsome I find you in return?"

He swallowed hard and tried to force the smile from his face. "You don't need to say that."

She shook her head slowly. "You need to know one thing about me. I don't say things to make people feel good. I wish I could, but in my position, that would be career suicide. So, when I tell you something, you have to understand it's because I believe it. And you are good-looking. I noticed right away before you opened your mouth and impressed me with your intellect and your passion."

Clark swallowed again, feeling the electric pull between them. "Well then." He smiled. "I guess you didn't notice my ears. They stick out something awful."

She laughed before she craned her neck and laughed as he turned from side to side. "I hadn't. And they're not that bad. I wanted to ask how you came by your passion for old movies, though."

"My mother. She's a huge film buff. She wanted to be a movie star but apparently got pregnant on her honeymoon and had to give up her dream. She's always blamed me for her failed career. I always told her if I ever made a movie, I'll feature her."

"So, she named you for Clark Gable?"

117

He grinned. "She wanted to name me Laurence, after Laurence Olivier, her favorite, but when she first got a look at me and saw my ears stuck out, she figured she'd better name me Clark instead."

Leigh laughed. "You're making that up."

He shook his head. "Nope. If you ever meet her, you can ask. My next eldest brother is Larry—Laurence. All five of us are named after movie stars. The fact that your name is Leigh would make her swoon. You're not named for Vivian Leigh, by any chance? The coincidence would be way too much."

She grinned. "Do you know how tempted I am to fib about that? But no."

Leigh was back to biting her lip, and suddenly he wanted nothing more than to smooth it with his thumb.

"So, about our dating—" he started,

She shook her head and then clasped her hands together. "Before we talk about that, can I ask you something? It's related, really more of a favor. It might change your mind about wanting to since we just met and all. This might be a make-or-break thing."

"Sure. Need a ride to the airport?" he asked. "Not that I like early morning flights, but I could make an exception for you."

She smiled. "No. This is a little more, uh, noteworthy."

"I don't own a shovel, so if you've got a body to bury, we can stop at the hardware store."

"What a vivid imagination you have."

"You've no idea," he wanted to reply. "I watch a lot of old movies."

"This is, well, you have every right to say no, of course. It's a huge imposition and all since we really don't know each other that well." Her big brown eyes looked into his. "Maybe forget I said anything."

He watched her fidget and wished he could take her in his arms to soothe her. "Whatever it is seems like it's a big deal to you. Go ahead. I can't believe you'll offend me."

118

She nodded, locked her fingers together, and then lifted her chin. "There's this big commemorative dinner. For work. Celebrating twenty-five years in business. It's a big deal for my mother. And me, and my sister, of course."

He let out a breath. "You need a date?"

She looked panicked. "Well, um, yes. High pressure situation, at least for me. And we hardly know one another well enough for me to ask you. The press will be there to cover it, and that will lead to all sorts of speculation, so forget—"

"I'd be happy to."

"It's black tie, very formal…"

"Okay."

"And there'll be lots of very stuffy people who are very full of themselves…"

"Leigh, I said yes."

She shut her mouth with a click of her teeth, and her eyes grew round. "You what? I mean, you will?"

"Sure."

"I don't want to impose on you. I mean, it'll be as friends because we aren't— we haven't— you know, really agreed to date. But people will make assumptions. I want to wait to see how it goes before we—"

She glanced at the mug in her hands, and he took her free hand in his and rested their clasped hands on her knee. "Let them assume whatever they want. I like you, and I like being with you. And if you need something or someone, I'm happy to assist. All as a means for us to get to know each other better."

"Really?" There was so much uncertainty, hope, and need in her voice he couldn't regret his offer. What the hell had Rocky done to her to make her so unsure of herself? He wanted to hit the guy, and Clark wasn't a violent man.

"Of course. I'll probably need a plus-one for university things, so you'll be able to return the favor. But I have a hard time believing you don't have anyone else you can ask before me."

She shook her head. "No. I'm sort of in charge of everyone in the IT division, which is pretty large. Even if we didn't have a no-fraternization policy, it would be kind of awkward." She turned her hand until they were palm to palm. "And Rocky is out of the question."

"I should say so," he said, more affronted than he expected. "I wouldn't allow it."

That made her laugh. "And the other former boyfriend I had is recently engaged. We're still friends, including his fiancée, but I don't think she'd approve. And my best guy friend was supposed to be on standby, with his husband's permission, but they're expecting a baby to arrive via surrogate around that time, so he can't commit."

"I guess I'm your last, best hope," he said with a dramatic sigh, causing her to laugh again. "You said this is a formal shindig?"

"Tux, if you don't have one, I'm sure I could arrange—"

He squeezed her hands. "Never fear. I happen to own a vintage tuxedo. Back when I was lucky enough to stumble upon Jerome Percy as a thesis subject and found his things in the library, there was a dry cleaner's ticket in one of his boxes. Believe it or not, despite it being almost thirty years later, they still had his tuxedo in cold storage. They couldn't bear to part with it earlier, given its provenance. But because I had the ticket and was willing to pay the storage fees, they sold it to me. It set me back so much I had to eat Raman noodles for a year. But even more wonderful, it fit. The owner threw in the alterations for free. I haven't had a chance to wear it. I've kept it in mothballs for the past ten years, but I can take it out to air it tonight."

Her eyes widened. "That's amazing."

He shrugged. "I was surprised myself, though they needed to let it out along the shoulders. Most film actors of that day were on the short, athletic side. Jerome was pretty tall. Some say that's why he never made it to the headliners." He stopped. "Hey, ouch."

He'd been kicked in the shin. Crap. He looked around. Was Jerome lurking? The ghost had promised he'd keep his transparent nose out of Clark's business. And it wasn't often the specter was able to physically impose himself in the world, but there were moments.

"Are you okay?"

"Uh, yeah. Just a weird cramp in my leg. I'm fine now."

"You got kind of pale for a moment."

"So, when is this fancy do?" he said, trying for a calming smile. "And do we want to act like a couple even though I haven't managed to get you to agree to seeing me yet? I'm not opposed, if that's what you want, I mean, need. I did take some acting lessons in my time."

"No, that's not needed," she said, looking at him through her lashes. "Going as friends is fine. In fact, that would be best for now, the event's next month. I don't want to put any pressure on you. If things don't work out between us—" She bit her lip before she could elaborate. "On a Saturday. I'll send you the details. You're not going to be traveling, are you?"

He shook his head. "Day trips only until spring. That's the advantage of this location. Plenty of libraries for me to research in a few hours' drive. Can you tell me more about who will be there?"

"Clients. Lots of folks from the company. A few dignitaries from the city and the university. Mom's done a lot of work with it over the years. A few people will fly in from California. We work with the film industry. That's how mom got her start, even though we're separated by a continent. We get requests from overseas studios too."

He watched her animated face and thought he'd never seen anything so charming. He thought he might be able to gaze at her forever. "I had no idea," he said after a short pause, hoping she didn't notice he was gawking.

"Yeah, well, she started out writing inventory systems. Mom had a connection in California who wanted her to adapt it for tracking props for an independent movie, and it kind of caught on from there. We then branched into bookkeeping, so we could track the purchase and sale of items, payroll, even some market research work, you name it. We're even doing some CGI stuff, which is so cool I can't even begin to tell you. It makes me wish I could start coding again rather than sitting making executive decisions."

He watched her, captivated by her spirit, wishing he could calm her unease. He wanted to reach for her hand but stopped himself. She seemed interested, but reluctant. He could take his time if she needed him to. "So, a lot of film people?"

She paused and pressed her lips together. "Quite a few. I don't know if there'll be anyone you know, but some might come. It might be a good chance for you to network."

"Oh, I wouldn't—" Clark stopped himself.

She looked so earnest he felt a pang.

"You wouldn't mind if I did?"

She shook her head, and her shiny hair caught the light. "Not at all. It's not like you're a starving student, right? But why waste an opportunity?"

"As a film historian, I'm always looking for leads on topics. And we can always use more funding." He laughed. "Okay, this is sounding more and more intriguing by the moment."

She yawned behind her hand. "I'm sorry. As interesting as this is, I was up early and need to get home." She struggled to rise. Clark stood and held out a hand to her.

"That's fine. I had a long day too. So, maybe we'll talk before the big day—I mean, date?" he asked.

She smiled and leaned closer. "I'd like that," she said when her phone rang in her purse. Leigh rooted around until she found it, looked at the display, and then pressed the cancel call icon on the screen. "That son-of-a-bit..." she closed her eyes for a moment as she composed herself. "See what I mean? That was Rocky.

Calling despite my having blocked him. I don't know how he does it and why he won't quit." She took a deep breath. "Sorry. What were you saying?"

Clark tilted his head. "I see I'll have to be patient with him too. But what I wanted to say was, depending on how it goes at your event, we can discuss seeing each other a bit more casually?" he asked.

Her hesitation went straight to his heart. Rocky had really hurt this woman, and he wanted to do nothing more than throttle the man. How dare he do this to her?

"Would you mind walking me to my car? It's kind of dark, and the lot will be mostly empty by now."

"Of course," he said as he helped her into her coat, then pulled on his own, well aware she hadn't answered him.

He took her arm as they went out into the blustery night. She pointed where she was parked, and all he could think of was if he should try to kiss her. He wanted to. Very badly. She looked so very kissable. And in need of one, or two, perchance three. And most of all, he wanted to be sure Jerome was nowhere near. He cast a stern mental thought into the universe, not that such had ever worked before. It would be like the old bugger to ruin an intimate scene for his own entertainment.

As soon as her car came into view, Leigh dug her keys from her purse and pressed the automatic starter. "This has been such a nice evening."

They stopped outside her door. "I'm sorry again about the dean inserting himself. You'll give my apologies to Berry?"

Leigh smiled. "I don't think she minded. And it might mean work for Moe, which is never a bad thing." She grinned at him. "Besides, we finally had a chance to talk."

He stepped closer and slipped his hands along her arms to her elbows, telling himself he was shielding her from the fierce wind. "We did. And I enjoyed your company. Maybe we can do this again sometime? Maybe without the movie prelude?"

"As friends?" she asked.

He gave as non-committal a shrug as he could, given his coat was not nearly thick enough to block the autumn wind. "Maybe, or more? But not until after your big night."

She grinned and stepped closer, looking up as he was so much taller than her. "I'll be back for your next film in a couple of weeks. The dinner is the week after that." She bit her adorable lip one more time, and it nearly was enough to warm his rapidly chilling flesh. "I'm afraid I'll be traveling a lot between now and then. I won't be home most evenings."

"Oh." He paused. "You might be a difficult woman to romance. Should someone such as myself be so inclined and given permission, of course."

Leigh smiled up at him. The tips of her boots touched the toes of his shoes, sending a spark through him. "Not so difficult, once you get to know me," she said in a husky voice, her lips slightly parted.

"Leigh—" His hands went to her lapels, snuggling them closer to her chin.

"Clark—" Her eyes drifted closed.

This was one invitation Clark was not going to miss. He lowered his head, fully intending to press his lips to hers.

"Excuse me," came a gravelly voice.

He bumped his forehead into hers. *No. It can't be. Why would Jerome do this to me? Jerome said he liked Leigh. Thought she was the right woman for me?* Gritting his teeth, Clark was aware that he and Leigh sighed together before turning their faces to the interloper.

"Excuse me. Sorry to bother you, but do you happen to have a match?"

"A match?" Clark had never heard that particular tone come out of his throat before. "You want a match?"

"Oh, I beg your pardon. You're a non-smoker? My apologies to you both." Jerome tipped his hat and faded into the dark night.

"I can't believe that guy," Clark sputtered as he stared into the gloom.

"I can."

Clark whipped his head to her.

"I've seen him here. I sat next to him the first time I came. He nodded to me in the theater earlier, and I saw him at the cafe." She gazed over Clark's shoulder. "Kind of funny that an old man like him would be out on a cold night."

She rubbed her gloveless hands together, and he heard her teeth chatter. Clark took her hands in his. "I'm sorry we were interrupted."

"Me too," she said as she beeped to unlock her door. "But I'm freezing, and I know you're not used to this kind of cold. Can I give you a lift to your car?" She slid in behind the wheel.

He shook his head. "No. Thanks. I'll walk to warm up. And maybe catch up with that guy. Give him a piece of my mind."

She shut her car door and opened the window. "I'll talk to you soon, okay? Even though I'm traveling, I have some evenings free. Maybe I'll give you a call?"

Clark stuck his hands in his pockets. "Yes. I'd like that. Very much."

"Well, goodnight," she said.

"Good night," he replied as her window rolled up and she drove off.

He rolled his head to loosen his tight neck muscles. "So," he asked the heavens. "How exactly does one go about killing an interfering old ghost?"

Tommy, I saw the way Blanche was eyeing you.

My love, she's nothing to me. You know I only have eyes for you. I'd sleep in your bed every night for the rest of my life if you'd let me.

Oh, you're just saying that.

Darling, you wound me. I would marry you tomorrow if it wasn't written into your contract you can't marry without the studio's permission. I don't know how you let them add that clause.

Blanche means nothing to you? Promise?

Come into my arms, Buttercup, and let me hold you. Now, isn't that better?

It is. So, you don't care for Blanche?

Blanche who?

Chapter Eleven

Leigh

"That dress reminds me of one I once wore."

Gram had never sounded so wistful.

"You like it? I thought it had a flapper vibe to it," Leigh replied.

The dress was beautiful. It was a soft, pale blue silk with a snug sheath that widened at her hips as the tone melded into a vibrant, cobalt blue. The bodice was beaded and shimmered lightly when she moved.

"It is lovely," Gram agreed. "In fact, I think I saved the half-hat that matched mine. It has just the right amount of—what do you call it—bling. Go run to my closet to get it. Third shelf down on the right. It's in a silver box."

Leigh brushed past her grandmother's wheelchair and found the headpiece exactly where she said it would be. She brought the box and opened it in front of the old woman.

The concave, blue silk oblong was as dark as the lower part of Leigh's dress. It was dotted with drops of small crystals and had a spray of indigo feathers fluttering over the long edge farthest from the comb. The effect was subtly glamorous. "Ah, yes, exactly as I recall. I haven't seen it in years. But I must have known you'd need it someday." The old woman smiled, her eyes tearing in pleasure. "Do you like it? Don't wear it if you don't. No need to spare my feelings."

Leigh slid her fingers under the antique piece. It seemed solid enough. She waggled the sewn-in comb a time or two to make sure it would hold, then brought it to the mirror. "It's gorgeous," she said in a hushed breath. "Of course, I'll wear it. Help me decide how to position it."

She looked deeper into the box and found a photo of her grandmother, in a dress very much like the one she now wore. Leigh held it up, realizing as she did that the photo was torn. All she could see was the elbow of a rather tall gentleman where their arms had been linked.

"That doesn't look like Grandfather."

Gram leaned back to look at the image. "Oh, no, my darling. That was, well, someone best left forgotten. I didn't realize I'd kept that old picture. Your grandfather would have been mad if he'd known. Terribly jealous he was."

Leigh turned the picture back to look at it again. "Did you give the other half to your boyfriend?"

Gram sighed. "No, Dearest. I ripped it in a fit of pique and must have thrown the other half away. Not sure if you young gals still have those—"

Leigh laughed. "I think we do, but we call them something else these days."

"I couldn't bear to part with it. I did look lovely that night."

127

"What was his name?"

Gram looked up. "Your grandfather?"

"Gram," Leigh said with a roll of her eyes. "This guy. Your date. If you and he were so gussied up, you must have known him pretty well."

Instead of answering, Gram closed her eyes. "He was—" Her eyes snapped open, and she stopped herself. "He was my past."

"A lover then. Star crossed?" Leigh prompted.

Gram laughed, but it sounded forced. "Foolishness. I was a foolish girl with grand dreams. And he was too good looking for his own good. Cocky, you'd call it now. Sure of himself. Goodness knows I've learned a lot since then."

"Tell me about him," Leigh said as she went back to the mirror and started to position the silk and feathered concoction. "I promise I won't judge."

"The past is best left where it was left," Gram said, her voice softer and sadder than before. "Come, set that on the left instead of the right. It's curved to fit there, as it did in that picture. Maybe that's why I kept the photo, so we'd know how best for you to wear it."

Once it was on, Leigh took a selfie—Gram could never manage it, and then she held it side by side with the old photo to show Gram. "I never appreciated how much I look like you," she said.

"More than I realized, though you are dark to my light. But you are so much more beautiful and accomplished than I. Certainly braver. You know your heart—"

"Gram—"

"Oh, you know it's the truth. I had charm, and I had presence, but I was hampered by restrictions you'll never know." Gram's eyes looked off into the distance.

"Do you ever think about him?"

"Your grandfather?" Those blue eyes snapped. "The least amount I can."

"Gram! I thought you loved him."

"At first, I thought I'd come to love that man — more wishful thinking. I don't mean to shock you, but he saw me as the means to an end rather than a wife. He wanted children — a dynasty to cement his legacy. I was available. And I was pretty. Young, hurt and in need of—of—"

"I can't believe I never heard any of this before," Leigh remarked. "No one ever said anything."

"I don't know how much your mother knows," Gram said. "My husband was gone by the time she was born, and there was no point in bad-mouthing him. I lived well enough based on his largess. I wasn't stupid, but he didn't love me. All his love had been given to his first wife. He built her this house."

"That's what mom said. Do you know what happened?"

Gram gave a one shouldered shrug. "She died before it was finished. He was too cheap to stop work on it. There wasn't another man in town who could afford to take it off his hands. He married me and installed me in my rooms. Visited when he felt like it." She leaned forward and whispered, "He knew he wasn't my first lover, which was his convenient excuse to see other women."

"You didn't—"

Gram shook her head. "I never took another, not even after he passed away. No doubt his first wife was waiting for him with open arms. She's welcome to him if he really loved her. There were others, you know." Gram sighed. "There's only so much a woman can stand, having her husband call other women's names in the throes of passion."

"He didn't!"

Gram shrugged as she turned, but Leigh caught a glimpse of unshed tears. "This isn't what you wanted to hear from me tonight. Not when you're about to go out with your new, young man."

Leigh's insides clenched. "I can't believe you're pushing me to see a man when your own treated you so badly."

129

"It was a different time," Gram said steadily. "I thought I knew what I was getting into but knew far more after the first week of my marriage. It was my choice to stay. And he gave me my child. I was happy enough to raise her. He was disappointed that she wasn't a boy—couldn't help that. I bore him other children, you know, all boys. Three of them. Each died in infancy."

"Oh Gram—"

"It was a very different time. I felt lucky to have the one. But you are so much smarter than I was. You have a career. You're independent, money of your own no man can take away. You had a bad relationship and were able to walk away from it before it ruined your life. And you have your entire life ahead of you." She smiled up at Leigh. "And for women of your generation, if a man treats you badly, no one, yourself least of all, will think less of you for leaving him. You don't know how many sleepless nights I spent wondering if you were going to let that bounder—that riffraff you were dating, go, or feel you needed to hold on to him. I was so relieved when you gave him his walking papers."

Leigh bit her lip. "Do you ever think—" She paused. "No. Forget I said anything."

"Go ahead, my darling. Do I ever think what?"

"After your being here so long—do you wonder what's waiting for you? Will your husband welcome you, do you think? I mean, if there's an after-life and all."

Gram's eyes lost their dreamy look. "Oh, I know there's an afterlife. I'm convinced. But no. No one's waiting for me." She looked off into the distance. "I was always told it was your own true love who'd meet you. My husband was not mine any more than I was his."

"But the young man in the picture?" Leigh prompted.

The old woman shook her head. "I was in love with him, but I don't for a minute believe I was the great love of his life, no matter what he said. He had many women after me. I was the one who suited him then." She looked up at Leigh. "I think perhaps that's

130

why I've stuck around all these years. Can't bear the heartache of having no one waiting to meet me on the other side."

"Oh, Gram," Leigh cried and wanted to give the old woman a hug, but she'd wheeled herself away.

"None of that. Don't ruin your makeup. I'm a tough old bird and can take a little melancholia. I want you to go and have a lovely evening. I expect you to tell me all about it in the morning." She turned the chair but stopped to look over her shoulder. "And don't think I'm not waiting for you to find the love of your life before I'm ready to go. Call me a foolish, hopeful old woman, but something tells me you might have met him. There's nothing saying you can't be a strong, independent woman and be happily in love at the same time."

"If I had to choose between you and a man—" Leigh started to say, but Gram held up a hand.

"Don't. Don't make that sort of comparison. You know I love you more than anything, but I can't give you a child to love. I can't hold you in my arms at night the way a lover can. I'm an old woman who's hung around way too long. You—you go find him, and I'll dance at your wedding and send up a toast. See if I don't." She looked left and right at the door. "Constance! Constance?" she yelled, then muttered, "Drat that woman. I'll do this myself." And she wheeled herself away.

Clark

He stood idly at a tall table where he'd been chatting with another guest and watched as Leigh walked across the ballroom holding glasses of champagne. She was stopped along the way by people wishing her well. There were smiles and air kisses as Leigh made slow progress back to him. She looked like a dream. There was something about her that night that he couldn't quite define, but her allure was hard to ignore.

131

It started when she picked him up. His old clunker wasn't nearly elegant enough to drive to the fine old hotel. The heater still didn't work, and the diesel stench that permeated the interior was enough to have him walk to campus most days. Leigh hadn't minded driving and had sat in the idling car as he hurried down the apartment's stairs, hoping not to slip on the soles of his new shoes. He'd been ready an hour before she arrived, too nervous to sit around. He'd gotten a haircut and had the barber trim his beard before he went home to shower and then don the tux that had come from the cleaners and was as fresh as if it were new.

Jerome had had a good laugh at Clark's expense over his preparations, but he'd had plenty of sartorial advice about the proper way to wear a tuxedo. The pants needed to break just so over the tops of his shoes; his white cuffs should show exactly the right amount beneath the black wool sleeves of the shawl-collared jacket—enough that the onyx cufflinks that matched the shirt studs would peek out. Clark's tie was raw silk, worn with a pleated, wingtip shirt. And his pocket square had to be folded to match. That had been the most frustrating part of all, for Clark's attempts to follow Jerome's instructions were futile, to the point where Jerome did his utmost to exert control over physical matter. Though successful, the exercise had exhausted him, and he lay prone, his chest heaving. The effect was ruined as he couldn't keep himself on the floor but slowly pinwheeled around the room, one arm over his eyes, the other thrown outward.

At least the ghost had been too tired to tag along.

But all that was forgotten when Clark walked into the hotel ballroom with Leigh on his arm. When the Maître'd took her coat, Clark had been rendered temporarily speechless. "You look—you look—wow," he'd sputtered.

Her brow furrowed. "Is my lipstick smudged?"

"No—not at all. You're going to laugh at me, but I have to say—it's that you look like something out of a dream or a movie.

I can't remember who, but the resemblance to an actress has me dumbstruck."

Leigh's shoulders relaxed as she let out her breath before she narrowed her eyes at him. "You had me worried. I thought you were going to remind me how smart and beautiful I am," she teased. "I didn't realize I was so nervous about this party."

Clark's hand rested on his heart, and he bowed his head. "You are every bit as smart as I first thought you," he replied. "And more beautiful than I could ever hope for in a woman gracing my arm."

"I don't really look like a movie star." She looked down at herself. "I'm much to plump. And short."

He took her hand. "You are the perfect type to have been a huge star in the silent era. Your face is the right shape, and your skin would have been incandescent under the lights. Many of the stars back then were short, athletic even."

She laughed. "No one's ever accused me of that before."

He smiled. "Back then, lots of people were always hungry, so a woman with some substance was the height of beauty." He leaned closer. "I find you very attractive if you must know."

He felt her shiver as she peered up at him with her large brown eyes. "Really?" she asked, clearly trying for sarcasm, but there was a wistful note underlying her words. He nodded and watched the slow smile spread across her face as she took his arm. "Good to know."

He leaned closer. "Now it's your turn to enumerate all my wonderful attributes."

Leigh threw her head back and laughed. "And here I thought you were the shy, bumbling professor. You're really quite the flirt, aren't you? A handsome, charming, not to mention smart, flirt."

Clark felt his ears redden, but he gave a nonchalant shrug. "Busted."

An hour later, they were drinking champagne and snatching canapes from passing waiters. A photographer had come by. Clark made him stop until he'd linked his arm in hers. The photographer then snapped their picture as they held up champagne goblets. "I want a copy of that," he told Leigh. "To remember this night forever." Leigh tightened her arm in his by way of acknowledgment, and they circulated. There were more air kisses for Leigh and many pats on the back for him as they promenaded about the glittering ballroom. Jerome would have been proud.

"Don't the two of you look adorable," a tallish woman in a silvery-white pantsuit gushed as they approached. "Leigh, you look wonderful, and who is this?" she asked as she leaned over and wrapped Leigh in a hug.

"Sarah, this is Clark Conrad. Clark, this is my sister, Sarah. She works with Mom and me at MirandaTech."

Clark held out his hand, which was gripped by a strong, feminine hand. "I'm glad to meet you. Leigh and I've been missing each other for weeks. I didn't know she was seeing anyone."

"Oh, we're not—" Leigh started.

Clark cleared his throat. "Leigh and I met this past summer and have been testing the waters," he said with a smile. "I hope she finds me to her liking."

The taller woman looked at her sister with a wide grin. "Oh, so gallant. I think he's a keeper. Has Mom met him yet?"

Clark winked at Leigh. "See, your sister approves of me."

Leigh laughed. "Mom's normally got very good judgment. We'll have to wait and see." She turned to her sister. "Where's Carole?" To Clark, she added, "my sister married last year."

Clark nodded. "Congratulations. I hope to meet her."

Sarah sighed dramatically. "She's galivanting around somewhere. You'd think we never go out the way she's working the room."

"Carole's a stage actress," Leigh told him. "She's far more social than either my sister or I will ever be. It's one of those opposite attract situations."

Sarah shrugged. "She's right. I'm a workaholic, and she's a drama queen. Luckily, she's in rehearsals now, or she wouldn't have been able to make tonight's event. I guess we have a thing about theater and film in the family. I took one look at her, and I was hooked."

Clark looked at Leigh, who shifted uncomfortably. He stored that tidbit away. "Well, I'll keep an eye open for her," Leigh said. She finished her champagne and took Clark's empty glass in her other hand. "Don't let us keep you. We'll have to have lunch one of these days when we're both in the office."

Sarah grinned at Leigh and winked at Clark. "And then you can tell me all about Clark. All the stuff you don't want to say in front of him."

Leigh laughed and took Clark by the elbow once more, tugging him back to the bar. Once they were out of earshot, she leaned in close. "My older sister. I love her dearly, but she's nosy. I didn't want her prying all your secrets out of you."

He lifted his brows. "Really?"

She winked. "Not before I have a chance to," she teased.

The band in the corner of the room started playing. Clark grinned. "May I have this dance?" He held out his hand and hoped he wouldn't embarrass himself. Taking dance lessons from a ghost had left something to be desired, and his confidence in his physical abilities were less than robust. But Leigh's face brightened, and she took his hand and let him lead her onto the floor.

This was the closest they'd been since the night he'd almost kissed her. His free hand went to her warm, silk clad waist. She smelled heavenly, like flowers that he hadn't a prayer of identifying. Leigh lightly touched his shoulder, her right hand cradled in his. A few bars in, she moved closer and rested her cheek against his chest, letting out a sigh he hoped was contentment. Clark lowered their clasped hand to rest against his free shoulder. Leigh was like heaven in his arms, soft and smooth, and an unexpected yearning opened to want more of this, more of

135

her, in his life. His heart began beating hard, and he feared she would feel it.

He didn't have long to worry, for moments later, a woman who looked like an older version of Leigh approached them. "Sweetie," she said as she tapped Leigh on the shoulder. Leigh unfurled herself from his arms, and the older woman quickly enveloped Leigh in a hug. "I've only got a moment—you know how it is, but I wanted to meet your young man."

The three of them stepped off the dance floor. Leigh blushed charmingly. "Mom, he's not—"

"I'm Miranda Mason," she said, holding out her hand. "Leigh and Sarah's mother."

He took her hand. Her grip was firm for its small size, warm and soft. "I'm happy to meet you, and congratulations on your achievement."

She smiled. "I know. I can hardly believe it myself, but here we are." She wrapped an arm around Leigh. "My daughter tells me you're a professor of film." She gave an unapologetic grin. "The two of you looked like Fred Astaire and Ginger Rogers in a slow movement of 'S'Wonderful.'"

He nodded. "Guilty as charged. Though if I had my druthers, I'd look more like Gene Kelly, but I'll take what I can get. Musicals are not my forte."

"My grandmother once had dreams of becoming a film star, or so I've always been told. I never had the chance to grill her about it." Miranda wrinkled her nose. "Unfortunately, my mother found the subject distasteful and refused to let anyone talk about it."

"Really?" Clark looked at Leigh.

Leigh rubbed her nose. "I don't know much," she said. "Two generations removed and all that."

Miranda laughed. "I'm sure Leigh can tell you loads. She was fascinated by those stories as a kid. Absolutely tormented my mother to tell her more than even she knew. Grammy was apparently rather closemouthed about the whole episode of her life. I always wondered if she was ashamed or browbeaten." Miranda glanced at her watch. "Sorry, but I need to run. I have a speech to make and need to look over my notes." She gave Leigh another hug and sent a warm smile to Clark. "I hope I see you again under less trying times. Even if you two are just friends." With a wink and a laugh, she was gone.

"And that," Leigh said with a sigh, "is my mother."

"I think she's charming, and I look forward to getting to know her better. But I didn't realize the theatrical aspirations in your family."

Leigh's smile faded. "It was all a long time ago. The closest we come these days is working with studios in Hollywood and elsewhere." She gazed at him with the frank expression he'd come to know. "I want another drink. How about you?"

"Only if you promise to save another dance for me. We didn't get to finish our first. I need more time to practice my moves," he said, trying to smooth away her uneasiness. "And you're definitely making me look good out there. So, deal?"

Leigh's smile returned, and she nodded. "You're full of it. You know you were the smoother one out there, making me look good, so, sure."

"Good. Because word on the street is, you're not a woman to go back on your word."

A moment later, another photographer approached them. Leigh linked her arm in Clark's, and they smiled for the camera, he doing his best to look like Jerome in that photo he'd pulled from the library box ten years before.

Tommy, the studio wants me to go down to Mexico for my next film. I'll be gone for a month.

You need to do what you need to do, my love. I'll wait here like a good boy and think of you every night.

But— do you think— oh, I'm too embarrassed to ask.

What is it, my Izzy?

Do you think you can be faithful to me while I'm away?

I'm crushed that you would even ask such a question.

I need to know!

Chapter Twelve

Leigh

It was late, and despite it being early November, a light snow was falling. Leigh sighed a deep, relieved breath as she stopped her car in front of Clark's building. "That was a lot more fun than I expected. So much could have gone wrong."

"Did you expect so little of me?" he asked with more than a hint of humor. "I swear I didn't stomp on your toes even once."

His faked outrage broke her reverie. "Oh. I didn't mean you. I meant all the speeches. Mom asked everyone to keep them short. There was only the one bloviator. I wanted to take a hook to him to get him off the mic."

Clark gave the deep rumble that was his laugh. "I could hear you grinding your teeth as soon as he started."

She covered her face with her gloved hands. "Was I that bad?" she asked, peeking out at him.

He shook his head. "I'm the only one who noticed. Which was good, given he's one of the deans I work with at the university."

She groaned and rested her forehead on the steering wheel. "Ugh. I hope he didn't see me. I'd hate to get you in trouble."

Clark chuckled. "I don't think he could see with the spotlight on him, which was a mistake. The spotlight, I mean. And the mic. And a captive audience. And here I thought staff meetings were bad—"

"He's like that at work?" Leigh asked.

Clark nodded in the dark, his face lit only by the dim dashboard lights. "'Fraid so. I heard through the English department grapevine that he's a frustrated actor. Any opportunity to orate is an opportunity to—" he gave her a half smile "—soliloquize. I don't think that's a real word, but it fits."

She gave a small huff of a laugh. "Well, I'm sorry to hear that. Maybe once they give you tenure, you can lead your own department and won't have to suffer his lectures anymore."

Clark rubbed his bearded chin. "Right, and then I'll be the one the others have to suffer through. You have no idea how much work it is for me to limit myself when speaking before those movies every other week. I could go on and on and on."

"And it's hard for someone to kick you in the shins when there's no table to hide under," she quipped.

He gave a startled burst of laughter. She loved his laugh. "You'd be surprised how one can get a proverbial kick when a physical one isn't forthcoming. But you're right. So, so far, my self-control seems to be working," he added.

"I'll give you a critique after the next film," she said with a straight face.

"You, on the other hand, were wonderful," he said. "Your tribute to your mother was lovely. Short, to the point, and it brought tears to her eyes."

Leigh turned to him. "I was too nervous to look at her until I was finished."

He nodded, his dark eyes dancing in the dim light. "As hard as it was tearing my eyes off you, I saw her wipe her eyes a few times."

"You needn't say that," she said, looking away.

139

He shifted until he faced her and rested his hand on the back of her seat. "That was no empty compliment," he said softly. "It's been all I can do to keep from telling you how lovely you look tonight. How much I loved dancing with you and talking to you and your friends."

"So, it wasn't horrible for you?" she said asked.

"Are you kidding? I like spending time with you, and I met a lot of important people. To be perfectly selfish, it was a great opportunity for me. I made a lot of contacts. Being associated with you didn't hurt."

Leigh's stomach clenched. So, there was something he wanted from her after all. Didn't it figure she'd find out once she got comfortable with him. She stiffened and tried to pull away, but he covered her hand with his. "But all that aside, being with you was what made it special. I hope you feel the same way."

His tone was straightforward, and his eyes were wide. There was no shiftiness to them. Rocky had never spoken to her from the heart. Perhaps Clark was sincere. Not knowing, unable to trust her instincts, was torture.

"You're not simply saying that, are you? Because you feel you have to? I really won't mind."

She could see Clark's jaw tighten. "Are you calling me a liar? I hope you're saying that out of some sort of misplaced insecurity rather than brushing me off. Not that you have anything to be insecure about. Hell, look at you. A big shot at your company and smarter than everyone else in the room. Beautiful in a way that's uniquely your own. And until five minutes ago, I would have said the most confident, powerful woman of our generation I've ever been with. And remember, I'm from California, where confidence grows on trees along with the oranges. Only you're the real deal, not phony in the least."

She looked at him then, seeing the honesty in his eyes. It was as if a switch went off in her head. "I'm sorry… I sometimes get a little gun shy. I like—" she cleared her throat. "I liked spending time with you too," she said softly. "It was easy. And fun. I, uh, like you. A lot." She shed her gloves and reached for his bare hands.

His fingers tightened around hers. "Good, because I'd like to spend more time with you. Maybe when we don't have to dress up and spend time in the spotlight." He pressed his lips together. "I want to kiss you."

She felt a smile form. "Do you?"

"I do. A lot," he affirmed. "But honestly, I'm kind of scared to go for it, given you're so powerful."

Her smile grew broader. "That's how you see me?"

Clark unbuckled his seatbelt and turned more fully toward her and took both her hands in his. "It's about the sexiest thing imaginable. I don't care who knows. It's not emasculating. It's the opposite. For a woman like you to want a guy like me... it's... it's—"

She pressed her mouth to his. There was silence as his lips moved against hers. Sweetly. Reverently. He accepted her kiss and returned it threefold, turning his head to change their angle, to better exchange one kiss for each she gave, and ask for another.

Clark pulled back slightly, and she watched as he looked down into her eyes, his fingers tenderly brushing a few strands of hair from her brow with his thumbs. "I guess we're not too old to make out in cars," he said with a smile.

Leigh gave a small, surprised laugh, then drew in a deep breath and came back for more. His tongue tickled her lips, and with a sigh, she opened them, inviting him in, where they waltzed intimately, as the heat between them throbbed and built.

Leigh pulled back, held his head, and pressed her forehead to his as she caught her breath. His hands held her cheeks and caressed her jaw above her scarf. "I—" She cleared her throat again. "I suppose I wanted to kiss you too," she said in a low voice. She looked up at him. "I still do."

141

He said nothing but pressed his mouth to hers once more, softly, gently, the heat between them enough for now until it grew, and his hands went to her hair. "Leigh—ooops—" He knocked the small fascinator off and caught it, presenting it to her with a chagrinned smile.

She sighed as she took it from him, brushing the feathers where they were ruffled. "Clark, I want you to know, the next time you want to kiss me, you don't have to ask first." She looked into his eyes. "You can pretty much assume I want to kiss you too."

She felt his smile against her cheek. "Yeah?"

She nodded and kissed him again. "Yeah."

His hands slipped around her in the tight space of the car. "It's late. And if I were to invite you in, I might not want you to leave. But even I know it's too soon for us to—you know—"

She kissed him again. "I suppose one of us has to be the adult here," she said wistfully.

He laughed and hugged her tighter, kissing with increasing ardor until one of their elbows hit the horn, and they broke apart. "That hasn't happened to me since I was a teenager."

"Making out in a car at midnight?"

He nodded, smiling in the dark. "And calling all sorts of unwanted attention to myself with my too large elbows and long legs."

"I'd say you grew into them pretty well," she remarked.

"You have no idea how glad I am you think so," he said ruefully. "But it's late, and you said you have things to do tomorrow—" He looked at his watch, "—later today. So, I'll go on up to my cold, lonely bed, and I'll talk to you. Very soon."

She pouted. It was too soon to assert herself, no matter how much she wanted to. She'd never slept with a man on the first date, and this was the first time she considered it. But there was Gram to think of. Leigh didn't want to scare Clark off, so instead, she pressed one more kiss to his cheek. "Okay, Professor, I'll let you go. I have a busy day tomorrow, and the whole week is going to be crazy, but I'm freeing up my Friday night so I can go to your film." She looked into his eyes. "Want me to save you a seat again?"

"At the risk of sounding too eager, yes. Yes, I do. And it's going to be a great night. I'll be showing Jerome Percy's one and only starring role along with the mysterious Isabel Standish. When I think about how awesome a couple they were— what they could have done on the screen if she hadn't disappeared—" He stopped and, clutching his hands to his head, groaned. "Gotta keep that obsession from taking over. I've been researching what happened to her. Did I tell you that's one of the reasons I came east? All the credible rumors say she came here."

Leigh quieted. "Oh?"

Clark nodded. "Yeah. Sorry about that little outburst. I need to work on that so you don't change your mind about me."

She laughed. "What? And miss the fun of watching your ears turn red."

"Seriously?"

She gave him another quick kiss. "I don't know. It's too dark to tell, but I do need to tease you a little."

"Leigh, I want a copy of those pictures they took of us tonight."

She smiled at him. "We do clean up good, don't we?" she joked, then looked out the windshield. "Will you look at that?"

Clark's gaze followed hers, and she felt him wince.

"Way too much of a coincidence, don't you think?" she asked, for it was the older gentleman from the University movie theater getting out of an old-fashioned checker cab on the corner. At least she thought it was he. It was too dark to tell, and the streetlight wasn't on, but he wore a wide-brimmed hat at a jaunty angle, and there was the faint glow of a cigarette dangling from his mouth. "When's the last time you saw a cab like that?" she said in awe.

Beside her, Clark stirred, and she glimpsed his jaw tightening. "Coincidence, sure," he muttered.

The cab drove on, its rear lights fading into the night as they watched the man lean against a light pole and light another cigarette, tossing away the match carelessly, like they used to do in movies.

"I need to go," Clark said. He reached for the door handle. "I'll talk to you—call you every night. Or you call me." He kissed her, missing her lips and landing on her chin, and then was gone, striding big, long strides over to the man at the lamppost. Leigh grinned at the sight and drove off as Clark confronted the ubiquitous man in her rear-view mirror.

Clark

"I can't believe you— I mean, you were supposed to be— if she starts to suspect who— I mean what you are— why can't you mind your own damned business?" Clark sputtered as he walked in circles before the stationary ghost. "Why?" he asked, running his hand through his hair when he finally stopped. "I give you your privacy."

Jerome laughed. "M'boy, I have no secrets left from you in this life or the one before."

"I never wrote about the really salacious stuff." Clark exhaled. "You know that."

"Not that it mattered," the ghost said with a trace of bitterness. "It had all been printed before. And given the modest success of the book, the stuff you left out got dredged up anyway."

Clark's shoulders sagged. "We knew that was a risk. You knew it from the time you offered to help me."

"Doesn't mean I like it." Jerome snatched the cigarette from his mouth and crushed it as the embers, bits of tobacco, and paper fluttered into nothingness under his ghostly sole.

Clark stopped his pacing. "I'm sorry about that. I was as scholarly as I could be. Even with the rewrite, I kept to the high road and didn't do more than reference all that. It *was* part of your story, after all. It's what made you a legend, kept you working even in the lean years, including in the fifties when you were accused of being a lefty has-been.

That got Jerome's attention. "Ha! I *was* a lefty. In my heart. Not that I did much for the cause other than attend a few rallies and midnight meetings, and part with a few greenbacks. I had to do something with my life. The damned scripts I was given those days were mediocre at best. I needed some excitement." He straightened his tie. "And I was *never* a has-been."

"You lent your support for workers' rights. That was plenty. Made folks think. And you never ratted anyone out, ever. That's more than can be said for some."

Jerome rubbed his chin. "That I did, and I'm proud of it."

"But none of that has anything to do with your spying on me and Leigh tonight."

"Hardly spying. What you two did in her car on a frigid night like this—it's not like it was back in California where the weather was always balmy and a midnight tryst in the backseat of a car would keep a man warm for hours, and the memory would stay with him for days—"

"You promised," Clark said again.

"It's not like you two did anything. Why at your age, I'd have…"

"Jer!" Clark roared. "Stop changing the subject. It's not all about you."

The ghost restored his meek mien. "So right, so right. Sorry 'bout that, son."

"So, you were spying."

"Let's say it was the tux. It's been a long, long time since that suit saw the inside of a ballroom. I couldn't help myself. I made sure no one saw me. I floated above the chandeliers. Nice party, for a bunch of stiffs that is. Not like the crowd I used to run with, that's for sure—"

145

Clark shook his head. "The period cab— I must say that was a nice touch."

Jerome gave a wide grin. "Like that, did you? I was quite proud of it."

Clark glanced up and looked at Jerome over his glasses. "Jerry, what am I going to do with you?"

"Well, forgive me for one. No harm done. And you did get to kiss the girl. I mean, she kissed you. Not a bad ending for the night. Sure, it could have been better, but you're not the type to take advantage of a warm, willing woman—"

"I was being respectful. We hardly know each other. And I wasn't about to invite her up when I thought you were hanging around, no matter how much I wanted to. She's, well, her last boyfriend was a real jackass. I don't want to scare her off by being too pushy."

"You know, Clark, you could take a page out of my book— take two and be a little more forceful. It's not like she didn't want you. You could have…"

"I wasn't ready to make a move like that, you old lecher. She came off a bad breakup. Really down on men. I don't want to blow it by moving too fast."

"More's the pity," Jerome replied, shaking his head. "Just make sure you're not moving too slow either." He looked around, seeing scraps of paper and a few brown leaves blowing along the sidewalk along with snow swirling in ribbons. "Now I think it's time for a nightcap. Not that I feel it, but you must be getting cold. I think I'll toddle upstairs—"

Before Clark's eyes, Jerome whirled himself around and swooped up to the picture window of their apartment, seven flights above the street. When another gust hit, Clark shivered, sighed, and headed for the front door. In a way, Jerome had been right. He could have pressed his advantage. Leigh seemed to want him as much as he wanted her. But he wanted more than a night of passion. He wanted mornings. Afternoons. Weekends. Long

146

walks, sweltering summer days where the touch of their fingers would suffice for an embrace, spring afternoons playing hooky with a picnic by a stream, autumn cocoa with a shot of bourbon by a fire, and cold winter nights when they'd lay entangled under downy quilts to stay warm.

He walked by the front guard's desk with a wave and then pressed the elevator button. Clark wondered if a future with Leigh was possible. Would she allow her affection for him to grow? Would he get tenure, allowing him to stay? Would he ever break the mystery of what happened to Isabel Standish, so he could publish his next Hollywood biography? And if he did, once he did, would Jerome Percy finally move on to whatever it was that came next for ghostly beings?

And what would life be like once he was gone?

Tommy, I'm going to Mexico tomorrow. I've given this a lot of thought. I think we need to break things off.

Darling, don't. I told you I'd wait for you. Celibate. I promise.

That's not what I heard.

What did you hear?

When I was having my makeup done this morning, all the girls were talking about how you can't go for a week without a woman!

My Darling Buttercup, I went without for months when I was waiting for you.

But I was right here. Next week I'll be hundreds of miles away.

Well, if you're so unsure of me, maybe you ought to go and find out when you return.

If that's the way you want to be about it, fine. Have your freedom. And see if I still want you when I return.

Izzy, that's not what I meant.

Goodbye, Tommy!

Chapter Thirteen

Clark

"I forgot how impressive your house is," Clark said as Leigh opened her front door the following Friday evening.

She hesitated as she looked at her phone before she stuck it in her pocket, then smiled and welcomed him in. "I'll be a minute. And it's just a house. A big house, but a house."

He stood in the foyer as she went for her coat. Looking up, he saw the grand staircase as it wound around, seemingly forever, until he realized the proportions were off. It was almost as if the second and third floors had lower banisters to give the appearance of greater height. The oak gleamed, and the sconces flickered as if lit with candles rather than electric bulbs. He squinted, trying to picture it when new—not difficult given the appointments appeared to be original. He thought he saw a movement out of the corner of his eye, but when he looked around, there was nothing.

His neck prickled. *Sure,* he laughed at himself. *I'm standing in this big, old, historic house, so, of course, I feel like ghosts are watching me. Clearly, I've spent too much time with Jerome.*

"Ready," Leigh said as she returned, wrapping a scarf around her neck.

He noted a large manilla envelope in her hand before he leaned over and kissed her. He intended it to be a welcoming peck on the lips, but she stilled and then returned his kiss, her hands clutching his arms as he deepened it. With a groan, he wrapped his arms around her. "You took off before I could do that," he whispered against her ear. "I've been wanting to since you left me last week."

Leigh leaned against him, her forehead pressed to the soft wool of his coat. "Yeah?" she asked, sounding breathless.

He nodded and pulled her tighter against him, despite all the layers between them. "Yeah." He laughed. "Aren't we the most articulate pair ever?"

She leaned back, secure with his arms around her. "You're making me regress. And remember how much I suck at flirting."

"Then we both are," he replied. "So, is that a good thing or a bad thing?" he asked, trying to keep his lips straight.

"I don't know," she replied. "But I like it."

He nuzzled her ear with his cold nose. "Me too."

She batted her eyes playfully. "So, how many times did you think of me this week?"

Her teasing caused his heart to leap, and he couldn't suppress his smile. "More than once."

"How many more times than more than once?" She wrinkled her nose. "Twice? Ten times? Twenty?"

He pulled her in closer and kissed her again. "More than that, if you must know."

"Oh, I must," she replied.

"How about constantly, or near to," he said as he pulled his keys from his pocket and held out his arm.

"Oh, this sounds better and better," Leigh said as she opened her front door. "Maybe I ought to ask when you didn't think of me."

Clark smiled. "Department meetings? No. Those were boring, so that's when I particularly needed to think of you. Maybe it was when I was in class, talking about Allegory in Westerns. I was going to say when I went out to eat, but every time I walked into a fast-food place, all I could think was you would never go to a place like that, and then I was off again. And at the risk of sounding crude, each and every night when I went to bed." He handed her into his car. "Is it too much for me to hope I got equal treatment?"

Her eyes sparkled as she turned to him. "Wouldn't you like to know?"

Clark rounded the car and slid into his seat. He leaned over and bussed her again. "I would—" Kiss. "Very—" A longer smooch that time. "Much—" Kiss again. "—like to know that you were thinking of me. Were distracted by thoughts of me. Daydreamed of seeing me again." He pressed his lips to hers once more and pulled back beaming.

She laughed. "I was. All of the above."

"How much?" he echoed, still grinning as he turned on the ignition.

"Lots and lots," she admitted. "When I got home last weekend, Gram waited up to ask about my evening and kept me almost until dawn. I thought about you during my vendor meetings when I should have been reviewing the contract. And during lunch with my sister, who asked about a thousand questions, so that wasn't officially distraction per se."

"Yeah?" They had pulled into the street and away from the university.

He saw her nod from the corner of his eye. "And did Gram and your sister approve?"

She laughed. "My sister and mother, definitely. They thought you were very handsome and gentlemanly. Old fashioned, my mom said."

"Yikes."

"She meant it as a compliment," Leigh insisted.

"Uh oh. That must mean Gram didn't like me."

Leigh laughed again. "It means she thought you were handsome, based on my description of you, and entirely *too* gentlemanly."

At the stop sign, he hit the brakes hard. "What?"

She shrugged slyly. "According to Gram, and I quote, 'he should have swept you off your feet, into his apartment, under his sheets to make mad, passionate love to you.'" She leaned closer. "I think she watches way too much daytime TV."

He gulped. "I hardly know what to say. Not that it didn't cross my mind—"

A car behind them beeped, and he stepped on the gas.

"Once or twice while you were thinking of me this week?" she said, her smile evident in her light tone.

"Well, to be completely honest—"

"Oh, yes, let's be honest with one another—"

"Then, yes." He managed to swallow despite his dry mouth. "I suppose that did figure into my thoughts."

"Good," she said. "Because to be honest—"

"Yes, we *should* always be honest with one another," he said with a smirk.

Leigh shrugged as they turned into the campus. "A wild, romantic gesture or two wouldn't be refused."

He pulled into a parking space and rested his forehead on the wheel. "Now you tell me," he said in mock anguish.

Leigh patted his back. "Maybe we'll have another chance tonight."

151

He shook his head. "It's more than I could hope for," he said, then looked around. "We're here. So, maybe we can continue this conversation later, say after a glass of wine or two? Just the two of us? If Dr. Davis tries to join us, I'll say you have a headache, and I need to get you home. Does that sound okay?"

She leaned over and kissed him. He could feel her happiness against his lips. "Well, so much for all that touted honesty." He wrinkled his nose at her, and she added, "But that sounds perfect."

She set the envelope on the worn car seat. "Here are your photos of the two of us. We can look at them later."

"Wait right there," Clark said as he got out of the car and raced around the hood to her side. With a slight bow, he opened her door. "Let's see if I can be an old-fashioned gentleman and a reprobate at the same time."

She stepped out and into his arms. "Oooh, the best of both worlds."

He locked the door and wrapped his arm around her shoulders. "Every time we talked this week after we hung up, I remembered you never told me about your, er, conversation with that man— the one who keeps showing up."

He tripped on the sidewalk, jerking his arm from her. "Damn it. Oh, ah, him. Yeah, that."

She wound her arm in his again and tugged him closer. "So?"

Clark pushed his glasses up his nose. "It wasn't much. It seems he lives in the neighborhood. In my building in fact. Nice guy. Harmless. Loves old movies. Just a coincidence."

She tightened her hand on his arm. "Is that all?"

"He finds you very pretty," Clark added. "I think his exact words were, 'You're one lucky bastard to have a woman like that interested in you. She's a looker, no two ways about it.'"

Leigh laughed and hugged him tighter. "Nicest thing anyone's ever said to me, and it wasn't even to me. At least he didn't call me a 'dame'."

Clark laughed half-heartedly. "I set him straight about leaving us alone. Or you, in particular. I don't want anyone to bother you, especially when I'm not around."

She stopped and put a hand on his chest and looked him in the eye, no small feat given she was six inches shorter than he. "Slow down, big guy," she said. "No need to go ape-man on me. I can take care of myself. He's a harmless old flirt who happens to love old movies and has questionable social skills."

Clark fought to control his breathing, not wanting to give away the game. "You're right. But I thought you wanted me to go all ape man on you."

She hugged his arm closer. "Hmm. You're right, I did say that. And a little bit of jealousy isn't a bad thing—"

"Who's jealous?" Berry said as she came from behind. "Nothing like a little jealousy to spice things up. How are you two doing?

They pulled apart, and Clark immediately missed having Leigh pressed against him. "Hey, Ber," Clark said. "Listen, I'm running a little behind and need to meet with the students running the projectors, and then check my notes." He leaned over and kissed Leigh. "Save me a seat, will you?" He pulled three tickets from his pocket and handed them to her. "For you two, and Moe. My treat for having introduced us." He kissed Leigh again, backed up, and looked at her before he moved in for a long, lingering kiss, then made his way through a side door.

Berry

As Clark walked away, Leigh nodded at me and then pulled out her phone and glared at it before she put it back in her purse.

"Work?"

She shook her head. "No. Yes. Sort of. Your brother."

"What's Rocky want?"

153

"I don't want to know." She looked around. "He's been texting me, asking if we can meet. He's called the office a few times too. I've told my admin to put his calls through to voice mail, so I can ignore them."

"I am so sorry, Leigh. I'm embarrassed to be related to such a jerk. If I see him, I'll tell him to stop. Not that he'll listen to me. He never has."

She shook back her hair. "Thanks, but don't bother. I'll handle him when I'm ready. I'm hoping he gets the message soon."

"Rocky's really good at reading people," I told her. "The problem is, he uses that knowledge for evil, not for good. He'll know he's getting under your skin. It might be better to tell him off to his face. Again."

"Do you mind if we don't talk about him anymore?" Leigh asked.

"My pleasure. Besides, it looks like things have moved along between you and Clark."

The kiss Clark gave Leigh made me wonder how far things had progressed. It had only been two weeks since I last saw them, and they hadn't been on kissing terms then. But I needed to be stealthy. No need to get Leigh suspicious I'd be writing a story based on her and Clark's romance. She and I hadn't yet had a conversation about how I got inspiration from the couples I matched, and I didn't want to spook her. Or Clark, for that matter. I didn't know if either of them would mind the local notoriety—people who knew me had caught on that there was often local flavor to my books, but it wasn't known to my readers nationally. When I went on one of my rare book tours, I didn't emphasize that. I didn't think Clark would welcome being made a sex god (I'm joking, of course. My books aren't all about sex gods, only the first one) since he was working hard for tenure. Or Leigh the attention as a femme fatale.

But I'm getting off track. I'll do my best to fade into the background. Oh, who am I fooling? I'll be right there, left of

154

center, scribbling away. Now that I got that out of my system, back to Leigh.

She looked at me, startled, but then her face turned to one of joy. "Well, sort of."

I nudged Leigh. "Come on, spill."

"We went out last weekend. He took me to the gala for my mother's company's twenty-fifth anniversary."

"And—"

"We finally had a chance to spend some time together. And we decided we like each other."

"Like, or are crazy about each other?" I gave her another nudge.

"Like, I guess." Leigh leaned closer. I could see her cheeks turning pink. "A lot. We've only kissed. Taking things slow. Clark's so— so— I don't think I could get him to rush." She muttered about the stupidity of waiting, to herself, mostly.

I laughed. "Oh, sure you could. But then you'd probably shock the poor man. He's not quite stuffy, but proper. As far as I know, he's the only one in the family. The Conrad men I know aren't crude, but they can be pretty earthy."

It was Leigh's turn to laugh. "No, that's not Clark. He's polished. Almost as if he's had deportment lessons. Maybe all those old movies've rubbed off on him. But I'm convinced he's serious about me, not fooling around or waiting to see how I can help his career. If he were, why not rush into things?"

"That's good. It really is. I can tell you from experience, there's nothing quite like being sure of the man in your life." I looked around to see my husband in deep conversation with the dean. "When we were first seeing each other, I suspected Moe was fooling around with a char— acquaintance of mine. He wasn't, and thank goodness it was all cleared up quickly, but that was hell to go through. And he wasn't happy I'd suspected he was messing around. So, you two have been seeing a lot of one another?"

155

"We're both really busy, so I haven't seen him all week, but we talk almost every night." Leigh's gaze flicked over my shoulder. "Oh. It's him." I started to turn around when Leigh stopped me. "No, don't. It's that older guy. It seems like he's always hanging around whenever Clark and I get together."

I managed to look around in what I hoped was an unobtrusive way. "The man with the mustache."

"Yes."

"Come on, he can't always be around. This is a public spot. I'll bet there are plenty of folks who've been to every film in the series."

Leigh laughed. "Well, yeah. But not only here."

"What? That's impossible."

She shook her head. "It was a few weeks ago when Clark walked me to my car. He was about to kiss me when that guy interrupted to ask for a match."

I couldn't help myself when a laugh burst out. "No way. Well, that's once, but you've seen Clark again, not here."

Leigh nodded. "That's when I felt as if he was stalking us. After my mother's event when I was dropping Clark off, the same guy got out of a cab, right in front of us."

I don't mind telling you, the wheels in my head started turning. "That is kind of a weird coincidence."

"Clark stormed off to confront him. That was odd because he doesn't seem to allow himself to get too emotional about anything. When I asked him about it, he said it turns out the old man lives in his building, likes old movies, and hangs around. It sounded like the man's lonely. You know how sometimes older people lose their social skills and insert themselves?"

Those wheels I mentioned? Starting to turn into gears. But of course, I couldn't tell Leigh that. I nodded. "I guess. Let's shift how we stand for a minute. I want to get a better look at him."

We did a little dance sideways for a quarter turn until I could see the guy from the corner of my eye. He stood along a dark wall

156

where a sconce bulb must have gone out. He appeared comfortable to be standing alone, not like he was waiting for anyone. He certainly wasn't checking his phone the way people do when they have no one to talk to. He looked amused, not making eye contact though he did look at Leigh as though he found her fascinating, but not in a stalkerish way. He was quite dapper with his double-breasted striped suit, his coat slung over his arm, and hat in hand. Without a doubt, he was the best-dressed man in the place. Clark was the only other one I'd seen who'd worn a suit, though much more modern. But even Clark's seemed to be a throw-back to an earlier day. Maybe it was the bow ties he wore.

"He seems to be a loner, but not dangerous. Maybe he's the only one of his friends who'll go out after dark. You know how a lot of elderly people can't drive at night." I dared another look at him while he was gazing elsewhere. "Come to think of it, he looks kind of familiar."

That's when the doors opened to the theater. Moe finished his conversation and came to my side. The three of us filed down the aisle to our seats. But I couldn't stop thinking about that older man and who he reminded me of. I kept my eye on him and saw he'd seated himself in the middle of the row at the very back of the theater. He met my eye and gave me a wink. Busted. At least his attention was on me and not Leigh.

The lights in the theater lowered, and I turned to face the screen as Clark came on stage. The spotlight found him. It occurred to me that if he'd shaved his beard, but kept the mustache, worn a wide-brimmed hat and suit with wide lapels, he would look very much like the mystery man at the back of the theater. That, or my imagination was really running away with me. It wouldn't be the first time that happened. And if I wanted to keep my writing career alive, I could only hope it wouldn't be the last.

I settled back and listened as Clark introduced the film.

"Ladies and gentlemen, friends, foes, and gentle beings, thank you for attending tonight's performance."

There was an appreciative murmur from the audience.

"Tonight's feature film holds a special place in my heart. Those of you who have been here before may remember my mentioning I wrote my dissertation on the long and storied career of Jerome Percy. Tonight's film, *Sin*, is the only one in which he had a starring role. He's paired with Isabel Standish, the up-and-coming actress who mysteriously disappeared shortly after the film's release. It was wildly popular in its day, but the beauty and subtly were overshadowed by the scandal, and it has rarely been appreciated for the work of art it truly is.

"The title is a bit of a misnomer. Most folks who've heard of it expect the main conflict is about the sins committed by the hero and heroine. Rather, it's a tender love story and social commentary on the social mores at the time this film was made and the assumptions the upper classes had about the morality of the working class. In it, both the hero and the heroine, childhood sweethearts, and now domestics, are enticed by their employers to be unfaithful to their true loves, in much the way the perpetrators are. It is more about the absence of sin in the hearts of the leads rather than the act of their sinning.

You may be aware that Percy left his first wife and was granted a quickie divorce just before he met Standish, whom he desperately wanted to marry. It was a small scandal at the time, but his intentions were pure. Pinnacle Studio had a morals clause written into Isabel's contract, and she wasn't able to marry a divorced man until her contract ran out. She essentially broke the contract when she disappeared and broke Jerome's heart at the same time.

"Unlike the end of the love affair on screen— no, I won't give it all away, the real lovers' became star-crossed, and as best we know, neither was ever able to find true love in their lives ever after. What we do know is that life, so many of those who were idolized, were far less than perfect in real life.

158

"By all accounts, Jerome was destined for stardom. Fate had other things in store for him, but as you'll see in the next sixty-odd minutes, he had tremendous charisma and appeal. That's why the studios clamored to keep him despite his reputation and the sad mystery that hung over him for the rest of his life.

"We tend to think of movie stars, both then and now, as larger than life, but also as two-dimensional figures who are little more than light and shadow projected onto a screen. In reality, they were real people with bigger than usual personalities, whose images were captured onto celluloid, then projected through the ether into the hearts of those like you and me, across the world. It was both their greatest gift, and their greatest failing.

"So, in a few minutes, I present Sin."

Applause filled the auditorium as Clark made his bow. The spotlight snapped off, and I watched as he jumped off the small stage and ran up the aisle to where Leigh awaited him. There he leaned over and kissed her passionately before taking his seat, his arm around the back of hers, and her free hand in his.

As the credits rolled, I glanced back at the mystery man. He watched Clark and Leigh with an avid eye and a satisfied smile. He sat in the flickering light in shades of black, white, and grey. When he noticed me looking at him, and with the light reflected from the projection room above him, he gave me a broad, happy wink.

I winked back, turned, and took some of my husband's popcorn as ideas began to swirl around my head, some of them possible, some farfetched, and others just plain ridiculous. If you've read my stories, you'll know I've encountered many absurdities in my life and never let the unbelievable stop me before. It sure as heck wasn't going to stop me now.

The film was engrossing. It was funny, sweet, and heartwarmingly tragic before its surprise happy ending. The chemistry between the leads was unmistakable. Isabel Standish was an unquestionable beauty. She sparkled up on the screen, and

159

I felt for the put-upon lovers. The scene that stayed with me was one where the two of them were dancing together at the wedding of their employers. They were in the kitchen, dressed in their servant's clothing. Jerome held Isabel closely, and they danced a few steps. The way he looked at her—my goodness! I only wish I could put into words the love that was shining in his eyes. And she, looking up at him through her fluttering eyelashes, well, it was clear to me she adored him. The two grabbed glasses of beer from a passing waiter and toasted each other, and then the audience—that was a sly trick if ever I saw one—before they kissed, barely, and were pulled apart by the butler and put back to work. Just those few moments in each other's arms, and I was as smitten as they.

Small wonder Clark loved these movies the way he did.

What the hell is going on in here?

Darling! Isabel, why didn't you tell me you were back in town?

What? Why would I do that and break up this happy little love nest? I knew it, Tommy. I just knew it. You couldn't be faithful to me. I was a fool to think you would.

Darling, Izzy, it's not what it appears. Don't go, Izzy—Damn it, get your hands off me, Blanche.

Oh, let her go, Jerry. You don't need her, not when you have me.

Shut up, Blanche. I told you I never wanted you here. You knew I was holding out for when Isabel returned.

Fat lot of good that did you, Jerry. Looks like she's gone for good. So, while I'm here—

Blanche, get out of here!

Chapter Fourteen

Clark

He sat back and gave silent thanks that Dean Davis didn't intrude on their small party after the film. He'd spoken to the man at length during the week and then saw Moe corner him in the lobby as Clark left Leigh behind when he went to speak to the film club behind the screen.

And, of course, Clark had a long talk with Jerome after the near fiasco following Miranda's party. Clark warned him he wouldn't put up with that nonsense again, not that he had any true leverage over Jerome other than stopping his research on Isabel Standish. The problem was, Clark had made enough public remarks about it, so he couldn't in good faith give up the quest at this point, but Jerry didn't need to know that.

The ghost conceded he'd remain visible but promised to remain in the shadows and not intrude on any conversations, or as he called them, interludes, between Leigh and Clark. Further, if he did follow them home (not invisibly in Clark's car as he'd admitted to doing in the past), he'd make himself scarce if Clark invited Leigh upstairs and remain so until she'd gone. Clark had high hopes he'd finally gotten through to Jerome and that his presence would not provide an impediment to furthering his relationship with Leigh.

But what do they say about the best laid plans? That night after the showing, Clark wasn't sure if he was the mouse or the man.

Leigh, Clark, Berry, and Moe had once again claimed a cozy corner of the coffeehouse. They'd been chatting about the film, and once they assured Clark he wasn't boring them, he expounded upon Jerome and Isabel's ill-fated romance. Moe had just returned with a second round of Irish Coffees when Berry moved her chair closer to Clark's.

"So, this Jerome Percy guy, he was quite the ladies' man," she said.

His neck prickling, Clark nodded. "His reputation was pretty well founded, though he kept to one woman at a time."

"But this was the only film he starred in."

Berry's intensity surprised him, but he couldn't fathom why. "It didn't take long to shoot movies in those days. He was making another the few weeks he and Isabel were apart, and then he was under contract for one more, in fact, one was getting ready to shoot when Isabel turned up missing. They booted him off the set, recast his part, and edited him out before the release, and canceled the third film. Jerome and Isabel were going to co-star, given the dynamic between them. When the studios realized a scandal was brewing, they replaced both leads. Jerome sued them over it and won. Those months were very difficult, er, or so my research showed, but then his contract was sold to another studio. It ended up benefiting Jer, as Pinnacle Studios folded soon after that. I

162

think the fact he was willing to fight the studios held him back later in his career. Even with the single starring role he proved too popular for any studio to cut him loose entirely. He had a reputation for talking to the press on his own, without a handler. They must have assumed it was safer to keep him under contract and under some control."

Clark took a sip of his drink. "That was a dark period for Jerome. The one and only time he drank too much. But he never went on a bender the way some of the others did. He always maintained control despite his sorrow. There were some diary entries from that time that broke my heart to read."

"I might have to read your book," Moe quipped.

Berry patted his knee. "It's not like my books, sweetie. It's based on fact."

Moe covered her hand with his. "Like yours aren't," he said with a good-natured wink.

"But Jerome married again, right?" Leigh asked.

"Four more times," Clark answered. "Divorced three of them. The last one died in childbirth. It was all so tragic. Even sadder when you consider he didn't truly love any of them. Only Isabel, as far as I could determine from his papers, news articles, and the few firsthand accounts I could get. And that doesn't include any of the lovers in between the wives."

"Jerome was very handsome," Berry said. "I couldn't stop looking at him in the movie the week before last, and he was the second lead. And tonight, it was even more pronounced. There's something about him that kept my eyes on him, even when the action was elsewhere."

Clark smiled. "You're not the first to think that. He had a lot of presence. He had an earlier career on stage. I'm sure he had the same sort of charisma there. It was a waste to keep him in the background. The studio heads were trying to protect themselves, but I think there was some spite involved. Rumor has it Jerry was involved with the wife of one of the studio heads. He wasn't a saint, and he'd had his fun, that's for sure."

"Jerry?" Moe asked.

Clark was glad of the dim light, so they couldn't see his blush. "I, uh, got kind of familiar with him when I was writing the biography. I'm not sure anyone other than his most trusted friends ever called him that."

"Next thing, Clark will be calling Isabel Standish Izzy," Leigh laughed. "If that really was her name."

Clark ducked his head. "That's what Jerome called her. Apparently, he was the only one who did."

"Well, it's not like she's around to object," Berry said with a laugh. "Or him. You can call him whatever you want." She took a sip of her drink and looked up at him over the rim. "He's not still around, is he?"

Clark's hand jerked, and he spilled half his drink. "What? Who? Jerome? No. He died a long time ago. Hit by a car. He'd be older than Methuselah by now. Well, not exactly, but he'd be over 130. And Isabel Standish was about eight years younger, so any hope she'll be found alive is highly unlikely."

Leigh set her own mug down with a clatter, and a small tsunami spilled over the side. "Ugh. I can't imagine being that old? Can you?"

Clark noticed that Berry looked sharply at Leigh, but she was busy cleaning up the mess she'd made and didn't see.

"The reason I was asking, and you'll have to forgive me for this, but that guy, the old one Leigh said has been hanging around?"

Clark set his mug down loudly. "What about him?" He gave a laugh that he hoped sounded nervous only to him. "Did Leigh tell you he and I had words?"

Moe cuffed him on the shoulder with a snorted laugh. "Words. That's funny. Next thing you're going to tell me is you engaged in fisticuffs."

They all laughed, but Clark couldn't meet their eyes. "What about that guy?" He looked around. "He's not here tonight, is he?"

Berry laughed. "I haven't seen him since the movie started. He was watching your presentation, but then I got involved in the film, and when it was over, and I remember to turn around to look for him, he'd vanished."

"I beg your pardon?" Clark said faintly.

"Well, not exactly vanished. He was gone, is what I meant," Berry said as she finished her drink. "People were standing up and getting their coats on and all. But I didn't see him in the lobby, or in the parking lot when we walked through."

Berry sat forward, and the three others did as well. "And I have to ask you this," she said in a low voice. "Don't you think that the old man—bear with me now and use your imagination—but don't you think he looks a lot like Jerome Percy would have looked about fifty or so years after tonight's film was made?"

Which is when both Clark, and Leigh dropped their mugs onto the floor.

"Oops." Leigh bent to retrieve hers. "Maybe he's a super fan—you know how some people can be about trying to look like their idols."

Moe laughed as his wife looked around their small table. "You'll have to forgive my wife. She sees drama and intrigue wherever she goes."

Berry smiled as she sat back, and a shiver of epic proportions ran down Clark's spine.

Berry

Okay, time for me to take you aside, my dear readers. Clark was hiding something. I knew that from the start. Secrets are like catnip to me. I cannot help myself, even if I wanted to, which most of the time I don't. I mean, what better way for me to get inspired for a new story than when there's some mystery waiting to be discovered? There was more to that mysterious old man than Clark was letting on, and his case of nerves confirmed it.

What really surprised me was how Leigh reacted. And it was up to me to figure out how to get to the bottom of that unexpected little mystery and not lose the friendship I treasured.

"Uh, well, that's an interesting observation," Clark sputtered. "Good thing those mugs were already empty?" He smiled at his guests, but it seemed Leigh couldn't follow suit.

"It never would have occurred to me," Leigh replied, "But you might be right." She turned to Clark. "Are you going to show any of Jerome Percy's later films?"

"I wasn't planning to, this year. Mostly focus on the silent films for this series." He stood and looked around for a waitress. "What a mess. Excuse me, please."

Leigh buried her hands in her lap. I could see her pulse racing in the vein in her forehead. She must have been wondering what I was implying. I could imagine what she was thinking: *That man couldn't possibly be Jerome Percy. Perhaps it was his son? And why would he be in their little city and not in California?*

Clark returned, and Leigh looked up in relief. He looked far more composed as he smiled at them. "Someone will be by to clean up the mess in a few minutes." He turned to me. "While I was at the bar, I figured it out. Jerome would be between 137 and 140 now, depending on which studio bio you believe, so that couldn't have been him. Besides, I visited his gravestone as part of my research. I even spoke to one of the nurses who was present when he passed away. There have been an unbelievable number of rumors about him in his afterlife. I think it's because he happened to die on Halloween."

What could I do? I grinned. "I'm sorry. I was making an observation. I never meant for anyone to take it so seriously."

"And that's our cue to leave," Moe said as he stood and stretched. He gathered me under his arm for a hug, then helped me on with my coat. "Good night, all. On our drive home, I'll remind my wife to keep her far-fetched ideas to herself in the future." He gave them a wink. "Not that it will work. We've had this conversation before, but her imagination pays the bills, given her royalty checks keep on rolling in."

"Wasn't that fun? I asked Moe when we were alone in the truck. "I can see why Clark's crazy about those old films. I want to see all of them." I didn't mind Moe's little speech to our friends. He likes to do that, but it doesn't mean anything. He happens to be one of my biggest fans.

My husband cast a wry eye toward me. "Sure, you do, hon. And the fact that there's a romance brewing that you can't help sticking your big toe into has nothing to do with it."

Does my husband know me or what? "Well, yeah, but—"

He laughed. "Yeah, but nothing. Why can't you leave well enough alone? You did your part and introduced them. Why not let nature do her thing and cheer them on from the sidelines?"

"What fun would that be?" I asked, a phony sulk in my voice. We both knew I couldn't sit back. How'd I get my story if I didn't involve myself?

"Besides," I added after an appropriate moment of silence, "There's something else going on."

He hit the brake a little harder than usual at the next stop sign. "Tell me you're kidding," he said in the dire tone only a long-suffering man could adopt. He hit the gas with the same amount of force he'd done the brake, and my neck hit the headrest as we took off.

"Moe, slow down. You know I'm never wrong about this stuff."

"Berry…"

"Did you see Clark's face when I started talking about spirits? He went pale as a ghost."

"Ber…"

167

"And Leigh's? At first, I thought it was all him, but I bet she knows something."

"B…"

"Everyone, and I mean everyone, is hiding secrets. You know that. You do, Moe. Everyone."

He shook his head slowly, and I'm certain if he hadn't been wearing gloves, I'd have seen white knuckles on the steering wheel. "No. Just no, Ber. I won't allow it. No more woo-woo stuff."

'Woo-woo stuff' was his code for anything even slightly, just the teensiest bit out of the ordinary. To be honest, the abnormal (no spooky stuff, I promise you) had pretty much become normal in our family circle. "It's not like either of them have ESP," I said. "And if your brother can live with a woman who can throw knives using only her mind—not that she does that anymore—then this should be easy." Note to readers, there is an explanation behind that, but not right now.

"But this isn't clearly in the family," he reminded me. "After we met, my mother and my brothers had all kinds of unexpected stuff to happen to them. Gradually. Clark's a great guy, but he hasn't had the past few years to get used to the weird stuff, and I sure as shit don't want to be the one to indoctrinate him into the woo-woo brotherhood."

"Woo-woo brotherhood?" I chortled, which I don't think I had ever done before. "Do you guys have a secret handshake now?" I laughed some more and saw Moe's lips turn up in a smile." We have a password," he said. I was full on laughing at that point, and so was he.

"You know what I mean, Berry." He tried to be stern. We had pulled into the driveway and needed to present ourselves as adults before heading into the house, given his mother was watching TV in the family room. "I mean it. No ghosts. I won't allow it."

I tried to stop laughing, but one more look at him, and I burst out again.

"It's not that funny," he tried to say but then cracked up all over again.

"I can't wait to tell Joey. And Paul. And Sammy and Pete," I said, barely able to name each of his brothers, I was laughing so hard. "And wait until I tell Rhea, and Annie, and—"

He shut off the motor and turned to me. "That's enough," he said, and leaned over to kiss me, and boy, it was a good kiss. We've been practicing, you see, for more than ten years (and in case you never read one of my books before, that's an inside joke, so you'll have to read the first one to find out). He looked up a long time later. "That's the only way I know to get you to stop."

I gave him my best 'come-hither' smile. "Yeah. Stop one thing and start another."

Which got him laughing all over again. He got out of the truck, still chuckling, came around to my side, opened the door, and helped me down (it's a big truck, and I'm not that tall, so this is sort of our thing). "As long as you promise you won't laugh at me in bed tonight, we're good," he said and kissed me again, this time with a bit more heat.

I gazed up at his eyes in the moonlight and gave him a wink. "Keep kissing me like that, Moe, and the only reason I'll laugh is if you tell me a knock-knock joke at an inopportune moment."

Which of course started him laughing all over again.

Juliet, bring me to the train station. We've got to hurry.

What happened, Lill—I mean Isabel? Didn't you see Jerome?

Isabel drew in a deep breath. *Blanche LaFleur was there. Coming out of Jerry's bedroom. Wearing his robe.* She dissolved into tears.

Juliet bit her lip. *Maybe it was a mistake. I kept my eye on him like you asked. He wasn't flirting with anyone that I could see. And you know how that Blanche is.*

I know what I saw, Juliet. Now, drive me to the station. I'll be back before my next picture is ready to start shooting.

Okay. But I'm using your car while you're away.

Chapter Fifteen

Leigh

"Who texted you?" Clark asked as they left the parking lot. "Which reminds me once again, I need to do something about my phone. I'm missing more and more calls and texts."

Leigh sighed. "I really don't want to talk about it."

He covered her hand with his. "You can tell me anything, you know. If that's an old boyfriend or lover…"

She gave a snort-laugh. "Hardly. It was Rocky, still trying to get on my last nerve."

He laughed softly. "Do you want me to talk to him? Tell him that you're mine, and I'm yours, and that he should leave you the hell alone?"

She smiled. "Yours?"

Clark shrugged. "You know what I mean. Not like a caveman. But if he needs to be set straight, and he's not listening to you—"

"He's not listening because he doesn't want to," she replied. "I thought ignoring him would send a message, but that's not working." She touched his arm. "I don't need you to talk to him. He's my battle to fight. Over and over again. And I mean it. I really don't want to ruin the evening by talking about him."

Clark steered the car into the turnabout in front of her home's grand front entrance.

Leigh folded her hands in her lap, unfolded, and refolded them. "I— I can't invite you in tonight. My Gram—"

He covered her cold fingers with his warm hand. "There'll be other times for us."

She'd thought she was falling for him based on the bright spark of intellect in his eye, not to mention his perpetually crooked bowtie, but his unaffected courtesy and old-fashioned manners that were making her heart race around her rib cage, wanting to burst out and drag him upstairs to her bedroom.

"Wait here—" he said as he unfolded himself from his car and came around to help her out.

"As cliché as it sounds, you're ruining me for other men," she said as he stood by her door as she emerged from the car and then closed her door.

A wickedly cocky grin graced his face. "And here I thought I was scoring points because the heater's working for once. I haven't even shown you my best moves."

Hand in hand, they walked up the steps to the landing by the front door. The grand brass knocker and handle gleamed. Clark took both her hands, keeping some distance between them. He looked down at her face, his own shadowed from the lights that were on either side of the portal, plus the one above. "I had a lovely time tonight." His hands tightened as he moved a minuscule step closer. "Every time we're together, I have a wonderful time."

She simply couldn't help smiling up at him. "Me too."

His grin grew. "Now I'm going to be the sappy one, but thinking of you makes me smile. I think I've got it bad."

It was Leigh's turn to step closer as she ran her fingers up his chest. "Well, it so happens that every time I think of you, I get a fluttery feeling in my stomach. And it makes me want to pick up the phone and call you."

He moved closer, his arms slid to her shoulders as hers wound about his waist. "I think I need to send you my schedule," he whispered hoarsely. "So, you know the best time to give in to that urge."

She fluttered her eyelashes with a coy smile. "You don't think it's too forward for a girl to call a boy?"

He leaned closer, grinning at her play, his lips brushing her cheek. "Maybe some unenlightened boys wouldn't like it. But not me."

"You won't think I'm fast?" she asked with another dramatic flutter.

His wolfish grin returned. "Oh, I didn't say that. I'm rather fond of fast girls." He looked over his shoulder with a wry grin. "Seeing as I'll never have a fast car."

Stifling a laugh, she leaned in further, and he snuggled her collar around her chin against the still and frigid night air.

"Really, Leigh. Tonight was great. You know how much I love spending time with you."

Her hands moved up to pat his chest as she looked up at him. "And I love spending time with you." She reached up and gave him a quick peck on the lips. "Even if we sometimes have to put up with my friend and her crazy notions and a lonely old man with terrible timing." She kissed him again, this time lingering until she let herself down from her tiptoes.

He rubbed his chin and blew out a nervous breath. "About that— I and Berry's insinuations tonight. I... uh... have to tell you something—"

Leigh waved him off. "Don't worry about it. I know Berry pretty well, and I've read enough of her books to know she has a wild imagination." She lifted her chin. "So, where were we? You were telling me how much you like me. And how you think about

172

me all the time. I want to hear more about that. And maybe some more kissing. And then I'll flutter my eyelids at you again."

Clark let out a small laugh. "No, I mean, yes, I do, but what I want to tell you—"

She reached up and kissed him again as she tugged lightly on his bowtie. "Now's not the time for talking, Professor."

He made a small, strangled noise before he gave in and held her close, kissing her back with a fervor equal to her own.

"That's more like it," Leigh sighed, and by the light of her front door, Clark kissed her nearly into a swoon.

Many kisses and a long good-bye later, Leigh tiptoed into the house. She didn't fear she'd wake anyone, given the bedrooms were on the second floor and at the back of the large house. She wanted to savor the moments she'd had with Clark. Eyes closed, she turned and pressed her back against the door as she listened to his car drive off. She sighed happily, her fingers gently touched her tender lips.

"I thought you two would never come up for air."

Leigh's eyes flew open at Gram's wry tone.

"Quite a scene out there. I can tell that boy's seen a lot of decent movies in his life given his suave moves."

"Gram, were you spying on us?" Leigh came away from the door, her hands on her hips. "I thought you were—" She looked around, but Gram's companion was nowhere to be found.

"Oh, pish, girl. I might be prehistoric, but I still enjoy a good love scene when I see one. And you and he— there's real chemistry there." She turned her wheelchair and began to roll away, "But he's a timid one. Too much of a gentleman. Why, in my day, a young fella'd press his advantage until a girl gave in. Or gave him a slap. He's waiting for you to give him the green light, more's the pity…"

"Gram, you weren't a slut."

"We called sluts something else back then."

"I know that. But you weren't—"

Gram turned with a wide grin. "I wasn't as fast as some, Leigh, but I wasn't a shy, retiring violet either. I kissed my share of Romeos. That's how I knew when I had the right one." Her gaze drifted off. "And like a fool, I let him get away. Next one I kissed was tolerable good at it, or he was at first. Not much imagination, but I allowed myself to be convinced security and social acceptance were more important than kisses. Marriage. A ring around my finger. Respectability. Status." She closed her eyes and shook her head. "All of that rubbish is overrated. I should have stuck around for love. Fought for it."

"Oh, Gram." Leigh knelt by her chair, but the old woman rolled away.

"I've got no time for pity. Felt plenty of it over the years. I'm done with that foolishness. Now, you need to tell me why you didn't invite that young man in. Not that you have to invite him into your bed, but at least to stretch out horizontal someplace else. Goodness knows we've got enough couches and bedrooms in this place."

Leigh dropped her purse on a table and hung her coat on a hook in the closet hidden by the front door. "I don't know. He seems to want to take his time. And I'm enjoying being courted, I guess."

Gram lifted a pale brow. "What's the matter? Don't tell me he doesn't feel the urge. He's not one of those fellas who's light in the loafers, is he? I'm not usually wrong about that sort of thing."

Leigh felt her cheeks heat up. "Oh, he felt it all right." She covered her face with her hands. "I can't believe I'm talking to you about this."

Gram laughed. "Your generation didn't invent desire. Or sex." She rolled closer. "And who better to talk to about this with? Not your mother. And your sister's love life is a bit different from yours. Bless her—I'm not being critical, but she doesn't find men attractive, though she'll be one hundred percent supportive of you.

She has a different dynamic with her wife. Now you, on the other hand—"

Leigh closed her eyes with a sigh, opening them only after her grandmother gave an impatient 'ahem.' "Gram, I really, really like him. He's kind. And considerate. Funny. And so smart. And he likes me, he really likes me for me. I don't think he's using me, but after being fooled by Rocky, I'm not trusting my judgement."

"You forgot handsome as all get out. Tell me, is his beard soft, or does it prickle?"

Leigh laughed. "Soft. He is handsome, isn't he?"

Gram nodded.

"You like him?" She looked into Gram's eyes. "I'm not fooling myself about him, am I?"

"I'd have to meet him," Gram replied.

Leigh bit her lip. "Oh. Well. Right. No, I mean. We don't want him asking too much about family history and all."

"You worry too much."

"Gram, you don't understand. Mom told him her grandmother wanted to be in the movies. He's not going to forget something like that. He might be the nicest guy I ever met, but he's also dedicated to his research. We don't want him coming here and asking awkward questions. I mean, I have my reputation to protect for work, and the family's always been so quiet about..."

"He's not going to ruin you."

Leigh folded her arms. "Ruin me?" She scoffed. "Gram, he's a historian. He's researching an old movie mystery. I don't want him to start prying into our family's history. I don't know him well enough to know how discrete he'd be. He's looking for tenure at the university. It means a lot to him. And as of right now, while I know he likes me, I can't count on the depth of his affection to stop him if he starts poking his nose where it doesn't belong. And you know as well as I do there's some inconsistent information out there should anyone look too hard."

Gram sat up straighter in her wheelchair, and for the first time in a long time, Leigh saw the beauty she'd once been. Gram might have always been short, but her stature had nothing to do with her presence. "Do you really think I can't handle a handsome young man's questions?"

Leigh pursed her lips, then let out a sigh. "Let me think about it, okay?"

"Okay, my darling girl. You go on up and go to bed so you can dream sweet dreams about your handsome young man. But don't you think you can fool me. I don't care how smart he is, if he's not easy on the eyes, there won't be any chemistry in the bedroom." Gram laughed as she wheeled herself out of the room. She stopped at the door and turned to blow Leigh a kiss. Leigh caught it and pressed it to her heart.

"Good night, Gram. Sleep well."

"Oh, I'll have plenty of time to sleep later. I think I'm going to do a little inventory of my past life tonight. I love you, my Lei-Lei."

Clark

He drove the city streets, barely registering stop signs and stoplights. Those kisses. Those sweet, hot, soul-consuming kisses at the door of the fanciest house in town. Leigh's face had been tender and so beautiful. Her skin was radiant in the dim lights of the portico. If he ever imagined he'd be living a romantic scene out of a movie, tonight was the night. He couldn't wait to get home so he could text her, to thank her again for her company and for her kisses. He wanted to beg for more of them. All of them. For the rest of their lives—and even longer, if such could be arranged. And he was kicking himself for having walked away from her.

Jerome popped into the seat next to him without warning. "I see you had quite a night."

Clark swerved in surprise. He wrestled the wheel to the left before he could go over the curb and into an inconveniently placed mailbox. "Jerry! What the hel—"

"Quite a hot little handful. I'm glad you don't follow the trend with one of those sylph-like creatures women turn themselves into. They make mighty attractive clothing hangers, but there's nothing to hold onto, if you know what I mean."

"Why are you—"

"You could have pressed her for more, you know. I'll bet she was willing. Seems to have taken quite a fancy to you."

"You promised not to spy on me," Clark raged as he pulled into his lot. "I can't believe you made yourself visible tonight. We agreed you'd stay out of sight. She's already suspicious of you. And Berry was insinuating all sorts of crazy ideas that are too close to the truth. According to Moe, she's not shy about paranormal stuff. Leigh's not likely to wonder too much, but Berry, do you really want her to nose around and find out who, I mean, what you are? I could lose Leigh over this. Not to mention my job." He got out of the car and slammed the door before stomping to the door.

"That's not going to happen. Humor me, old chap. Your Leigh reminds me of my Izzy. You gotta give a fella a chance to ogle a woman. It's not like I could snatch her away from you." Jerome followed Clark into the elevator and bopped around the ceiling like a balloon as they rode up.

Clark folded his arms. "Oh, don't you dare pull that 'poor me' schtick. Her family's been in this town for generations. There's no way there's a connection. They're all strait-laced old puritans…"

"You need to look into it. I'm telling you. I think there's something there."

Clark turned his back on the ghost as he marched down the hall. He stopped and turned suddenly "No. And you know why? Because you've been disrespectful to her. And to me." He rattled his key in the door. "You lived in a different time. Men were able to get away with stuff they can't anymore. Being famous, you had more leeway than most. I'm not like that. I'll never be like you." Clark turned and trod on.

"Yeah? Well, you really overplay that in your little book, boyo. Don't think I was happy about it, after all, I did for you. And I wasn't disrespectful to women. Hell, I was far more respectful than most men I knew. And you only wish you could be like me."

"That's right. Like I want to be a womanizer—"

Jerome dropped from the ceiling, which made Clark rear back rather than walk through the ghost. Jerome frowned, his hands on his hips. "Yes, I was a playboy. At times, I was what you fellas today so cavalierly call a man-whore. It was expected, and damn it, it was fun. I make no apologies. But you know darned well I always treated my women with respect."

"All but one," Clark said as he kicked off his boots. "And look what happened to her. Oh, wait. We don't know what happened to her, do we?"

Had he been capable, Jerome would have inhaled a great, calming breath before slugging Clark in the nose. Instead, he stopped and hung his head. "You're right. All but one—but not my Izzy."

"I'm starting to think you were never in love with her," Clark said.

Jerome's mouth hung open. "Clearly, only someone who's never been in love would say something that ridiculous."

Clark folded his arms and glared at his ghost.

Jerome was silent, his fingers twitching in annoyance, looking like he was holding his breath. "Never doubt I loved her," he said at last, his voice low and urgent. "Never question that I love her still. But I was talking about Blanche," Jerome insisted. "She's the one who lied to Lilly and caused her to run away before I could stop her. That bitch got everything she was owed. But I can tell you this: I never used those women one jot more than they used me. I won't lie and tell you I loved all of them. Or any of them.

178

Everyone understood the score. We had fun while we used each other, and when we were done, it might have gotten heated for a while, but we parted with a kiss and no regrets. But don't for one minute think I didn't love my Buttercup from the bottom of my heart. And only my Lilly." Jerome stepped away, his voice picking up speed. "I was a man, and I liked sex, so I pursued having sex as often as I could after she was gone. But I was in love, really and truly in love with my Lilly, and I don't appreciate your belittling it or disrespecting her. And no, those aren't lines I borrowed from one of my films. Those are from my heart." He twirled his phantom hat in his transparent hands. "I miss her, Clark," he said softly. "After all these years, I still miss her like hell."

Clark's arms dropped to his sides. "What did you just say?"

"What do you mean, what did I say? I miss her like hell—"

"You didn't call her Izzy or Buttercup. You called her a different name. Twice."

Jerome stood and scratched his head. "I did? I don't recall."

Clark ran frustrated hands through his hair as he strode around the room. "I knew you were holding out on me. The missing link. What did you just call her? What was her real name, damn it?"

Jerome stood there, looking contrite. "I don't know. Damn it, boy, don't you think I'd tell you if I did?"

"I can't believe you got me all worked up like this," Clark shouted. "I'm sorry. I'm sorry about all of it. And it was the publisher of the popular version that had me gum up the works and paint you in unflattering colors. But I'm not sorry I published it. I needed the money, and the prestige, so I could go on to the next step. And I'm determined to write the sequel like we planned. And I need you to remember her name. And to stop following Leigh and me around."

"Oh, calm down." All evidence of passion faded from Jerome's voice. "If you must know, I was waiting, silently and invisibly, I might add, right there on the sidewalk in front of her house, waiting for you to come home."

"So how did you know—"

Jerome shook his ghostly head and sighed. "M'boy, you've got her lipstick on your face. And I've never, ever seen you so distracted, which is saying a lot given how long we've known one another. And you were mooning over her so hard I could practically read your mind."

Clark fell into a chair, his head in his hands. "Don't tell me you can read my mind now. That's not fair."

"Calm down, sonny. I said practically. I may be many things— actually, I may not be many things— but a mind reader I'm not." He flicked an invisible piece of lint from his wide lapel. "Not that I'm not sure she wouldn't have welcomed some more advances from you, but there'll be another time for that."

Clark leaned back and stretched his long legs. Jerome floated beside him, prone, with his elbow resting on nothing while holding up his head. "You haven't been around much, and I want to know how you're making out with the research. As much as I like your new tootsie, I don't want her taking up all your time."

Clark sighed. Jerome began to slowly pinwheel around the room, his feet temporarily disappearing into the ceiling, but they'd cohabitated for so long, Clark was past being disturbed by the sight. As long as there were no shrieks from the apartment above.

"I am. I've sent emails to every library and historical society in the state asking what sort of social news they have on file from those years. My research assistant is preparing a list of towns in the neighboring states so we can ask the same of them. We know Isabel came east, Jerry. It's simply a matter of finding the right reference to her in one of those papers. She was too darned famous for someone to not remark on it—hometown girl made good and came back to live her happily ever after with the boy next door."

"What about the other—you know, theory. That she never made it back?"

Clark closed his eyes and laid his head back. "I've been thinking of that too. Next week I'll have my assistant trace the train routes Isabel might have taken. We can check the town libraries along the way to see if there were any mysterious women who stepped off at the stations and made a new life in one of them. Anyone as pretty as Isabel would be noticed, even in a small farming town." He opened his eyes. "I don't think we'll find anything. From all we know about her, she was strong and healthy. She wouldn't have done anything stupid or gotten sick. And she was angry enough and had enough self-possession she wouldn't have gone off with a strange man."

Jerome shuddered. "Imagine if she ended up in the town I came from. Wouldn't that be rich. Or poor, as the case may be. A little speck, a nothing of a town." He lit a cigarette as he floated on his back. "Makes me wonder if the place is even there anymore."

Clark hung his coat in the closet and kicked off his shoes. "You never gave me a straight answer when I was writing your story. Did you ever go back?"

Jerome shook his head. "I wasn't ever sure of the name of the place. I don't imagine any of my people were left anyway. No one to welcome the prodigal home, if they even associated the semi-famous Jerome Percy with little Tommy Judson. Gads, there must have been a thousand boys like me out there, and to think I'm the one who made it out alive—"

He sat on a chair of his own imagination, head in his hands. Clark let him be. It didn't happen often, but there were times Jerome reflected upon his early life and became morose for days. There was no living with him then.

"We'll check obituaries for lost women as well. From everything we know about her, she wasn't the suicidal type."

Jerome lay back in the chair, his eyes closed. "Not suicidal. She was angry, and hurt, and rightly so. But I've never had a woman want to kill herself over me. I wasn't worth it. Disease was a greater threat in those days than now. She could have caught a cold, had it become pneumonia and died alone—"

"It was July," Clark reminded him. "Unlikely. I still think she wanted to forget all about Hollywood. She went home and lived out her life in an ordinary way. Probably married a local boy, had a bunch of kids, and died surrounded by her loving family."

The ghost shook his head. "That's not what happened. I don't know how, but if that was her fate, I think I'd've known. I'd have felt it back when— when I died. I wouldn't have stuck around waiting for her."

"You can't know that," Clark said gently. "You've told me a thousand times you didn't get an instruction book."

"I'd've known about it, especially then. They've got my name on a list somewhere, whoever they are, and I can feel it in my bones they would've called me on the carpet to tell me when she arrived. I may not have a physical body any longer, may not feel the same urges as when I was alive, but there are things I know that I can't explain to you. There are no words I've learned to describe what senses I possess that living beings can't begin to imagine."

Clark shivered. "If it's all the same to you, maybe we can talk about that some other day. It's not the kind of thing I want to think about when I'm going to sleep."

Jerome nodded. "Right. I've lost the capacity for squeamishness."

"We'll find her, Jer. I promise I'm doing everything I can think of." Clark looked around the apartment, but apparently, the ghost decided it was too much work to remain visible, even in the dim light. Clark could still feel his presence. It was a strange thing to be able to sense an incorporeal being. And it wasn't just Jerome. There'd been many times since they'd formed their association when Clark felt the presence of other spirits. Jerome brought his pals over from time to time for one of their epic card games that involved plenty of phantom gin, sleeve garters, baize tabletops, and lots of trash talk. Those spirits occasionally made themselves visible to Clark. Others did not. Not a one of them bothered him or asked for anything. Only Jerome.

"These things take time, and there's always red tape. But I'll find her for you," Clark said again. "After all, it's the only way I'll ever rid myself of an old nag like you. Get my privacy back and all that." He made his way into the bedroom to text Leigh.

Jerome laughed out of the darkness. "And that, m'boy, is where you and I differ. I lived my life playing by my own rules. Other people's rules are for the suckers who believe in them. Not me. I play strictly for fun."

"Right," Clark said as he switched off the light. *That's how you've gotten to where you are.* But he didn't say that out loud. He'd gotten very fond of his old nag. "Remind me again why you're still hanging around?"

There was a laugh in the darkness. "Oh, to make your life interesting, my boy. I never had a son—not really. I figured you were my one and only chance to mold a life into one worth living, and I must say, you've been quite a challenge. More than I expected. It's a wonder I haven't given up on you."

As Clark pulled back the covers and turned to Jerome one last time, he asked, "Do you really think Leigh'd have let me—I mean, that she wanted us to…"

There was a ping, as she answered his text with one of her own. Clark looked at it and smiled.

Jerome appeared in the dark room. He grinned, his ghostly teeth gleaming in the gloom as he tossed his hat up into the air, high enough that it rose through the ceiling. Clark spent a breathless moment before it returned, where Jerome caught it and deftly set it on his head at its usual jaunty angle. "No doubt in my mind. Not one little bit. Like I said, you need to learn to take a risk now and then. A slap on the cheek doesn't hurt forever, you know."

"That's a very unenlightened attitude," Clark said.

Jerome shrugged. "Oh yeah? Just try and sue me." His laughter trailed off as he faded into the night.

Hey, Lilly, do you want this magazine? It's good reading while you get your hair done. You sure have been quiet since you got back. Maybe it'll cheer you up.

Sure. Thanks, Mary. Who's on the cover?

Oh, you know, that Jerome Percy? Did you see any of his films while you were overseas? He's such a dream. Anyway, the big story is he ditched that Isabel Standish while she was away making a movie, and he took up with that floozy Blanche LaFleur. I'll tell you, I'll never forgive him for this. How could he? They were perfect together.

Uh, well, on second thought, I don't care much for magazines anyway.

Chapter Sixteen

Clark

The following week was a frenzy of classroom and research activity. The late-night argument with Jerome scared and inspired Clark. He gave in to contemplating what life would be like without the ghost by his side and couldn't decide if he was looking forward to or dreading it. Sadness won the sorry contest, and he kept busy to keep from dwelling on it.

His research assistant used her ten hours a week sending inquiries to various libraries about their local news archives, and because she was as intrigued by the mystery, put in unpaid overtime, but despite her efforts, responses were slow, and they made no tangible progress.

With the arrival of a single new lead from one inquiry, Clark expanded his search into local theatrical groups from that time, both amateur and professional, to see if there was a suggestion that Isabel Standish was among the players. Any actress with the same initials caught his attention, but one by one, the possibilities dried up. There had been one in particular and close to home, but by the date on the news article, the actress would have been young enough to be Isabel's daughter. And there were no leads to follow that story. At the end of the week, he didn't know what was worse—the lack of anything substantial or having to tell Jerome he was no closer to solving the problem than he'd been at the start of the week.

With each disappointment, it seemed Jerome's spirit faded a little bit more. Clark tried to talk to him, but the ghost refused to speak about it.

Clark was glad when the weekend finally came. He and Leigh had spoken almost every night and were to get together for dinner on Friday.

They agreed to meet at a small bistro, mid-way between her office and the university. He arrived on time and sat at a table for an hour as he nursed a beer and wondered if she stood him up when he saw her rush through the door.

"Clark, I'm so sorry. My last meeting ran over, and the more I tried to shut it down, the more determined that SOB was to keep me." She pressed a kiss to his cheek, then looked at him with worried eyes. "I tried calling, but it went to voice mail. Are you angry? Is your phone on?"

He caught her hand in his. "My phone is on… I've been staring at it constantly, but it's old and doesn't always connect. I'm sorry. I was worried you'd come to your senses and decided to ditch a poor excuse of a man like me."

Her eyes twinkled. "As if. And I love when you talk like that—so continental." She laughed and sat down, tossing her coat on an empty chair. "I wanted to kick that jerk where it hurt to get him to move along. But there were others in the room. Can't have a witness."

A waiter handed her a menu and poured water in a goblet. "I'd like a Pinot Noir, nothing fancy," she told him before she turned to Clark and, with a gentle touch, brushed a lock of hair from his forehead. "You look like you had a difficult week."

He shrugged. "It's the tail end of class presentations, and we're getting ready for finals. The students are getting restless. And my research is stuck. I'm running out of ideas. If I don't show my department head a draft of my next publication in the next few weeks, I can kiss my chance of getting my contract renewed goodbye, no matter what else I've done."

She cocked her head. "That's so unfair. You're doing so much with that film series. I saw the write up in the paper. They were gushing about it and you." She thanked the waiter who delivered her wine and took a sip, closing her eyes in pleasure. She opened her eyes and looked into his. "I hate to say, but I needed that." Leigh took his hand. "Is there anything I can do to help? I know all sorts of people in town if you want to talk to anyone. I know you were trying to research someone local. An actress, right? I know I should remember more details, but my mind is fried. Sorry."

Clark squeezed her fingers and brought them to his lips for a quick kiss. "I don't expect you to remember everything about my work. But yes, I'm looking for a local actress. The problem is, I don't know her real name. Her stage name was Isabel Standish."

"Right. The love interest of that actor—what was his name—Jerry. The one you wrote about. She was the great love of his life and died mysteriously."

He grinned at her. "You got most of it. Jerome Percy. I admit to having an obsession with him. And Isabel was the true love of his life, so she's my new obsession. No one's discovered her real name. She boarded a train one day and vanished. There were hints she came from around here, so this is where I came to find her." He kissed Leigh's fingers once more. "I almost feel as if I owe my career and our meeting to Jerome. I was a struggling student when I first... er... encountered him. Through sheer dumb luck, I came

187

upon the papers he'd left to the school. They'd been misfiled from the start, so no one knew what became of them until I found them."

She grinned at him. "Luck's a funny thing."

He leaned over the table and kissed her lips. "I'll say. It was pure luck that allowed us to meet."

Leigh batted her lashes at him, making him smile as it did whenever she was playful. "Luck, and Berry Conrad."

He laughed. "I'll give you that. But my dissertation was picked up by a publisher, and with a few months' work, I was able to transform it into a commercial biography, and that took off bigger than anyone expected, so I was able to pay off a huge chunk of my student loans. It's not only the dean who wants me to do more. The publisher's been after me to solve the Standish story. Why they think I can do that is another mystery. But I kind of feel like I owe it to Jerome to solve it."

She smiled at him. "You think of him as a real person, don't you?"

He blinked and paused. "I guess I do. You can't immerse yourself in a man's life, even posthumously, and not feel like you know him inside and out." He squeezed her fingers again and leaned in. "I, uh, well, I really do know him."

She nodded, but to his dismay, his nerve left him. Telling Leigh about his friendly ghost in a public restaurant when he'd already had one beer on an empty stomach was not the best idea he'd ever had. He needed to tell her but at another time.

She tucked her other hand into his. "And that, I think, is one of the reasons I find you so appealing, Clark Conrad. Not just any man would admit to something like that. Nor have such a sense of responsibility to the dead."

He leaned back. "I, uh, I'm no hero." He rubbed his beard with his free hand. "I'm not sure I'm not in it for the money—another book would be good, and there's still rumors of an unclaimed bounty for finding Isabel. I've been making inquiries into that. Not to mention the chance to earn tenure. The university has a great national reputation. I'd love to be associated with it long term. And I feel like I owe it to Jerry. But…"

She shook her head. "You can't talk me out of thinking you're a good man, Clark. You can admit to being caught up in the mystery, wanting to solve it, see if there's a reward, even if it's merely acclaim, or results in a job offer. But I think I know you better than that. You want this for your Jerome. It's wild, romantic, and honorable."

He hung his head. "And thankless. I don't know that there's anyone left alive who knew her as Isabel, no matter what name she went by before or after her acting career. And if there is, I haven't a clue how to find that person, or if they'd know more than the local newspapers published back then. Leigh, I'm inquiring at every public library and historical society on the east coast for any hints of her in their society pages, their theater productions, obituaries, wedding notices, you name it. I've been at it for six months, and I'm coming up empty. For all I know, my hunch was wrong to start with. She could have gotten off the train at the very next station and lived her life out in California. Or Nevada, or anywhere else along the line."

She patted his hand. "I think you need a good meal. And time to decompress. Sometimes things come to you when you stop thinking about them."

He leaned forward and pressed another kiss to her lips. "Have I told you recently how smart I think you are?"

She smiled at him. "I believe you might have done exactly that. But I'll let you in on a secret." He leaned closer, and she whispered in his ear. "I don't think I'll ever get tired of hearing it."

He looked into the depths of her eyes. "And right now, all I can think of is all sorts of interesting places where I might be able to remind you of that fact."

Leigh

Drinks led to appetizers, and those segued into dinner, which became dessert, and dessert led to after dinner drinks. Leigh was feeling warm and cozy, for Clark had slipped into the seat next to hers and draped his arm around her. He used it to good effect, bringing them together for the occasional kiss. And that became one long hot one. His hand stroked her arm, scrambling her ability to think. His lips were warm and soft, and she opened hers to allow the kiss to deepen. Clark took advantage of her offering and pressed closer, heating her from the inside out.

"To sound totally selfish, you're good for me," he said as he brushed a warm kiss below her ear. "I hope you're feeling as good as I am right now."

She snuggled closer. "I am. Just the thought of you waiting for me made putting up with Rocky's nonsense into perspective before."

Clark stiffened. "You saw him?"

She nodded, hating the sudden distance between them. "I was meeting with Rocky, my former and current adversary, and one-time brief romantic interest, at a business meeting. He's the reason I was so late." She laughed at herself. "I sound like I'm writing a movie trailer. He came by to see if he could revive the takeover he started earlier this year. Wanted to start fresh. New terms. Let bygones be bygones." She took a sip of her amaretto. "He didn't know Mom's talking to another company about a merger, and I didn't clue him in." She laughed harshly. "He never expected I'd have plans tonight. Thought he'd take me out on the town, show me a good time, and no doubt end up in his bed."

She saw Clark stiffen. "That son of a bitch—"

Leigh set her hand on his shoulder. "As flattering as your reaction is, there's no need to worry. I set him straight. Told him I was seeing you. And that any hopes he had for merging our companies was DOA." She took a sip of her cordial. "I had one of our corporate lawyers with me. Rocky asked her to leave, but she stayed put. Thank goodness. I will never be alone with him again."

"You told him about us?"

She nodded. "Briefly. Not that it's any of his business, but if I only said I was seeing someone, it would sound like I was lying." She frowned. "I know we didn't exactly discuss our relationship or declare we're exclusive or anything like that. I didn't want to overstep, but I also didn't want him to think he had room to maneuver."

"I don't mind." His warm hands took hers that were suddenly much colder. "I like the idea that we're exclusive. I like it a lot. I hope you do too."

She met his gaze in the dim light of the restaurant. "I do. You know I don't have a lot of opportunities to meet men socially, but you see hundreds of women every day, and if you wanted to, oh, I don't know, see me, and them, well then I guess—"

He leaned over and kissed her. Her lips opened, allowing for a more intimate kiss. His hands were at her cheeks, cradling her face before they moved to her head as he threaded his fingers through her hair. When she pulled back to catch her breath, he looked at her and kissed her once more. "Leigh. It kills me that that guy was so horrible to you that you hesitate to trust me. I'll do whatever I can to make you believe me, will wait as long as I need to. I want us to be exclusive. I thought you knew that. Isn't it obvious I'm interested? And as for juggling multiple women—not my style. I'm too disorganized for one thing, and more importantly, I'm a one-woman man. Always have been. I guess Jerome and I have that in common. Of course, he was a serial lover. I'm more like if I find a woman I like, I'm going to stick with her forever if she lets me. And with you I feel like I've found everything I could ever hope for in a woman."

"Clark—"

"Shhh. Let me tell you this." He brushed a curl from her face. "You know how I feel about you. How smart you are. That I love

191

how sassy you can be. And don't think for one minute I don't know that you don't need me half as much as I need you. A woman like you, independent, strong minded, you don't need a man in your life to feel successful. I get that, and I respect the hell out of it, no matter how much it intimidates me. But the fact that a woman as strong, and smart, and as beautiful as you wants to be with me—do you have any idea how thrilling that is?"

She looked at him for a long moment, staring into his wide, earnest eyes. "You mean it."

He nodded. "I don't want you to ever doubt that. Or doubt my regard for you. I didn't want to tell you this, but I was crazy about you the first time we met."

She laughed, unable to suppress the scoff that crept in. "I was the first single woman you met when you arrived."

He smiled. "That's not quite true. But I took one look at you, and it was all over for me. You were the one I wanted, and it killed me that you were with that— that bastard. So, when you mentioned his name, it made me want to find him and beat the hell out of him and tell him to stay away from my woman. And you can ask anyone who knows me—I'm no fighter."

A grin spread across her face. "Your woman," she breathed with a smile. "And you're my man."

He rubbed her nose with his own before she pressed a kiss to his lips. "You asking, or are you telling?"

She laughed and grabbed his tie in her fist, pulling him closer. "I'm telling you." She leaned back and eyed him. "And you are, until further notice, buster. If anyone questions that, refer them to me."

"Including Rocky?" he teased.

"Especially Rocky," she told him with a roll of her eyes. "Unfortunately, he's nothing if not persistent. I'm afraid I haven't seen the last of him, so I might need to call on you to have my back from time to time."

He rubbed her shoulder with his large hand. "It would be my honor."

The waitstaff were all gathered by the bar and looking around. Leigh realized they were the last patrons in the restaurant. "I think it's time for us to leave," she said quietly.

Clark looked around, clearly startled. "Right. So, let's continue this discussion outside."

He held her coat as she slipped her arms into the sleeves and then took his hand as they walked out into the cold November air.

"Where's your car?" he asked.

"Over there," she said and pointed to the lone car on the street.

"Come on, I'll walk you to it. I think we need to call it a night. But tomorrow evening, there's a jazz place I want to take you to. We'll do dinner first and then go to the club. Does that sound good?"

She stood on her tiptoes and pressed a kiss to his cold lips. "As much as I don't want this night to end, I'm beat, so I guess so. Call me and let me know how we'll meet up."

"One of these days, we'll be able to kiss without our coats," he mumbled.

She winked as she unlocked her door. "One of these days, we'll be able to kiss without our clothes."

He gave a startled laugh. "Okay. You've gone and ruined the good night's sleep I had planned. I won't be able to get the image out of my mind."

She laughed and got into her car. "Sweet dreams, my man," she said with a wave.

"Let me know you got home okay," he called after her. "And I mean it."

"I will." She got out of her car and kissed him once more."

"And tomorrow, maybe we can talk about your grandmother. Your mother mentioned she once had theatrical aspirations. Maybe I need to talk to your mother about it sometime. Who knows? Wouldn't it be something if somehow one of you will have the kernel of information I've been looking for? Maybe I could even talk to your grandmother myself. For all we know, she might have once met the Great Isabel Standish."

The bubble of joy Leigh had been floating on burst suddenly. "Oh. Well. I, uh. Well, goodnight, Clark."

She fell into her seat and shut the door, then drove away, biting her lip.

He didn't know what he was asking for. And the truth was, she wasn't quite certain either, other than for the fact that the idea scared her to pieces.

Blanche, I don't care what you think. We are not a couple. Never were. Never will be.

Jerry, you're no fun. Why don't you just stop thinking about that Izzy...

Don't you call her that. Her name is Isabel.

She's gone, Jer. Can't you get that through your head? No reason we can't take up now. She's gone, and she's not coming back.

Blanche, why can't you understand I love Isabel? I love her. Not you. I have to find her. I gotta explain what she really saw, not what you wanted her to think. This whole story is getting out of hand. The head honcho is starting to worry this could ruin my career, even the studio. Why did you have to tell the reporters you spent the night?

Well, I did.

Because you were too high to get home. And you were in the bedroom alone, and I stayed on the sofa.

Ha ha ha. Like anyone's ever going to believe you, Jer. Certainly not your little goody-two-shoes.

Chapter Seventeen

Leigh

"Good morning, my darling. How was your evening with your young man? Tell me, has your mother met him? Of course, she has. At the big fete. She likes him, I assume?"

Leigh looked up to see her grandmother in the doorway. The light behind her made her features indistinct, and her voice seemed somehow fainter. But her spirit was as buoyant as ever.

"Hey, Gram. Yes, Clark's great. We had a wonderful time last night. Closed down the restaurant."

195

Gram's eyes twinkled as she was wheeled into the room by her silent companion. "I half expected you to spend the night elsewhere." Her brows raised. "You know I wouldn't think the worse of you for it." She looked over her shoulder and lifted a brow at the woman, daring her to think otherwise.

Leigh forced a smile. "Well, no. I mean, we had 'the relationship talk' last night. He wants us to be exclusive, and so do I. But he was very clear we weren't going to sleep together—yet. I'll see him again tonight. Who knows what will happen then?" She pushed her cereal away and focused on her coffee.

"So, what's wrong, sweetheart?" Gram rolled up to the table, the light still at her back. "Anything I can do to help?"

"I've told you that Clark is doing research, right?"

"Yes, darling. Old Hollywood or some such nonsense."

"He wants to talk to mom. She mentioned her grandmother was interested in movies way back when. He's looking for a specific actress who went AWOL."

Gram looked down at her hands, folded in her lap. They were gnarled but still beautiful, her nails freshly polished. "Is he?"

"I don't want him poking his nose in family business. I don't want this to be an issue that keeps us from seeing one another, falling in love and all that. But I want to keep our history private. He's going to get suspicious, especially after mom talks to him." Leigh pushed her coffee cup away and rested her chin on her fist. "Not that I expect our family has anything to do with what he's researching, but until he knows for certain, he's going to keep asking. I don't want to have to keep secrets from him."

Gram sighed. "Darling Lei-Lei, everyone has secrets."

Leigh frowned. "I know."

"And everyone's entitled to their secrets. Even ghosts."

Leigh shivered before she looked up. As lovely as Gram looked, she appeared more translucent than ever. "I know that too. But not everyone's respectful of those secrets. And keeping secrets is hard work. I don't like to lie. I especially don't want the

196

foundation of what could be a wonderful relationship to be based on lies."

There was a long pause from across the table. "What about telling him the truth?"

Leigh looked up. "You must be joking."

Gram smiled. "Never more serious in my life, my darling."

Leigh shook her head. "I can't. There is so much to lose. My privacy. *Your privacy.* Life would never be the same, and I hate to think what effect that would have on you. And then he'd know, and he'd never look at me quite the same way again. If he looked at me at all." Leigh rubbed her eyes. "He might think I'm a crackpot.

"Gram, you should have heard him. He seems to think I'm some sort of perfect super woman who is absolutely comfortable in her own skin, in control of her career and her projects, and running her life exactly the way she wants it to be. He doesn't know anything about how awful it is that I don't fit into the clothes I wore last year. That my breath smells after I eat garlic. I still have to tell him I snore." She covered her face with her hands. "How in the world will he still want me, knowing that?"

There was a gay laugh from across the table. "Garlic, my Lei-Lei, really? For heaven's sake, it's been some time since my nose worked correctly, but darling, who's breath doesn't smell after eating spicy food? And as for snoring, you can have him leave, or you leave, before the night is through. Stop making excuses for not finding the love of your life. You'd miss out on the wonders of truly being in love— when all those things don't matter because all that does is waking up in the arms of the one you adore. That, as I recall, is one of the best parts of new love. Not to mention the act itself, which was wonderful, of course, when done properly. None of the rest matters. His breath could be twice as bad as yours. He could be a restless sleeper, or worse, talk in his sleep. But if he loves you, and you love him, what does it matter?"

Leigh rubbed her eyes. "I know. I want that. But I don't want you to lose your privacy. I don't want memories you cherish to become fodder for mindless readers. And I don't want to scare him off."

Gram laughed. "What if it became fodder for avid, intelligent readers? One doesn't reach my state in life without thinking about leaving some sort of legacy. One day, I'll be gone for good. We both know that. What will it matter then if my name is drawn through the mud?" Her eyes sparkled. "You, of course. You'll be left. And I can see it now, folks wanting to talk to you about your daring, scandalous old Gram. My wish for you, Lei-Lei, is that when that day comes, you'll hold your head up high and say, 'Yup, that Gram of mine was quite a broad. They sure don't make 'em like that anymore.'"

A laugh burst from Leigh. "Oh, Gram, I love you so much." She wanted to reach out and hug her very own ghost, but the memory of touching Gram when she was younger lingered still. At age three, she hadn't known better, and the shock to her put her in bed for a week, to the worry of her family. Not to mention the psychiatrist her family forced her to see when she told them that she had seen and touched her great-grandmother. Leigh hadn't dared try to touch Gram since.

The old woman blew a kiss across the table. "And I love you. We'll get you through this, even if I have to meet him myself."

"But Gram—"

"I know, I know. I've allowed myself to become a hermit. Maybe it's time to let one or two more people in. You'll have to tell me what you told him, so we can keep our stories straight."

"Are you sure?"

"I'm not that fragile, am I? I can run a brush through my hair, put on my best clothes. And I promise I won't eat any garlic."

Leigh gave a startled laugh. "But Gram, I do think of you as being fragile." She pursed her lips. "And as far as the rest of the world is concerned, you don't exist. Mom and Sarah think I use you as an excuse to keep men away."

"Well, perhaps for one hour we'll let him satisfy his curiosity and be done with it. And then you can kill me off once and for all." She looked up coyly. "It's not like I don't know how to keep a secret, Darling."

Leigh rose and cleared her things from the table. "I'll think about it. And only if he asks again."

"That's my girl," Gram said with a smile. "And when all else fails, distract him with sex. It certainly worked for me."

Another laugh escaped Leigh's somber mood as Gram was wheeled into the light streaming through the doorway and disappeared.

Clark

He held her elbow as they walked down the steep concrete stairs. "This place is open until two," Clark said as he held the door open for Leigh. The small jazz club was in the basement of an old building near the university. The lighting was just bright enough for them to find their way to a table. Paintings of Billie Holiday, Benny Goodman, John Coltrane, and other jazz luminaries were on the walls, along with battered brass and woodwind instruments. Small tables were scattered around a small wooden stage. "And I hear the performers sometimes jam even later, though they stop serving."

Leigh had been quiet when he picked her up and hadn't spoken much during dinner other than to comment on the food. Worse than her thoughtful mood, though, he worried she'd changed her mind about him. Had she gotten wind of Jerry's true nature? Or was Clark himself too quirky? He'd done his best to be a gentleman, waiting until he was sure his advances would be welcomed for the long term. Maybe he should have gone all caveman on her and tried to seduce her. Damn it. Why the hell was falling in love so difficult?

She smiled up at him. "Noted."

He touched her shoulder. "If you're not in the mood, we can go somewhere else, or I can take you home."

Her eyes opened wide. "No. I've been looking forward to this. I'm feeling a little… I don't know, not down exactly."

"Maybe some good music will help?"

She took his hand. "And good company. I'm sorry I'm being so quiet. If you want to leave—"

Clark squeezed her fingers. "I don't want to leave. I want to be here with you. And maybe help cheer you up."

"You're great," she replied and squeezed his hand back. "Let's stay and enjoy the music and the company. I promise I'll try to shake my mood."

"I'm not afraid of a little melancholia," he said. "I'm somewhat familiar with it myself, though not so much these days. Maybe, for a laugh, we can tell each other the most embarrassing things that ever happened to us—"

She grinned. "Oh boy. I've worked hard at suppressing those memories."

They were shown to a table and ordered drinks and dessert as the band warmed up.

"Okay, I'll start," Clark volunteered. "Most embarrassing thing. I was my high school class's biggest nerd. President of the AV club, thick lenses in dark, square frames, pencil neck, big ears that stuck out. Tall and uncoordinated. No one, and I mean ever, considered asking me to try out for the basketball team."

Her eyes danced as she gazed up and down at him. "I can't believe that. In my imagination, you were always a hunk."

"You have no idea how happy I am to hear you think that, but when I was seventeen, I was skinny, pale, and pimply. I was into old movies instead of sports. And I tripped over dust as I got accustomed to the size of my feet."

"So, what happened?"

He took her hand. "Well, watching those old movies, I got ideas about what romance should be between a man and a woman. I always thought of myself as the Jimmy Stewart type, awkward and bumbling but good at heart, the hero who would prevail at the end. And in order to do that, I needed to make sure the prettiest girl at school noticed me."

"Uh oh. This can't end well," Leigh muttered.

Clark grinned. "Well, yeah. That's the whole point. And that's exactly what happened."

She squeezed his fingers.

"I was determined to clean myself up. I got the acne under control, sort of. I told myself I was growing a beard as if ten chin hairs counted. I made sure I learned proper hygiene for a young adolescent male—thanks to my mother. Plus, she taught me to iron a shirt. My dad coached me on how to ask a young woman out on a date—even promised to help fund it if I was successful." He looked into the distance. "I should have known he didn't expect me to succeed. Dad wasn't exactly generous. I guess he was betting I would strike out." Clark took Leigh's hands in his. "He wasn't a skinflint, but he didn't have much considering he had a bunch of boys to raise. But at the time I took it as encouragement, that he believed in me and that's what I needed.

"So, the big day arrived. I was going to ask her to the homecoming dance."

"Was she pretty?"

Clark nodded. "The prettiest girl I'd ever seen. The perfect Southern California type. Long blond hair. Big blue eyes. She had the clearest skin, and her braces had come off the year before, so her teeth were perfect. Tall, slender. And most importantly, she'd broken up with her boyfriend, so I knew I had a fighting chance—"

"Let me guess, she was built," Leigh said with a smile.

"Let's say she had a beautiful figure," Clark said with a grin.

"Okay, let's," Leigh agreed. "What happened?"

"I approached her during lunch. She always ate with a bunch of her friends. I usually ate alone. But I was too nervous to eat. And I didn't want to chance there was any bologna stuck in my teeth. I waited until she was done. I used some breath spray, got up, and went to her table."

Leigh cringed. "It's like watching a train wreck. She turned you down? She was mean about it? Why do I want to punch her?"

Clark laughed. "I went over to ask her out. I had my speech prepared. I'd practiced nonstop all morning, muttering to myself through calculus and world history. I made my way over to her, all the time watching her watch me as I came over. In fact, I never took my eyes off her the entire time."

Leigh bit her bottom lip, her gaze never leaving his eyes.

"Which meant I didn't notice her ex-boyfriend stick his foot out and trip me."

Leigh's hands flew to her face. "Oh no."

Clark shrugged. "I fell at her feet. Let's say I got the sympathy vote that day. My glasses went flying. My nose was bloody, and that jackass and all his friends were all laughing. I was about as humiliated as you could imagine." Clark pushed his glasses up his nose. "When I lifted my head, I saw she was laughing too."

"She turned you down?"

"I didn't bother asking. I suddenly saw her for what she was, a beautiful, empty shell. I turned to her friend, Olivia, who handed me my glasses. She's the one who turned me down. Said she was going to be out of town but thanked me for asking. She was really nice about it."

"Oh, Clark," Leigh crooned. "You poor thing." She squinted thoughtfully. "I'll bet that nasty girl regretted it when she's seen you since. Oh, I hope she wanted you to ask her out, and you refused. I hope she felt that rejection down to her toes."

Clark took her hands. "Are you always this fierce?"

Leigh laughed. "I guess I am. But did you? Did you crush her? Say yes, even if you have to lie."

It was his turn to laugh. "No, but I remained friends with Olivia. We were undergrads together and stay in touch. I've gotten multiple requests from the mean girl to be friends on social media. Each of which I turn down." His smile turned into a cocky grin. "I did see her once after that. She came to one of my book signings right after I appeared on a national talk show. She tried to get friendly. I, uh, didn't accommodate her."

"I'll bet that's the meanest thing you've ever done in your life," Leigh said. "Am I right?"

He nodded. "Yeah. And I won't lie. It felt great."

"Not revenge, though," she said. "You didn't plan it. Serendipity. Karma. Call it what you will, but the universe has a way of helping even the score. So, had she aged badly? Wrinkles? Bad hair?" Leigh leaned forward. "Had she gotten heavy? That's what I always wish on the mean girls who used to tease me about my weight."

"No. She was still beautiful. But she was as arrogant as ever. Her eyes were cold. I remember she pushed her way to the front of the line, made a big deal about knowing me way back when I was nothing. I wonder if she even realized she was being insulting when she was trying to suck up. I saw the looks on the face of the woman she'd shoved and pretended I didn't remember her. I signed her book but misspelled her name."

Leigh burst out laughing. "On behalf of all the girls who've been shoved aside, I thank you."

"Olivia called me to say it was all over social media how I'd snubbed her. It could have been a disaster, but my agent was there and captured the whole thing on a video. She posted it, anonymously, of course."

"Even better," Leigh said.

"So, your turn," he said to her.

203

"Shhh. The music's starting." She sent him a wink and held his hand.

He leaned closer. "I won't forget. When they take a break, you're going to spill all your secrets."

Leigh

An hour later, the band walked off the small stage, promising to return in twenty minutes.

"Okay," Clark said as he squeezed her hand. "Your turn. I want to know your secrets."

Ugh. That word again. Leigh signed. "Must I?"

He nodded and squeezed her hand. Leigh sighed. "My story isn't as interesting as yours. But it was in high school and about the mysterious world of mean girls and clueless boys."

Clark's hand enveloped hers and held on.

"I wasn't one of the popular kids. Despite my grandparents living in the big house on the hill and having once been the most prominent family in the city, my circumstances were pretty bleak. Everyone knew it. My dad had died years earlier. My mother's parents didn't help her out financially even though they could afford to. We never knew my dad's family. Mom was doing her best as a single parent, working long hours to keep her new business afloat. I consoled myself with food.

"What was supposed to be a bright spot was when Mom convinced my grandmother to pay my tuition at a private academy. I was a smart kid, and my local high school didn't have much to offer. Going there was the only way I could excel and hope to get a scholarship to a good college. I arrived my sophomore year. Most of those kids had been together since kindergarten. I was shy, overweight, and didn't belong to any country clubs like they did. I didn't go skiing in the Alps or to the Caribbean on winter break. I had to work at a fast-food place after school, weekends, and during the summer."

His warm grip tightened.

"The only thing I had going for me was a strong sense of my own worth. I was smarter than most of those kids and nicer, so some of the teachers liked me, those who weren't toadying up to the rich kids' parents for side tutoring jobs. None of the kids appreciated a smart girl coming in and excelling. It was about as bad as the stories you hear about prep schools. I wanted to go back to the public high school, but neither my mother nor grandparents would allow it. My sister was already off at college, having endured the same hell. They figured if she could, so could I.

"So, there was this boy my senior year."

Clark cringed. "Ouch?"

Leigh nodded. "Yeah. He was really cute, and I had a crush on him. I was told by one of his friends that he wanted to meet me behind the gym after school."

He held her hands tighter. "Don't tell me this if it's too painful."

She shook back her hair. "I don't think I've ever told anyone. I met him, all starry-eyed. He was there, looking dangerous with his leather jacket and pretentious swagger. Why I thought he'd be interested in me, I have no idea, but I've never had good sense when it comes to men."

"Until me," Clark said. "You have very good sense when it comes to me."

She grinned. "I do. This is why I'm so cautious. Anyway, he was supposed to meet me there and ask me out. The plot line was murky, but I was in love and wanted to believe that a cute, popular guy was interested in me. I think I was supposed to somehow put out for him—like lift my shirt so he could see me. Not go all the way, my friend said. Just a sign that I'd be worth his while.

"Anyway, the deal was this. He agreed to meet me as a joke. He'd get me alone and do whatever it was he was supposed to do to get me to humiliate myself. And all the popular kids would jump out and surprise us."

"Oh, Leigh."

"It turns out he wasn't the sharpest tool in the shed. Apparently, he thought he was the one who was supposed to expose himself. So, there I was, about to lift my shirt, when he pulled down his pants. That's when everyone jumped out."

Clark guffawed. "Oh, honey."

She shrugged. "No one saw anything of me, but he was pretty embarrassed. I ran away. It's a good thing cellphones weren't prevalent then. I hear there was a big party that night when they all were talking about it. He didn't lose any friends, but I realized I really didn't have any real ones. I went back to school Monday and ignored all of them. It was difficult, but I continued to work hard and graduated first in my class. I got my scholarship and went to my top choice school and excelled in the program, earning my MBA a few years later."

"There's got to be a comeuppance here somewhere."

Leigh shrugged. "I wasn't the only one from my class to earn a degree in computer science. Like in so many places, who you know means more than what you know. Over the years, there've been plenty of my old classmates who've shown up, looking to network. And despite the fact I advanced my career on merit, they assume I'm still the dumb, gullible fat girl I used to be, who works there because her mother's the CEO, and that I'd be grateful to hire them so we could relive old times."

"Yeah, right," he snorted. "So—"

"So, I make sure I interview them. Kindly and gently."

"Let me guess, you're killing 'em with kindness?"

She shrugged again. "Usually. One or more of my department heads will walk in asking about something. I keep an open door, you see. No secrets."

"I'll bet you impress them."

She laughed. "I'm afraid I'm not that nice. My goal is to impress them if I can. If someone on my team comes to me with a problem, I ask my interviewee what he or she would do to solve it. We all listen to their answer. If they admit they're over their heads, I respect them. If they venture a guess that's reasonably coherent, even better. But if they start to BS me, we all sit around and encourage them to dig themselves in deeper before we expose them, but kindly."

She laughed. "I don't believe ignorance is a disease, but stupidity can be fatal. I think almost everyone on my team today was a misfit way back when. We're seeking some sort of reprisal in our current success, in one way or another. If I think my classmate is any good, I might recommend another place for them to look for work, but I will never hire them." She let go of his hands and took a sip of her drink. "So, in light of what you said about me yesterday, I'm not all that nice. I'm not proud of it, but it's true." She blinked up at him. "Still want to date me?"

He gazed at her steadily. "One favor?"

Leigh nodded.

"Don't let me dig myself a hole."

She smiled. "You've already proven you're the kind to admit when you don't know something. As long as you're honest with me, I'll be honest with you."

He held out his hands for hers, and she took them. "Leigh, all my life, I've wanted to be the hero of my own movie. I never knew if it was going to be a mystery, drama, or screwball comedy. I've taken acting classes, I've learned to fight with swords and rapiers, and even my fists, so I'd be able to fairly judge the skill of Errol Flynn and Basil Rathbones. I've learned how stunts are done, so if I trip over my own feet again, I know how to roll and recover with at least some dignity. But mostly, I've wanted to play hero across from a strong, determined, smart, spunky, sexy, and beautiful heroine. I want someone capable of standing by my side or at my back, with a sword in her own hand. I want that journey, setbacks, success, and during the final roll of the credits, I want to kiss the hell out of my heroine before I wink at the audience before the screen fades to black and have the words 'And they lived happily ever after' scroll across the screen. And you know what else I want? I want to hear the satisfied sighs of the audience as they walk out of the theater."

"Oh, Clark."

"You can imagine how well an earlier version of that went over on the playground when I was six. Or high school drama club, the only other club I belonged to, where I longed to be the lead, but was cast in a minor role, or relegated to stagehand."

"Aren't you glad we're grown up now?" she asked wistfully. "That all that drama is behind us?"

He nodded. "I haven't had a girlfriend for a few years. I'm still a quirky guy. I might have grown into my feet, and I can grow a full beard now, but inside, I'm still that awkward little kid standing out in the field with an oversized glove on his hand, imagining he's directing a movie scene when he was supposed to keep his eye on the softball hurtling toward his head." Clark ducked his chin. "I'm thirty-two years old, and if I haven't outgrown that tendency to lose focus, I don't know that I ever will. But I want you, Leigh. Very much, so I'm laying my cards on the table. Will you take me into your life, knowing all this stuff?"

She placed her hand over his. "And will you take me, knowing I can be bitchy from time to time? I don't have the best track record when it comes to men."

His tender smile melted her heart. "As long as you stay smart and sassy, yes, absolutely, I can. And you can throw Rocky out of your office any old time, and I won't mind a bit. I'll even help if I can." His eyes twinkled. "Even Berry hates her brother, so how bad can your perceptions of that jackass be?"

She smiled back. "I can work on the bitchy thing, you know."

He shook his head, never breaking eye contact. "Don't you dare. I like you exactly the way you are. And really, how many former classmates can be left still looking for a job?"

She bit her lip to stop from laughing as he moved in closer for a kiss.

They were startled apart as the drummer began her opening paradiddle.

Clark leaned in closer with a grin. "You can't scare me away, Leigh Mason. I know who you really are inside."

Lilly, darling. Come meet Mr. Sprague. Remember dearest? I told you about him over breakfast? He lost his wife last year. Mr. Sprague, this is my daughter, Lilly Manning. Isn't she as lovely as I promised?

How do you do, Mr. Sprague.

Miss Manning, I've heard so much about you. Your mother has kept me abreast of your exploits in California. We even saw some of your films here in town. But mum's the word that you are her.

Lilly's put that all behind her now, haven't you, darling? Why, just last week she told her father and me she wanted to go back. Of course, we said no. And do call her Lilly. Isn't that so, dear?

His eyes swept up and down her body, lingering below her collarbone.

She shivered. *Yes, Mother.*

And to prove it, we will never again mention the name of Isabel Standish. Very posh, of course, but it won't do to have people remember her by it. Especially since that name was linked to that horrible man. Lilly has assured me that was all a lot of hokum that the press made up.

Well, Miss Manning, if that's true, perhaps you and I might get to know one another a little better, hmmm?

Chapter Eighteen

Leigh

She didn't need to look up to know her sister was standing in her doorway.

"I think Clark's trying to make you crazy," Sarah opined.

Leigh's gaze remained on her computer screen as she tapped the last few words of her email. "That's funny. I don't remember asking your opinion." She reread the contents, pressed send, and leaned back in her chair. "Exactly how do you know my business, anyway?"

"Carole and I happened to be driving by the old place last night, on our way home from the theater. Since that spruce came down last winter, it's not hard to see the front door from the street, you know. And the two of you were in the clinches. I thought for sure you'd open the door and crook your finger for him to follow. But no. One very long, very passionate kiss, and he bolted." She shook her head. "What gives? Did you tell one too many risqué jokes? Or maybe no jokes at all. Answer me this, did you tell him to take a hike?"

Leigh groaned and hung her head. "No. I wish I knew what was going on. He professes to care about me. A lot. And he kisses me like he means it." She looked at her sister. "I know you don't have recent experience with this, but when a man finds you attractive, and you're in close quarters, you can tell he's interested."

Sarah laughed. "I recollect something about male physiology."

Leigh smiled. "But then he claims he needs to be a gentleman and leaves."

"Maybe he believes your story about living with Gram. Doesn't want to run into an old lady when he visits the bathroom in the middle of the night. I can't believe you still tell people that. I mean, if anyone were to check, it would be easy enough to figure out when our grandparents and great-grands died. It's not like there's anyone left who knew them."

Leigh bit her lip. "I know, I know."

"You told him, though. He thinks you live with your great-grandmother."

"Sarah, lay off, okay? If you can't say something helpful, maybe you can shut up?"

Her sister laughed. "Fine. You created this mess, so you can fix it. When are you seeing him again, and are you going to finally sleep with him? I mean, he's pretty good-looking, for a guy. And he does seem to be into you."

"I want to. I'm not sure how to force the issue. If he's not willing, it would be as bad as a man trying to force a woman who isn't."

"There's that," her sister agreed. "Maybe you can ask him what he's waiting for. If it's permission, give it to him. If he's got a communicable disease, then get it all out there so you can send him packing. Or for a dose of penicillin."

"I guess I'll have to," Leigh agreed. "Damn, why is romance stuff so complicated?"

Her sister laughed. "All the stuff leading up to love is complicated. Once you fall in, the rest is easy." She gave her sister another wink. "Or I should say easier. So, this weekend. You'll push the issue?"

Leigh nodded. "Berry asked us to dinner before the film. I can ask him while we're in the car or after the film. He has to speak at the event, so I don't want to distract him before that."

"Oh, Lei-Lei, from what I can tell, you distract him plenty. One little push. That's all he needs, and he's going ass over teakettle for you. Mark my words." She turned to leave. "I want a full report Monday morning and not a minute sooner, 'cause I want the two of you to spend all weekend in bed. Together. You can come up for air, food, and bio breaks, but that's it."

Berry

Okay, Berry here. Yes, I invited Leigh and Clark for dinner. I knew something was up between them, but I couldn't blatantly stick my nose into their business. So, I did the next best thing, which was to make it easy for them to tell me what was going on face to face.

I made an early dinner. My kids know how to behave with adults, so it was a family style meal. My mother-in-law, Rosemary, who's my go-to babysitter, was at the table with us.

It didn't take long after they arrived for Moe to invite Clark into his basement workshop. Rosemary was with the kids, who were telling her all about their school projects, so it was me and Leigh in the kitchen as I put the finishing touches on the roast and made the salad.

"So," I started out all nice and casual. "You and Clark?" What points I don't get in subtlety, I make up for in being direct.

Leigh shrugged. Ah, she was going to make me work for my info.

"You two have been seeing a lot of each other? We had dinner with my parents and brother. He mentioned he'd seen you and, you wanted to get back together. I pushed and pushed, and he finally mentioned you said something about Clark. I couldn't tell if you were using him as an excuse because you two are only friends or if something was really going on."

Leigh bit her lip, then laughed. "Yeah. Your brother's a real pain in the butt. And a liar. Clark and I are seeing each other, but we're taking it slow."

I gave her a look that implied my doubts, concerns, and confusion.

"Clark is a gentleman," she explained, sounding rather irked.

"Clark needs a kick in the pants," I retorted. "Need me to say something?"

"Get in line. My sister said pretty much the same thing." She blushed down to her roots. "I was going to." She cleared her throat. "I am going to."

"I don't mind," I told her. "I have a lot of experience in bringing couples together."

Leigh finally laughed. "Moe's mentioned that once or twice."

It was my turn to shrug as I shook a jar of vinaigrette. "Hey, I'm good at it. Both in real life and on the page. Just let me know if you need any help."

I needed to change the subject, or she'd catch on to how interested I really was. "So, has that interesting older gentleman been bothering you lately?"

"I haven't seen him in two weeks," Leigh answered. "But if you're right and he's a ghost like you were teasing Clark, maybe he's been hanging around invisibly. And if that's true, maybe that's why Clark's keeping his distance, so the spirit world can't peep in on us if things go in that direction." She stopped. In fact, she stopped for a very long moment as if she were thinking hard. Then she tossed her head and laughed. "Right. That makes a whole lot of sense. Not. But no. I haven't, and Clark hasn't mentioned it even though they live in the same building. Maybe we'll see him tonight."

So, that was the end of that interrogation. Not my finest hour, I'll admit.

I couldn't help noticing the way Clark was sending dark, brooding glances at Leigh across the table during dinner and how she was returning them with interest. I concluded they didn't need any help from me. But I was prepared to give my brother a swift kick in the as… let's say the pants, if he didn't stay out of Leigh's way. As much as I loved her as a friend, I'd much prefer to see her become a happy cousin-in-law than a miserable sister-in-law. Then again, I wanted to kick my brother as a general principle.

One last note before I stop this first-person stuff. I was still convinced something didn't seem right about that old guy. I was sure Leigh was aware of the anomaly, but as she had no experience with the paranormal, she couldn't quite articulate whatever she was feeling. I planned to pay close attention, in case we saw him. Very. Close. Attention. I couldn't mention to Clark that I thought Leigh was hiding something until I knew more. And, of course, I had no idea exactly what it was she was hiding.

So, Berry out. For now.

Clark

"Did Berry give you the third degree while I was downstairs?" Clark asked as they drove to the university.

"There's a lot of interest in our relationship," Leigh replied lightly. "Where it's going? How do we feel about one another? Are we sleeping together?"

He choked out a laugh. "Yeah, well, Moe was just as nosy. Wanted to know my intentions."

Leigh snort-laughed and covered her mouth. "He's been married to a romance writer for a while. He was bound to have picked up questions like that."

"I know, right. But I think you and I kind of covered my intentions when we talked last week. And it's not like we haven't spoken every day though I'd have preferred for us to see each other."

"We'll be able to see more of each other soon. My calendar is freeing up some with the holidays," Leigh said. "A lot of my speaking engagements are at colleges, but they're winding down. It'll pick up in the spring. But you've been traveling a lot for your research. Any progress this week?"

He shook his head in the darkened car. "Not a bit. I had a few nibbles, but I haven't been able to follow up on all of them. It's going to be tough next semester when I have to train a new research assistant. The one I have is really into the mystery, but one of the other professors wants her next year." He sighed. "I'm starting to wonder if an answer can be found. It'll be awfully disappointing to us if we can't solve it."

"Us?" she echoed. "We?"

Clark cleared his throat. "Sorry. I meant my assistant, Bonnie. And me, of course. And a number of other folks who've expressed interest." He cleared his throat again and gripped the wheel tighter. "And I suppose I assumed you were interested as well."

"Oh. Okay. I mean, I am. Mostly because it seems like it's consuming you, and I know it's important. But have you thought about another topic, just in case? What about early moviemaking on the East Coast? I heard that a lot of the early stars came from here and moved out to California later."

He did a double take. "You knew that? Most people don't."

She gave a small apologetic smile. "I think, um, that someone once told me. Or I read it. I assumed it was common knowledge."

"It's not. But it gave me a thrill that you do." He pulled into the parking lot closest to the theater. "And I want to remind you if I begin to sound obsessive and won't shut up, you need to call me on it." He ran his gloved hands over his hair. "In fact, I wish you would distract me."

"Like this?" she asked as she leaned over and kissed him. "Or like this?" Her lips traced under his jaw where the skin was smooth, to his ear. Her hands roamed beneath his coat, and the feel of them so close to his skin made his breath quicken. His fingers fumbled with her buttons to find the softness below. "I think we need to spend a few hours after the movie doing something other than talking."

Clark's pulse skyrocketed. "Leigh, are you saying—"

She gave him a bright smile. "That's exactly what I'm saying. Not that I want to force you. But those midnight kisses either need to stop or to turn into something a little more—lasting?"

He laughed. "Nice ambush when I'm doing all I can to keep my hands to myself and my mind on the little speech I have to give in thirty minutes."

Leigh kissed him again. "You know how I like your introductions to the films, but maybe later, after the film, you can skip all that after-movie chatter and drinks. We might go someplace a little more private."

He leaned into the kiss, his hand going through her hair. "You're mean it?"

She nodded, and he pressed his forehead against hers. "If you're sure, then there's nothing I would like more." He pulled back far enough to look into her eyes. He was unable to stop his smile. "So, the only remaining question is, your place or mine?"

Leigh

She watched as her soon-to-be lover strode onto the stage. She barely heard what he said about that night's films. Her place, or his? Her place meant Gram would potentially hear them and come to investigate. Or his place. Did that older man live on Clark's floor? He seemed nice enough, but was he nosy? Did his bedroom share a wall with Clark's?

She glanced around and saw the old coot. He was focused on the stage, but as if he could feel her gaze, he turned and nodded, a pleasant smile on his face. Was that a gentle wink? Her neck prickled uncomfortably. Leigh turned back to Clark as he was finishing his introduction. The old man seemed harmless, but there was something about him that she couldn't quite put her finger on — something familiar beyond his resemblance to a long-dead movie star, and at the same time, not.

"We're trying something new tonight. As so many of you have stopped me in the lobby after the past several showings, we'll do a brief Q and A here in the theater right after the film." Clark's gaze shifted to where Leigh sat before he returned his focus to the auditorium. Several people glanced at her, and she felt her cheeks heat. "And now, please enjoy tonight's films."

The spotlight shut down, and the curtains behind him lifted. Clark jumped off the stage and came to sit by her, kissing her warmly and wrapped an arm around her shoulders. "I could barely think, let alone talk up there," he murmured before he pressed a kiss to her forehead. "I hope I didn't make a total fool of myself."

"I didn't notice," she whispered back, then lifted her face for another kiss. "Nervous about later?" she asked.

217

He grinned at her. "Terrified."

She nodded. "Good," and smiled. "Me too."

Berry

When Clark got up on stage after the films, I moved into the seat next to Leigh. "I was looking for that old man. He disappeared again."

Leigh looked around and found him still there. "I see him," she said.

I turned, and it was the weirdest thing. One moment there was an empty seat, and the next, that old guy was looking at me — grinning. It was almost as if he and I shared a private joke, only I wasn't sure what the punchline was.

"Oh. I must have looked the wrong way." Not my greatest fib, but I don't think it mattered. Leigh only had eyes for Clark. "How's your grandmother?" I asked.

Leigh flinched. "She's uh, good. For her age. Sharp as anything."

"I'd still like to meet her," I said. "I don't get to meet too many really old folks, and I'd love to pick her brain. I'm thinking of writing some flashbacks to the twenties for my latest book, so maybe she can help. Oh, wait, maybe she wasn't born then."

"We'll see," Leigh murmured as the house lights came up. Clark was still up on stage, talking to a young woman standing in the aisle. He gestured to Leigh, and she rose. "Excuse me."

I watched as Clark made introductions. Then the young woman walked away, and Clark helped Leigh up to stand with him on stage as he pointed to something in the wings. The theater emptied, and the lights came down. I stayed where I was. I'm like that. At the end of a movie, I watch until the credits are all done, and that night it felt like something more was about to happen. Besides, Moe was off talking shop with someone he knew, and I didn't have anyone else to chat with.

I wasn't disappointed. There were only a few of us left, and the lights dimmed again. Before my eyes, Clark took Leigh into his arms. His hands cupped her jaw lightly, and suddenly a spotlight was on them as he kissed her tenderly at first, and suddenly she was bent over his arm, and he was kissing the heck out of her. I wanted to sigh. I knew they were heading for a happy ending.

I turned because the little hairs on the back of my neck started to stand, and I saw that man, still sitting right where he had been. He and I were the only ones left in the audience, and he began to applaud. I'm not sure if Leigh and Clark could hear him, but I could.

And what's more, despite the dim light, I was pretty sure I could see right through him.

Leigh wasn't the only one with some explaining to do.

Finch, I read your last report. Still no word on what happened to Miss Standish?

No, Mr. Percy. I've got guys looking from here to New York, Boston, Philly, and San Antone. Not a trace. We've been checking the papers every day — no stage actresses by the name of Isabel anywhere.

Well, keep looking. It's only been a few months. She's got to turn up somewhere. My career depends on it.

Will do, sir. And of course, our invoice is enclosed.

I'll see that you're paid.

Thank you, sir.

Ah. Alone again. Yes, my career depends on someone, Jerome said to the empty room. *Finding her, but my peace of mind as well. And my heart. Oh, Izzy, why couldn't you believe in me?*

Chapter Nineteen

Clark

They were putting on their coats after bowing to their small audience. Berry had winked at them and quickly left, but to Clark's consternation, Jerome made a production of shaking out his overcoat and setting it on his shoulders, then putting on his hat at just the right angle before he sauntered out of the auditorium.

Once they were alone, Clark started, "So," but it came out more like a wheeze. "About that—"

Leigh stopped him with another kiss. "Doesn't matter. I'm not exactly ashamed to be seen with you," she teased. "Unless it's unseemly for a university professor to be seen kissing his girlfriend on stage?"

Clark laughed. "If anything, being seen with you will give me added stature around here." He shook his head, then took her hand

and pressed a kiss to the back of it, then the palm. "I'm serious. Let them know how high I set my standards, and some of the more assertive sophomores will leave me alone."

"They hit on you?"

He shrugged. "Once or twice. I usually ignore them, but I've mentioned it to the dean in case one of them gets more aggressive. I let them down easy. Tell 'em I have someone in my life, and she's terribly jealous and doesn't like to share." He looked into her sparkling eyes. "Right?"

She stretched onto her toes and kissed him again. "Damned right. If any of them get too close, remind them I don't get mad, I get even."

Clark laughed. "So, I'll add territorial to your description."

"Fierce and protective," she affirmed with a smile. "And you've kept me waiting long enough. Your place or mine?" She looked around the now empty theater. "I was thinking yours—"

He lifted his brow.

"Because I haven't seen it yet."

Clark pulled her into his arms, then rubbed her nose with his. "And I don't have a nosy grandmother who might make things uncomfortable?"

Leigh pulled back, and her smile faded as if a drip of poisoned uncertainty contaminated her joy. "That too. One of these days, we need to talk about her."

Clark wrapped his arms around her once more. "But not tonight. I don't want to talk about anything other than how beautiful you are and how happy I'll be to have you in my arms. Not to mention in my bed." He kissed her.

"Are we really going to do this?" she asked, her voice small and oh-so wonderfully hopeful.

He nodded, refusing to let his nerves get the better of him. "Unless you change your mind." He kissed her again. He pulled her closer, deepening the kiss until urgency overcame his nerves.

He started searching for a secluded, horizontal surface closer than the fourteen blocks to his apartment.

There was a polite clearing of a throat, and they broke apart, hands behind their backs.

"Sorry, Professor," the janitor said. "Union rules say I have to be done by midnight. Can't start cleaning until everyone's gone."

Clark fumbled his glasses which had half fallen off. Leigh ducked her head. "We'll be on our way then," he said. "Good night."

"Night, Professor, Miss," the janitor said, a smile in his voice. "Enjoyed that movie tonight. Like that Jeremy fella. Seems like a good guy."

"Er, right," Clark said as he took Leigh's elbow, and they hurried up the aisle and into the darkened lobby. "My place?" he asked one more time. "It might be kind of messy."

"Are the sheets clean?" Leigh asked.

He shivered at the low purr of her voice. "Uh, yes."

"Do you have a roommate?"

Clark bit his lip. "Not exactly." She raised her brows. Clark cleared his throat. "There's a neighbor who stops in from time to time." He almost laughed when Leigh squinted her eyes at him.

"Does he have a key?" she demanded.

He shook his head. "No key."

"So. If he knocks, we won't answer the door," Leigh said firmly.

A smile formed he could not stop even if he'd wanted to. "No. We won't," he agreed. "Follow me."

Ten minutes later, they were in his parking lot. He pulled the key from the ignition and turned to kiss her, and she responded with a hot, open-mouthed kiss that sent his pulse thumping. He scrambled out and around the car, and when he opened her car door, she pulled him down into the car by his bowtie and kissed him again. She kissed him long and hard, but the cold wind was biting through his trousers. "Woman, let me get you inside," he growled in her ear. She laughed and kissed him once more before allowing him up, where he pulled her out of the car and into his arms. "It's cold out here," he grumbled as he held her close.

"Your blood's too thin," she teased. "That's what growing up on the left coast does to you."

He took her hand and tugged her toward the back door. When they reached the building, he lightly pushed her against the metal security door, his hips pressed forward, and there was no mistaking his interest. "Still think my blood's too thin?" he asked with a laugh. He leaned down and kissed from her temple to nape, taking small nibbles along the way. She gasped and shivered against him and pressed closer, lifting her chin to grant him access to her tender skin.

He found her lips once more, and as he kissed his way to her brow, Leigh gave a low, sultry moan and rubbed herself against him. "I'm the first to admit when I'm wrong." She slid her arms around his neck again. "Tell me why we're still outside?"

He rubbed his nose against hers. "Because I couldn't get you to move fast enough."

"Oh, right." She kissed him lightly. "I'm ready now."

Clark swiped his key fob at the door, and they made their way inside, their arms around one another, their lips locked until they encountered another tenant, banging a laundry cart into the hall as they waited for the elevator.

Leigh straightened as Clark adjusted his glasses. "This is nice," she said in a slightly strained voice as they made their way into the elevator with the older woman, the pungent scent of bleach about her.

Clark cleared his throat and tried to slow the hammering of his heart. *Try to sound normal*, he commanded himself. He cleared his throat again when he saw the gleam in Leigh's eye. "It turns out Berry owns a unit on another floor. This is where she lived when she first met Moe. Did you read the story she wrote about that time?"

223

Despite the interest of the interloper, Leigh pressed closer. "I did. It was hysterical. I can't believe Moe's okay with her writing all that. And the stuff about the characters who came to life—" She wrinkled her nose. "It almost sounded real the way she wrote it. Can you imagine?"

The elevator came to a stop, and he held the door as they stepped out. Despite his best wishes, the woman wheeled her cart out after them, so he continued his charade of normalcy. "It was preposterous. Stuff like that can't happen," he said, biting his lip. A wisp of a memory of something Moe said in the fall flittered around in the back of his head. "But it's entertaining."

Clark took Leigh's hand and walked her to his door, the woman following. They nodded as she passed them, but she turned back to stare once more before unlocking a door at the end of the hall.

"I wasn't expecting company," Clark said as he fumbled with his key. His blood was still humming despite the interruption, but he didn't want to press Leigh right into bed in case the mood was broken. "So, don't expect too much." He unlocked the door and held it open. "It's clean, but when I'm working, I'm not the tidiest person."

Leigh stepped over the threshold, and he watched as she looked around. The framed movie posters were askew but not dusty. His desk was littered with CDs and DVDs. Papers and books were on every surface, including the small galley kitchen counters. And his laptop was open with the screen saver of multiple images of Clark's favorite silent era stars cycled around. "So, this is where the magic happens," she said with a saucy smile.

Clark closed and locked the door. "Not yet, but I'm hoping…"

Leigh unbuttoned her coat and threw it over a chair full of books. "Does your research extend into the bedroom?"

His smile grew as he shed his overcoat. "Not that sort of research."

Her brows rose. "Oh?"

He strode to her and cradled her face in his palms as he smiled. "Tonight, I'm embarking on a brand-new project. More mathematical than cinematic or historical."

"Tell me more."

"I want—" He kissed her, then kissed her again as his hands slid down her back and up again. "To see—" Another kiss. "How many times—" His hands stroked over her shoulders to press her close. "I can kiss you—" He felt her shiver as his hands held her bottom and pulled her close.

A long moment later, she leaned back in his arms, breathless. "Is that all? Simple arithmetic?"

He turned them and started walking her backward into the bedroom, kissing her between every word. "Nothing simple about it, for I plan to multitask. You see, I also want to determine how many times I can make you come in one night." He leaned down and kissed her deeply. "Purely an educational exercise, you see."

When he kissed her again, he felt her smile.

"How many times do you hypothesize, Professor?" she asked as she kicked off her shoes and allowed herself to be pressed onto the bed.

He kicked off his own, loosened his tie, tossed his glasses on the nightstand before he crawled over her, brushing her soft hair away from her face. She was so lovely in the dim light. Her hair shone, her eyes sparkled, and her smile was welcoming and warm. "I hypothesize we will kiss one thousand times before I let you out of this bed tomorrow morning," he said with all the gravity he could muster. It wasn't much.

One pert brow quirked upward. "And the other?"

Clark rose on his knees and looked around. There was no hint of Jerome's presence in the apartment. He sighed in relief before he gazed into her eyes once more. "Lots and lots, and many more. Innumerable if I'm lucky. Even more, if we both are."

Leigh reached up and tugged one strand of his bow tie and flung it away. Her soft fingers undid the top button of his shirt, and then the second, spreading it wide and then placed a kiss on his Adams Apple. She licked downward until she was momentarily stopped by a layer of cotton shirt. "Well then, I think we need to start counting, don't you?"

Leigh

She snuggled next to Clark's long, warm body. She'd known before that he was tall, that he was fit, but his strength and stamina last night had been a delightful surprise. Her scholar clearly wasn't warming library benches all the time. Their kisses had indeed approached one thousand, were one to count every time lip met lip or lip met flesh. And oh, one absolutely ought. Nothing about their lovemaking had been awkward as it sometimes was between lovers the first time. She'd felt no shyness about her imperfect body. He'd delighted in her every curve, every bit of bountiful flesh, and drank in her sighs. And she'd thrilled in his body. Muscle and tendon, sinew and flesh—all of it was hers to enjoy. Over and over again.

As a hint of daylight slipped from behind the drawn curtains, Clark stirred, his arm tightened around her waist. She snuggled beside him, propped on her elbow to better see his sleeping face. She wanted to count every faint freckle that dotted his cheeks and nose, to spear her fingers through the closely cropped beard that was softer than expected and which he'd used to excite her. She wished to run her fingertips down his neck, across his broad shoulders, over his chest. But more, she wanted to examine him, and because touching him would awaken him, she wanted him to sleep a few minutes more, so she could enjoy the gift of his still body.

They'd made love throughout the night. Every time she'd consigned herself to slumber, his hand had come wandering, his lips not far behind, and each time she'd turned to him gladly.

Unless, of course, it had been she who'd sought him out with her own wandering hands and greedy lips.

Leigh stretched in his arms, loving how he kept her warm. She snuggled down and tucked herself under his chin, her back to his front when he began to stroke her hip.

"You awake?" She felt his basso rumble more than heard it.

She nodded. "Um. You?"

His hands wandered farther, exploring her back, and further down, then stroked up and in. She winced before she could stop herself. "You're sore," he said. "I'm sorry about that." His arms cradled her closer, and he kissed the top of her head. "You're so irresistible."

Leigh turned and curled an arm around his neck. "Not so sore, and not unwilling," she whispered.

"Had I known, I would have, we should have—"

She placed a finger on his lips, which he sucked into his mouth. "No regrets for last night. Or this morning." She felt his smile around her finger. "No regrets for last week or last month, and not a single regret for right now," she added as she scooted down in the bed, kissed his chest, and ran her tongue down the center of his body to his navel. She looked up at him, her eyes bright. "As long as you're willing."

He soon showed her just how willing he was.

Clark

When they next awoke, Clark proposed to take Leigh out for breakfast and then home. He hated the idea of parting, but she'd said something about needing to be on a call that afternoon, and he had research he needed to do. They stood on her doorstop with kisses that felt almost desperate at the thought of not seeing each other again for days despite their promises to speak again that night. At last, Leigh broke from his arms. Her fingers trailed slowly down his arms until, with almost an audible pop, they were apart. Her smile sad, she opened her door and slipped inside.

Clark heaved a deep sigh. With slumped shoulders, he walked back to his car. If Leigh was going to work that afternoon, so would he. That meant he needed some otherworldly assistance. As soon as he was back on the main road leading to his place, he yelled, "Jerome?"

And like that, the ghost appeared beside him, translucent in the pearly grey gloom of the late autumn day.

"You sly dog, you," was Jerome's greeting. "You finally got the girl into the sack. What I don't understand is why you're not still there?"

Clark scowled at him. "None of your business."

The ghost's frown was fierce. "Tell me, was she no good?"

"Jerome—"

"Or were you lacking?" Jerome shook his head, chuckling madly.

"I'm warning you," Clark said, but his shoulders sagged. "Who am I fooling. I can't threaten you other than with one thing. And at the risk of saying too much, Leigh was everything I could have hoped for and more. And I wasn't lacking either. She arranged for an overseas call weeks ago and couldn't cancel it given there are about a dozen folks dialing in from England and various parts of Asia."

Jerome grinned. "Remembered everything I told you, did you? You left the lady satisfied."

Clark couldn't help but grin. "None of your business, you dirty old man."

Jerome threw back his head and laughed. "That good then."

"That's not why I yelled for you." Clark chanced a quick glance at his companion, then back at the street, for it had started to snow lightly.

"I'm at your disposal," Jerome said affably.

"I want to talk to you again about the morning Isabel Standish left you."

The ghost's face turned sullen, or as sullen as possible given the wan light. "I've told you everything I know," he said softly.

"Not everything."

"Clark, m'boy—"

"Something occurred to me last night when Leigh and I were together."

Jerome sniggered.

"None of that. I mean, when I was holding her. We talked last night, and not about what she likes and what I like. We talked about things that are important to us. We're not the types who fall into bed with other people. We both like— no, need to, connect with one another at a deeper level."

Jerome's nose rose several degrees into the air. "I hope you're not implying that my affairs were merely physical flings." He relented with a small laugh. "Well, some were. But not all. I genuinely cared for the women I slept with. Other than that Blanche. I just used her, the poor, wretched woman. Not proud of it, but there you have it. She made herself convenient. And persistent. And Isabel had insisted we break things off between us before she went to Mexico. She thought I wouldn't be faithful to her, so she wanted to give me an excuse to appease my wandering eye." He looked down. "I wish she hadn't. Izzy that is. I *was* faithful to her." He turned to Clark. "It hurt. Rather a bit, to think she thought I was that weak." He looked out the window. "But to my credit, if such things matter, I waited until Izzy was good and gone before I laid a hand on that woman."

"Really, Jer? You took up with Blanche quickly enough."

Jerome hung his head further. "I suppose I did. But it was to make Izzy jealous. If she had so little faith in me, I'd— I'd— " He looked out the side window. "I don't know how this helps find what happened to her."

"Jerome, I'm staring at a bunch of dead ends. You've evaded answering some of my questions for years. Every lead I've followed has turned up with nothing. If you really want to find your Isabel, it's time for you to come clean with me. You have to give me something new, or we'll never find her."

Jerome stared straight ahead. "And if I told you I've already given you everything I remember?"

Clark shrugged as he pulled back into the driveway of his apartment building. "Then I'm done. Finished. I start looking for a new subject for my next book, and you have to figure out how move on to the next world."

He shut off the car and opened the door, not looking back. There was work he needed to do, no matter how much he'd rather still be laying in Leigh's arms. Not all his inquiries had hit a dead end, but the most promising ones had.

Clark went into his apartment, only to find Jerome beat him to it. The ghost did his impression of standing by the bedroom door, wistfully gazing at the messy bed Leigh had left less than an hour before.

"She's in love with you?" Jerome asked without looking around.

Clark ran a hand through his hair. "The words were not exactly spoken." Oh, Leigh had said things to the effect of 'I love that,' and 'do it again,' and quite a few utterances of 'more', but there was not a single 'I love you' spoken by either of them despite his having bitten them back a time or two.

"I always loved the look of a bed after Izzy and I left it," Jerome said sorrowfully. "I know you'll think I'm a fanciful old fool, but to see the imprint of her body in the sheets, to imagine her there still. With me." His hand went to the vicinity of where his heart once beat, and he sighed. "Did you know she and I never got to spend an entire night together?"

"I didn't."

Jerome shook his head again. "She was afraid to. No matter how many times I told her no one would care. No matter how many times I told her I loved her, wanted to marry her. She was a good girl at heart. Had the crazy idea that if we didn't spend all night together, the fact that we slept together without being married wasn't a sin."

Jerome stood there, longing and bereft. Clark wanted nothing so much as to pat Jerome on the shoulder, but in all their years of acquaintance, the two had never touched—or come close to even a brush. It was an unspoken agreement they wouldn't occupy the same physical space, even if there was nothing physical about Jerome.

"What I wouldn't give to be able to see my Izzy again," Jerome sighed softly. "To hold her, kiss her." He hung his head. "I was so stupid. So arrogant. I thought I had all the time in the world. Thought I'd teach her a lesson that she could trust me while she went off to make a movie without me." He looked up at Clark. "I never, ever once thought she'd actually desert me, m'boy. I believed she loved me as much as I loved her."

"Maybe not coming back wasn't her choice," Clark said softly. "Maybe she wanted to, but things changed, and she couldn't."

"She never wrote me. I never heard from her again."

Clark's head rose. "Are you sure? Maybe she did, but you never saw it."

Jerome spun around. "What?"

"Fan mail. Maybe she wrote you, but it was lost in the volume. The studio or your fan club might never have sent it on to you — especially if she used her real name. Or the studio did it on purpose to get back at you. Or get back at her. Or for the publicity…"

The ghost thrust his hands in his pockets and paced. "It never— I didn't think— I suppose it's possible." He hung his head once more, his face a tragic mask. "All of which makes me feel worse. What if she did, and the letter was intercepted?" He looked up, and there were phantom tears in his eyes. "What if it was all

231

one big misunderstanding?" He sank to his knees, his hands covering his face as his hat fell into oblivion. "Clark, Clark, why did she leave me, and why did she not come back?"

Unspoken rule or none, Clark couldn't take his mentor, his friend's pain any longer. He sank to his own knees, leaned over, and wrapped his arms around the grieving ghost as gently as he could. But there was nothing there. Jerome had vanished.

Dearest Tommy,

It's been months since we last saw each other. I want you to know I've had a lot of time to think about what happened between us. I'm back home, and my life has picked up pretty much as it would have, had I never gone away. I shall leave you to draw your own conclusions about that. Except for the boy I was keeping company with. He's got another girl now. Won't even look at me.

I hope you haven't forgotten me, and maybe can forgive me for acting so recklessly. I should have believed in you, and I deeply regret acting so rashly. I can't tell you everything that had gone on in my mind that day, but trust me, there was a lot, particularly after what happened on the way back from Mexico. I wanted to tell you, but seeing you with Blanche—well, it was very difficult for me. What I need to tell you now is how much I miss you. And that I forgive you for having strayed.

What you also need to know is that I've received a proposal of marriage. He's a very kind man, but I'm not sure marrying is the right thing do to. If you have any feelings for me, please write back, and I'll break the engagement. Somehow, I'll find a way to return to you. I always intended to go back to California, but my parents confiscated my money, and I haven't found a way to buy a ticket. I'll rob a bank if that's what it takes to return if you'll have me.

I can't tell you how much I regret not writing sooner, but I was so confused and angry. Suddenly things are much clearer, and I realize how foolish I was. The wedding is set for June. That should be plenty of time for you to write back to me. I know you have always disdained playing the lead—the hero, but I could really use one now.

I love you and always will.
Lilly

Chapter Twenty

Leigh

She looked across the kitchen table at Gram. She seemed smaller than ever, her dear face paler. Leigh blinked. Was Gram even really there? And why had she hung around all these years, with Leigh as her only human company?

"You look troubled, Darling," Gram said.

"I'm afraid things are catching up to me," she replied. "Fact and imagination are starting to confuse me."

Gram laughed. "Oh, well, that. You know more than anyone that imagination is powerful stuff. Why, there are some who make entire careers out of it."

"Why can I see you?" Leigh blurted. "Why me and not Sarah? Or Mom?"

Gram looked down at her hands in her lap. "I often wonder that myself, Dear Lei-Lei. It's not that Sarah never knew me. I expect she remembers me better than you from when you were small. But I think you were so young, you didn't understand the concept of death. Perhaps it's you who has kept me here. Or it's only you to whom I wish to be visible. I dare say, if I cared to, I could be so for others. When I passed, I was certainly surprised to find that I never really left, although my status did change significantly. I believe that's why I'm still in this wheelchair when we both know I can't possibly need it as a ghost. It's how you remembered me." She gave a bright smile despite her translucence. "I think because of you, I've never had the urge to move on." Her smile faded. "But I'm not certain I'll be here much longer, my dearest, darling great-granddaughter. I fear that soon not even your love will be enough."

"Gram—"

"It will be fine, Lei-Lei. You will keep me in your heart, and I shall keep you in what serves as one for me. I am determined to, you know. No matter what comes next."

Gram smiled again, and Leigh returned it, though a tear fell. "I'm not sure how I'll get on without you." She wiped her face. "And Berry's been asking to meet you. How do I delay her?"

"Well, you could kill me off," Gram said with a laugh. "Though it will be a bit difficult given my obituary was published decades ago."

Leigh gave a watery laugh as she hid her face in her hands. "It's not funny."

"I beg to differ, Darling Girl." Gram leaned forward. "I think you might be able to trust Berry to keep your secret."

Leigh lifted her head. "What?"

Gram smiled. "Given her stories, I have a hunch she may not be a stranger to the extra-ordinary."

Leigh groaned. "Even so, what do I do about Clark? He wants to meet you too."

"I'll have to give that more thought," Gram said. "Eat your dinner. We'll talk again tomorrow."

Berry

"Do you like teaching at the university? Is your research is going well?"

Seeing a golden opportunity, I pulled Clark into the kitchen for some coffee and gossip when he'd stopped by to ask Moe for advice about snow tires. Fortunately for me, Moe was at a basketball game with Max and Maddie. I was hoping Clark would find it in his heart to confide in me, so I planned to test the waters to gently hint what I knew, to see how he'd react.

He shrugged. "I've hit a few dead ends. There's something out there I need to follow up on, but it keeps eluding me."

I frowned. "Want to talk it through?"

He nodded vaguely. "There's something I'm missing. I have all of Jerome Percy's papers. He searched high and low for Isabel Standish for years, but there was never a single verifiable lead. I think I have all the reports from the private eyes. Just about every single report and invoice."

"So—"

He drummed his fingers on the table. "All of them, including the last from the primary firm. The report from that last month was different, though, as if the PI was giving up. For some reason, there was no bill. Jerome fired that firm and picked another, but again, nothing. He paid them for years. I think they were bilking him, to be honest. The trail had gone cold within weeks of her leaving."

I poured coffee and pushed a mug in his direction. "What if that one month was an anomaly?"

"Huh?"

I put myself in plotting mode. "If I were writing this, I'd ask myself what if that report was intercepted?" I said. "If Jerome was married, and if I were his wife, I'd be plenty pissed if my husband was spending thousands of dollars a year looking for another woman. What if whichever wife he had at the time took the report, paid the PI, and then hid the results and sent a phony one in. Only she forgot to send an invoice."

"I thought of that and dismissed it. The record is so complete otherwise. I'll have to give it more thought."

"Really?" I felt rather proud of myself. It occurred to me that perhaps I should start to write mysteries. I squashed that thought then and there.

Clark shook his head. "It makes me wonder what else I might've overlooked. Or missed seeing right before my very eyes. Thank you." He pulled out his phone and made a few notes."

"So, things between you and Leigh, they're going well?"

His dreamy smile said it all. "She's wonderful."

"Comes from an interesting family," I added. "It really doesn't surprise me that the two of you hit it off, what with her family having an interest in the movie business and all." I picked up a cookie and took a bite. "So, you two are exclusive, right?"

He nodded. "We're both so busy, neither of us would have time to juggle multiple partners even if we were inclined. We agreed to total honesty between us."

Was that a twitch I saw on his brow? "Oh, well. Right," I said before I leaned closer. "Take it from someone who's been in a long-term relationship— there are times when a secret or two are perfectly appropriate. Or necessary." I gave him a wink. "I don't mean cheating. But surprises on birthdays, or romantic weekends away, that sort of thing." The twitch on his brow flickered again. "Or family secrets. Nothing harmful. Things you don't want to let out that might embarrass someone else. Adds a little mystique, you know?"

Moe was right about Clark. He was clumsy as his coffee sloshed as he set it back on the table. "Family secrets?" he said with the tiniest hint of a squeak to his voice.

I shrugged. "Well, I didn't let Moe meet my brother until he and I were a committed couple," I said with a laugh. "You've met Rocky. If you had a ghastly relative like him, wouldn't you wait until you had a ring on Leigh's finger— metaphorically, of course— before you introduced them?" I covered my mouth with my fingers. "Oh, I'm sorry. I haven't met your brothers."

He laughed. "My brothers are all fine. Not a one of them's horrifying. Annoying, maybe." He picked up his cup and then set it down. "What did you mean when you said Leigh's family is in the film business? I know her mother works with film producers, and she hinted at something, but I never got a chance to follow up with her. They do some specialized CGI work. Is that what you meant?"

"No. I think it was one of Leigh's grandparents who had gone out to Hollywood and then came back. I don't know the details.

She mentioned it once in passing when we first met. Do you think she might have been the woman you're researching?"

Clark came about as close to doing a real-life spit-take as anyone I've ever seen. "I remember someone saying something," he said weakly as he mopped his face with his napkin. "I'll have to follow up." He took another moment. "But that would be the mother of all coincidences, don't you think?"

"Funny she's never mentioned it to you," I added. "Leigh would if she knew."

"Not a word," he said, looking around and then stood. "Listen, I need to go. Can you ask Moe to call me? I need to get some snow tires soon, or I'm going to wreck my car."

"I will." I stood on my toes to press a kiss to his cheek. "You and Leigh should come by for dinner again soon. Maybe some week when you don't have to run to show a movie, so we're not rushed."

He smiled faintly. "Sounds good. I'll see you around."

Clark let himself out the back door and practically ran to his car. As disappointed as I was that he didn't spill his secrets to me, his was a very interesting reaction. I couldn't wait to find out what would happen next.

Leigh

She paced between the grand hall and the kitchen. Clark was expected for dinner and to spend the night. She and Gram had not resumed their conversation of the other morning, though the old woman promised to stay out of sight for the duration of Clark's visit, even if it extended into the morning.

Walking the distance from the front door to the kitchen, Leigh rued the fact that the house was too darned big for one person to manage. It was designed with expectations for a staff, including a cook, maid, and butler who would man the front door. She'd never hear the doorbell from the back of the house where the kitchen lay.

She checked on her roast and switched the oven to warm. She wouldn't heat the vegetables until he arrived, and the dinner rolls were wrapped in foil and ready to go into the oven at the same time.

Hurrying back to the front door, she saw Clark's tall silhouette in the sidelights. The bell sounded as she reached for the knob.

"Hi," she said and presented her face for a kiss.

He leaned down and pressed his lips to hers. "Hi, yourself."

"Come on in. It's freezing out there." She held the door wider, and he walked in, taking in the grand foyer with its oak staircase.

"Let me take your coat, and we'll go to the back. This house is too big this time of year. Even with most of the rooms shut off, the heating bill is ugly. We'll eat in the morning room if you don't mind. I have the dining room's radiators turned off, but I'll show you around if you'd like."

She hung his coat in the closet and held out her hand. "Quick tour first. Are you hungry?"

He took her hand. "I'm always hungry. I was a starving grad student for too many years to ever turn down a meal."

She laughed. "Okay. Let me point out where we are. To the right is the formal parlor. It's full of antiques. I keep it cold this time of year. On the left is the small parlor, which is the only modern room on this floor. That's where I spend most of my waking hours when I'm not at work. Just past it is the music room. There's a water closet here. Original antique plumbing I'm afraid, but it works, and it's heated. Past the formal parlor is the dining room. This is where the Trust's board meets quarterly. I turn on the heat for that, though I missed the last meeting." She opened the door and a cold chill swept over them. "I promise to give you a more extensive tour another day. Let's hurry through to the kitchen."

She tugged him through the door, walking quickly in the frigid air. They went through another door into the cozy kitchen.

"Wow," he said. "This is amazing. It's such a mix of old and new." He ran his hand along the stainless-steel countertop that ran below a string of original glass-fronted cabinets. In front of one was a sturdy wooden worktable.

"We had to modify it for the functions we hold. The old iron stove wasn't doing it for us. We kept it, though, down in the basement along with the original cabinets. If we ever turn this place into a museum, we'll put them back."

"Is that part of your plan?"

She shook her head. "Not any time soon. The basement is huge and dry since I replaced the water heater. But it's scary as anything. I always hated going down there. My sister used to dare me when we were kids, so of course, I had to try. She said it was haunted." Leigh swallowed despite her dry throat. "Kids are pretty crazy."

Clark laughed, but his smile seemed forced. "Ever see a ghost while you were down there?"

"I can honestly tell you I never saw a ghost in the basement," she said, forcing a laugh. "I can't say that about the rest of the house."

She spun to the oven before he could reply and took out the pan and set it on the stove. "This roast needs to sit for another twenty minutes. I've got some appetizers set out on the worktable." Leigh slipped the foil-wrapped bread into the oven and turned up the heat under the green beans. She turned to find him at her back.

"Come here," he said softly as he took her into his arms. "I've missed you." He bent to kiss her, the kiss growing in intensity as the moments ticked by. His hands spanned her back, stroking warmly as his tongue sought entrance to her mouth. She opened for him gladly. His kisses spread to her neck, and she regretted wearing the thick, turtleneck sweater, but that didn't stop him from bestowing kisses along her jaw, making her shiver.

She leaned back and cupped his face. "I've missed you too." His answering smile warmed her.

"Yeah?" he asked.

She nodded. "Talking on the phone's okay, but I missed this," she said, pointing between them.

Clark didn't wait for permission. His grip on her tightened as their kisses turned hotter. "Is your grandmother likely to come in here?" he asked heatedly before claiming her lips again.

She shook her head as she reached for the hem of her sweater. He did the same with his. "She never comes down here at night." Leigh encircled his neck in her arms and dragged his head down to her. "Or her companion."

Clark grunted as his hands slid around and down. "Will you think I'm a complete pig if we—"

She reached for his belt. "Not a chance."

A moment later, he'd helped her yank her skirt up and her tights off as his jeans puddled around his ankles. "Back pocket," he said, panting, his hands full of her breasts.

Leigh reached for his wallet and pulled it out, found what she was looking for, and dropped the leather to the floor. Clark turned and shut off the stove burner before lifting her onto an unused countertop, tugging a kitchen towel beneath her. She gasped as her bottom hit the cold, but then he sheathed himself and then pressed against her. "I can't believe I'm acting like a beast," he said.

She laughed. "Shut up. I like this side of you," and pulled him closer.

His hands came around her bottom. Leigh leaned back, and he slid into her with a groan. "You feel so damned good," he grunted.

"So do you," she groaned, leaning back on her elbows as her head fell back. He changed his angle and pressed home. "Oh, right there," she cried as her body clenched around his. She shuddered, and he grasped her lest she fall.

Clark pressed forward, surging and retreating until he was panting, then scooped her into his arms with a tremendous groan, his hips pressing once more, hard. His face fell to her heart. "Oh, Leigh," he sighed, breathing hard.

She sat in his embrace, sated and trembling, cradling his shoulders, and lightly ran her fingers through his hair. "That was about the most exciting thing—ever," she said dreamily.

A laugh erupted from Clark's chest. "I thought it was more like desperation." He pulled himself upright before helping her sit up. "So, you don't hate me for acting like an animal?"

She grinned as she reached down to adjust her clothes. "You're kidding, right?"

He looked so chagrinned as he did up his fly, she had to wrap him in her arms again. "I loved it. You can surprise me like that almost any time you want."

His gaze changed from abject horror to admiration. He reached for her and held her close, resting his cheek on top of her head. "You make me an offer like that, and I'll take you at your word."

"Promises, promises," she said lightly and heard him laugh again. "Dinner should be ready in a few minutes." She looked at him over her shoulder. "Unless you want to do that again."

He nuzzled her neck. "The next time, I want to take my time and savor every inch of your luscious self. In a bed." He reached under her skirt and her eyes fluttered as he touched her. "I want to make you moan for hours."

Leigh closed her eyes and pressed against him. She felt him grow harder behind his fly. His hands didn't stop, and she hugged him harder against him, and he ground his hips against her sensitive core as she leaned on the edge of the table. She was suddenly unsure her legs would hold her as his hand did its magic. "Clark," she whispered until she cried out and sagged, his arms holding her upright.

"Easy," he said as he nibbled along the line of her ear as he helped her down. "You make that much too much fun."

She took her time, breathing slowly as the room stopped whirling. "Are you sure you even want dinner?"

Clark laughed and spun her around to kiss her. "You mentioned appetizers. I wanted you more." He kissed her again. "So, let's eat and regain our strength. I think we're going to need it."

Leigh looped her arms around his neck and lay her ear upon his chest until she could hear his heartbeat. "Do you think we're moving too fast?"

He tightened his arms and nuzzled her ear, pressing a soft kiss on it. "Absolutely not." He pressed back and ducked his head to look her in the eye. "This isn't about sex, Leigh. If it were, you and I would have done this weeks ago."

She shuddered and met his gaze. "I don't want to feel like a fool again."

Clark's arms tightened around her. "If the only way for me to prove that I care deeply about you is for us to stop being intimate, then we'll stop." His voice was ragged. "I don't want to. But you mean so more to me than sex. We'll go as fast or slow as you want."

Leigh burrowed her face in his chest. "I don't want to stop either." She looked up at him. "Why don't men seem to worry about this kind of crap?"

His eyes crinkled as he smiled. "Says who?"

"What?"

She felt his laugh deep in his chest. He cleared his throat and said, "Ugh. Do you really want to know how many times I agonized over making a move on you? It's not that you're intimidating, but you're so sure of yourself. I needed to know you wanted me as much as I wanted you—or wanted me even a little before I dared try to kiss you."

"Were you afraid I'd call the cops on you?"

Clark shuddered. "No, but I have a reputation I'm trying to set in this town, and I didn't want to have anyone—you especially, mistake my intentions for anything other than honorable."

She grinned up at him. "If I'd have known, I might have—"

He stopped her with another kiss. "That's history. What we have is right now. Tonight. Tomorrow. Next week." He kissed her again. "I don't mind talking long term, but you know I may not be here this time next year."

Her joy diminished as she nodded. "I try not to think about that. But you're right. We have right now. Tomorrow, I fly out for a conference. After that, except for Thanksgiving, I'll be home at least until January."

Clark lowered his face to kiss her again. "Then let's not waste any more time thinking about what ifs and maybes. Let's take tonight, right now, and make it our own."

They kissed until the sizzle under the green beans reminded them that dinner was waiting. The two broke apart with a laugh.

Much later, they cuddled in the warm cocoon of their lovemaking, drifting off while holding hands, not thinking of what-ifs, and what-might-have-beens, but reveling in their what-I-have-right-nows.

Hey boss, get a load of this letter. Boy, those crazy fans of yours'll try any angle to get your attention. This one's a doozy. Says she's getting married unless you declare your undying love for her. The nutty thing is, she don't even get your name right. Calls you Tommy. Says she's Lilly. Must not'a heard you got yourself hitched. I guess news don't travel that fast cross country.

Hey, boss, you listening to me?

Ah, cripes. He's passed out drunk again. Mack, Jerome's assistant, grumbled around his stogie. *Guess he had a big fight with the second Mrs. Percy last night. Again. She musta thrown him out like she did last week. We'll be lucky if he wakes up in time to go on camera. I'll just send the dame an autographed picture of Jer and be done with it. Wish her luck with her noo-pitals and all. I'll just put this one in the discard pile with all the rest of 'em. What he don't know won't hurt 'im.*

Chapter Twenty-One

Leigh

"Lei-Lei, it's about time you got back."

Gram was in the in the foyer as Leigh opened the front door then lugged her suitcase inside. A wheel had broken off the bag on her way to the airport days before. She'd had to carry-drag it since.

"Hey, Gram." Leigh blew her a kiss. "I'm glad to be home. Four-hour delay because of fog." She grimaced. "Remind me not to book so many trips next year. The thrill of travel has worn off."

Gram laughed. "That's because you're traveling alone. If you had your handsome man beside you to carry your luggage, you'd feel a little different."

Leigh raised a brow. "Really, Gram?"

The old woman smiled. "Yes, really, darling girl," she replied with a touch of sass. "There's nothing like lying in your lover's arms in a strange city, a different bedroom, a new bed." She sighed. "There's a thrill to it, like it's something clandestine."

"I think you've been watching too much TV," Leigh said.

"Ugh." Gram shook her head. "I cannot abide what's on these days. And changing the station is so complicated. It takes both me and Constance to accomplish it." She closed her eyes. "Back when I was young and in love, we didn't have distractions like television. The radio sometimes, but neither of us cared for it much."

"Then what did you do with yourselves?" Leigh asked as she hung her coat and kicked off her boots.

"Why, we talked, of course." Gram raised a brow. "And when we ran out of things to talk about, we read to one another. Poetry, prose, the newspaper." She closed her eyes and sighed. "He had the most marvelous voice for poetry. Deep and rich. He'd recite gobs of it. Oh, his laugh—I still get shivers thinking about it." Gram's eyes grew dreamy. "But he loved to have me read to him." She fluttered her eyelashes like the ingenue she once was. "He always told me he loved the sound of my voice and that it was such a shame I never acted on stage—"

"You told me he could hardly read, whatever his name was."

"Oh, don't ruin this for me, Lei-Lei," Gram said with a touch of annoyance. "He memorized the poems. Where's your sense of romance? Speaking of which, what happened with your young man Sunday night? I must say, he's quite the looker, and if I'm not mistaken, seems to know what he's about." She gave a broad wink."

"Gram! You promised you wouldn't meddle—"

The old woman waved a ghostly hand in the air. "I didn't see anything if that's what you mean. I just wanted a good look at him. How was I to know he'd be so hot for you he'd want you right there in the kitchen?"

"Oh my god," Leigh cried and covered her face with her hands.

"It's not as if I never saw the suchlike before," Gram said. "I wasn't exactly a shy, blushing-maiden, you know. Now your grandmother, my daughter— that one was as strait-laced as they come. Never did enjoy her husband—not that he was any bargain. I don't think he cared for her more than a little himself."

"But Gram—"

"Oh, get down from your high horse, missy. I left before anything interesting happened. More's the pity." She wheeled herself backward. "And trust me, Tom— my love and I, well, we were far more daring in our day." She waved an arm. "Pish! We met underneath restaurant booths, in powder rooms at parties, once in a backyard pool—" She closed her eyes. "He was certainly inventive. And considerate. Not like your great-grandfather." Her eyes snapped open. "Dark room. Under the covers. Him on top. Always him on top. Right from the start, he resisted my attempts at creativity—thought it wasn't ladylike for me to enjoy sex." She shuddered. "If I had known that before the wedding, I never would have married him. I would have found a way to run right back to— " She stopped. "Never you mind."

"No, this is getting interesting," Leigh said. "Would you have left great-grandfather and gone back to your lover?"

Gram sighed. "I didn't. I always thought my true love would follow me, but I must have left a poor trail of breadcrumbs. It makes me wonder if my letters ever reached him. By the time I wrote to say I was getting married, turns out he'd already married someone else. All I received was a form letter wishing me well." Her shoulders sagged as she looked at her veiny hands. "I never should have left. I should have stayed and fought." She cast her eyes up at Leigh. "Don't be a fool like me. If you love your Clark with all your heart and something happens between you, go after him. Fight for him. Sacrifice something, especially your pride."

Leigh scoffed. "I hardly think I'll need to do that."

"You never know what the future will bring," Gram said fiercely. "No one does. You must tell your lover what he means to you, and he must sacrifice something for you in return, so you know how much he values you. But I'm telling you, my dearest Lei-Lei, once you find that someone you want, you need to be ready to fight for him. Never assume life is going to give you a second chance."

"Why didn't you marry your lover in the first place? Did he cheat on you?"

Gram shook her head. "I'd set him free as a test. I'd hoped and dreamed he'd remain true to me, but instead, it seemed he'd taken the freedom I gave him and ran with it. I should have expected more. I should have asked for— no, demanded more. I didn't trust him, and he was angry or disappointed—" Her faded lips trembled. "And I... well, while I was away... things happened to me that I couldn't share." She clutched her arthritic hands together.

Gram seemed to waver before Leigh's eyes. Leigh dropped to her knees before the phantom wheelchair. "Are you okay?"

The old woman gave a weak smile. "I haven't worked myself into such a lather for some time. I'll be fine. I need to rest. There are some memories I will cherish forever and others that keep me so angry—it keeps what passes for blood in my veins pumping. And still there are other memories I wish I could leave behind." She looked around. "Where's that dratted Constance when I need her?"

A moment later, the tall, silent ghost appeared and took the handles of the wheelchair. She did not acknowledge Leigh but did her mistress's bidding.

"Good night, Gram," Leigh called.

A transparent wave was her only response, and Leigh was alone in the dim, drafty hall of the house.

Her heart hurt. Was Gram getting ready to leave at long last? Tonight's feisty response had been so like the old girl, but then she'd waned so quickly. And before she revealed too much of her mysterious first lover. Who had it been? And why, after all this time, was it such a mystery? How could Gram bear to have survived with a broken heart for so many years?

Leigh's thoughts went to Clark. They'd parted early Monday morning on the front stairs as Leigh was about to fly to the west coast, and Clark was heading for his apartment and an early morning run. They'd spoken a few times while she was away, but their timing was always off, making her uneasy. When he'd called, she was heading off to her symposium. And when she'd called back, he had been about to begin class. They'd missed each other like that most of the time she was gone. Each failed connection was like a knife chipping away at her confidence. Leigh never knew if it was the fault of his old phone or his schedule. She'd never expected to miss him so much. And now it was late, and her internal clock was jammed from the long flight and the conversation with Gram.

Inside her purse, her phone vibrated. She pulled it out and glanced at the display. Clark. No doubt wanting to know if she was home. With a weary finger, she swiped to answer.

"Clark, hi."

"I've been watching the airline app all night. Are you home? Can I see you, or is that asking too much? God, but I've missed you," he said in a rush.

"Yes. I want to see you too. Can you come over? Spend the night? Gram's gone up to bed. I've missed you so much."

She heard a car door slam on the other end of the call. "I'm on my way."

Clark

Leigh was silhouetted in the open doorway when Clark pulled up. She looked so lovely as the light shone down on her hair. Snow fell softly all around. He'd barely stopped the car when he was out of it, running into her arms. He held her tight, and she clung to him. He caressed her soft cheek with one hand before he kissed her, softly, then harder, mindless of the cold wind that whipped around them. "I missed you so much," he whispered. Her answer was another kiss.

"Come in," she urged.

"I have to get my things." He broke from her to collect his backpack and lock his car. She stood waiting for him, shivering.

When he stepped inside, he noted her suitcase listing on the floor, her coat and gloves tossed on it. "You really did just arrive."

She looked up at him, her eyes wide and sad. "Gram and I were talking," she replied. "It got intense fast. I didn't have a chance to put anything away. And then you called."

"I'm glad I did. I didn't want to bother you, but I couldn't help myself. You must be exhausted." He knelt to open his backpack. "I stopped to get this earlier. It's not much but let me warm it up for you." He offered a container of wonton soup.

Her smile made his detour to get the soup worthwhile. "That's perfect." She took his hand and led him to the kitchen. "We'll leave our stuff there for now. No one's going to trip over it."

Clark looked over his shoulder to make certain Jerome hadn't trailed after him. There was no sense of anyone in the house other than the two of them. He squeezed her hand and followed. In his mind, it was like a scene with Carey Grant, where he was tall and suave, chasing after some beautiful starlet.

Once in the warm kitchen, he watched as Leigh's gaze fell to the far counter where they'd made love when last they were together there. Her cheeks heated to a delightful pink. "Are you thinking what I'm thinking?" she asked. "Let me get this in a pot, and we can relive that moment." She gave him a saucy smile and winked. "I know I want to."

He loosened his grip on her but kept his hands on her hips as she moved about. "I was thinking more about making new memories," he murmured in her ear. "Maybe upstairs, later. Once you've had a chance to relax and eat something." He took her hands. "I've missed sitting across a table, looking at you, and talking with you."

She nodded. "We'll have to, uh, be more careful. Gram almost caught us last time."

"No." He sprung away as if stung. Definitely Cary Grant in one of his bumbling, lighter roles.

She grinned. "She says she left before we did the deed, but she's pretty stealthy."

"I didn't hear anything." He rubbed a hand on his jaw. "Was she angry? I mean, I wanted to meet her, but now I'm afraid I'll be embarrassed."

She shook her head as she put a lid on the soup pot. "She wasn't. I got an earful about how she and her first lover had all sorts of sexual escapades. Trust me when I say this: talking about sex with one's grandmother is only slightly less weird than talking about sex with one's mother. But weird in a whole different way."

Clark laughed. "I'm not sure I want to know."

Leigh shrugged. "I didn't, but I got to hear it anyway." She reached for two soup bowls. "But that wasn't what got to me."

He stepped closer and took her into his arms once more. "Tell me, Leigh. Tell me anything." She leaned into him, and he tightened his hug. "I want to help."

She gripped his back through his sweater and shirt. "I'm afraid she's going to go soon."

"Her health is bad?"

He saw her look of hesitation before she shook her head. "It's hard to explain. It's like she's fading. Every day I lose a little bit more of her. I'm afraid one day there won't be anything left."

"Because you were gone, you saw it more?"

She nodded against his chest. "Something like that."

"I, uh, well, I know what you mean." He bit his lip. Had he said too much? It all sounded so much like his fears about Jerome.

She looked up at him, tears in her eyes. "There's so much more I want to ask her. She's so wise. I've had her all my life. I'm not sure what I'll do without her. I've always thought her life was exciting, but she's always been stingy with the details."

His heart thumped hard, and he stepped closer, wrapped her tighter in his arms. "I know, sweetheart. I know. But you've got me."

She murmured something against his chest, and the plaintive sound crushed him.

"What?"

"How long will I have you?" she asked against the wool of his vest.

He stepped back. "I, uh, I don't like to think about that." Clark rubbed his neck with his free hand. "Ever since I met you, I wanted to get to know you better. In a perverse sort of way, I was almost glad to find out you had a boyfriend because it gave me an excuse to not pursue you." He took her hands. "And then you were free and interested. And I was intrigued and turned on, and there was no way in hell I could resist you." There was no mirth in his laugh. "Sweetheart, it's been on my mind constantly that I need to nail this biography and solve the mystery. It's the best way I know to achieve security at school. But I don't want to talk about that tonight. I don't want a long-distance relationship. Phone sex might work for some, but there's nothing like holding your hand across a table and talking to you, seeing the spark in your eye when you tell me something funny, or having you squeeze my hand when I tell you my worries." He brushed a lock of hair from her cheek. "And holding each other after we make love."

Leigh's arms wound around him. "That's all I needed to hear." She kissed him before pulling back to look at him. "We'll figure it out, okay? Just don't hold back on me because you might not get the job."

"I love you, you know," he murmured into her hair.

Her breath caught in her throat. "You do?"

252

He nodded and gave her a warm smile. "I can't help it, not that I want to." He brushed her nose with his own. "If I don't get the job, there are other schools I could apply to. Or I could write full time and become a guest lecturer and make this my home base. It would mean travel, but it would mean coming back to you." He kissed her lightly. "I want to always come back to you, Leigh."

She reached behind her and turned off the stove. "Let's go upstairs now," she said. "I'm not hungry anymore." She took him by the hand and led him up the narrow back stairs, the ones the servants once used, and into her bedroom suite, where she showed him exactly how much she wanted him to always come back to her. And along the way, she told him every way she knew that she loved him too.

The bride wore an elegant gown of ivory Brussels lace. Not a conventional choice, but 'so' Lilly Manning in her daring fashion choices, just like in days of old.

Several guests mentioned how calm the new Mrs. Sprague was for a bride. In fact, several specifically mentioned how composed, even sad she looked, and how she turned around several times during the ceremony to see who was attending—

Chapter Twenty-Two

Clark

After being together since Monday, Wednesday morning began with an apology as they vied for space in front of his scratched bathroom mirror.

Leigh held her lipstick against her mouth. "Clark, I'm so sorry about the mix up. I thought I mentioned that Mom, Sarah, and I are flying to Iowa to spend Thanksgiving with Carole's family."

He rubbed his neck in frustration. "You did. I forgot." He sighed. "I can't get a flight back home now. Everyone's booked. I don't have the patience to do stand-by."

"Do you want me to see if I can get you a seat with us? We're not flying out until this evening."

"That would be pushing the limits of hospitality. Berry asked me over. I'll go there. But I think she invited her immediate family, not the Conrads."

"Ugh. Be sure not to give my regards to Rocky. I assume he's mooching a meal from his sister. Unless he's roped some poor, unsuspecting woman into inviting him."

Clark rubbed the back of his neck again. From the corner of his eye, he saw Jerome make a slashing motion across his neck as he shook his head. When Leigh's attention was elsewhere, Clark jerked his head toward the front door, a clear sign for Jerome to leave. With a raised brow and a wince, the ghost disappeared.

"I'll be back on Sunday," Leigh said. "Can you hold the evening open?"

"Say no more. Need me to pick you up?"

"No. We'll have Mom's car. When I get to work later, I'll send you my itinerary and text you when we land."

He slid his arms around her and pressed her back to his chest as they locked eyes in the mirror. "I'm going to miss you, my lovely Leigh."

She spun to look at him rather than his reflection, then wrapped her arms around his neck. He gladly lowered his head to kiss her. To hell with her lipstick.

"And I'll miss you, but it's only for a few days." She kissed him back, then broke free to look at her watch, gasped, and hurried out the door. "Clark, we'll talk every day, okay? I swear next year we'll plan it better. After this year, all our holidays will be spent together. Starting with Christmas and New Year's." She flew down the small hall, grabbed her coat, and then she was gone.

Just a few days. It seemed like a lifetime. He and Leigh had spent every night together since she'd come home. They'd shared not only beds, showers, breakfasts, and dinners, but more and more of themselves and their hearts with every hour. The prospect of a long, lonely weekend was disheartening. He didn't mind seeing his cousin and family, but the thought of spending it with Leigh's former boyfriend held no appeal. Maybe he could have Jerome tag along and haunt the house for a few hours, maybe chase Rocky off. That sounded promising.

The object of his thoughts popped into the room, smoothing his mustache. "Count me out, m'boy. I'm off for a long-delayed card game with the fellas. Got a new recruit last month. Different vintage, of course, but the poor chap died broken-hearted and didn't want to… well, you know… move on to the next place. Not sure what he's waiting for. None of us really talk about it, not when there's cards to cheat at and heavenly booze to guzzle."

"Did you read my mind about haunting Rocky?"

Jerome chuckled. "The look on your face said it all. Still, it might be fun to play a trick or two on that rotter. Overheard plenty about him. Tell you what. If you need my help, hit the loo, and call my name. The boys 'n I'll pop on over and see what we can do. Deal?"

"Go have fun." Clark waved Jerome away. "I'll be fine. If I can tolerate my department chairman, I can handle a blowhard like Rocky for a few hours. I'll have allies in the room."

"That's the spirit. Just be subtle. Don't give away too much about your lady love. No one ever gained anything by bragging, no matter how happy the two of you are."

"Not to worry. I'll get caught up on my research. Uninterrupted time means I can go over the correspondence and news articles again. Maybe I'll find something I missed."

"Cheerio then, old bean. I'll expect great things from you upon my return."

Jerome dropped his trusty fedora onto his head, draped a camel hair coat around his shoulders, and with a twirl of his cane, popped from view.

Having no classes that day, Clark pulled up his electronic research files and started plowing through the accumulated documents. He kept going back to the social pages, certain anyone as lively as Isabel Standish wouldn't settle for a humdrum life no matter where she found herself. If only Jerome remembered her real name. It always struck him as preposterous that Jerome forgot that detail, but then the man had spent most of his fortune trying to find the woman. It was hard to believe he'd wasted it on a whim. Even worse, the one time Jer dropped another name, Clark had been too focused on something else to retain it.

Late that night, after a dinner of take out, Clark tracked Leigh's flight on his phone. Twenty minutes after the app showed she'd landed, she sent a text to let him know she was fine. It was only after he sent her an image of hearts and flowers did he go to his cold, lonely bed.

Thanksgiving morning, Clark awoke early. Berry told him he wasn't responsible for bringing anything other than himself, but rather than arrive empty handed, he'd bought two bottles of wine the day before. That was easy enough for a bachelor who couldn't cook. He wasn't expected until four, so he sat down to do more research in his quiet apartment.

Hours in, he reached for a manila folder full of articles he'd printed off microfiche. He studied the photostats of society pages of the local paper from August 1925 until the end of the year. There were no parties with an Isabel attending, though there were many mentions of a Lilly Manning that sparked his interest, but no pictures. Early on, there was mention of her having arrived back home after being abroad for two years, and her new sophistication and fancy French gowns really set the tone for parties going forward. "No, no, no. It can't be her," Clark mused to himself. "Wrong name, but why is it so damned familiar?" He looked some more. *The time frame is right. And they described her gown—it sounds like one Isabel wore to a movie opening.* He thought back to the ripped photo of Jerry he saw when he'd first met the ghost, where only a hint of a woman's dress could be seen along the torn edge. "Damn it, I wish there was a picture of Lilly."

He called out into the room. "Hey, Jer, can you hear me?"

There was no answer.

"Jerome?" he tried again.

"Tommy?" No reply. "Crap. He must be deep in his game. I'll have to wait 'til tomorrow."

He flipped pages until he came to another article. There, before him, finally was a photo with the caption 'The Glamourous Lilly

Manning at the Library Gala, on the arm of her Gallant Future Husband, Roger Sprague."

The small photo featured a posed line of men and women, each dressed for an evening out. The two at the center faced each other, so only their profiles showed against a dark background.

Clark held the small image away from himself before moving it closer. The grainy image would not release its secrets, but if he closed his eyes, he could imagine it was Isabel. When he blinked, it looked like Leigh, but with lighter hair. At arm's length it was once again a blur. "What the hell?"

He glanced at the time. "Crap, I'm late." He set the manila file on the table, but when he rose from his chair, his elbow hit the folder and its contents scattered over the floor and under the furniture. "Shit," he muttered as he ran for the bathroom to run a comb through his hair. In a rush, he picked up his phone, grabbed his coat, the wine bottles, and ran for the door.

"Hey, Clark, glad you could make it."

Berry gave him a kiss on the cheek as he came through the kitchen door. "Everyone's in the family parlor. Go join them."

He handed her the wine. "I hope these are okay. If not, save them for another occasion. The guy at the store said the red would be good with dessert."

"Any wine is welcome by me," she told him with a grin. "Especially today. My folks aren't big drinkers. Moe prefers beer, and my brother brought a bottle of scotch since we don't stock his favorite brand." She wrinkled her nose as she leaned forward. "I think he's trying to shame us. Not working."

Clark laughed. "Maybe I'll take some of his fancy stuff with a drop of water, so you don't get stuck with it, okay?"

"He probably plans to bring the rest home with him. If there's anything left, so you might as well help yourself." Berry nodded him over to the open bottle by the door to the dining room. "I'm up to my armpits in mashed potatoes right now, so help yourself."

Clark did as she asked, shrugging out of his coat first. "Hang it on the rack by the back door and catch your breath. You look like you ran over," she told him. "Glasses are to the left of the sink."

He nodded, poured a generous amount, and then took a deep gulp. "I made some unexpected progress on my research. The time got away from me, and I ran almost every red light between my place and yours."

Berry laughed. "You're a Conrad all right. The stories I could tell you, but you don't care about that. Go on in and make yourself comfortable. I've got appetizers on the table, assuming the kids didn't eat them all."

"Are you sure there's nothing I can do to help?"

"You can get out of my way," she said with a smile. "I've got it under control. Go make sure my brother isn't telling any off-color jokes in front of the kids. You can tell me what you found later, when everyone else is conked out or watching football."

Clark checked his phone, but it was once again acting up. He tried to send Leigh a text, but it wouldn't go through. He slipped it into his pocket, determined he'd try again later.

He found his way through the house to the cozy room. Moe greeted him with a good-natured slap on the back. He nodded at Berry's parents and brother. The two children were over in a corner, quietly playing a game. "Hi Mr. and Mrs. Samuels, Rocky. Nice to see you again."

"Likewise," Berry's mother chirped as she perched on the edge of her chair, her folded hands on her knees. Her husband grunted as he kept his eyes on the TV.

Clark looked at Rocky, who was absorbed with his phone. "How are you?" he asked as he took a seat and held up his tumbler. "Good scotch."

Rocky glanced up with half a shrug, then went back to furiously tapping on the screen. Moe poked at the fire. "'Scuse me.

I need to check the fire in the dining room," he said and headed out.

Clark rubbed his hands together. "Kind of chilly out there. I need to start remembering gloves."

"You're from California." It was a statement rather than a question from Berry's mother.

"Yes. Southern end of the state." There was an uncomfortable silence in the room. "Have you ever been?" Clark asked politely.

"Oh no. We don't travel that far," she replied. "Florida, maybe."

Clark nodded and wondered if he could somehow magically acquire some kitchen skills to help Berry in the kitchen.

"I'm looking forward to dinner. Your daughter is a wonderful cook. And hostess."

Mrs. Samuels preened. "She is, isn't she."

"The turkey smells great."

Rocky snorted, then muttered an expletive as he read something on his phone.

"Rocco!" his mother snapped.

"Sorry, Mom. Trying to close a deal here."

"On a holiday? You should be enjoying your family. Those children are your only niece and nephew. And until you—"

Rocky rolled his eyes. "We are not going there today. You know I'm not having any. Bug your daughter if you want more grandchildren."

Mrs. Samuels sighed. "Do you have any children, Mr. Conrad?"

Clark nearly spilled his drink. "Me? Ah, no. Though I want some. Someday."

"Won't happen if you're seeing Leigh," Rocky said under his breath.

Clark cleared his throat and was relieved when Berry came into the room. "Dinner's ready, everyone. Kids, go wash your hands. Rocky, help dad out of his chair, please."

She looked at Clark, an unspoken apology in her eye. "We'll seat my father closest to the fireplace. Mom will go next to him. Rocky, do you want to sit next to Maddy or Max?"

Rocky didn't look up from his phone. "Who cares?"

"Finish what you're doing. No phones at the table."

Rocky sighed. "Yeah, yeah, sure." He typed some more and then pocketed the device. He rose and walked across the room to his father and tugged the older man's arm before he readied himself and his cane. "Up you go," he said and yanked the man to his feet to the point he pitched forward.

Clark offered the arm that didn't already hold Mrs. Samuels' hand. "Easy does it," he said as he steadied the elderly man. Rocky, his task now complete, exited the room.

"Don't move so fast anymore," Mr. Samuels said with a chuckle. "My son seems to think he can turn back time by force of will. Lives his whole life that way. Every time I think he'll change, he surprises me. Digs his heels in. Kids!" He shook his head slowly. "You ever disappoint your parents, there, uh, what's your name again?"

"Clark. And I hear about it if I do," he said with a laugh.

The meal proceeded in fits and starts. The food was wonderful, but no one other than the children had much to say. Clark silently worried the latest twist in his research around and around in his mind. He'd need to talk to Leigh as soon as he could. Wasn't Lilly her grandmother's name? Or was it her Great-grandmother? He wanted to go online to check but didn't want to be rude. Had he somehow stumbled upon something that would blow her mind the way the possibility was starting to blow his? Maybe even that night. His fingers twitched, wanting to call her, but unlike Berry's brother, he wouldn't pull his phone out at the table.

At last, the interminable meal was over, and everyone was shooed back to the parlor as Berry and her mother did the dishes together. Moe took the children out to play in the yard. Clark hadn't worn his heavy overcoat, so it was too cold for him to join

261

them no matter how he would have preferred it to sitting in the family room with a dozing Mr. Samuels and a petulant Rocky.

After twenty minutes of watching the dying flames, Clark looked up as Rocky threw his phone to the floor in disgust. "Losers," he muttered. "Stubborn jackass."

There was a snort from the sofa, then the return of soft, ,rhythmic snores.

"Problems?" Clark asked.

"Stupid client wants my blood," Rocky replied. "Idiot. Nothing you'd understand with your cushy job. What do you do all day? Stand in front of a bunch of college kids and spout a bunch of crap. That's not real work."

Clark grinned despite himself, imagining Rocky being thwarted by anyone. "Right. That's all it takes. I talk out of my ass day after day. No research to be done or decisions to be made. I fly all over the country and repeat it for a pile of money."

Rocky snorted. "Sure seems that way. Waste of time." He stretched and gave his phone a kick, but it was wedged in the carpet's pile. "So, you're seeing Leigh."

"We've had dinner a few times," Clark acknowledged.

"Yeah, well, you want to keep it light with her. She's not an easy woman, believe me. Thinks way too much of herself."

The hair on the back of Clark's neck stood up. "Oh?"

"Cost me a bundle. I mean, I lost a huge deal when things turned sour between me and her. I lost the merger because she's so prickly. My manager nearly fired me over it. Damn, but it was a done deal until her bitch of a mother pulled out because her little girl's feelings were bruised. I'm sure she's told you all about it."

"News to me," Clark said, doing his best to sound bored.

"And she's crazy to boot. Went on and on about her grandmother. Said she lived with the old woman. I figured the old broad would be worth a bundle when she died. But when I asked the mother and her dyke sister about her, they both told me the old broad'd been gone for years. Seems Leigh likes to make up stories

262

about the old woman to keep people away." Rocky shook his head. "Just to be sure, I got her good and drunk one night and asked about her. Crazy Leigh stuck to her story that her grandmother was still living in the house. Went to Hollywood as a kid to be in movies. She made such a thing about it, I looked it up, thinking I could spin it to sweeten her mother up. Couldn't find a damn thing about it. When I asked Leigh the next time, she acted like it was some big secret, and I wasn't supposed to tell anyone."

Clark did his best to falsify a yawn as his heart started hammering. Gram wasn't alive? Leigh was lying, or— or— what? "No kidding?" he managed. The memory of that photo flitted through his brain, his desire for meaning making the resemblance to Leigh stand out more than it had in the first place.

"Yeah, whole family's full of shit." Rocky shook his head and gave his phone another kick. "No matter how drunk I got her, she hardly put out. So, a word of advice, don't even bother. Stone cold woman, that one. Probably a lezzie like her sister, only won't admit it."

"She seems nice to me," Clark said.

"Probably 'cause she thinks she can use you. No offense, but someone like you can be led around by his dick—"

"Don't let your mother hear you talk like that," Mr. Samuels muttered.

Rocky snorted. "Fine, lead you around by your... er... nose. Not me. No woman'll ever control me."

"But you dated her—" Clark clamped his mouth shut. He needed to get back to work. He had to find out—

"Sure. I thought she was loaded. Lives in that big house. Only way I had of getting an in with her mother. She's got a sweet little company there, ripe for the plucking. I was angling to give them a few mill, then have the new board of directors boot their asses to the curb so we could break it up and make something off it when we sell their technology and contacts. But they got gun shy.

Who'd'a thought they'd be so principled?" He spat out the word as if it were dirty. "Not to mention crazy."

"I'll keep that in mind," Clark said, his fingers tapping on the edge of his chair. Had Leigh lied to him? Why? Impossible. Why the hell was he taking Rocky's word for anything. But the story about Gram...

"Yeah, well, don't think you'll get your hands on any of the family money. Her great grandfather tied it all up nice and neat for generations to come. Leigh's only got what she earns. Can't get her hands on the principal. None of them can. Lost cause." He set his head back and closed his eyes. "But my damned boss won't let it go. Wants me to try again." He pointed at the phone with his loafer. "I've been back and forth with her sister all day." He paused a moment. "You know Leigh was cheating on me, right? All the time, I was trying to bang her, and she was banging some other dude. Pissed me off."

"W-w-what?" Clark sputtered.

Rocky's leaned forward with a sly smile. "None of this leaves this room, right?"

Clark's fingers fumbled on his tumbler. "Who is he? The other guy?"

Rocky shrugged, but his gaze remained on Clark as if to gauge his response. "Some dude she meets at the conferences she goes to. Darren. Acts all high and mighty, telling everyone she goes to mentor girls. It's just one big orgy. I got tired of waiting for her." Rocky smirked. "And besides, who knows what sorts of diseases she's pick up."

Clark downed the remainder of his drink and pushed his glasses up his nose. "Sure. Makes sense."

Rocky bent his elbow, and the rest of his scotch disappeared. "So, none of this leaves the room, right? My sister would be crushed to learn her friend's such a slut. I wouldn't want to hurt Berry for anything." He eyed Clark hard. "Or tell anyone else for that matter."

"Oh, I'm nothing but a lowly college professor. No head for business," Clark feigned. "I don't know anyone in Leigh's profession. So, you're going to approach her again? But why not go to her mother? She's the owner or Sarah. Leigh's into the technology."

"Yeah, right," Rocky snorted. "I've got no ins with Sarah, being she's married to that actress now. No chance of romancing her. Real shame. She's way hotter than her straight sister."

"Do you always use sex to get business?"

Rocky sat back with a smirk. "Only when dealing with women. And then only the pretty ones. I mean, Leigh might have an extra-large caboose, but it's quality caboose, if you get my meaning."

Clark opened his mouth, but the rest of the family returned with Berry who bore a tray of coffee and pie.

Clark made his excuses early and returned home on a tear, calling out for Jerome as he stepped into his apartment.

The ghost appeared, smoking a cigar and holding a fan of cards. He was wearing a green visor, and his sleeves were held up with garters. "What the hell, boy? I've got a royal flush. Your timing is appalling."

"What was Isabel's real name?" Clark shouted. "Tell me, damn it."

"I don't—"

"Don't tell me you don't remember." Clark looked around and picked up the papers from the floor, turning them over until he found the image he couldn't stop thinking about. It had been under the couch and was wreathed in dust bunnies. "Is this her? Is this Isabel? Or is her name Lilly?"

Clark hadn't thought it possible for Jerome to get any paler, but the phantom bobbed closer to him to look at the wrinkled paper in Clark's hand. One by one, the cards fluttered out of Jerome's hand, vanishing as they fell.

265

"Son of a bitch," the old man wheezed. "You found her. You found my Izzy. I need a drink. I need a whole bottle. Two bottles. Hell, I'm going on a bender for the next week."

And just like the cards, Jerome whirled around and disappeared.

"Jerome?" Clark bellowed. "Where the hell are you? Don't you dare fade on me now." He looked around the empty apartment. "Crap," he muttered.

What do you mean you won't visit my room anymore?

Lilly, he said with a forced chuckle. *My dearest wife, surely you don't expect me to sleep in your bed while you're carrying my child. It's not seemly. And, your shape— it doesn't appeal. I'll admit it was interesting the first time you were pregnant, but the novelty has worn off.*

You're not taking a mistress. Roger? Answer me, damn it.

Lilly, you can't expect me to go without. We'll be discrete. And it's only Constance. I won't shame you. Not the way you led me on to think you were a virgin when we married.

I never claimed that. And I never cheated on you. I never would.

You can be sure of that, wife. I'll visit your room again once you've safely delivered the child. And not a moment before.

Chapter Twenty-Three

Leigh

She returned to her office Monday morning. She felt haggard, having gotten home close to three in the morning. Her Sunday afternoon flight had been canceled due to snow, and her text to Clark with her revised plans had gone unanswered. His damned phone. That, or he had fallen asleep waiting. Leigh's heart sank at the thought, but she would have grown weary waiting if the roles were reversed. In fact, every time they spoke, he'd been distracted. There was an air of expectation about him, but every time she probed, he said it had to wait until they saw each other.

Maybe they'd be able to see each other that night and fall asleep in each other's arms watching TV. It was unlikely she'd be good for more than that. And as luck would have it, she felt sniffles coming on. "Damned packed airplanes and recycled air," she muttered.

She opened her laptop and quickly scrolled through the list of calls and emails she needed to return, and the meetings that had been set up. She stopped halfway down the list.

"Rachel?" she called. "What the hell—"

Her admin came running. "What?"

Leigh pointed to a line on her monitor. "Who authorized me to meet with that scumbag tonight?"

The young woman came around Leigh's desk to see where she was pointing. "Oh. That. He was very insistent."

"Well, you can call and cancel."

Her assistant looked stricken. "I can't. He told me Miranda's office called him specifically to make sure it got on your calendar."

"Well, you can call them all right back and tell them I refuse."

"I can't tell your mother that!" Rachel gasped.

"You work for me, not her."

"But she's the owner. And founder—"

Leigh sighed and hung her head. "Fine. I'll do it. Let me know as soon as she shows up."

"Who shows up?" Miranda asked as she walked in with a smile that was far too bright, given she couldn't have gotten any more sleep than Leigh. "Rachel, I hate to ask, but Leigh and I need coffee. Would you be a dear and get us some?" She handed the woman a twenty-dollar bill. "Just regular with milk for me. You know how Leigh likes it. And treat yourself too."

Rachel sidled out of the office, avoiding Leigh's glare.

"Mom, you know I never want to see that weasel again."

Miranda sighed and sat across from her daughter. "I know. I know. But they dangled a very tempting offer over the weekend. Far better terms where we'd keep much more control, guaranteed."

"Mom, it's Rocky. You know we can't trust him."

268

"It's not just him. His boss will be there. And Sarah and me." She gave a smug smile. "I want to see how far they're willing to go."

"You can't trust them."

"Well, I know that," Miranda admonished. "But it's a free dinner—" She gave a broad wink. "And think of the entertainment value."

"I wanted to see Clark tonight."

"You can see him later." Her mother's eyes danced in the bright morning light. "After Rocky foots the bill for a nice vegetarian dinner."

Leigh gave a startled laugh. "He hates everything but steak and potatoes."

Her mother grinned wider. "That's why I insisted we go vegetarian." She picked at a bead on her sweater. "I wasn't cruel enough to insist on vegan. This is how we'll play it out: we'll let them wine and dine us, make us all sorts of promises alongside the organic wine. They've agreed I can record the conversation, so anything they say can later be used against them. Then they give us the contract, and we have our lawyers tear it apart."

"And then?" Leigh asked.

"Then we let them dangle for a week or three. Run down the clock. Make noises that we're going to do business with them."

Leigh nodded hesitantly. "And—"

Miranda grinned. "And then we squash their hopes and dreams by merging with the firm I want to do business with." Miranda laughed. "I know I taught you better, but payback's gonna be a bitch for them this time."

"Can't you do this without me?" Leigh asked.

"But, sweetheart, won't it be that much more fun for you to be in on it? Let that idiot hope his schemes will work, and then we reveal him for who he is when it'll hurt him the most."

"I never knew you were so diabolical," Leigh said.

269

Miranda gave her a wan smile. "I had to be to survive. As long as men think it's still a man's world, a woman's got to do what she must to hold her own. As much as I hate to say it, I don't think that'll change in my lifetime. Maybe in yours. You know that as well as I do, otherwise, you wouldn't be flying all over the country to encourage young women to enter the field. Don't get me wrong. I hate the sexual politics of this. Hate it with a passion. But I've got more of a passion to succeed in life. Long before my hair started going grey, I stopped caring what people thought of me, other than to further my ends and make a decent living for you and your sister."

Rachel returned with the mugs of coffee. Leigh took hers and sipped with a grateful groan.

Miranda breathed in the fragrant steam from her mug. "It's never too late to turn over a new leaf. So, yes. You, Sarah, and I are going to that dinner tonight. Call your young man and tell him he needs to wait until Tuesday to see you. It'll make him more eager for your company. Now, I've got to run. I have an all-day meeting across town, and Sarah's coming with me. We'll meet you at the restaurant."

"Fine, fine," Leigh muttered.

"Take a nap at lunch, dear," her mother said before she left.

With the door closed, Leigh picked up her phone and called Clark. Naturally, she got his voicemail. "Hey, it's me. Listen, something came up, and I need to go to a business dinner. I hate to ask, but do you mind waiting until tomorrow to get together? Okay, bye."

She frowned as she set her phone down. Something didn't feel right, but she didn't have time to call him back. He'd understand the pressure she was under. He had to.

An hour later, her phone buzzed with a text. She called a quick break in her meeting and picked it up.

Got your msg. Deep in research and have questions
for you. Must meet with a student. Waiting is fine.
Will text you later if I get a chance. Clark.

Miffed he hadn't called, didn't say he missed her, said nothing personal at all, she set the phone down. She was so very tired, and she dreaded the coming dinner. Leigh tried to focus on planning for the upcoming year, but her concentration was broken.

At six-thirty, Leigh drove to the restaurant. As she parked, she realized she was a block away from Clark's apartment. Not that she expected to see him that night. He'd made that perfectly clear by his continued silence. Frowning, she checked her makeup in the rear-view mirror before walking in. "Good thing I'm not trying to break any hearts tonight," she muttered, for the dark circles under her eyes had their own dark circles. Her suit was wrinkled, and she felt out of sorts as if she needed a good fifteen hours of sleep and a gallon of coffee to approach feeling normal.

At the hostess' station, Leigh gave her name and was shown to a table for two. Rocky stood when he saw her approach, and his smirk raised every hackle she possessed and a few she borrowed on the spot.

"What the hell—"

Rocky shushed her. "Calm down, will ya?"

"What are you trying to pull? Where is everyone?"

"Sit down, Leigh," he said through his teeth. "People are staring."

She glared as she pulled the chair from his hands and sat. "I told you I was through with your games."

Rocky reached for his glass but found it empty. He held it out to a passing waiter. "Double scotch. Rocks." When the man looked to Leigh for her order, Rocky waved him on.

Leigh folded her arms and glared as hard as she'd ever glared in her life.

271

"You can at least take off your coat," he said through his teeth.

"Table for two? Where is everyone?"

"My boss had to cancel. He sent out an email, but he got your address wrong. I didn't notice until it was too late. I figured I could take you out to dinner anyway. So we could talk."

"That hardly seems possible. Even if so, why didn't you forward the email? Or call me?" Her fingers drummed on her sleeve. "Or text?"

He shrugged. "Dinner and drinks on the expense account— why would I?"

The waiter returned with his drink and looked inquiringly at her. She shook her head, and he left.

"You mean drinks, and dinner, don't you?"

Rocky sighed. "Already with the nagging, Leigh? I thought I told you that was a very unattractive quality in a woman."

"As I recall, there wasn't much about me you found attractive, other than my money and connections."

He sighed and rubbed his brow before taking a big swallow of his drink. "Yeah, you're right. I was pretty hard on you. Wasn't until I heard you were involved with that professor guy that I realized I messed up big time. I guess I owe you an apology."

Leigh didn't take her gaze off him. "Okay."

"Okay what?"

"You said you owe me an apology. I'm waiting to hear it."

Not meeting her eyes as he spun his glass on the table, Rocky said, "I just said it.".

Leigh shook her head. "No, you didn't. You said you owed me one. But you haven't said you're sorry or what you're sorry for."

"Hell, woman, what do you want from me, blood?" He grabbed the drink and upended it.

Leigh shrugged and leaned closer. "I want what's owed me, so let me give you a hint about what to say. You are a jackass. You lied to me. You feigned interest because you wanted me to convince my mother to sell her company to yours. Oh, and you thought I had money. Let me tell you, that last one was especially flattering. You talked about me behind my back and tried to undermine me every chance you got. Further, you tried to humiliate me to my face, with an emphasis on tried because you never succeeded." She sat back with a smirk, watching his dissolve. "You tried to undermine my confidence. You were generally unpleasant, overbearing, boastful, and immoral every chance you got. Plus, you're selfish in bed. So, you can pick one or all of the above, or maybe something else you're feeling remorse over. Start talking. I've got all night, thanks to you and your conniving ways."

Rocky lifted his glass to drink, but it was empty. He looked around wildly but found no succor in a room full of strangers. "All of the above, I guess."

Leigh laughed. "Seriously? Still taking the easy way out. Can't quite bring yourself to say the words."

"Hell, Leigh, you think groveling's easy for me?"

She shook her head. "You haven't actually groveled. You know, this has been easier on you than it should be. I think a little humility is what you need. I'm still waiting for that apology, by the way. Three little words. Repeat after me. 'I'm sorry, Leigh. Oh, and make it as loud as your derogatory comments were."

He scowled at her. "I'm sorry, Leigh," he said under his breath before searching for the last drop in his glass.

Leigh sighed. "Not exactly from the heart, was it?"

He shrugged. "Best I can do."

The waiter brought a platter of appetizers to the table. She slid several onto her plate and ate one. When she finished chewing, she asked, "What do you want from me?"

Rocky frowned. "I want to reopen negotiations."

"Over my dead body. What else?" She took another bite, finding her appetite, then looked across the table. "You honestly expect I'm going to trust you?"

"Come on, Leigh. My job depends on this."

She felt her smile grow. "Really?" Her phone buzzed in her purse, but she ignored it.

He narrowed his eyes.

"Isn't that too bad for you."

"Come on, give me a chance. You owe me that."

She laughed. "I'm not sure how you came to the conclusion I owe you anything."

"You lead me along. Let me think you were an heiress."

She nearly choked. "Seriously? Wow. You really know how to flatter a woman, don't you?"

"Come on, you know what I mean."

She shook her head. "I'm afraid I do, and if you don't stop with the flattery, you're going to owe me another apology."

"Hey, you know me now. And I know you. I'll make a good offer this time. Don't you see? If I want to keep my job, I have to do this by the book."

"And what's in it for me to see to your gainful employment continues?"

His confident smirk resurfaced. "You liked me once."

"You were nice to me once. Until I found out it was all lies."

He lifted a shoulder. "A guy's gotta do what it takes to make a buck."

Leigh stared him down. "Let me repeat my question: what's in it for me?"

Rocky's gaze shifted around the room. She glanced over his shoulder to see the familiar form of the old man from the theater, perched on a barstool. He seemed to waver in the dim light, or that could be her tired eyes playing tricks on her. He had a full glass in front of him. He turned and looked at her. Well, didn't it figure that that old man was there spying on her. He gave her a friendly nod and a two fingered salute. She ignored him and turned her gaze to glare at Rocky.

Clark

274

He'd rushed home to continue his research. He'd wanted to see Leigh, but her curt voice mail left him uneasy, especially after he'd been stewing about Rocky's words since Thanksgiving. Was Leigh cheating on him? Was their relationship a farce? He didn't believe it, but Rocky seemed earnest. Clark didn't want to trust him, but really, how well did he and Leigh actually know one another? They needed to talk— about many things, but she wasn't available. And then Jerome had disappeared. He'd done it before, but never for so long. And how the hell could a ghost go on a bender?

Clark forced himself to focus on his research and pieced together more clues. A long while later, he glanced at his watch. It was late enough that Leigh might be home from her dinner. He dialed her cell, but it went to voice mail. He then called her home number.

The phone rang several times. There was a long clatter before a cheerful, warbly voice answered, "Sprague House."

"Is Leigh available? This is Clark Conrad."

"Mr. Conrad, so glad to speak to you. This is Leigh's Gram."

Wait— what? His pulse raced. Rocky said she didn't exist. There were so many questions he wanted to ask this woman about her mother, but he promised Leigh he'd go through her before doing so. "I'm happy to finally speak to you. Leigh's told me so many wonderful things about you."

There was a soft laugh on the other end of the phone. "Likewise. But I'm afraid Lei-Lei's still out. Have you tried her cell phone? Dratted contraptions, but terribly handy."

"I did. She might be driving or still in her dinner meeting. Would you tell her I called?"

"I'll do that, young man. And you tell my granddaughter to introduce us the next time you stop by. She's much too protective of me. Thinks I'm going to flutter away to nothing if I talk to anyone."

"I'd like that very much."

275

"I'll tell her you called when she gets in."

"Thank you, Mrs.—"

"Oh, call me Gram," the kindly voice replied. "And have yourself a pleasant evening, Mr. Conrad."

He set his phone down and returned to his computer screen with a smile. Gram sounded like a dear old woman, her old-fashioned manners the same vintage as Jerry's courtliness. And if he was right, the two of them both had someone in common in their lives—Isabel Standish, a.k.a. Lilly Manning Sprague, Gram's mother.

Morning, handsome.

His head pounding like thunder, Jerome squinted at the woman lying backward in his bed, from her toes that were tickling his shoulder to her mussed titian hair. She was quite naked, other than the finger she wiggled, sporting a golden band.

With a sigh, he curled away from her. *Oh god. How did this happen again? I just got rid of one wife, and now I have another? Oh, Izzy, what happened to you? Why did you leave me? None of this would have happened if you'd come back to me. Where are you, my love? Are you safe? Are you well? Are you even alive?*

Chapter Twenty-Four

Leigh

She needed to settle things with Rocky once and for all. Leigh set her hands on the table while her nemesis ordered another drink. She would kill for a cup of coffee but didn't want to be there that long.

"Why me? Why not talk to my mother. I'm the IT side of the business."

He sighed. "Your mother won't talk to me unless you give the nod."

She rested her head on her fisted hand and rolled her eyes. "Tell me one good reason why I'd want to be stuck with you as a business partner?"

"Because I'll make you a rich woman. Your mother can retire. Hell, with what we're offering, you'll never need to work another day in your life. Just walk away from it all with a fat check. Spend time with your cheating professor and start to pop out little professor babies for him."

Her heart stuttered. Leigh folded her arms across her chest. "What did you say?"

"Babies. Isn't that what you said you wanted," he said, eyes wide.

Leigh took a deep breath. Damn, she had to take the bait. "You said my cheating professor."

Rocky looked aghast. "What? No. I didn't say that." He looked at his empty glass and then back at her. "But since you brought up the subject, you know all guys cheat, right? It's in our DNA." He gave another shrug. "But you like those brainiac types. And he's the type to be discrete. Face it. He thinks you're an heiress and wants your fortune. Except you aren't one. And there is no fortune. Until you sell MirandaTech to me. So, if you cooperate, everyone gets what they want. I get the company. You get your professor and babies. And he gets you and the money you'll make from the sale. Everyone gets what they want and lives happily ever after."

A trickle of doubt etched a furrow in her conviction about her relationship. She took another deep breath. "Clark isn't the type to cheat. We're committed to one another. That's not something you'll ever understand."

Rocky snorted. "Sure. You go right on believing that." He leaned forward. "It's not like you're not a pretty girl—"

She gritted her teeth before opening her mouth to refute him, but he continued, unabated.

"—But you've a few extra pounds on you. And you'll have more as you get older. I know your type. Besides, he's a college professor. Reasonably good-looking. He's got all those young chickies in his classes, willing to do anything for a good grade. He practically said so at Thanksgiving."

Leigh's mouth shut with a snap, her mind whirling the unsavory mix of fury and exhaustion, and she wanted to howl as Rocky sat back in his chair. She tightened her arms as he hooked an elbow over the back of another chair. "Come on. You and I've both been around the block. You know how things work in the classroom. Trust me, if I'd've thought I could've gotten a better grade by coming on to a professor, I would've done it. Hell, I'd flirt with my boss for a raise if he swung that way." He paused and flicked some lint off his sleeve. "Don't tell me you never considered it. Oh, but I forgot who I'm talking to. You're too proud, aren't you? Too pure." He sat forward and tented his hands on the table. "Way too ethical. So, let's stop this chitchat and get down to business. You're only human, and you want what you want. What you're owed." His voice carried throughout the restaurant, and patrons turned to look at their table.

Her hands shook in anger. Leigh crumpled her napkin tossed it on her plate. "I never— he's not— it's— we're not—" She pressed her lips together and stood. "I wish I could say it's been a pleasure, but I'd be lying. It's clear you won't negotiate in good faith, so I'm ending this conversation. Good-bye Rocky. Don't bother calling me or the office. Tomorrow morning, I'll be telling my mother exactly what our conversation consisted of."

"Wait, Leigh— I didn't mean—"

Leigh whirled on Rocky as she shot her arms through her coat sleeves. "What didn't you mean? Calling me fat? Or thinking me so stupid I wouldn't notice? Did you really think you were turning on the charm tonight because I've got news for you, you've lost your touch. Once upon a time, I might have given you the benefit of the doubt, but no more. In all honesty, you're a terrible actor. So, if you think I give a rat's ass that your job is on the line, you really need to examine your ego. The only reason I wouldn't want you on the unemployment line is that I'd regret having my taxes pay to support your lying ass." She spun away, aware of the eyes upon her.

"Leigh—" He grabbed her arm, nearly jerking her off her feet.

Behind her, the old man leaned over the bar to get the bartender's attention and pointed at the table where the two quarreled and pantomimed dialing. The bartender glanced up and nodded as she reached for the phone.

Leigh stopped and looked at his hand gripping her and then back at him. "Take your hand off me."

He tightened his grip. "Leigh, I'm sorry. Really, I'm sorry. It's the booze. It gets the better of me. I didn't mean half of what I said."

She tugged her arm, but he didn't loosen her.

The hostess ran over. "Sir. Miss. I have to ask you to take your argument outside…"

Behind her, no one noticed the old man slip through the front door and whirl himself into nothingness.

"Leigh, don't do this. I didn't mean it. Please stay. Let's talk this out. Come on. It was the booze talking—"

"You're blaming the scotch? Then stop drinking. But it's not the booze, Rocky. It's you. Now let me go."

"I can't. If you don't help me, I'm going to lose my job. I can't. I can't do that. I'll be humiliated."

She tugged at her arm. "Tell someone who cares," she said through grit teeth.

Clark

It seemed only moments after he'd hung up when Jerome finally popped into the apartment, waving his hands and yelling. "You've got to go. The Hippie restaurant down the street. Leigh's there with a troglodyte who's man-handling her."

Clark nearly fell out of his chair. "What? Where the hell have you been?"

"Go. Go, I tell you! Get your coat and run. I'll tell you on the way. There's no time to lose."

"This isn't a Keystone Kop movie," Clark said as he settled into his chair and picked up his pen.

"Damn it, boy, I said move." Jerome gave a kick that set the chair to vibrating.

"Huh?" Clark rose from his seat, stunned. "What the hell? I'm following up on this lead. This is the breakthrough we've been waiting for."

"Screw that. I told you Leigh's in trouble with that jackass Rocky, and you're just sitting there? Get your hat and your coat. Come on."

All the worry that had been simmering since Thanksgiving burst out boiling. He'd done his best to tamp it down, but niggling doubt had made a nest in his memory, made worse when Leigh had canceled on him. He never thought she'd fool around with that idiot again, but he found himself moving despite his reservations. "Leigh's out with Rocky?" Clark headed for the door. He felt his coat lining tear as he yanked it off the hook by the door with one hand and grabbed his keys with the other.

"Business meeting as best I can tell," Jerome said, panting, as the act of physically moving matter had worn him out. "He started in on her, and she's ready to punch his lights out. Then he grabbed her. Not sure if the cops are on the way. You need to go there and keep her from slugging him. She won't want to spend the night in the slammer."

Clark stopped in his tracks. "She won't want me to interfere. She can take care of herself. If she wants him— my research— it's important. If I get this right, it means I can stay here."

Jerome shot him a disgusted look. "Get your head out of your ass, you dope, and move!"

Clark picked up the pace, and Jerome soared past Clark and headed down the stairwell and out onto the frigid sidewalk, Clark not far behind.

"After all these years, a body would think you'd have learned something at my knee," Jerome muttered. "Women want to be appreciated. Even the strongest needs a show of support. Hell yeah, she can take care of herself, but a little show of jealousy is never a bad thing."

And with that, Jerome gave Clark one more push, which poofed Jerome out of sight, and Clark was through the restaurant's front door, watching the woman he loved in the middle of an altercation.

Leigh

"Please, I have to ask you to leave," the restaurant manager begged.

Rocky released Leigh, his hands in the air. "It was nothing. A misunderstanding. It's over," he muttered.

Leigh's mouth dropped open to protest when a woman from a nearby table stood up.

"I saw it all," the stranger said breathlessly. "He was so mean to her. And she finally couldn't take it any longer. And then he grabbed her and wouldn't let go. I heard every word. I even got most of it." She held up a glittering phone in a trembling hand.

"Do you want me to call the police, ma'am?" The manager asked Leigh.

Leigh kept her eye on Rocky. "Do I need to?" she asked him. "Or will you back off?"

He continued to hold his hands up. "I won't bother you again," he mumbled.

"I got that on video too," the woman said from the other table. "I wouldn't trust him. He's as slippery as my first husband. I'd press charges if I were you. Teach the bastard a lesson."

The manager looked to Leigh for direction.

Leigh thought a moment. "I'd like to think he's learned his lesson, but I'm not taking any chances. Ma'am, if you could share that video with me, I'd appreciate it. I will be more than happy to share it with his employer, his parents, and his sister if need be."

"Sure, honey. Just give me your information, and I'll send it to you."

Rocky hung his head.

The manager addressed Rocky. "Sir, you settle your bill, and I'll escort you to the door. You've had a lot to drink, so we'll be calling you a cab."

"I can drive my goddamned car," Rocky yelled.

Which is when Clark burst into the restaurant, his coat half off his shoulders, his glasses askew and his hair looking like it hadn't been combed in a week. "Leigh— what the hell's going on. Jer— a friend saw everything and told me you were in trouble. I got here as soon as I could."

"Whoa, so you and this bitch *are* more than just friends?" Rocky said, his smirk back in full force.

Before Leigh's startled eyes, Clark grabbed Rocky's shirt front. "What the hell are you trying to pull with Leigh this time, you prick? Give me one reason why I shouldn't deck you?"

He pulled back his fist back until he was stopped by the hand of the manager standing beside Leigh.

"Sir, don't touch that man, or I'll really have to call the police."

Leigh's heart soared at the sight of Clark before her. It hammered down in anger. Her head ached from exhaustion, and now this? How dare he rush in and play the hero, the cheating liar? If he'd only told her he wanted to see her, she would have canceled this dinner. But now the drama was over, and she wanted to put it behind her, take a hot shower, and fall into bed. Leigh's shoulders sagged as she turned her back to both men.

"Leigh?" Clark said as the manager took Rocky from the table to the reservation desk. He glanced at the women staring from the next table. "I'm her boyfriend. Do you mind giving us some privacy?"

Leigh sighed and nodded. "It's okay. He is my boyfriend. Or was."

Clark startled at her words. "What?"

"This is all your fault," she said before shaking her head and slumping into a chair. "Oh god, I don't even know what I'm saying anymore. I'm so tired."

Clark

He stared at his fingers as he painfully loosened the muscles of his fist and then lowered his hand to his side before he sank into a chair next to Leigh. How in the world had he gone from peacefully conducting his research to being ready to punch a man for the first time in his adult life? In a crowded restaurant? That was something his middle brother would do. Or Jerome. But not Clark. Not proper, rule-abiding Clark. If he'd done it, he could kiss tenure goodbye. But would he have gotten the girl? It would all be worth it if he did. But he didn't know if she still wanted him.

Bewildered, Clark pushed his glasses up his nose. "I don't understand." Which was perfectly true, Jerome's warning coming back to bite him.

"If you'd wanted to see me—" she started, then puffed out her cheeks and sank lower, holding her head in her hands. "That's not right."

He knelt by her side. "Leigh, what's going on? Why were you here with Rocky?"

She shook her head as her hands dropped to her lap.

He took them in his own. "Tell me. Please?"

Leigh sighed. "It was supposed to be a dinner meeting. My mother and sister were going to join us. But Rocky— I should have known. He canceled with them and tricked me into coming. He wanted— he wanted—"

"You and he weren't—" He couldn't bear to finish the thought.

The look of outrage on her face eased the jealous ache over the line into embarrassment.

"I'm sorry. I shouldn't've thought that. I need to tell you what—but that can wait." Clark tugged her into his arms. "He's the same man he's always been, darling."

284

She nodded against his shoulder. "I didn't want him to romance me. He acted like I should be grateful for the attention. He accused you of fooling around with your students—"

Clark laughed. "Why in the world would I want to do that when I have you?"

She looked at him, his face so close to hers. "You mean it?"

Clark brushed the hair from her face. "Of course, I mean it. Damn, but that guy did a real number on you if he makes you doubt me even now. Even me. Leigh, I thought you knew how crazy I am about you."

"But you didn't want to see me tonight."

He blew out a breath. "I was mad… I thought you didn't want to see me. And despite the progress I've made, I've regretted not forcing the issue." He stood and took held her hands as she got to her feet. "I've finally gotten the break I need to solve the mystery. And it's very close to home. I needed to compile all the information I could, and despite how mad I was, your being busy tonight gave me the time. I never want to get in the way of your work or ask you to put me before it. No, that's a lie. I do want to ask you to do that, but I love and respect you enough that I won't. Not when you would never ask that of me."

She pressed closer. "I've thought about it a time or two over the past few weeks when I try to call, and you're in class or a meeting."

He laughed and held her near. "Leigh, what are we going to do?"

"I don't know. I'm just so mad."

He reared back. "At me?"

She shook her head. "You. Me. Rocky. My mother and sister."

"Why?"

"Because I wanted you to want to see me no matter what, to give me an excuse to not be here." She laughed harshly, sounding more like a sob. "At Rocky for being himself, and me almost falling for his lies. And I feel like such a jerk for allowing me to doubt. And at Mom and Sarah. They should have known he'd pull something and stopped me before I came." She rubbed her eyes. Clark had never seen her so exhausted. "He tried to convince me to tell my mother to bargain with him again for another merger." She closed her eyes and took a deep breath. "I should have walked out as soon as I saw him." She shook herself. "No. What I should have done is tell him off as soon as I saw him here."

Clark gripped her hand. "What would you have told him?"

She took a deep breath, her eyes hardening. "What would I have told him?" Leigh repeated. She set her shoulders back and took a deep breath. "What would I have said is this: 'You call me proud as if that's an insult? The truth is, you're not man enough for me. You have to tear others down in order to make yourself feel good. That's not a man. That's an immature child. It's shameful and embarrassing. That was the worst thing about my time with you— it left me embarrassed that I let you get to me. Let you convince me I wasn't good enough, that you were doing me a favor by looking at me. And you weren't. That's the kicker. You were using me because a man like you can't see the worth of a woman like me, and you never will. So instead of being mad at you, I feel sorry for you. I pity you and whatever poor woman falls for your lines.'"

She lifted a hand and held it to Clark's cheek, and her whole mien softened. "And then I would have said: 'But Clark isn't like that. He doesn't need to tear anyone down to feel like a man. He knows he has a woman like me by his side because I want to be there, and that's enough for him. He's earned the right to be my boyfriend. He knows he's strong enough to put up with me—a sexy, proud, beautiful woman. But you, Rocky, you only can get women who want what you can buy them. They don't really want you. They want your bank account. How's that make you feel, hot shot? Especially since you're running low on money and even lower on prestige. The truth is, you're running low on charm, and all that's left is sleaze. See how far that gets you.'" She took a breath and hung her head.

Clark wanted to take Leigh under his arm, but this was her moment, and he didn't want to ruin it for her. "I'm proud of you, sweetheart," he said softly. "And trust me, I'll do everything I can, so you never have to talk to me like that. And I would never, ever cheat on you."

Leigh's smile crept out as the woman at the next table burst into laughter. "He's a keeper, dear, so if you don't want him, I know someone who'll scoop him right up."

Leigh linked her arm with Clarks. "I'm not even halfway done with him yet. Not sure I'll ever be."

Leigh

An hour later, she was half-asleep when Clark lifted the blankets and snuggled closer. "You didn't have to come home with me," she sighed as she pressed her back to his chest.

She heard his laughter as his arms tightened. "No way was I going to let you drive. You're exhausted."

She rolled over and curled against his chest. "You just wanted an excuse to drive my car. Admit it."

His arms came about her again. "You got me there. I've been waiting months for the opportunity to fumble with your stick shift and stall your car out to impress you with my mighty masculine aptitude."

Leigh closed her eyes as he pressed kisses to her forehead. "If I'd have known you didn't know how to drive a standard, I would have insisted on driving," she told him.

"What?" He kissed her ear. "Now I have a new skill to add to my resume. Doctor of Film History, holder of Aluminum Ladders, and able to use a clutch in an emergency. I'm just thankful there aren't any real hills between the restaurant and here." He kissed her lightly. "Go to sleep. You're exhausted. Let me hold you."

She turned over and snuggled down as his arms tightened. "You said you'd made a breakthrough?"

"Shhh. We can talk in the morning. And you can introduce me to your grandmother. She was very nice when we talked earlier."

Leigh stiffened. "What?" she spun to face him on the bed. "You spoke to her?"

"Yeah. I was so focused on driving the car, I didn't have a chance to tell you. Right before J… my friend told me to come get you, I called the house. She answered."

She sat up. "Gram actually answered the phone?"

Clark pulled her back down. "Well, yeah. Said she wants to meet me."

Leigh shook her head. "Gram never does that."

Clark shrugged and lay back, resettling their cuddle. "She did tonight. We had a very pleasant conversation. We have one thing in common. We both adore you."

"But she can't do that."

Clark pressed another kiss to her cheek. "You're talking nonsense. Sleep, Leigh. We'll talk again tomorrow." He squeezed her hand. "Sweet dreams to the love of my life. Think about that. One way or another, we're going to make a go of our romance. I think I've made the breakthrough that I need to in order to solve the mystery. We need to talk about it tomorrow."

"And I love you too," she said as she drifted off.

Jerome

Hours later, when the full moon began to set, Jerome peered in the window of Leigh's second floor bedroom. He'd been able to trace Clark's psychic trail or some such nonsense. After all this time, he still didn't exactly know why he could travel to some places and not others. All he understood was he knew where to find his friend. Jerome smiled to himself as he saw the lovers entwined in each other's arms.

"That boy's done well. Even I can tell it's cold outside. No wonder they're under the blankets," he whispered to himself with a grin.

Jerome floated down to the ground and peered around at the park-like setting as he caught his phantom breath. He was more tired than he'd ever been. "Interesting house. I'll have to quiz the boy when he gets home tomorrow. Funny how I can't get through the walls or peek in any window but the one. I know Clark's found Izzy, but I was a fool to run out before he could tell me more. I need to find out what he knows. It was a shock to see her in that photo. I couldn't bear to stick around. Now I'm too weak to look through those papers myself. Who'd' ever have thought it was so much work to flip through 'em. And that's if I could read better'n I can."

He sniffed, or tried to, wishing he could smell the fresh air, feel the bite of the cold, to once again feel anything. It wasn't hard to remember his early years when he'd suffered thin blankets and not enough food. Hunger—that had been a motivator for sure, but the sensations faded over the decades. He looked up at the night sky, where a million bright lights winked at him. "Stars, they called us," he muttered. "Only one of us could rival what I see. Where are you, my Izzy? Where are you, and will I ever see you again?"

His chin dropped until it rested against his chest. "I miss you so much," he cried, and with a whirl, gathered what was left of himself and flung himself away.

He didn't see the ghostly face pressed to a far window, looking out at the same icy night and the same distant stars. He didn't see the longing stare, nor the sorrow of another broken heart, so close to his own.

Mrs. Sprague, I'm so sorry, but the child died last night. The doctor said nothing could be done to save him.

Constance, why didn't you wake me?

Mr. Sprague didn't want to disturb your sleep. He's here and wants to see you.

But I don't want to…

Her attention was cut when her husband strode into the room. *There, there, Lilly, we'll try again. We'll have you pregnant again before the year is out.*

Roger, don't you touch me. Don't you dare. How can you be so unfeeling?

Perhaps it's the sins of the mother coming to visit her. Hummm? You should feel privileged I'm considering giving you another child.

How can you say that? My baby just died. Did you feel nothing for him? And why aren't you claiming it's the sins of the father? You've had far more women than I've ever had men. It was only Jerome before you. That's all.

Now Lilly, don't be foolish.

Get out, Roger. Get out and never come back.

Chapter Twenty-Five

Leigh

"Sorry we needed to rush this morning." She glanced at Clark as she shifted into third gear. "I can't believe I didn't set the alarm."

He touched her arm lightly, and a tingle ran up it, despite the leather of his glove and the layers of wool between them. She wondered if it would always be that way. "I don't have to be on campus until afternoon. I could have called for a ride. You didn't have to cross town to bring me home."

She shook her head, loving the calm look on his face. "Not after you were my Galahad last night."

He shrugged, but his grin grew wider. "My pleasure. And this way I get to observe your technique— driving, that is."

She shot him a grateful smile. "I know you wanted to meet Gram—"

"Don't worry. There'll be another time."

Leigh wasn't so certain. After being woken by an early morning call from Berry, she'd gone to check on Gram first thing, but her ghost was so weak and transparent, there was no way she would chance having Clark encounter her. Not without a whole lot of explanations that would likely cause Clark to run out the door and her life. It must have been the effort of answering the phone the night before—any activity that involved moving even the lightest physical object had always exhausted her. Manipulating a phone receiver was monumental for the ghost. Leigh hated having to leave Gram, even for a few hours, but there was no reasonable excuse she could find for working from home. Gram had insisted she'd be fine by the time Leigh got home. What sort of restorative could a ghost use?

"Does Berry always call so early?" Clark asked.

Leigh downshifted as she approached Clark's apartment building. "No. She said it was the only chance she'd have until tonight and was afraid she'd forget. She volunteered for a field trip with Maddie's class and wanted to get an early start."

"What did she want?"

Leigh grimaced. "It's kind of funny, actually. She wants to interview Gram. I think Berry's got some plotline she's researching and wants to talk to someone old. I'll call her back in a few minutes. She'll be on the school bus but said she can talk then. Speaking of which—"

"No worries. Maybe this weekend. We can have dinner at your place. I'll bring take-out, so you don't need to fuss, and we'll invite your grandmother to join us."

"She's very limited on what she can eat. Gram's companion prepares—"

"She can join us at the table then," Clark assured her. "Maybe we can invite Berry and Moe if they can get someone to watch the kids. Kill two birds with one stone."

Leigh glanced at him as she pulled into a parking space.

His nerves must have shown on his face, for he quickly amended his thought. "Or maybe not. I'm not sure if they'd be interested in my questions."

Leigh yanked up the brake. "Let's talk later. Can we meet for a drink or something? I have to talk to Mom and Sarah about last night, and I'll need to reward myself after."

Clark reached over and kissed her. "Whatever you want. Text me when you're free, and we'll talk when we can."

She nodded and kissed him back, holding on to his lapel when he would have exited the car. "Clark, about last night. I know I wasn't grateful at the time—"

He took her hand and kissed it. "Extenuating circumstances. And you let me take you home, so it's all good in the end."

"I don't deserve you," she said.

Clark laughed as he got out of the car but then leaned back in to give her one more kiss, this time with a lot more heat. "I don't know about that, sweetheart. I think we're good for one another." He stood and blew another kiss as he shut the door.

Berry

Hey there. I've been trying to keep a low profile lately.

That field trip really wore me out. The good news is that it also wore Maddie out, so she didn't argue when I put her to bed an hour early. My son, Max, can't tell time yet, so he didn't suspect a thing about turning in when his sister went to bed, so I have a few minutes to write.

Anyway, after talking to Leigh, I couldn't wait to get home and finish my research into her family. I'm kicking myself for not doing it sooner. Here's the thing. I Googled Leigh and her mother. And from there I went to *her* mother. After all, I had all their names. And what I found was a shocker.

Leigh's grandmother died in 1993. Her name was Chloris, and by all accounts, she was an unpleasant, cold-hearted woman who was very impressed with herself, but not about anyone below her economic level or who dared disagree with her about virtually anything. That included her only child. This was not the woman Leigh described so warmly as her Gram. For the record, there was scarcely any information about Leigh's paternal family, and none of it led me to believe Leigh's beloved Gram came from that side of the family.

Grandmother Chloris lived her entire life in the big mansion on the edge of town, the one her father had built for his first wife but settled his second wife into after the first died. I was searching for some sort of mystery about how the first wife died, but there wasn't a hint of scandal there. No one knows for sure, but all hints were it was an ectopic pregnancy. More about family scandals in a moment. One notable fact was this Chloris was so stuck on her family's consequence, she insisted her husband take *her* family name when they married. Maybe it was once a more common practice. I don't know, but I doubt it. It might make an interesting plot point someday.

Apparently, Chloris' husband took over the family business along with its name, but times were tough, and it began to lose money. A lot of money. He spent most of his later years battling the courts, trying to free up funds from the trust his father-in-law created to perpetuate the family estate. From all accounts, Mr. Chloris was careless with money and would have wasted any he pried away from the trustees had he won, much as he'd run the family business into the ground. His wife had a separate trust fund from her father that supported her lavish lifestyle despite her husband's mismanagement of the family business. Her husband wasn't able to tap into that either, though he benefited from it. But it was due to Leigh's great-grandfather's forethought that the house and grounds were preserved by the trust. But none of that was what interested me.

What I found confounding was that Chloris was angry with her daughter Miranda for marrying a handsome, talented, but penniless orphan. For all intents and purposes, Chloris disowned her daughter, not deigning to help even after her Miranda was unexpectedly widowed with two small children. This was not the kind, generous and loving grandmother Leigh described to me.

Anyway, this means the old besom of a grandmother died at age 89, no lascivious scandal associated with her, only her spendthrift husband to sully her memory. But this is where things got interesting.

There was a single mention of this in one of the news articles I found when researching Chloris, but it seemed her mother, Lillian Sprague, nee Manning, lived to the ripe old age of 92. What's more, she lived in the same big old house with her daughter and son-in-law. Which means Miranda, Leigh's mother, would have known her, in fact, grown up with her grandmother in the house. Leigh and her sister would have met the old woman when visiting as children, assuming they visited from time to time. And great-grandmother Lillian, also known as Lilly, was the fascinating one. Fortunately for me, the local paper was digitized and available online.

I read far into the night about this interesting woman, though the news stories dwindled over time. In her youth, she was a well-renowned beauty. As the only child of a successful department store owner, she had no trouble dressing in the latest fashion and leading a pack of other privileged young women and men in society. There was one mention of her going to New York on a lark (that's how they spoke back then) and appearing in a movie reel as a walk-on with some famous actor. I can't recall who it was. I'll ask Clark about it when I see him. That caused great excitement. In the months that followed, it seemed she formed a party every week to go to the movie house with all her friends cheerfully tagging along, even pantomiming along with the actors on screen, Lilly being the most ardent of the imitators. There was never a theater opening she didn't attend, a concert, or a recital where she was not in the front row. She hosted boat outings on the river and parties at which she excelled in charades. Clearly, Lillian liked to see and, more importantly, be seen. But there were no ill feelings about it. It seemed she was the soul of kindness. Everyone loved her and her hijinks.

And then she disappeared from the papers. Not a word about her for two years.

Not. One. Word. Trust me, I read those papers from cover to cover, including the police reports and the obituaries, just in case.

Of course, I assumed the worse, that she'd gotten knocked up and sent away to have a baby in shame. If it had been whispered about, it never made the papers. But the timing was off. If she'd had a child, it wasn't the unpleasant Chloris whose birth in 1928 was well documented. I couldn't find a single insinuation to that effect. And then, about two years later, Lillian was back.

There was no big ballyhoo about her return. She was casually mentioned as having attended a boating party in July 1925. More attention was paid to her gown and shoes than to the fact that she suddenly reappeared. Lillian's name continued appearing in the papers, party after party. She was no longer the ringleader. She was older than most of the single girls and boys at this point, most of her contemporaries having married, but there were plenty of observations about her quiet beauty and demure disposition setting a standard of elegance and poise, all quite different from the gay and vivacious Lillian of old.

I read one story that stuck out for me. The reporter had expected Lillian to form movie parties the way she used to, but it seemed the fair maiden had lost her taste for the medium and no longer joined her friends at the cinema. When asked to take part in amateur theatrics, she demurred. In fact, she'd become camera shy, and though others of her social class had their photos in the paper, she never did.

Then I read through the social reporter's raptures of the attention the new widower, Roger Sprague, was paying the fair Lillian. He was at least ten years her senior. And then, months later, there was the engagement announcement.

Lillian's wedding had been reported in ecstatic terms. She was the only daughter of a wealthy man, and she was marrying another wealthy man. No expense had been spared in her wedding trousseau. It was the social event of the year, and the couple's European honeymoon itinerary was outlined in great detail.

I read of the birth of their daughter a year later—the haughty Chloris. Lillian's social engagements and appearances diminished. There were then the reports in the succeeding years of the births, then deaths of three infant sons. It seemed with each, the once popular Lillian faded from society and then from life. There was a decades long gap before she appeared again when her daughter made her debut, and then at her daughter's ostentatious wedding, and finally disappearing once and for all while wearing her black crepe and veils after the funeral of her husband. Her obituary was but a brief mention in the paper. Apparently, her daughter spared every expense when it came to her late mother.

Chloris, it seemed, was never her mother's equal in beauty, grace, or élan. While there were no outright comparisons in the social pages during her youth, there were a number of mentions of her mother's heyday with the disclaimer that, of course, it had been a different time.

I stopped reading when Moe came to complain it was after two AM, and I needed to be up with the kids in a few hours. I realized how exhausted I was. I promised myself I'd reread every story the next day.

So, who was Leigh's beloved Gram? Chloris? Or was it Lilly? Or the better question, *what* was Gram?

I was prepared for what I'd hoped would be my meeting with her and knew what questions I wanted to ask. If only I would be given a chance.

And all that made me wonder if I should let Clark know what I'd found? There was not a single outright statement that the original Lillian was Isabel Standish, but the timing was uncanny. And as Moe will tell you, I'm not shy about reading between the lines.

I couldn't help but wonder if I'd stumbled upon the answer to Clark's mystery. Or was I the victim of my own wishful thinking? In the back of my mind, I could hear Moe's voice telling me to mind my own damned business, so I decided I would hold off on sharing any of this with Clark. Even if I was right, what would I gain by ruining the excitement of his discovering it all for himself?

Clark

He was putting on fresh clothes after his run and a quick shower when Jerome wafted into the bedroom.

"Did I tell you?" Clark asked as he buttoned his shirt. "Over the weekend, I reached out to your ex-wives estates and asked for permission to look through their papers. I should be hearing back any day now. Hey, do you want to go to school today? It's been a while since you've ogled the girls. You always enjoy that." Not to mention Jerome's habit of confounding Clark by talking to him in the classroom when only he could hear, particularly when someone else was speaking.

Jerome propped himself in the corner, looking exhausted and more transparent than usual. "I appreciate the thought, m'boy, but it's much too cold for these old bones."

"Come on, Jer, you can't feel the cold. It'll perk you up to make fun of Dean Davis. There's a staff meeting today. You know you love to stand behind the old windbag and make faces." It was true, reminiscent of a scene from <u>Singin' in the Rain</u>. It had been all Clark could do to keep from laughing the first time it had happened, and every time since, until Clark had forbidden Jerome to accompany him.

"Sorry, old chap. Not in the mood." The ghost seemed to wilt into the woodwork before he pulled himself out again. "Maybe leave the radio on for me today? That station that plays the old tunes. I'm feeling nostalgic."

"Sure, Jer. Whatever you want. And if you'd like, I'll stay in tonight. Maybe invite Leigh over here for dinner?"

Jerome didn't reply. His eyes were closed, and he was still as death.

"Jerry?"

The ghost's eyes fluttered open, and he made a face as if someone had given him a whiskey sour instead of a dry martini.

"You are *not* going to wear that monstrosity of a sweater vest with that jacket."

Clark laughed. It had been weeks since Jerome had chided him about his wardrobe. He quickly shed the offending garment and slid his arms into a worsted waistcoat. "How's this?"

Jerome nodded. "Better. I still say you should acquire a pocket watch. It would lend you gravitas. Since it seems I've failed to make you a dandy, the next best thing would be to have you impersonate someone with some stature."

"Hey, I resent that," Clark said, not bothering to hide his smile. "I'm too young for that. Or for gravitas."

Jerome waved a transparent hand at him. "And I've tried so hard," he said faintly.

"Hey there, Jer, don't leave me now. I'm so close to finding what happened to your Izzy. Come on now. Stay with me, buddy."

Jerome closed his eyes. "I fear you'll have to hurry, my dear boy. Don't know why, but there's not much left in this lifeless husk. No one ever gave me a timetable for how long I could stay here." He sighed, and it was the saddest, most dramatically natural sigh Clark ever witnessed. "I fear what once seemed an eternity spent in this condition is about to come to an end. I don't understand why now any better than I have anything else that has transpired since I left the mortal coil."

Clark's heart began to pound, and he felt the blood drain from his face. "Come on, just a few more days, Jer. Give me that, will ya? I'm so close."

"I'll do my best." Jerome's eyes drooped again. "You'd best run along. You don't want to be late for the old windbag's bloviation. You'll tell me all about it when you get back." He gave a vague smile. "I'm going to take a bit of a rest in the in-between. Have I told you about it there? Used to hate it, so dark. So lonely. Now, I rather like it. So restful."

"Just come back to me, old man. I'm not done with you yet. I mean, what are you going to do next?"

299

"Hell if I know," Jerome said with a sigh before he faded away.

A knot of worry soured Clark's belly. He needed to wrap things up and fast. He was so close to proving who Isabel Standish was, but the last bit of proof eluded him. It was all circumstantial. The site that held the news clippings wouldn't load on his damned phone when he last tried to access it. He needed this, needed to prove his theory, but no longer for his own sake. He needed to give Jerome his peace of mind and whatever happily-ever-after he could wrench from the universe and bestow to his resident ghost and very best friend.

To figure it all out, he needed to talk to Leigh and confess it all to her. He needed to know what she knew and what she'd been hiding from him. Surely, she'd heard some stories growing up. The question was, why was she hiding it from him when she knew how much it meant to him?

And if he was going to tell her what he knew, he was going to have to tell her about Jerome. All about Jerome.

How that would go over, he hadn't a clue.

What, another hundred dollars? Jerome, how much money are you going to waste looking for that woman. She's been gone for years.

Go away, woman. You don't understand.

Darn tootin' I don't. All I see is that you're wasting money on those cheatin' private eyes. They ain't doing nothing but smoking cigars and drinking cheap hooch while they send in phony bills.

Don't start with me Delores.

I can't believe you're still pining over a dead woman. Isn't it time you wised up and started living in the present? You've got me. But if you don't snap out of it soon, I'll be gone. And you can be sure I'll take you for everything you've got in a divorce settlement. See if I don't, you second-rate has-been.

Get out. Do you hear me? Get out!

Chapter Twenty-Six

Leigh

She woke up alone. She'd put Clark off with the lie of a headache the night before. He'd been disappointed but understanding. He said there was something he needed to discuss. He'd sounded almost agitated, but she'd made him leave. What she'd needed was more time with Gram, who was waning before her very eyes. For the first time ever, Leigh dragged her mattress into Gram's room so she could check on her throughout the night. Gram's companion looked on, her face impassive. Leigh had promised Berry a visit with Gram, and the old woman was determined to keep the appointment despite Leigh's fretting.

"We'll have tea in the blue parlor," Leigh decided Saturday morning. "It'll be at four, so the sun will be mostly down. You can keep your hands under your shawl. And we can have a teacup on your table, already poured so Berry won't suspect a thing." *Hopefully.*

"Don't worry, my darling Lei-Lei," Gram said in her faint voice.

"Are you sure you're up for this?"

"My love, it's now or never. No one knows what tomorrow will bring. And this friend of yours seems interesting. I've read some of her books, you know. It took some doing to learn how to use that electronic gadget of yours, but between Constance and I, we can turn the pages easier than any physical book." There was a twinkle in her eye. "I want to meet a woman who can write a hot love scene. Think she'll do a reading for us?"

Leigh gave a laugh that sounded too much like a sob. "Oh, Gram."

"Sweetheart, you'll be fine. I'll be fine. You'll see. After all this time, I don't think the universe is going to deny me a happy ending." She looked down at her transparent hands as she turned them over to look at her palms. "Of sorts. One's idea of what constitutes that changes over time."

"You should never have answered the phone the other day. That took too much out of you."

"Oh, pish. It was the only way I would ever get to speak to your young man. And don't for a moment think I'm going to evaporate before I get to meet him."

"You do too much," Leigh insisted.

"My dear girl, I've done practically nothing for the past twenty-five years. Surely you will allow me the joy of speaking to a handsome young man."

Leigh huffed another sigh but said nothing. She stayed with Gram's until it was time for Berry's visit.

"Come now. Go fix your face and put on the hot water. I'll do as you ask." Gram blinked hard, and suddenly, the image of a steaming cup of tea sat at her elbow. "Your friend will be none the wiser about what I am. I may be weak, but I don't expect to check out today or tomorrow. Now scoot. Pinch those cheeks and put some color in them. And put on that red sweater. It flatters you like nothing else in your wardrobe. Plus, it's warm. I swear, even I can feel the chill in the air these days."

Glad for a chance to escape, Leigh changed her clothes and freshened her scant makeup. She took a deep breath and braced herself for the next hour. Then, and only then would she call Clark. She owed him that much.

Berry

Leigh ushered me inside quickly. It had started to snow—not hard enough to justify canceling, but enough that Leigh might try to shorten the visit if things started to go awry. I wasn't leaving without a fight, so I had Moe drive me. It would take longer for me to depart that way. I had questions, and I was determined to get my answers.

We exchanged hugs at the door after she took my coat. "Thanks for having me," I said. "I know how protective you are." I leaned closer. "You have my permission to kick me if I get too personal."

That made Leigh smile, though her face remained a study of worry. "Deal. Come on to the back of the house. I've got tea in the family parlor. It's kind of dark, but it's the least drafty room."

I rubbed my hands together. "Thanks. Moe dropped me off. He doesn't trust me to drive in this weather, the big galoot." That made her laugh. "I'll give him a call when it's time to go. He wanted to stay and explore the house while we talked, but I told him that was even ruder than my inviting myself over. I swear, that man would take an x-ray machine to these walls if he could."

"Considering how much work he's done for us, I should let him," Leigh said. "Come on, let's get you warm. I have a fire going back there."

I was surprised how small the parlor was, but that made sense. There had never been a large family living there despite the number of bedrooms the house boasted, and this small room was downright cozy. There was a cheerful fire in the tiled fireplace. And beside it sat the most elegant and beautiful elderly woman I'd ever laid eyes upon.

Her hair was snowy but still thick, set back in a neat bun. Her dark eyes sparkled with intelligence and laughter in the depths of her lined face. She was swaddled in shawls and blankets, but her smile was warm.

I approached her, Leigh at my elbow. "Mrs. Sprague," I said with as much warmth as I could muster, and let me tell you, I was plenty nervous about how this would go. "I can't tell you how glad I am to meet you. I've never met a ghost before. I'm sorry. I hope that's not a deregulatory term. I'm afraid I don't know what else to call you."

Leigh gasped and swayed. I reached out and held her hand as her Gram beamed at me. I heaved a mental breath of relief. You don't need to tell me how many ways that all might have gone wrong.

"I'd be terribly insulted if you called me a spook," Gram said, laughter clear in her voice. "I've done my best never to scare anyone. Especially this dear great-granddaughter of mine when she was a tot. I think I've done a good job. Don't you?"

Leigh made her way to the nearest chair and more or less fell into it. Fortunately, she fell away from the silver tea service. "How— what— when—" she sputtered.

I shrugged. "I, uh, have some experience with the paranormal." I turned to Gram. "You will pardon the expression."

She nodded graciously, clearly enjoying herself.

"As I mentioned, I've never met someone of your persuasion before." It was the truth. I hadn't yet met the ghost that dogged Clark. As best I could tell, even Leigh hadn't figured out what he was. It would be up to Clark to fess up to that phantasm. "But I've met people with extraordinary abilities." I looked down at my hands. "I'm not exactly innocent, you see." I sat down and leaned closer. "I have some powers of my own. To make imaginary people real. Temporarily that is. When I write my books."

"What?" Leigh asked breathlessly. The poor thing looked ready to expire.

"You know the first book I gave you to read of mine? Trista and Brad's story?"

She nodded faintly. Her grandmother perked up. "You mean that sexy couple who couldn't keep their hands off each other?"

I grinned. "Yes, ma'am, them."

"And they were featured in the story you wrote about yourself and that big strong, handsome husband of yours."

I grinned at Gram. "You like Moe, do you?"

Gram gave a hearty laugh for one so translucent. "I'll admit, I've spied on him a time or two. Quite the charmer. And easy on the eyes, as you kids say. A gentleman through and through."

"Do I need to worry?" I asked with as much gravity as I could muster, which honestly wasn't much.

"Were I in my youth, yes. Yes, I believe you would." Her face grew serious. "Of course, were I in my youth, my parents would never have allowed me to look at a man who worked with his hands. Such a shame. Things are so much better now. I tell that to my Lei-Lei all the time. A modern woman can choose her own destiny, within reason, of course."

I nodded. "I think it's probably still easier to be a man, damn it all, but I guess it's all relative. And yes, my Moe's a good man."

"You were saying about your characters—" Lillian prompted.

"Oh, er, right. Well, that part in the second book, the one where my heroine was able to talk to her characters in real life, and they escaped and were living wild lives of their own. It's all true."

"Oh, god," Leigh said. She looked shocked enough that I wanted to check that she was still breathing. She closed her eyes and covered her face with her hands. "I don't believe this."

I reached over and patted her knee. "I know, and I'm sorry to spring this on you. You realize this means that I trust you, right? I don't mention this to just anyone. What I'm trying to say here, is that it wasn't that much of a stretch once I did a bit of research and realized that all your grandparents had passed away. You were so adamant about living with your grandmother, and I had to tell myself; 'Leigh isn't crazy.'"

"Thank goodness for that," she said behind her hands.

I turned to Gram. "But it was confounding. So, I thought and thought about it until the only logical explanation was either Leigh is a colossal liar, or you're a ghost." I sat back. "Really, when you think about it, it was the only plausible explanation."

Gram turned to Leigh. "You see, my darling. I told you everything would be all right."

Leigh nodded, but I could see her hands trembling, so I did the unthinkable and took it upon myself to pour the tea and start the interroga— conversation.

We spoke a while. Gram was kind enough to give me permission to call her Lilly. Poor Leigh was able to shake her surprise long enough to pour a second round of tea (I asked her to get some brandy to add to it), though she was remarkably quiet. I asked questions of Gram, letting her talk about her childhood, her father's grand emporium, and later of her marriage and the children she'd lost.

I believe Leigh was as enraptured as I was at the stories. Lilly's marriage had brought her much unhappiness, as did her daughter. But her granddaughter, and later, her great-granddaughters, brought joy enough to make up for it.

Then Lilly spoke of her husband and of befriending his mistress after his death. She had given the poor woman a small fortune, seeing as she'd given up her life for the man. Lilly had more than enough money to live on, even given the stingy stipulations in her husband's will.

We talked about the mores of courtship and what it was like to be a young, fashionable matron after her marriage. She'd traveled some, once her daughter had been old enough to be left with a nanny and governess.

"And that is why I so envy you women of today," Lilly said as she finished her tale. "No one sets boundaries for you but yourselves. I did my best with my granddaughter to make her independent. Oh, her mother and I argued over it, but in the end, I prevailed. My Miranda did well for herself. It broke my heart that once I passed, she could not see me as my Leigh does. But that is as it should be, I suppose. And you, my Lei-Lei: had I yet a beating heart, it would have burst a hundred times over, so proud I am of you."

Leigh hung her head before sitting up straight and gazed adoringly at the ghost in the old-fashioned wicker wheelchair. "Thank-you, Gram. You've said it so many times, but I never really understood it until now."

I will admit I wiped away a tear or two, watching at the two of them. I could practically feel the sorrow pouring from Leigh at the thought of her Gram's upcoming departure, for it was clear to me that would be soon. I needed to hurry. And it was clear to me I needed to talk to Clark, but I needed Leigh's permission for that. I didn't want to chance rocking the boat for them— and if she were keeping Gram a secret— I mean, who wouldn't keep their ghostly grandmother from prying eyes...

I was reassured that Leigh accepted someone else was in on the secret. I think she was relieved to finally share it. I can't imagine holding on to something like that, and she had for most of her life. When she let down her guard, she was bright, funny, and warm, and oh, so interesting in her own right. She'd been so tense when I arrived, but she was more relaxed now. I couldn't imagine what was going through her head initially, and I wasn't going to try.

I hadn't glanced at my watch since I arrived, and it was only when the door creaked open and Moe strode in, that I realized I'd overstayed my visit. The silent nurse glided over to her mistress's side, and the light clearly shone through her as she stepped before a lamp.

"Hey, Leigh," Moe said before he looked at me. "Ber, you were supposed to call an hour ago. The weather's really turning nasty—" He turned to Gram and nodded at her. And at her companion. "Ladies—"

Have I described my husband to you? He's a brawny, fit sort of guy. He's tall, around six feet. Handsome and, as Lilly described him, a natural gentleman. But he's got a soft spot in his heart as big as all outdoors. He and I have been through a lot together. His patience is practically endless, as is his sense of humor. But he's got this incurable weak spot when it comes to the paranormal. It doesn't matter how often he's encountered it at my side. That day was no exception. Moe greeted everyone with his charming grin and only then stopped to take a good look around. I saw it happening as if in slow motion. He did a double take at Gram and her companion. His face turned ashen, and a moment later, he was flat on his back with his head smacking the floor, out cold.

Naturally, that put a damper on the party. I was used to it—not that it happened all that often, but seeing a grown man faint can be pretty upsetting if you've never experienced it. I checked to make sure he hadn't hit his head on anything. The good news is that he has a good head of hair and was wearing a thick woolen cap when he hit the Persian carpet. He was blinking before I got to him, and yes, he was plenty embarrassed. He sat up before Leigh could go to the kitchen for ice.

"Sorry to break up the party," he said, nodding to me and Leigh. He took a quick glance at Lilly and turned green before turning away. "Ma'am," he added on a whisper.

"Think nothing of it. I suppose it's my duty as a ghost to scare at least one person before I, well, head off to greener pastures." She gave a girlish laugh. "But I'm sorry it had to be you."

Moe sat up further and rubbed his head. "I'm sorry it had to be me, too. And glad I wasn't on a ladder at the time," he replied with a lopsided grin. "Just when I thought Berry and I were done with all— all—" He stopped and shook his head before lumbering to his feet. "When I thought I'd seen it all." He rubbed his head once more and winced as he pressed a tender spot. "I suppose I've got to stop making those sorts of assumptions."

I gave him a hug. "I was getting ready to leave when you came in. Are you okay to drive?"

Moe, being Moe, puffed out his chest. "Of course. Though I might need a little extra TLC when we get home." The other women in the room gave him sappy smiles at his crooked grin, just as he intended.

Yeah, I knew he was okay. He'd never pass up an opportunity to play on my emotions.

"Okay. We'll go in a minute." I patted his chest and reached up to give him a kiss on the cheek. "I have one more question for Lilly."

"I'll go to the kitchen for that ice," Moe said. "Leigh, you stay here. I know the way."

She nodded and sat back in her chair.

I turned to Leigh, Lilly, and to the nurse who'd spoken not a word.

"What's your question, Berry?" Lilly asked. She had a resigned look in her eye. It made me feel bad about asking, but I had to know.

I looked at Leigh, sad to see the tension was back in her eyes. She gripped the wooden arms of her chair and closed her eyes.

I looked from her to Lilly and back again. "I'm really sorry to ask this, but why? Why have you hidden the fact that you were once Isabel Standish?" I looked at each of them again. Leigh gasped her shock for the second time that afternoon, but Lilly—Lilly sat up straighter, and it was almost as if the years were falling away from her face and form.

"I'd say you were an impertinent baggage," Lilly said in a haughty tone, but her shoulders relaxed, and a small, playful smile appeared. "But the truth is, you're not. You're curious. And you've asked what no one else has dared ask me for more decades than I can count. And the truth is rather sad, I'm afraid."

I waited. Dare I say, I held my breath. One glance at Leigh's pale face next to me made me sure she was holding hers as well. "I didn't know," she mouthed. "I didn't want to guess. Clark's Isabel Standish?"

Lilly frowned. "My mother, my husband, and later my daughter, drat them all, were embarrassed by my foray into the American cinema, as well as the fact I took a lover before my marriage. They could not bear to have a hint of scandal touch the family." She shook her head. "I thought it more of a shame they didn't recognize my husband's immoral behavior as being far more shocking, Or my daughter's husband for his flamboyant and very public incompetence as a businessman, mayor, husband, and father. No, for them, it was my having lived away from home for two years and having fallen in love with a wonderful, handsome and exciting man."

She looked from me to Leigh and back again. "When I praised you young ladies for living your independent lives and not giving a fig about what others thought of you, I meant every word. My only regret is that I let the fears and prejudices of others color my actions for so long. I could have lived the life I was meant to live up on the silver screen, instead of hiding inside this mausoleum as if I were ashamed of myself." She shook her head. "I could have returned to the man I loved, the one who loved me, to find out if what we had was real. So much wasted time. So many wasted lives. It's a terrible thing, my dear girls, to live with regret. A terrible, horrible thing. Far worse than any pranks I ever played, or the love I once dared to act upon." She looked at her great granddaughter with tears shining on her transparent cheeks. "I'm sorry I never told you."

I sighed.

Leigh came to her feet. "Berry, you can't tell Clark. Please. You can't."

I was stunned. After what Lilly had said, Leigh wanted to perpetuate the lie? "But this is what he's been searching for all this time. Finding out the truth about Isabel Standish's disappearance will make his career."

She shook her head. "I can't— can't see Gram shamed after all these years."

"Darling, Lei-Lei—" Lilly tried to say, but Leigh shook her off.

"It's not that. My mother's about to close on a very important merger. I can't let anything distract from that. She's worked too hard to have anything get in the way." She hung her head. "And me. No one will ever believe I've lived all these years with a ghost." She lifted her apologetic eyes to Gram. "Worse, I'll be shamed when people find out that I believed in a ghost. They'll think me a fool, and all that credibility, all the respect I've achieved will be for nothing." She closed her eyes and wrung her hands. "I'll tell him myself. I swear I will." She looked up at me, her eyes huge. "Promise you won't. Just give me time."

I hung my head. "I won't tell Clark. I promise."

"What about Moe?"

I bit my lip once more. "He won't like it, but he'll do as I ask. Besides, it's almost Christmas. Clark'll be flying home soon, and we won't see him. That'll make it easier not to say anything."

"Lei-Lei, don't wait, dearest."

Leigh turned a tear-stained face to her dear Gram. "I have to."

Mrs. Sprague? Mrs. Roger Sprague?

Yes?

311

Ma'am. My name is Jones. Bertram Jones. I'm a private investigator.

Lilly's stomach gave an uneasy lurch. *What can I do for you, Mr. Jones?*

I'm looking for a woman by the name of Isabel Standish. You know anything about her?

Lilly was struck dumb before little Chloris grasped her skirts. *Mamma? Mamma, who's Bel Stansh? Isn't that what Father calls you when he's cross?*

The man squinted at her and then at the picture in his hand. *Wait a gol-darned moment. Are* you *Isabel Standish?*

I'm afraid I can't help you, Mr. Jones. Good day.

She tried to shut the door, but he stuck his foot in it. *Just confirm or deny. That's all I need. Were you once known as Isabel? The actress who disappeared?*

Lilly gasped, her hand to her throat. *I cannot speak with you. Kindly remove yourself from my door. If my husband hears you speak that name…*

That's all the confirmation I need, ma'am. Sorry to trouble you.

Chapter Twenty-Seven

Clark

He was anxious to return to Jerome. The ghost had adamantly refused to travel, and for the first time, Clark wondered if Jerome was too weak to appear wherever he wanted. Something Jerome had been able to do years before, even across large distances, providing Clark was there to anchor him or had been in a place once before. Now it seemed he dared not try.

Arriving home from the airport, Clark ran into the apartment to find Jerome floating in the living room, so transparent it was hard to see him. It didn't help that the blinds were open and late December daylight flooded the room. Clark bit back the crazy thought that ghosts faded in the sunlight, much as old photographs did.

"Welcome back, m'boy," Jerome said with barely a nod. His eyes remained closed. "It's been five days already?"

"Four. I cut my visit short. I was worried about you."

"Thank you, son. I have to admit, I was getting lonely. The guys and I got together to play cards. I think they cleaned up after themselves. I was too tired to enjoy myself—" The ghost weakly held his hand out to Clark.

Panic struck as Clark looked at the outstretched hand, and for the first time in ten years, without thought, reached out his own to touch Jerome.

The contact startled them both. There was no actual physical sensation of heat or cold in the grasp of the ghost's hand, but a strange sort of fizzle started in Clark's heart and ran down his hand into Jerome. The old man's eyes blinked open in surprise. Jerome snatched his hand away with more vigor than he'd shown in weeks, but not before Clark's heart received a ping of its own.

Jerome practically pulsed with new energy as he righted himself. "Great Scott, m'boy, what was that?"

Clark rubbed his tingling fingers against his pant leg. "I— I'm not sure. I suppose there's some way to find out, but I'm not sure how to look it up." He stared at his hand. It looked and felt normal as the sensation faded. "Whatever it was, it seemed to have done you some good."

Jerome laughed as he executed a full body twirl. "Ha! I feel like I'm eighty-seven again," he shouted in glee. "Now, get back to work. I want to know what else you've found about my Izzy."

Shaking his head, Clark picked up his suitcase. "Mind if I unpack first? And call my girlfriend?"

"Details, details." Jerome spun again and popped out of sight. "I'll be back later. Things to do, people to see. Go on, do your thing, and I'll do mine. But I'm expecting great things from you, m'boy. Always have, right from the start."

A half hour later, freshly showered and with the wash started in the laundry room down the hall, Clark messaged Leigh.

I'm back. Want to see you. Let me know when and where.

He set the phone on his desk as he opened his laptop and began to review his notes. When she called, they spoke briefly and agreed to meet for dinner. Satisfied, he returned to work. When he saw Leigh, he'd ask one last time to talk to her grandmother. He wanted to round out his work with an in-person interview with perhaps the last being on earth who'd known Isabel Standish. This was too important for his research. He knew Leigh was protective of her grandmother, but this couldn't wait much longer. And finding out what happened to Isabel was the only way he could ensure that he'd keep his teaching position so they could be together. She had to understand that.

A few hours later, Leigh arrived with bags of take out. A mass of cold air radiated around her and lent a chill to the room.

He met her at the door and swept her into his arms. "I've missed you so much," he said as he took the bags.

Leigh's brown eyes gazed into his. Despite her smile, she looked solemn. "I've missed you too. It's been so crazy. The merger agreement happened so suddenly." She wiped her eyes. "We're trying to keep it a secret, but there are meetings all day long. It's been all I can do to not mess up any of my projects while keeping up with everything. My mother and sister are frantic."

She took a breath. "And Rocky keeps calling, trying to weasel information out of anyone he can. I don't know how he managed it, but he's gotten past my admin a dozen times. He's not giving up." She pulled back, her eyes shining. "And I had to keep on—

and Gram is getting weaker, and I can't do anything. And then Berry came to meet her—" She broke down then, and Clark held her closer, whispering into her hair, kissing her over and over again. He wiped her tears before taking the bags of food to the kitchen.

"Would you think I'm a complete ass if I suggested we skip dinner and head to the bedroom? I need to hold you, love you," she asked.

He grabbed her hand and tugged her into the other room. "I think you'd be the complete opposite of an ass," he said. "I need you too."

They shed their clothes in a moment and crawled under the covers and into each other's arms, shivering. "I want to hold you," Clark whispered, his arms around her tight. She shivered again, and he rubbed her back. The bed began to warm. "My darling, my poor darling. You should have told me. I would've come home sooner. I wouldn't have left you to face it all al—"

She kissed him. "I'm a big girl," she said with a tearful laugh. "You needed to see your family. And I should be able to handle this on my own. I'm supposed to be able to handle everything on my own."

Clark pressed his forehead to hers. "It doesn't mean you have to. I may not understand your work, but I understand people. I understand you. I want to be here for you, if only as a shoulder to cry on, or someone you can vent to. Don't you understand, Leigh? I want to be the one you come to. Every day. Every night. I love you."

"Oh, Clark," she sighed as she kissed him.

"Don't ever think you're not my priority. The job, the research, Jerome, my parents— all of that is secondary to my loving you."

She wrinkled her nose. "Jerome?"

He laughed to cover his error. "Slip of the tongue. I spent so many years researching him, he's still on my mind. But, Leigh, I can't say this any plainer. Everything I do from now on is so we can be together. When we met, my priority was to write a new book for my own glory, not to mention the promise of a secure job. But since then, my priorities have changed. Yes, I want the job, but it's so I can stay here. With you."

She laughed. "I'm overwhelmed, you know." She kissed him. "You're more than I ever dreamed of."

He grinned. "I am wonderful, aren't I? But it's you who makes me so. Who could blame me for wanting to stay here, in your arms, for the rest of my life?" He kissed her once more. "You know, all this research, seeing how sad some people's lives were, even with great wealth and notoriety, it makes me so much more grateful for what we have. I'll never be famous—"

"Says the one who was on all those talk shows when your first book was published," she said.

He shrugged. "My fame was fleeting. None of that matters to anyone looking to hire me. But what we have, what *we* can be, that's my future. That's my goal."

He kissed her once more. "You're the one I want, too," she whispered. "I haven't allowed myself to believe that what we have will last. But I'm beginning to. I'm beginning to believe you are my forever."

He felt her smile under his lips. "Then let me show you how much I adore you."

They made feverish love under the covers, then rested, only to make love again, languidly this time, until hunger pangs drove them out of the bedroom and into the tiny kitchen. She was wrapped in his plaid robe, thick woolen socks on her feet, and a sated smile on her face. Clark grabbed his sweats, and they walked arm in arm back into the kitchen, where Leigh put their dinner in the microwave.

"It's not as good as if it were fresh," she said with a frown.

He smiled as he reached for her hand across the small table. "I don't care. We needed to be together more than we needed hot

Crab Rangoon. I only wish you could have come with me for Christmas. My parents want to meet you. I need to prove to them that someone as wonderful as you wants me, and you're not a figment of my imagination."

She laughed around a bite of eggroll. "I would have if you'd asked."

He shook his head. "I knew you didn't want to leave your grandmother. Next year. Or in the spring, when my family comes to visit." He waggled his eyebrows. "Besides, I was sleeping in my old bed—"

"I wouldn't mind sharing a twin bed with you," she protested.

"Yeah, except my brother Larry was across the room in his. That would have made making love a little awkward."

She laughed. "Okay. We'll stay in a hotel when we go."

He grew serious. "I need to tell you something, though."

Her smile fell away, and he wanted to kick himself for that.

"It's about my research."

"Oh?" she gasped.

"I've come to a point—I need to ask again to meet your grandmother. I think she's related to Isabel."

Leigh dropped her chopsticks, and her cheeks paled. "That's impossible."

The wontons felt like lead in his stomach. "I can't tell you too much about what I know—what I think I've learned until I've verified it. But I think she can help. And if nothing else, I'd like to meet someone who's so important to you."

"Clark—"

"Leigh. Please." He took her hands and squeezed them lightly. "I need you to trust me. It's important. To my research. My book. Our future. I would never do anything to harm your grandmother. It's tearing me up thinking that you'll lose her soon. I know exactly what you're going through. I'll be here for you."

Her face went from a pinched, stricken look to sad and resigned.

317

"Sweetheart?" he asked.

She nodded. "Okay. New Year's Eve. You can come for dinner. I'll let Gram know."

"I don't want this to be weird between us."

"Too late," Leigh said quietly. "I can't help but think it's not going to go well."

"Hey, I know my salad fork from my dinner fork," Clark joked. "I promise I won't slurp my soup."

That won him a small smile.

"Leigh, I love you, and I would never do anything to hurt you."

Leigh nodded. "I know. It's that I have a bad feeling about this, and I'm not sure what I can do to make it go away."

He stood and lifted her into his arms before reseating himself with her on his lap. "Leigh. I love you more than I ever thought I could love anyone. It'll be fine. I promise. It will all turn out okay in the end."

Leigh nodded, but her body was so stiff, so unyielding, he knew she wouldn't believe him until it happened.

And he wasn't entirely certain he wasn't lying. All he knew was this was not the time to tell her about Jerome. But he needed to, and soon. Jerry didn't have much time left, and he wanted to clear up the mystery for him before he left.

Leigh

The next morning, she hurried home after lying sleepless beside Clark much of the night. It was only the thought of how upset he'd be if she'd left that kept her beside him.

"Gram!" she called as she rushed in the door. "Gram, I'm back."

Gram was transparent as she sat in her chair at the top of the grand staircase. "My dear, Lei-Lei, why in heaven's name aren't you lounging in the arms of your lover?"

318

"I couldn't—" She was breathless as she ran up and knelt at the old woman's feet. "I couldn't. He wants to meet you. We have to go through this again. I'm not sure I'm up for it. The pretense…" She bowed her head. "I should never have told him about you."

Gram laughed. "I'm— how do they say it… your dirty little secret?"

Leigh scowled. "You know that's not—"

"I'm joking, darling." She reached out to cradle Leigh's chin, stopping short of touching her. That was something they had only done once when Leigh was a small child. It had shocked her terribly and the small child had been sick for a week. Gram never dared cross that barrier again in all the years since. "I like him. It will be fine. You'll see."

"What if he's scared of you?" Leigh bit her lips. "What if I lose him because he can't see you and he thinks I'm a mad woman? What if he tells the whole world I think I can see ghosts? And they believe him?"

"You know perfectly well he'll see me if I want to be seen. Even in these waning days, I can make my presence known. You worry too much, my darling. You saw how Moe reacted, and then he was fine. A charming devil, that one."

"Moe's used to weird stuff. Berry's stories are full of funny, paranormal things. It's not like that in real life."

"This isn't real life?" Gram asked with a saucy wink. "You worry way too much."

"But Gram—"

"I know you're scared. Trust me, I know what keeping a secret is like." She paused and looked at her gnarled knuckles. "I allowed the foolishness about hiding my past, being ashamed of it, go on for too long. I hid in this house like a scared, old woman because I was so conditioned to be one, and now in what passes for my afterlife, I can't leave it. But I never thought you'd be ashamed of me too."

"Never!" Leigh cried. "I love you. I don't know what I'd do without you. But Clark…"

"Tell me this, young lady," Gram waved a finger in the air. "Say you didn't have me—never knew me. If you found out your Clark was harboring some supernatural power, would you love him less?"

Leigh frowned and wrung her fingers until they popped. "That's not a fair question. I can't honestly answer it because I've always known you. But he hasn't had the same experiences."

"He believes in the power of old movies," Gram said calmly. "Believes in all that make-believe. Did you know that when people first saw movies, they thought it was magic? Their standards were different from yours, but they were so very willing to believe. Surely a man who can suspend his disbelief to watch— to love old movies—can accept that the woman he loves has a Great-grandmother who's a ghost."

Leigh looked skeptical. "I don't know."

"He loves you."

"He says so."

Grams tsked. "He loves you, heart and soul."

Leigh nodded. "And I love him," she said in a small voice.

"You haven't made yourself the easiest woman in the world to love, you know. And yes, there are good reasons for that. But he does love you. So, you're going to need to trust him. From every single thing you've told me he's the kind of man who keeps his word."

"Clark is kind of old-fashioned," she agreed. "He's very trustworthy."

"Then let him prove it to you, Lei-Lei. My darling girl, I so wish I could give you a hug right now. You need one so desperately." With that, Gram held out her translucent arms and floated up from her chair to embrace Leigh.

The contact startled them both, and they parted, only to look at one another and grin. Gram shone brighter than she had in months. "I should have done that years ago," the old woman said with a shake of her head. "One more thing I've missed out on by playing by the rules. Shame on me." She looked at her great-granddaughter held out her hands, and Leigh gently placed hers in the space above them. "You can bet in the time I have left, I'm not going to miss out one more thing. And for your information, missy, that includes seeing you settled with that professor of yours. Capiche?"

Mrs. Percy? I'm Bertram Jones. I've been working on a project for Mr. Jerome Percy and got a package for 'im.

Just give it to me. I'll deliver it to Mr. Percy.

Ma'am, your husband was very specific that he's the only one I'm to give this to. He's been waiting for this for years.

I said I'll give it to him. Delores grabbed the manila envelope.

Breathing hard, she clutched it to her chest. *Damned man. It's like I'm living with a ghost. I'll put an end to his wishing for his long-lost love once and for all.* She ripped open the package and scanned the sheets quickly and laughed out loud. So, his little dove flew away home, did she? Married a rich man within the year? Maybe I ought to tell him. Let him know she didn't love him after all. Not that that will ever make him love me or any other woman. I don't think anything can. No. Better he doesn't know. If he did, he'll divorce me to go after her, and we can't have that. Now, where can I hide this, so I'll have it available in case I ever need it?

She looked at the PI. *How much?* She asked.

Ma'am?

How much for you to agree that you never delivered this report to me? How much for you to go back to your office and type up another report. Tell Jerry you can't find the girl, and it's a lost cause. Or that she died. I don't care what the hell you tell him. How much for your silence?

He gave her a squinty-eyed stare.

You might as well. You deliver this report, he ain't gonna need your services any longer anyhow.

The man hung his head before he looked up at her with a gleam in his eye. *A thousand. Gimme a thousand, and it'll be done.*

Chapter Twenty-Eight

Clark

He stood on the grand doorstep and took a deep breath before ringing the bell. A bouquet was sheltered under one side of his open coat, pressed to his heart to keep it safe from the bitter wind.

Leigh opened the door, looking lovely and solemn. "Clark, Come in. You must be freezing."

He used the snow scraper on his shoes and presented the blossoms as he stepped over the threshold. "For you and your grandmother. I'm afraid they're a little worse for wear."

Leigh held them up to her nose. "The carnations are still spicy," she said with a small smile. "Thank you. They're beautiful. I'm sure Gram will love them, though she can't really smell anymore."

"My father once told me I can't go wrong giving flowers to a woman," he replied. "I want her to like me." He reached over and gave Leigh a peck on the cheek.

"She already does." Leigh set the bouquet down to take his coat. "Wow. You clean up good," she said.

Clark looked down at his dark suit, white shirt, and tugged at his modestly striped bow tie to straighten it. He checked that his pocket square was in place. That had been an argument with Jerome in which the ghost had prevailed. In fact, everything lately had been an argument with Jerome. The only round Clark won was to insist that the ghost stay home and out of mischief as Clark handled the interview.

"For you, I'd wear a tie even when I'm not working." He leaned closer and kissed her until they were both breathless. Clark managed to pry himself away. His gaze took in her deep blue sweater and black skirt. "You look lovely."

She rubbed her arms. "Thank you. I don't know why I'm so nervous tonight."

He took her arm. "It'll be fine. I'll mind my manners."

"It's not that, Clark. It's – well -- have you spoken to Berry? Or Moe?"

He shook his head. "I texted when I got back, but that's it. Berry usually invites me over at least once a week. I guess she's tired of entertaining after the holidays."

Leigh's shoulders came down a notch. "She probably is. She does a lot for her family. I haven't talked to her either."

He gave her a hug. "Sweetheart, relax. We're going to have a nice dinner with your grandmother. And then I'll leave. As much as I'd like to stay, I don't want this to be awkward for you."

Leigh leaned into Clark and took a deep breath. "I'm sorry I'm such a wreck."

He lifted her chin with a gentle finger. "You weren't nervous about my meeting your mother and sister."

She smiled. "I know. It's stupid. So, come in, and I'll pour you a drink in the kitchen. Gram is still primping. She'll join us when it's time to eat."

"Maybe it'll be better if I stay sober, and you drink," he quipped as they walked down the echoing hall into the kitchen.

"Don't tell me you're going to prepare dinner," she said over her shoulder.

"Yeah, right. About that — still can't cook. Mom's given up on me," he said with a smile. "Okay. So, one glass of wine for you, one for me, and we'll see what happens."

Leigh squeezed his hand.

"Something smells wonderful," Clark said as Leigh opened the kitchen door. He saw a frosted cake on a pedestal on a windowsill.

"Nothing too fancy," Leigh replied. "Salmon, greens, and wild rice." She went to the stove and stirred a pot. "Why don't you pour?"

There was an open bottle of wine on the table paired with two glasses. He filled one for each of them and waited until she was ready before he took a sip of the crisp rose.

"It's the wine you brought last time," she said. "You have very good taste."

"I have a wine merchant with very good taste. What can I do?"

She placed the flowers in a vase then turned to set her hands on his lapels. "Nothing. The table is ready. I'll put the flowers out there and then serve." She kissed him lightly. "I want you to stay tonight. Our first New Year's Eve."

He bent down to her lips. "The first of many," he whispered as he feathered kisses along her jaw to her ear. "I never want us to be apart on New Year's, ever."

She curled into him, a wooden spoon still in her hand. She lifted her chin. Clark didn't hesitate to take her offering until the buzzer went off. Pulling away with a smile, she pressed an enamel button that was in a row on the wall. It was below a row of bells. "I buzzed Gram to let her know we're ready. These old servants' bells are very handy."

"Let me take the flowers out while you finish in here."

She nodded as she slipped on oven mitts.

Clark carefully lifted the cut crystal vase and pushed his way into the dining room through the swinging doors.

"Hello, young man."

He stopped before slowly turning around to find a small woman sitting in an old-fashioned rattan wheelchair. She was swaddled in blankets and shawls. A formidable woman stood behind her in the shadows.

Clark set the flowers on the table and bowed. Her hands were buried in blankets, so he didn't offer his. "Good evening. Mrs. Sprague? I'm Clark Conrad."

She nodded, her eyes twinkling. "I know exactly who you are. You'll have to forgive me for having spied on you a time or two."

325

He felt his face heat. "I'm only sorry it's taken us this long to meet."

"My granddaughter is very protective, as I'm sure you've noticed. And not without good reason. I had the pleasure of meeting one of her good friends a week or so back. A relative of yours, or so I believe. I've decided it's time for me to stop isolating myself. Good heavens, what's the worst that can befall an old woman such as myself? Death?"

She laughed gaily as the door from the kitchen swung open once more. "Gram!" came the shocked voice of Leigh. "Gram I didn't—"

"Not to worry, Lei-Lei. Your young man and I have taken care of the niceties. I dare say, he's even more handsome close up than he is from afar. You have good taste, my dear. Very good taste."

"Oh, Gram."

Leigh

Her worst fears ran through her mind as she watched Clark and Gram chat. Couldn't he see how transparent Gram was?

"Darling. Did you see the flowers your young man brought? So lovely. It's been ages since anyone was so thoughtful."

"They're beautiful," Leigh agreed, hating how her voice shook. The small sip of wine she'd had soured in her stomach.

Clark looked abashed at his accomplishment. "It's nothing, really."

"And all dressed up. That's what young men did when they courted women in my day," Gram continued as she beamed at him. "There's nothing quite like a man who cares about his grooming."

"Oh, well," Clark said, flustered. "I happen to have an, er, acquaintance who's helped me over the years. An older gentleman who takes pride in his appearance."

326

"And all those old films you watch," Gram said. "Not that I approve of them, mind you, but they did set a certain tone for what makes a man look good. Cary Grant. Don Ameche. John Gilbert. Clark Gable, whom you resemble if not for the beard, and one or two others whose names escape me—"

She looked into the distance, but her act didn't convince Leigh. "Gram, for someone who doesn't like movies, you seem to know a lot about them."

Gram flapped a corner of her shawl. "Well, yes, I suppose it's hard to avoid them altogether when one's been around as long as I. And I *don't* approve of them. So many sad stories." She gave a small shiver before her face brightened. "But you're the expert on that, my Leigh tells me. Why, you could tell me far more than I could ever tell you."

Clark cleared his throat. "I'm not sure about that. I do have some questions I'd like to ask, but let's wait until after dinner. Leigh's gone to so much trouble, and I don't want to ruin her efforts by asking questions when we should be enjoying this meal."

Gram's nurse wheeled Gram to the table as Leigh went back for more dishes. When she returned, she observed Clark warming his hands by the fire.

"All set?" she asked with more cheer than she felt. One by one, Leigh passed the covered serving dishes to Clark as she loaded small portions on a plate which she set before Gram.

"Back when this house was first built, there would have been a half dozen servants to attend to guests during dinner parties," Gram said. "Oh, those were fancy affairs, where people were so concerned about appearances, they barely ate a morsel. The servants feasted on the leftovers." She looked at Leigh, who scowled back. "Or so I'm told, of course," she added with a laugh. "Different times. This is so much cozier."

Leigh could barely taste her meal. Gram kept the conversation going from one frivolous topic to the next. She would touch her

327

fork to her lips from time to time, but the food on her plate never diminished, nor did the wine in her glass. Clark didn't seem to notice as he answered questions about his family and interests.

Leigh found a new appreciation for what her Great-Grandmother must have been like as a young woman, full of gaiety and charm. Small wonder she'd been popular. And there was an unmistakable something about her that must have caught the eye of a movie producer at that time.

When dinner was over, Clark helped clear the table. Leigh had a bad moment when he held the door for the aide, but she swept through it and into another room as Leigh put the water on for coffee. Clark didn't seem to notice anything out of the ordinary as Leigh bore the cake into the dining room, and he trailed her with a decanter of brandy and two snifters.

"This has been delightful," Gram said as she waved off dessert. "I can't recall the last time I had so much fun." She looked from Leigh to Clark, mischief clear in her eyes. "Oh, well, I suppose talking to your delightful cousin and her husband should count. Such a lovely couple. That Berry had a thousand questions for me." She leaned closer. "I think she wants to write — what did she call it — a fictionalized history about my life." Gram leaned back again. "I do hope I'm here long enough to read it." She glanced slyly at Clark. "As well as some other, shall we say, momentous events, perhaps for the two of you?"

Leigh wanted to sink into the floor. "Gram, let's not get ahead of ourselves."

Clark laughed and took Leigh's hand, kissing the back of it. "I won't say it hasn't crossed my mind. I'll know in a few months if my contract is extended. I can't ask Leigh to commit or make promises before then." He looked at her with shining eyes. "But don't doubt it's on my mind."

Leigh's heart fluttered. "Clark…"

He turned her hand over and kissed her palm. "Just so there is no doubting my intentions."

Gram beamed at them. "Just so. Only in my day, long engagements were frowned upon. Too much mischief could result."

Clark cleared his throat. "Speaking of which—"

Leigh's euphoria vanished in an instant. "Do you have to—"

Clark squeezed her hand. "Sweetheart, only a few questions. I promise."

She withdrew her hand and hugged herself, slipping her suddenly cold hands up her sleeves, but nothing could stop her shaking. She glanced at the clock on the mantle. It was a quarter to twelve.

"I'm curious about your mother," Clark said.

"My mother?" Gram looked bemused. "What an odd question. Not even that very inquisitive Berry asked about Mamma."

"Clark, what are you—"

"It's my research, you see. It's quite amazing when you think of it. I never expected it when her name came up. And since you're here, I thought I would be able to take advantage of speaking to you about her."

Gram batted her lashes. "I fail to see what interest Mamma would have to you. She was a rather ordinary wife of a successful merchant." She looked at Leigh. "The building that housed their emporium stood until a few years ago in fact."

Leigh looked sharply at Clark, who in turn looked confused. "I'm sorry. I was speaking of your mother, Lilly Manning." He looked at Leigh with an apology in his eyes. "I believe, and I want to try to confirm, that she was also known as Isabel Standish. Surely you're aware of her brief career as a film star."

Leigh's hands flew to her face. Gram's flirtatious smile deepened. She glanced at Leigh with a wink and then at Clark. "Young man, I'm afraid you have your generations confused."

Clark's mouth dropped open. "I beg your pardon."

Gram shook her head, her white hair gleaming in the dim candlelight. "Not at all. You see, my mother never traveled further west than Poughkeepsie. You have her confused with another."

"Was Isabel your aunt?" Clark asked.

"No, my dear boy." She again glanced at Leigh with a shrug. "I'm afraid I will shock you. I don't mean to, of course, but you've asked after all."

Leigh held out a shaking hand. "Gram, please don't," she asked plaintively.

"My dearest, Lei-Lei. He's going to find out sooner or later. Best it's from me, don't you see?"

She turned back to Clark as Leigh choked back a sob. "Young man, my mother was not Isabel Standish, nor was my aunt."

"But it was someone in the family?"

The chocolate cake Leigh had picked at turned to acid. "Gram—"

"Hush, child."

Every muscle in Leigh's body tensed.

Clark slumped in his chair. "I'm confused."

"Indeed," Gram continued with a regal nod.

There was a pregnant pause as Leigh hid her face in her hands while Gram beamed at Clark. "Young man, *I* was Isabel Standish."

Leigh wanted to bolt as she watched Clark's astonishment.

"But that would make you—" He counted silently in his head. "That would make you well past one hundred—"

"Or," Gram said with a laugh, "It would make me a ghost."

Leigh burst off her chair. "Out!" she shouted. "Get out," she yelled at Clark.

"But Leigh—"

She could stand to hear no more as her world crumbled around her. Hands over her ears, she cringed, "Get out, Clark. Out. I knew this was a disaster."

330

"Lei-Lei—" Grams clipped words were barely audible against the rushing in Leigh's ears.

"Leigh, darling—" Clark tried to say.

She shook her head. "I can't stand to hear another word. Get out. It's a mistake. All of it. How much more damage do you plan to do? You don't love me. You were only using me, just like all the others. I should have known better. Oh god, how many times do I need to learn this lesson?"

She closed her eyes, tears falling as the clock struck twelve.

There was a commotion around her, voices that were more noise than sense. As if from a distance, she heard Gram gently chiding Clark. There were footsteps, slow and hesitant, that faded.

And then there was silence, a blessed, empty hush.

No more children, Roger. I can't take it. We have our daughter. It would seem our sons are not strong enough to survive. I cannot bear to bury another child.

It's you, Lilly. You're a weak woman. I should have known better than to marry an actress, no matter how beautiful you were. And now you're losing your looks. You're no good to me. Better I see if I can get a son off another woman. Then we'll adopt him.

You cannot force me to take another woman's child into my home!

You'll do whatever I say, damn it. You're my wife. You promised to obey. You will do this.

Over my dead body!

That can be arranged.

Chapter Twenty-Nine

Clark

At the sight of Clark coming through the door, Jerome sprang from his favorite chair. "M'boy, what's amiss? Why are you home? Did you meet Izzy's daughter, or was it another dead end?" His hand went to his brow. "No. Don't tell me. I can't bear another disappointment. No matter what you did the other day, I'm fading. I fear I don't have much time left. Damn it all. Tell me. Tell me, boy!"

Clark slumped against his front door. "It was her."

Jerome stopped mid-tirade. "What?" he asked, a whisper more than a word.

"I found her. Leigh's Gram wasn't her actual grandmother. She *is* Isabel Standish. Also known as Lilly Manning, then Lilly Sprague."

After a startled silence, Jerome sank to his knees, head in hand. "My god. After all this time. I don't know if I want to know more." He lifted his head. "Do I?"

Clark pried himself away from the door and headed for the kitchen, coat still on, his shoes wet through. "I can't bear to tell you."

"Is she— was she— what is she—?"

"Dead?" Clark barked out a laugh. "Come on, Jerry. You know as well as I, she'd be over a hundred by now. Of course, she's dead. It's just that she—"

"—was murdered? Hanged? Killed by her husband? Died of heartbreak?"

Clark shook his head as he reached for the bottle over the sink. He was about to reach for a glass but unscrewed the cap and put the bottle to his lips instead, and swallowed, then swallowed again. He held it at arm's length and shuddered before he took another belt and held the bottle to his chest. "None of the above," he managed as he caught his breath despite his burning chest.

"You picked a fine time to turn from a teetotaler into lush," Jerome remarked with a raised brow.

Clark closed his eyes as he took another healthy swallow, then grit his teeth at the burn. "I was in a bar when we first met," he gasped.

Jerome's left eyebrow rose. "And you were no better suited for a life of debauchery then than you are now. So put that bottle down and tell me what happened."

Clark took a defiantly long final slug before he doubled over, coughing.

"At least tell me where she's buried. I want to go pay my respects—"

"It's after midnight on New Year's Eve. I had wine at Leigh's, and it's colder than— than—"

Jerome folded his arms. "I don't care."

"I do. The last thing I want is to get arrested on top of everything else. How exactly am I s'pposed to explain to a police osifier what I'm doing tromping aroun' drunk in a cemetery in a snowstorm, at the butt crack of the new year? Should I tell 'im a ghost made me do it? Would ya make yourself visible before he arrests me?" Clark slurred.

"Don't be absurd. You know I'd never willfully help a constable unless it was to keep my own caboose out of the hoosegow."

Bottle in hand, Clark staggered from the kitchen, struggling to disassociate his arms from his sleeves, but the coat would not cooperate. "M' point 'zactly. Besides, I don't know where she's buried. She didn't say." He shook the coat until it was off his shoulders, but it caught on one wrist. His other hand still clutched the bottle and was enveloped in wool. Clark fell into Jerome's chair and winced as the spring poked his back. Contorting his body, he tipped the bottle back again.

"That's a shame. But it's a matter of simple logic. What's the fanciest cemetery in these here parts? We'll go at first light. We can make plans right now—" Jerome's voice trailed off, and he stood stock-still for a moment. "Wait a gosh-darned moment. What in blazes do you mean, 'she didn't say?' Who didn't say what?"

Clark gave his hand another wiggle. The mostly shed coat was under him, and he couldn't feel his hands. He gave up trying, leaned back, and closed his eyes. "We dinn't get that far 'fore Leigh threw me out."

"Why'd you agree to such a harebrained thing like leaving?"

Clark looked at Jerome over the top of his glasses. He wanted to push them up, but with one trapped inside his coat sleeves and the other holding the bottle, it didn't seem worth the effort. Yet he tried, and missed, the neck of the bottle hitting his left lens. "This is the twenty-first century. When a woman tells you to leave, you leave."

Jerome shook his head. "In my day, a real man would've—"

"In your day, a man would've grabbed the woman and slugged her—"

Jerome stopped short. "Not all of us."

"Most of you," Clark said sullenly. He squinted at the bottle before he drank again.

"You've been watching too many old movies," Jerome replied. "I was going to say, a real man would've grabbed her and kissed the living daylights out of her until she saw reason. Or stopped yelling. Either would do."

Clark shook his head against the back of the old chair. "Okay. So, I'm not a real man. I don't measure up to your standard, and damn it, I prob'bly never will." He shut his eyes, and with a grimace, swallowed more bourbon. "You don't need to shay it. I'm a complete failure as a man. As a lover. Probably as a teacher, and I'll never get tenure now, 'cause the last thing I can do is publish this schtr-story. Leigh already hates me for what I discovered. Doesn't trust me, and she's probably right. I didn't set out to make her a laughingstock. But that's what she thinks."

"Clark— m'boy— son—" Jerome said softly.

"I'll finish out the spring semester, keep m' head down. Slink off at the end of the school year. I'll start searching for new positions tomorrow."

"But your research— your book— our book—"

"I scholved your mystery, Jer. That was our deal. You never said I had to publish. There's plen'y other topics to research." Clark put the bottle on the floor and flopped back in the chair, wincing.

"You can't give up. Not after all this time. All my hopes and dreams—" Jerome frowned. "After all I've done for you?"

Clark opened his eyes and stared at his ghostly companion of the last ten years. "That's what failures do, isn't it? We quit. Try and stop me."

"I— I—"

Clark tried to get to his feet, but his foot tangled in his coat, and he fell back. "I can't even do this right. You should have left me alone in that bar, Jerry. Gone off into the world on yer own. I would've made a first-rate dishwasher. I bet I'd be th' head dishwasher by now."

"Clark, dear boy, I never meant you were a failure."

"Right. Thanks, but it's a bit late for that now."

"I mean it, son. Look at what you've accomplished."

Clark gave Jerome a one-eyed stare. "Face it, Jer. Meeting you was my lucky break. I'd never've done it without you. Maybe you were right. I should've let you come with me tonight. At least then, Leigh would've known I'm not scared of ghosts. That I wouldn't make fun of her."

Jerome fell silent. A long moment later, he asked, "Wait one minute here. Are you telling me my Izzy is a ghost? In that big old house your girlfriend lives in?"

"Former girlfriend," Clark muttered. "I'm pretty confident given she threw me out an' never wants t' see me again. That means break up to me."

"You're missing the point," Jerome muttered.

Clark closed his eyes and moaned. "You're missing my point. Leigh ditched me because of your girlfriend. Your deceased, but still kicking girlfriend."

"But—" Jerome fell silent.

The two sat in the dim room for what felt like forever. Clark sighed and managed to shake off one coat sleeve. He grasped the bottle and held it up, but he'd lost the will for more drink.

"I never said you were a loser," Jerome said eventually.

Clark rocked his head up from the chairback to look at the ghost. "It was implied from time to time."

"Your skin really that thin?"

Clark rubbed his face with his now free hands, his glasses falling off all but one ear. "Tonight, it is." He sighed again. "Seems I devastated th' woman I love. And I was doin' it all for

336

her." He shook his head. "I wanted to solve this mystery so I could stay here. With her. I didn't know it would lead me to her front door. Hell, because of what I learned— doesn't mean I have t' expose her as having lived with a ghost. The very thought—"

"It's not like you haven't done the same."

"But she didn't give me a chance to explain that."

"Rotten luck, old chap."

They endured each other's silences for another while, listening to the ticking of a clock. "I don't suppose you mentioned me to her," Jerome asked.

Clark's answer was a snort. "Do you think I'd be shi-sitting here now if I'd had a chance to tell them I've been plagued by a ghost of my own for the last decade?"

"That's rather harsh."

Clark shrugged, changed his mind, and upended the bottle once more.

The ghost frowned. "I haven't been that much of a burden, have I? I've tried to make myself useful. Teach you a thing or two. How to be a gentleman, dress well, and all that."

Clark closed his eyes. "You haven't been a burden. A pain in the ass, yes. But not a burden. At least I didn't have to feed you or buy you drinks. Mos' of the time, I was hardly able to feed myself."

"Well, not for nothing, but you're not quite as hopeless as I might have implied," Jerome replied. "You've certainly upped your sartorial game."

Clark gave a ragged laugh. "Thanks, I think."

"And you're not bad with the ladies. This little snafu will pass. You'll see."

"You didn't hear her tonight." Clark's voice cracked. "I think I broke her heart. An' worse, her trust. All because of a damned coincidence."

"More like cosmic serendipity," Jerome mused. "I think it was meant to be."

"I was meant to break the heart of the woman I love?"

"You were meant to love the woman whose heart you just broke. Temporarily."

Clark sat up at the sound of Jerome's wishful tone.

"I'll be damned if your life is ruined by a misunderstanding the same way mine was," Jerome said. "I'm determined it won't be."

"What do you mean?"

"I'm going to fix this. One way or another."

"How?"

"I'm not sure. I need to think." Jerome paced up and down the wall and across the ceiling, one arm across his chest, the other propped on it as he stroked his chin. He stopped and dropped to the floor. "I know. You'll march right back in there, me by your side—"

"Not going to happen, Jer. She'll call the cops on me."

"You're probably right," the ghost mumbled as he resumed his pacing. "I've got it!" he said at last. "You're going to call your cousin's wife and have her do this for you."

"Berry?"

"The very same," Jerome said. "Go on. Give her a call."

"It's after one in the morning. I can't wake her up for this."

"Is it an emergency or not?"

"It's not life or death," Clark said.

"I'll be the judge of that." Jerome peered at Clark. "Just how pale and translucent was my Izzy? Hell, I didn't even ask how she looked or what she sounded like. You have to tell me, boy. I need to hear it."

"She didn't look like she was going to fade away before morning, if that's what you mean. But how am I going to 'splain this to Berry?"

"You're going to tell her the truth. If she's half as on the ball as I think she is, I'll bet she's already guessed."

"You think she'll help? Won't she be mad at me? She's been Leigh's friend longer than I've known her."

Jerome shook his transparent head once more. "After all I've taught you? Don't you know most women can't resist a romance? And think of it, m'boy. It will be catnip to the woman who writes love stories for a living."

Clark sat forward. His head was starting to pound from the bourbon and the stress. "Okay. I've got nothing left to lose. My pride's in the gutter, and my future isn't far behind."

And with sudden clarity, he remembered the conversation he and Moe had had all those months before about Berry and her uncanny abilities.

It was certainly worth a shot.

*God-damned woman lied to me. Took my money and lied. And
now Izzy's trail's grown cold. Again. Damned PI won't return my
calls,* Jerome muttered. *Yes, yes, hello? Is this Global Travel? I'd
like to book a flight to Las Vegas. Yes. Tonight, if possible. I need
a divorce. I hear they can be granted quickly there. Yes, I'll hold.
My name? Jerome Percy. And if this gets into the papers, young
lady, I'll have your job. And put me on one of those aeroplanes
that don't crash if you don't mind.*

Chapter Thirty

Berry

"Shhh. I don't want Gram to know you're here."

Leigh let me in the kitchen door on New Year's afternoon. We
tiptoed into the family room, where she had a teapot and cookies
ready. I noticed an unopened bottle of champagne. It listed sadly
in an elegant silver bucket, half-filled with water.

Given the state she was in, I was happy she agreed to see me.
I won't go into details, but Clark had called late that morning. I
suppose he thought Moe and I would be sleeping in after a night
of carousing. Clark must've forgotten it snowed all night, so rather
than toasting the New Year together, I sat alone while my husband
and his brothers were plowing driveways and parking lots. Given
my sisters-in-law all have children younger than mine, none of us
wanted to venture out to keep each other company, so we texted
all night and kept each other laughing.

My Moe came home at dawn, woke me up to kiss me hello,
and then fell asleep on top of the blankets. But enough about me.

Clark called, and after I said hello, he began to talk—much of
it was incomprehensible. I had the feeling he was talking to me
and someone in the room with him at the same time but didn't say

who. To be honest, I think he was a little drunk, or he was crying. Or both. Yeah, I think it was probably both.

After much coaxing, I got his side of the story. He'd correctly guessed Leigh's ancestor was Isabel Standish. I didn't mention I already knew. And the fact that he didn't mention meeting Lilly was telling. He clearly wanted to keep Leigh's secrets.

To say Clark was troubled would be an understatement. I realize how deeply he loved Leigh, and he took it terribly hard that she thought he'd deceived her. In fact, he said he'd scrap his research and go on to a different subject if only she'd take him back. Talk about devotion—his job and his career prospects were all on the line, and he was talking about throwing them away for her. I might have told him to cut back on the dramatics. I don't quite remember exactly what I said, but I'm quite certain I thought it. Out loud.

He'd tried calling and texting Leigh, but she wouldn't reply, and he was concerned about returning in person. So, he did the next best thing and asked me to talk to her.

Which was why I was sitting on the sofa in her family room a few hours after noon.

"Berry, he lied to me." Leigh plucked a tissue from the box nearby. "He lied and schemed and used me. Just like Rocky."

"Oh, honey," I said and gave her a hug. "I find that so hard to believe. He's a great guy. Kind of dorky, but so are you."

She wiped her tears. The poor thing was a mess. There were dark circles under her reddened eyes, and her nose looked as if she'd been blowing it for hours.

Leigh shook her head. "He did. More fool me for not seeing through his façade." She turned her watery gaze to me. "I know he's your cousin and all, but— but—"

Poor Leigh dissolved into tears before she could finish. I held and rocked her. I figured this would be good practice for when my kids grew up and had their hearts broken. It's something everyone

I know has gone through a time or two. Or three, if they're a slow learner.

"Tell me what happened."

She shushed me again. "I don't want Gram to hear. She's been giving me a hard time about it."

"Now, I'm really curious," I whispered.

"She thinks I overreacted."

I kept mostly silent. Reserving judgment and all. I know how it can be when a guy acts like a jerk. Especially when he doesn't know he's being a jerk. Long story. "Did you?" I finally asked. I don't know why. It kind of slipped out.

"Not you too." Her face crumpled.

"Leigh, all I know, and I hope I'm not giving too much away, is that Clark called me this morning, absolutely beside himself."

She snorted. "No doubt because his little scheme blew up in his face."

I shook my head. "Tell me what happened."

"You won't judge me?" she asked and sounded so much like a little girl my heart broke all over again for her. "What did he tell you?" she asked.

"I want to hear from you before I say anything."

Leigh grabbed a handful of tissues and mopped her face. And then she told me her tale.

It took a while, with breaks for crying. All her insecurities brought on by my brother were on full display along with angst left over from her unhappy high school days and other failed relationships. It's awful how those things stay with you no matter how much you try to overcome them. There was the tension about the merger and worry about her grandmother. In the end, she admitted she'd panicked and was as embarrassed as she was devastated.

The events were pretty much as Clark described, though he hadn't mentioned meeting Lilly. Leigh filled in that part, as well as telling me Gram had admonished her after Clark left. It sounded as if it was the first time in years that had happened, and it had stung.

An hour later, she sagged against the cushions and wiped her eyes once more. "So, I hardly slept. Gram was still mad this morning. Told me I'd acted like a spoiled child because I wouldn't listen to Clark." She sniffed back a sob. "Gram was so pale— so— so transparent. But I know he used me to get to Gram. And you know what she is. He's going to exploit that now. He's going to besmirch her reputation, and mine— and— and— I'm going to lose her too."

"Leigh—"

"And he's going to tell everyone I've been living with a ghost or that I'm crazy and only think I have been. He's going to make me a laughingstock. And because you're his cousin, you're going to take his side, and I'm going to lose my friend as well as my boyfriend, and my Gram, and my reputation, and my job— and I fell in love with him. I knew better, and I did anyway."

And then Leigh was off crying once more.

I waited her out. "You're not going to lose me," I told her gently. "Clark may be Moe's cousin, but that doesn't dictate my friendships. I mean, come on. Don't you know me?"

That got a small hiccupping laugh from her.

"I don't think Clark is so devious that he found out who your grandmother was, got to know you, and then did the big reveal. I mean, from what you told me, he got it wrong."

Leigh hiccupped again.

"If there's one thing I've learned about having a psychopath for a brother, it's how they operate. Everything they do is all about them and for their greater glory. If Clark was cold-blooded, why'd he want you back now?" I paused a moment. "And by the way, did you know my brother was fired?"

Leigh didn't say a word but gave a small smile as she smoothed a tissue on her knee.

"It seems this thing about Clark is more a matter of coincidence. And circumstance." Then I told her that Clark hadn't mentioned meeting Lilly, but I wasn't certain she heard or appreciated the significance of that.

"Sure," she was all she'd said. I didn't trust that her tone conveyed her certitude.

I cocked my head. "Come on, Leigh. If he already knew the answer to his mystery, then why would he woo you unless he really cares? He could have accomplished his goal without getting involved. I'll bet he never expected her spirit would still be hanging around. And it's not like you were dropping hints or leaving clues for him to find."

"He wanted my sympathy," she said. "He wouldn't have been able to prove anything without meeting her. Or get his hands on Gram's papers."

I gave a half-hearted laugh. "You think he knew all along that Lilly Manning and the great and mysterious Isabel Standish were one and the same? But he didn't know she was your Gram or that she's a ghost living... haunting... I mean, whatever it is she does, under this roof."

She pursed her lips. "I guess when you put it that way—"

"And there's no reason he needs to reveal her state of being in order to publish her story. No need for him to mention you at all, other than as a footnote."

"But Gram's always been so private. No one in the family ever talked about it, other than in whispers—"

"And I've told you that was a mistake." Gram glided into the room and startled us both. I think ghosts are the quietest beings on earth. Quieter than a two-year-old plotting to get into the cookie jar when your back is turned. "The time for secrets is over, my darling Lei-Lei."

"But for all these years—" my friend sputtered.

"All these years, I allowed the wishes of my mother and husband, and my ungrateful daughter, to dictate how I lead my

344

life, even unto death. No longer. I'm dead, Leigh. None of this can hurt me. Surely you can understand that."

"But it can hurt me," Leigh sobbed. "I know that's selfish, but it's true."

"Oh, pish," Gram said with a scowl. "You have all the power here. You can dictate how my story is told. There's no value in his announcing to the world that I outlived my death." She laughed. "Truly, do you think his reputation would survive if he spouted what would be sure to be seen as nonsense by 90% of the population? I thought you were smarter than that."

She came closer. "My darling, beautiful, unhappy, Leigh. He isn't Rocky. Clark really and truly cares about you. I saw it in his eyes every time he looked at you. He doesn't care that I'm a ghost. All he cares about is you. He loves you. Deeply. All that nonsense about my past that my husband started and dratted daughter continued is pure rubbish." Gram shook her head. "I should have truly haunted her before she died, the selfish thing. She needed to be taught a lesson."

I wanted to laugh but managed to hold it in.

"I was proud of my films," Gram continued. "I wished I'd made more of them. I wish I'd given Jerome a chance to talk to me— allowed me to forgive him. So much time wasted, love lost."

Leigh closed her eyes, and more tears coursed down her cheeks. "But how—"

"You might have missed it, but Clark didn't run screaming from the room when I told him what I was, my darling girl. And come to think of it, don't you think his casual acceptance was a bit odd?"

Leigh bit her lip as she nodded slowly.

"He's an intelligent man. And from what you told me, his book about my Jerome was well written. Thoroughly researched and made my Jerome out to be a sympathetic character despite his many flaws."

Leigh gave a giant sigh. "I suppose."

"Maybe you need to give Clark a chance to explain," I suggested softly.

Leigh closed her eyes. "I was awful last night, wasn't I?"

"If there's one thing I've learned, life is too short for regrets. Or undue pride," Gram said softly. "The occasional bout of humility is good for the soul."

"Maybe I could call him." Leigh's hands flew to her face. "But I'm so embarrassed. He saw the absolute worst of me. And it's not like he's blameless."

"You didn't know I was Isabel Standish until recently. But you were keeping secrets from him, even if you didn't mean hurt him with them," Gram reminded her. She looked up slyly. "Perhaps he has some secrets of his own."

Leigh sat up straighter, about to defend herself, so I knew it was time to interject. "Something tells me he'll understand." I gave Lilly a wink. "It's not every day a man encounters a ghost, you know. I mean, he didn't pass out or anything. Not like Moe. Maybe he's familiar with your, er, uh—"

Lilly winked back. "My kind, you mean? Specters? Phantoms? Wraiths?"

"Oh, I wouldn't call you any of those things."

"But I was so mean to him," Leigh whispered. "I don't know if I could bear to face him again."

I put my arm around her. "Trust me. After I heard how devastated he was over losing you, he'll be over here on his knees if he thought it would do any good. So, give this a little thought, and then maybe give him a call? Invite him over?"

Leigh sighed and looked at the pile of tissues in the wastebasket. "First, can you tell me more about Rocky getting fired?"

I grinned. "I don't know the whole story except when he opened an envelope thinking it was his annual holiday bonus, instead of a check, there was a pink slip." I couldn't help my grin. "It was all I could do to keep myself from cheering when I heard

346

the news. I think ultimately it was because your mother decided to merge with that other firm." I glanced down at my fingernails. "And I think a well-founded rumor about him in a particular restaurant being horrible in public to a particular person I know and like, might have had something to do with it."

Leigh clasped her hands together. "That's the best news I've heard in a while."

"So, can I call Clark and tell him to stop by?"

Her smile faded. "I need a minute to think about it. I'm not done being upset yet."

"Moe likes to joke about having learned to eat humble pie for breakfast when we got married. I don't mention this too often, but so have I. It's part of being in a successful relationship, my friend." I looked across the small table at Leigh's great-grandmother. She was noticeably more transparent than when I arrived. "So don't take too much time," I said softly.

How dare you touch me. You broke the lock, tore my clothes, and now I'm bloody and aching. Roger, I never thought you so low as to assault me.

Lilly rubbed her aching chin with one hand, the other pointed at her raging husband. You touch me again, and I'm leaving. I'll take Chloris, and I'll go. I don't care if I have to scrub floors to support her. Oh God, I should have stayed in California. What a mistake I made. I can't bear it. For all his faults, Jerome never hit a woman. He never had to, you monster.

No matter that, Lilly. You're mine. Now until death and beyond. You'll do as I say. You'll never leave this house again. I'll beat you again if I have to. Every damned day. Do you understand me? He swung at her once more, and she saw stars.

Lilly hung her head. Taking a deep, painful breath, she nodded. *Yes Roger. I understand.*

Chapter Thirty-One

Leigh

She saw Berry to the door, promising to make up her mind by evening. The day was as gray as she felt, the air cold and damp with the promise of more snow on the wind.

Leigh went to her bedroom and eyed the mess there before deciding it was too much work to clean. Instead, she took two pain relievers and a shower.

As the hot water poured down, she thought of Clark. His shy smiles, his awkward, old-fashioned ways, and his hot kisses. She knew he wasn't evil. He was driven, just as she was. It was more the thought of facing him again that troubled her, her own embarrassment more an impediment to forgiveness than anything he'd done or said.

348

She got out of the shower when the water ran cold. "Fine, I'll see him again," she said as she toweled herself off. "My pride be damned. I'll call. He better be prepared to accept Gram as part of our relationship or the deal's off."

After she dressed, Leigh knocked on Gram's door. She found Gram staring at the contents of her closet, at the fine, old dresses hanging in transparent garment bags, boxes of jewelry, and albums of photographs. There was a look of melancholy in her faded eyes.

"You know, darling, the worst thing about being a ghost is that I can't touch my things." Her hand passed through a thin bundle of letters tied in a faded yellow ribbon.

"I've seen you read those dozens of times," Leigh said as she crouched by the wheelchair. "Were those from Jerome?"

Lilly waved her hand carelessly. "Oh, those weren't real. Those were things I conjured to keep my memories alive." She clasped her hands at her breast with a sad smile. "Jerome wasn't much for letters. There were little love notes he left for me in the studio. Not a one of them wasn't riddled with spelling errors. But his heart— his heart was in each and every one of them."

"Why didn't you ask for help?"

Lilly looked up at a single shelf high above. "I don't know. Pride perhaps. I always felt so ashamed about running home over a misunderstanding and then staying when I knew I'd left my heart behind in Los Angeles. I think I could even have forgiven Jerome if he had strayed. I was ashamed of how foolish I was and wanted to keep it a secret. Finally, there was love. I was denied so much of it in my life, I wanted to keep the memory of what little I had, strong and close to my heart. And away from prying eyes and sticky fingers." She laughed; her eyes filled with phantom tears. "Do you know that after my death, my daughter and her husband couldn't enter this room? I made sure of it. I made sure I died in the main foyer. Once they were gone and you were old enough to understand, I told you where the key was hidden."

349

"I remember," Leigh said. "When we first opened the door, the air smelled kind of musty, but I never really thought about it. This room had been off-limits for so long, it never occurred to me to poke around."

"You know this is all yours now, darling. My will has long since been executed. The jewelry is the only thing that might be worth something, so when I'm finally gone, split it between yourself, your mother and sister."

"Gram, I can't bear to talk about this."

Lilly made to pat Leigh's hand but stopped before they touched. "No more of that. I fear my time here is coming to an end. Make no mistake. I want your young man to publish my biography. Let's set the world straight on what really happened. Let me be an object lesson to foolish young lovers, to think twice before abandoning that which they wanted most in the world in a fit of pique."

"Gram—"

"And my papers. I dare say those would be worth something to someone. Give 'em all to your Clark. You have decided to forgive him, haven't you?"

Leigh nodded.

Gram beamed at her. "I'm proud of you. He'll know what to do with them. Let him put them in his book. My diaries, my few letters. They do no one any good there on the shelf." She shrugged. "I dare say, it'll cause a stir to the town fathers to see what my husband and son-in-law were really like, the old buggers. Not that anyone will care anymore. I only wish I could see Roger squirm at the notoriety. It would serve him right." She gave Leigh a distracted smile. "Perhaps I'll have some sort of revenge yet. Who knows? This after-life of mine came with very few instructions."

"I had no idea you were so vengeful," Leigh teased. "Like my mother."

"I was, once upon a time. But I got it beaten out of me," Lilly said sadly. "A bit of posthumous shaming is the best I can hope for. That won't be comfortable for you, Miranda and Sarah, but so be it."

"We'll be proud of all that you lived through, Gram. But what about the trust?"

Lilly shrugged. "The trust was for the house and its furnishings. Though no one could access them at the time, my jewels and letters were left to my granddaughter and her descendants. If anyone on the board makes a fuss, you can override them as the presiding family member."

"Gram, I love you. You know that, don't you? Maybe if we touch again, it'll rejuvenate you like it did a few days ago."

Lilly shook her head, her hand once again reaching for, but not touching, Leigh's cheek. "I thank you for the offer, Lei-Lei mine, but I'm already on borrowed time." She closed her eyes, and a hint of a tear leaked out. "I only wish I could stay long enough to see you wed that tall, handsome man of yours."

"That's getting a bit ahead of things," Leigh said with a nervous laugh. "I mean, Clark and I still have a lot of things to say to one another. And he doesn't know if he's staying at the university."

"Oh, he's staying," Lilly said, her eyes open and shining. "The grant that got him here in the first place— that was my doing."

"What?"

Lilly smiled again, her face solidifying for a moment before fading. "I whispered in the ear of a few of the board members when you weren't around last year. Told 'em to fund a film studies professor."

"You couldn't have known—" Leigh exclaimed.

"Of course not. But it occurred to me that someone of that ilk might find himself— or herself— curious about the family. I suppose it's been in the back of what's left of my mind that I wanted my story to come out. It was a bonus they found Clark to fill the seat. You have every right to tell the board you wish to continue to fund his chair."

351

"Wow. But wouldn't it look funny that the man I love—"

"So, you do love him," Gram said, clasping her hands.

Leigh bowed her head. "I do. And I hope he still loves me. But wouldn't it look funny if the family trust happened to fund his permanent professorship?"

"Oh, I don't know about that. There've been far more nefarious doings in this family to dwell too long on that. In fact, it's all in my diaries. Clark will ferret them out. It doesn't exactly have anything to do with films, but so what? He's proven himself capable. And the two of you met and fell in love quite by accident. Who can argue with that?"

"I can think of plenty of people."

"Well, none of them are worth a fig. You pay them no mind," Gram said. She settled her hands in her lap. "Now, don't you have a call to make? And put on some lipstick, for heavens sakes. You look paler than me. And how many times I have I had to tell you, beige does nothing for you. Put on something red. Or that pretty purple sweater from your mother. That brings out the highlights of your hair."

Leigh rose. "Okay. But I want you with me. I want you to tell Clark what you told me about giving him access to your letters." She grinned as she walked to the door. "So maybe you should change out of that old frock you've been wearing. I want to see you in something pretty. Fluttery, like you wore in those old movies. Goodness, but you were gorgeous back then. I can't believe I sat in that theater a half dozen times and never recognized you on the screen. And you aged so beautifully. Gives me hope I'll do the same." She shook her head."

"Do you think I should?" Gram asked wistfully. "It's been ages since I dressed up for a man."

"Dress yourself up for yourself," Leigh said with a smile. "Here, catch." And she blew her grandmother a kiss. Lilly caught it and pressed it to her cheek before she blew one back to Leigh, who pressed it to her heart.

Great Scot, my head aches. What the hell happened last night?

A naked blond stretched luxuriously before she batted her eyelids at him. *You married me, sugar.*

Jerome scrambled from the bed as nimbly as his sodden brain would allow. *Who the hell are you? You're young enough to be my daughter.* He shuddered, then clutched his pounding head. *No. No. This is all a mirage. Why is it whenever I get drunk, I find myself married the next morning?*

Don't you remember, Mr. Percy? We met last night. At the casino. You said I was the prettiest girl you've seen in years. Said I reminded you of someone. Some Lilly or Izzy or sompin'.

Oh God, I never want to hear you say that name again. I'll give you a thousand bucks if you agree to a divorce by nightfall.

Nope. She reached across the bed with a smile and plucked a piece of paper from the nightstand. *See, I've got a prenup. And we didn't use any protection last night. For all we know, I could be preggers.*

There was a knock at the door. *Mr. Percy, can you come out and give the press a statement?*

With an anguished groan, Jerome fell into a nearby chair. *Shoot me now. Just do it and get it over with.*

Chapter Thirty-Two

Clark

With the mystery solved at last, Clark planned to work on his book as soon as his hangover eased. He tried not to think about the fact Leigh hadn't called him back.

Despite his plan, most of his day was spent at solitaire or watching inane videos online. Jerome had been moodily silent, wafting about the small apartment, apparently at the whim of whatever draft snagged him. Parts faded out of view as if his soul no longer had the glue to keep his ghostly form intact.

The living room had grown dark, lit only by the blue glow of the computer screen when Clark's phone suddenly dinged with Leigh's ringtone. His hands shook as he reached for it, then dropped it with a crunch. A new web of cracks crossed the screen. He picked it up carefully, praying it hadn't finally given up the ghost. With a careful finger, he pressed the on button.

Clark jerked away when he sensed Jerome peering over his shoulder. "Do you mind?'

"What? You have no secrets from me, m'boy. Tell me what she says. My future is at stake here, every bit as much as yours."

"I'd like to at least read it before I share it with you," Clark said through gritted teeth.

"Oh, very well. Don't mind me as I sit here, fading away. Go right ahead, deny me the pleasure of seeing if your lady love, and mine, want to see us—"

"See me. They don't know about you," Clark said as he shook the phone gently when it wouldn't light up. He grit his teeth.

"Is it busted?" Jerome asked, was once again hovering.

"Can you shut up, old man, for two minutes? You're distracting me with your amateur theatrics."

Jerome clutched the place where his heart once beat. "You wound me, son. You know how anxious I am to see my Izzy after all these years. Why, I don't know why I haven't tried to go there on my own—"

"You know that's impossible," Clark said, glancing at Jerome.

Jerome did look much worse for wear. It wasn't simply his presence fading. For the first time Jerome's clothing was less than pristine. His normally bright, white shirt was dingy, and one tail was untucked, his trousers wrinkled. His shoes, when they were visible, had no shine. Even his normally trim mustache looked ragged. "You don't look like you have the strength to float across the room, let alone across town."

354

Jerome hung his head. "I dare say you're right. So, tell me. What does she say? Is she giving you the old heave-ho, or do we have a chance?"

Gingerly, Clark gave the phone a harder shake, then gave a mighty whoop. "She wants to talk. Says to come over tonight."

Jerome looked about himself madly. "A chance. We have a chance. To forgive and forget. After all this time, a courtin' we will go."

"I'm going alone," Clark announced. "You'll only cause trouble."

Jerome slumped. "Clark. M'boy. Son, I implore you—"

"I can't trust you around Leigh."

"It's not your Leigh I'm anxious to see," Jerome growled. "Please. You know what sort of state I'm in. For all we know, I'll have gone pfft by this time tomorrow. Lost my chance. Suffering forever in purgatory, never again to see my lady love." He hung his head. "After all this time, maybe she doesn't want to see me. Or wants to slap my face." He looked up, his expression mournful. "Don't I deserve a chance to let her slug me?"

"I'm afraid seeing you would be such as surprise, you'd kill her," Clark said. "And I have no idea what Leigh's thinking. I couldn't tell a damned thing from her text."

"I hate to break this to you, son, but my Izzy's already dead. As am I. Can't get much deader than dead, you know. As best I can tell. So far, at any rate. I already suffered that fate once," Jerome responded. "It brought me here. With you. For longer than I ever expected. Not that I'm blaming you, of course. You did your damned best, nose to the grindstone and all that. Couldn't have asked for a better partner."

"Jerome..."

The ghost sank to his knees. "Please, m'boy. I promise I'll hang back. I'll stay in the car until you give me the signal. I only want a glimpse of her. Just one. Please. It's been so long."

Clark bit his lip. "You'll behave?"

355

"On my honor,"

"You'll have to do better than that."

"Okay, on your honor. The one I taught you but never practiced myself. Is that okay?"

Clark nodded. "Fine." He picked up his coat and keys. "Come on. Let's go."

When Clark turned at the opened front door to stare at Jerome, the ghost hung back and frowned at Clark. "Surely you don't intend to call on your lady love dressed like that?"

Clark looked down at his sweatpants, ragged tee-shirt, and mismatched socks. He rubbed his chin and realized he hadn't yet shaved his neck, nor was he sure he'd brushed his teeth that morning. Or showered. "Right. Okay. Let me clean up, and you help me figure out what I'll wear."

Jerome tsked as he drifted into Clark's bedroom. "You know, I thought I'd taught you to dress yourself." He heaved a dramatic sigh. "I guess it's a good thing you'll be married to Leigh soon. I hope she doesn't mind delivering sartorial remediation."

"Be nice, or I'll change my mind about bringing you."

"Ha!" Jerome shot back. "This is me being nice. And don't think you won't miss me when I'm gone."

Clark looked at his long-time, transparent companion and knew he'd miss his best friend terribly. And it seemed that day might be sooner than either of them expected. "What makes you think Leigh would marry me?" he asked with a put-upon snort.

"Because she's a smart woman, and she recognizes quality. Which you have in spades, young man. Other than your fashion sense. That, I fear, is dreadful and always shall be."

Thank you for your services, Mr. Reynolds. You're certain this door cannot be broken?

Yes, Ma'am. Best oak door we make. And the lock is steel. This here's the only key. Not even a hurricane'll knock this baby down. The whole house can blow away, and this door'll still be standing a hundred years from now. Only thing that'll get through this baby is a ghost. Ha ha ha.

Chapter Thirty-Three

Leigh

She paced the front hall as she waited for Clark's noisy old sedan. What would they say to one another? Should she apologize right off or wait for him to speak? Was he still angry? Hurt? Or would all be forgiven? She wondered if she'd ever be able to trust him with her heart the way she longed to do.

It had been more than an hour since he'd replied to her text, but as yet, there was no rattle and clang outside her door. Despite the driveway having been plowed after last night's snow, there were bumps and grooves that could shake Clark's old car to pieces. And it was starting to snow again, hard.

"Is he here yet?" Gram asked. She sat in the grand foyer, a fluttery, feminine dress on her thin frame and a lace shawl about her shoulders. Despite the gloom of the formal space, her white hair gleamed, and a smile graced her beloved face. She sat before a flickering sconce that echoed the original elegance of the house.

Leigh turned to look at her cherished Great-grandmother. She stifled a sob at the sight, for despite her glamorous efforts, Gram was more transparent than ever.

"Are you sure you should be here in the cold?" Leigh asked.

"My darling, Lei-Lei. You must realize those blankets and shawls I don are for show. I cannot feel the heat or the cold. Why, but for your modesty, I'd be happy to float about the room buck naked."

Leigh couldn't help her grin. "But you love your pretty frocks. I never understood why you bothered with that wheelchair. It's not like you were entertaining and needed to appear frail."

Gram shrugged. "Habit, I think. And I needed to do something to so Constance would feel needed all these years."

"Where is she?"

"Packing," Gram said with a shrug.

"Packing? What? Where do you think you're going?"

"One can never be too sure," Gram answered. "I needed her out from underfoot. She's been a steady companion all these years, though not much of a conversationalist."

"I never heard her speak a word," Leigh mused. "To be honest, most of the time, I almost forgot she was there."

Gram laughed. "She doesn't mind. Feels it's her penance."

"For what?" Leigh asked.

Gram ignored the question and held a hand to her ear. "Is that him I hear?"

Leigh returned to the door and looked out the side window. Headlights flashed along the beveled glass, making rainbows as Clark's car rounded the drive. She noted the myriad of tiny snowflakes glittering in the wind.

"When he moves in, you'll have him use the port cochere," Gram mused. "Much handier and warmer, too."

"Who says he'll be living here?" Leigh asked.

"Oh, come now, darling. You love him. He loves you. It's the sort of love one feels once in a lifetime. If he doesn't ask you to marry him, you'll have to be the one to ask him to move in. In sin if necessary. I promise, I won't mind." She gave a sly smile. "Though if your great grandfather were hovering, he'd be apoplectic and not be able to do a single thing about it." She gave a merry grin. "Just the thought makes me giddy."

"I'm not certain what Clark and I will be to one another when tonight's through."

"Hush with that talk. You know you love him. And I expect he'll be more than willing to meet you halfway. Now pinch your cheeks. You look paler than me, and we can't have that. That's him at the door if I'm not mistaken."

The doorbell gonged.

Leigh smoothed her hands down her jeans and plucked at her sweater. She swallowed hard before she reached for the door.

Clark stood there. Tall. Solemn. His eyes looked sad and shadowed. His brimmed hat was in one hand, the other sported a bouquet of wilted flowers. Snowflakes whipped about his broad shoulders.

"These are for you," he said as he thrust them at her. "I'm sorry they're so awful, but the gas station was the only place open, and it was either these or withered hot dogs."

Leigh gulped back a surprised laugh. "Come in, Clark."

He stepped forward, but not before glancing back as if to assure himself he'd shut off the headlights. She peered around, but the car was dark as she shut the door. "Is it bad out there? We could have waited 'till morning."

He shook his head. "Not yet, at any rate. No one's out since they're predicting it will get worse. And I wanted to see you. Leigh, there's so much I want to—need to—tell you. About how sorry I am. And other things."

"Ahem," Gram said, and startled, the two turned to look at her. "Good evening, Mr. Conrad," she said formally.

Clark spun to face Lilly. He bowed his head. "Mrs. Sprague."

"After all these years, I believe I prefer to be called Lilly," Gram said with another nod. "Or Gram. Yes, that's my favorite."

359

"You look lovely," Clark told her before he turned to Leigh. "And you. I'm sorry, I should have said that right away. You look so beautiful. You're always beautiful to me."

Leigh took the flowers from his hands. "Should I see if a little water might revive these?"

Clark gave a small laugh. "I'm not sure anything can. Maybe I should have gone for the giant chocolate bar instead."

"These are better for my waistline," Leigh said as she peered into the cellophane cone.

"There's nothing wrong with your waistline," Clark said abruptly. He rubbed his nose and pushed his glasses up. "Uh, sorry. I hope that wasn't too… er… I don't want to say the wrong thing…"

Leigh's cheeks warmed.

Gram cleared her throat again. "I'm glad to see you, young man. I hope the two of you can see past your differences. You're such a fine couple, and I wish the very best for the both of you." She beamed at them. "And for heavens sakes, you two've been lovers. It's hard to step back from that sort of intimacy. I'd suggest you give Leigh a kiss, even if she seems prickly."

Leigh glanced at Clark to see his cheeks a fiery red as he looked at his shoes. She wanted to slip through the marble floor.

A gust of wind hit the door, the sound of icy pellets hitting the glass of the side lights pinged through the echoey foyer, and the moment was lost.

Clark turned his hat in his hands and nodded before he cleared his throat. "I felt terrible last night. I never wanted to hurt you." He turned to Leigh and took her hands in one of his. "I've decided to give up the research. And the book. You mean more to me than it ever has. If I lose my job as a result, so be it. There are other schools where I can teach. I've started looking around for another position. The last thing I ever want to do is to hurt you or bring embarrassment to your family."

"Clark, I—" She stopped and bit her lip. "I overreacted last night. Badly. Gram and I talked. She's— she's okay with your writing the book. And so am I." Leigh turned to her grandmother. "She wants you to go through her papers. Her letters and diaries. No one's ever seen them."

Clark sent a stunned look past Leigh to Gram, who nodded regally.

"I have to discuss it with the trustees, but I think they'll agree," Leigh added.

His eyes gleamed before he shook his head and returned to his study of the floor. "No. I can't. It would be taking advantage."

Lilly cleared her throat. "Young man, I want you to."

He looked at her, hope lighting his eyes. "Are you sure?"

Another gust of wind blew against the house, whistling loudly. Clark looked about himself before focusing on Leigh and Lilly once again.

"I insist," Gram said as she wheeled herself closer. "It's not every young man who doesn't faint at the sight of a ghost. Why, your cousin Maurice—"

Clark looked at Leigh. "You've met Moe?"

She nodded. "Actually, it was Berry and then Moe. And he passed out. But only for a moment."

"She didn't say anything…"

"Berry knows how to keep a confidence," Leigh said.

Clark dropped his head. "I can accept that. And it's not like she's going to beat me to the punch. I mean, she might write a ghost story. A ghostly love story, not a biography." He stood up straighter. "If— I mean when I do this, wouldn't mention anything supernatural. It's too hard to explain, and I beg your pardon Mrs. Sp— I mean, Lil— I mean, Gram, but no one would believe me." He squeezed Leigh's hands. "In fact, I know a bit about…"

Another great gust hit the house, and the lights flickered. Leigh held her breath until they steadied.

361

She squeezed his hands right back. "Thank you. I should have known. It's that Gram hasn't been herself lately, and I was so worried last night about how you'd react. I still can't believe you're taking this so calmly."

Clark took a step back until he lurched into the paneled wall. "Well, there's something I need to tell you, too," he said. "You see, I'm not entirely unfamiliar with ghosts. In fact, I've known one for a number of years. Lived with him, in fact."

Leigh shivered as she wrapped her arms about her middle. "What?"

He blinked hard. "I tried to tell you. So many times. Before I knew what your grandmother is." He sighed. "My roommate. The old man you kept seeing at the movies—"

A gust blew the door open. Leigh cried out in surprise, and Clark hurried to shelter her from the cold air by wrapping his arms about her.

Time slowed as the snowflakes spun across the marble floor and kissed Leigh's cheeks. Her eyes darted across the room. Lilly gasped, and they turned to find a shadowy figure standing at the portal. The bright headlights from the car shone behind him.

He swept the hat from his head and held it in both hands, his feet braced wide against the wind, as his long coat whipped about his legs. After a long breath, he looked up, his eyes focused on one figure in the vast hall. "Izzy?" he asked.

Gram grasped the handles of her chair and slowly came to her feet, blankets and shawls sliding in a heap that disappeared before they hit the floor. Slowly her arms reached out, trembling.

"Tommy. Oh, Tommy," Lilly cried as the house was buffeted once more, and then the lights flickered and went out.

362

How dare you call that woman's name when you're in bed with me.

I'm telling you it was an honest mistake. I haven't seen Isabel in decades.

Don't matter, Jer. You still love her. For all you know, you're in love with a ghost.

He clutched his head in both hands. *You're right. I am. Always shall be. But you knew that when you married me. Did you honestly think that would change with four wives before you?*

You bastard, she cried and chucked her dinner plate at him. *I've got news for you. Someone else around here finds me attractive. If you think that child is yours, Jerry, you've got another think coming, you washed-up has-been.*

Chapter Thirty-Four

Clark

He slammed the front door shut behind Jerome and then hurried back to Leigh. The dark front hall was silent but for the wind howling outside.

Held in the circle of his arms, Clark felt Leigh's shock at the sight of Jerome. He feared she'd stopped breathing until she spoke. "You always did know how to make an entrance," he admonished his ghost.

"Wha— what's going on?" Her voice little more than a breath.

"Jer, you promised you'd stay in the car," Clark said.

In the bowels of the cellar, a generator rumbled to life. A moment later, a lone emergency light shone from the ceiling. Clark's arms reflexively tightened on Leigh, but she would have none of it as she broke free.

Her footsteps echoed as she walked across the marble tiled floor, where she confronted Jerome. He didn't blink as he turned his attention from Lilly to the foe before him.

"Who are you?" Leigh demanded. "Why are you here?"

Jerome turned his hat in his hand, looking from Leigh to Lilly and back again. "I— I—"

Clark stepped forward. "This is—"

"Let him speak for himself," Leigh snapped, her eyes never leaving the ghostly form before her.

Lilly sauntered forward. "His name is Jerome Percy." The years fell from her as her shawls had earlier. There she stood, an elegant, mature woman. "Tommy Judson. Jerome Percy. Washed up movie star. Womanizer. Happy-go-lucky-bastard. Breaker of hearts."

Leigh gasped and stumbled back into Clark's arms as her grandmother came between them.

Silently, they watched the scene play out before them.

Lilly stood before Jerome, seeming taller than her five-foot frame. "Where have you been all these years?"

"I— I—" Jerome looked down, frowning, then up again, his smile a study in fear and bravado. "I've missed you, Buttercup."

Lilly's eyes didn't waver. "Missed me?" In a flash, she slapped him hard. Jerome staggered before he regained his footing. His hand went to his jaw, waggling it, an appreciative light in his eyes.

Leigh flinched in Clark's arms. "I don't understand," she whispered.

"Shhhh," Clark whispered.

"You've got quite an arm there, Izzy. Especially for a ghost. You still mad?"

Lilly's fists went to her hips. "Mad?" she tossed her head. "Just giving you what you deserve."

Jerome nodded, his eyes never leaving the specter before him. "I guess I do." His chest expanded as if he'd taken a deep breath. "I suppose it's too late to say I'm sorry?"

Nose in the air, Lilly asked, "What are you sorry for? That you were caught with that awful tart?"

"Yes, but not in the way you think. I'm sorry I was stupid enough to allow Blanche to create a scene you'd misunderstand. Nothing happened between us. I swear."

Lilly whipped her palm across his cheek a second time. It echoed in the hall. "Which is why you took up with her less than a month after I left." Clark imagined she pulsed with anger. "The fan magazines were filled with it by the time I got home."

Jerome hung his head. "I suppose it wouldn't help if I explained she got me drunk, and I was shocked to see her when I woke up the next morning." He looked up. "She *was* there the night before. But I slept on the sofa. I swear I did. And I wanted to go after you, but your friend Juliet wouldn't tell me where you'd gone." He turned his hat round and round in his hands, finally pinching the crease in the crown. "I sent private eyes all over the country. I was under contract and couldn't leave. I begged the studio to let me go, but they wouldn't release me. Juliet wouldn't talk to the snoops either." He turned his hat one more time. "She thought that's what you wanted."

"But you married Blanche."

Jerome's broad shoulders drooped. "I did. First in a passel of colossal mistakes."

Lilly's shoulders lost some of their starch. "You could have come after you divorced her."

Jerome hung his head. "If the professionals couldn't find you, what chance did I have? I could barely read. Never did much get the hang of it. You know that from the few scribbled love notes I sent before you took off." He gulped. "I was a weak man. I know I was. I convinced myself you were better off without me. Small wonder the studios refused to let me play the lead. I was never hero material."

Lilly stood silent.

"I didn't know where you were, Izzy. I swear I didn't. It tore me up inside, worrying about you all those years. Missing you. Loving you. Knowing I was a fool to ever let you go. I never had a day go by when I didn't question what would've become of us.'" He shuffled his feet. "I wondered if you ever thought of me or if you'd gone on to make a new life for yourself. A part of me hoped you had. Hoped you'd met a fella worthy of you. One who could make you happy. Give you children. Make up for the crazy life we lived back then. I wanted you to have the happily ever after you deserved."

Lilly stood straight as phantom tears glistened as they rolled down her cheeks. "That's not what happened, Tommy."

Jerome stepped closer, tossing his hat into thin air as he dared take hold of her hands. "Tell me, Darling," he bade in a hushed voice.

Clark heard Leigh catch her breath.

"Before I came to you that morning, on the train back from Mexico—" Lilly started. "In the parlor car after dinner, there was a man. He recognized me." She hung her head. "He wanted to talk to a movie star. He bought me a drink. We talked. He bought me another. And then, when the car emptied late that night, he accosted me. He would have raped me had the conductor not come through and helped me."

"Lilly…"

"We made it home the next morning. I went straight to you. To tell you what happened. I wanted your arms around me, to hold me and tell me everything was okay." She looked up, anguish in her eyes. "And I found you with *her*."

"Dear God in heaven, sweetheart." Jerome stepped closer, but Lilly backed away. "I ran home, a dog with her tail between her legs." She sniffed. "Mother wanted me to forget all about it. Forget about you and everything that had happened to me while I was gone. I let her convince me I could forget it all. I never could get

366

to my money. And then I married. To please my mother. To be safe."

"Izzy—"

She looked at their clasped hands. "He was rich and handsome. A widower. He wanted a family. He promised to take care of me." Lilly stole a look at his face. "On paper, it was the perfect storybook ending."

"Buttercup—"

Lilly shook her head. "It wasn't too bad at first. He knew I didn't love him. He'd heard the rumors about us. I never denied it. He knew I was no virgin on our wedding night."

"Sweetheart—" Jerome whispered.

"He said it didn't matter, at first. But later, it made him angry. Said if I delivered a child sooner than nine months after we wed, he'd divorce me. It would have shamed me, not that it was possible. My parents sided with him. Said I was to never mention my time in California again. I was to burn anything I'd brought back with me that would remind my husband of the life I'd lived before."

Clark watched Lilly tremble, felt Leigh quake in his arms.

"I destroyed my things— some of them. Enough that they thought I complied. The rest I hid. I dared not look at them for fear of being discovered. I had to be so careful. The maids were my husband's spies. I discovered there were hidden compartments in my closet, so I stashed my things in there. Your few love notes. My scripts. The gifts you'd given me, pictures, the pressed flowers—"

"Oh, my darling, Izzy." Jerome tried to clasp her to him, but Lilly stood firm.

"He never found them. But Constance did. His secretary. His lover." Lilly looked around to find her companion standing quietly at the end of the hall beside a pile of ghostly suitcases.

"Roger allowed her free reign in the house, and she found my things. She blackmailed me. Made me promise to always take care

367

of her since my husband couldn't be bothered to divorce me and marry her."

Lilly blinked slowly. "After a few years, it no longer mattered. No one remembered I'd once been Isabel Standish or cared if they did. And revealing myself to the world would have made me a curiosity. I couldn't bear the thought of having to feed myself by cashing in on my fleeting fame."

"I would have—" Jerome tried.

Lilly scoffed. "Constance knew all my secrets. And in the end, I knew hers. Including the fact that Roger didn't love her any more than he loved me. She was convenient is all."

Leigh made a sound. Clark wrapped his arms around her, and she quieted, listening still.

"Roger became angry when Constance confronted him on his philandering. He told her if she wanted to be included in his will, she'd have to stay with me, forever. His terms were such that it was not until my true love found me that either of us would be free." She gave a scornful laugh. "I can't believe a self-respecting attorney would write that, but Roger paid and paid well."

"Izzy," Jerome crooned.

"I tried and tried but could not leave. I had no access to money, even to write another letter that was sure to go astray. The only thing he gave me was a child."

She took a deep breath. "There were other babies. Each named Roger Junior. Not a one survived more than a month or two. He wanted a son. He threatened to foist a bastard on Constance and force me to claim it as my own. No one would know. My friends had long stopped calling. I was alone. My parents didn't care, and then they were gone."

She glanced at Constance. The tall, silent ghost, dressed for travel, stood stoically by the valises. "She bore him a son. It didn't survive its first day, and then he was on her again. She miscarried when he forced himself upon her in her sixth month, and it rendered her unable to have another child."

368

By the grand staircase, the tall, silent woman bowed her head.

"It was shortly after that, that he died. I was stuck, without family, other than my daughter, who was the tool of my husband, cruel and uncaring. My parents were gone. My friends had moved on, and I was too bitter to care. My only option was to stay in this house. Then my daughter brought home her husband."

For the first time, Lilly's gaze softened as it went to Leigh, wrapped in Clark's arms, and then she glanced back to Jerome, her eyes misty.

"Every day— every single day of my life after I left you, I regret it. I tried to find a way back, but I was too weak and scared to set off on my own. I grew older. Heard of your marriages and knew you'd forgotten me."

She bowed her head. "And then a miracle occurred. My daughter had a child. There was joy in this house for the first time, ever. Miranda was a sweet girl. She defied her parents by marrying the man she loved. They cut her off. I did what I could for her, bound as I was by age and infirmities. I couldn't get my hands on any money, but I could nag my daughter into helping her child's family. And then I died, regretting until the end that I'd left you, that I didn't stay to fight, and that my few letters to you went unanswered."

She stood still; her eyes closed for a long moment. "I'm not sure how it happened or why, but moments after I died, I came back and wasn't able to leave this house. Little did I expect my husband's edict would follow me unto death. You know how it is, Tommy. No one explains anything to you. One day you're dead, and the next, you're not quite as deceased as you'd expected. Or hoped." Her head bowed. "I'll never know if it was his wish or my weakness that prevented me from leaving. Regardless, Constance had taken ill in caring for me, and she too died and returned in her current form."

Lilly turned now fully to Leigh. "And my great grandbaby, the youngest, by some miracle was able to see me. I wasn't alone

369

anymore. She became my playmate, and I, her confidant. Fate was not kind to her. She lost her father at a young age. It took all my powers to whisper in my daughter's ear while she slept to help provide for her grandchildren. Education at the very least."

"Oh, Gram," Leigh said softly. Clark held her tight, and one hand came up to caress his arm.

Lilly turned to Jerome. "The years passed. And now, by some other miracle, you're here."

As if a springtime breeze swept the room, the last of the years fell from Lilly, and she looked as she had when she was last captured on celluloid, a young, lithe, stunning woman with light hair and gleaming eyes. Jerome shook himself, and he was a young man, clean-shaven and dark-haired, with well-defined lips and rock-like profile, wearing a tuxedo. "My one true love," she whispered.

"Izzy," he said softly. "My Izzy. My Isabel. My Buttercup, I am so sorry. So utterly, contemptibly, completely sorry. I wanted so much…"

"I read your biography—I looked over Leigh's shoulder as she read it."

Jerome bowed his head. "So, you know how much I've always loved you, always mourned the loss of you."

"I do. How I wish things had turned out differently."

They joined hands, clasped between them as they stepped together under the bright light from above. They raised their hands, and he kissed her fingers while she kissed his.

"So, what does it mean that you're here now?" Lilly whispered.

"I don't know, my love, only that I've spent all the days before and since my death searching for you." He kissed the fingers held in his own. "Clark was my only avenue into the world. All I knew, all I desired, was that I spend the rest of eternity making it up to you."

"Tommy—" she whispered.

"Izzy—" he breathed, and then his lips lowered, and he kissed her.

Lilly's arms slid up his lapels until they draped about his neck, and he wrapped her in his arms, slanting his face to meet her in a kiss for the ages. "I forgive you, my dearest love," she said. "Wherever we go next, you are mine."

"Gram, don't leave me," Leigh said under her breath. "Stay, the both of you. Be here, with me, with us."

The lovers broke apart to smile at one another and then turned, cheek to cheek, to smile at their family, their faces wreathed in gratitude and joy. Lilly blew a kiss to Leigh, who caught it and pressed it to her heart. Jerome saluted Clark, placing his other hand upon his chest, his head bowed. Clark nodded, his own smile all he had to respond.

And then the lovers returned their attention to each other and kissed again, until they pressed their cheeks together and faced their audience one last time, eyes focused on the heavens.

With an ominous rumble, the generator gave out, and the circle of light embracing the lovers narrowed and shrank until it flickered out.

With another groan from the basement, they, and the light, were gone.

With the haunting intonation, *'ashes to ashes, dust to dust'* ringing in her ears, Lilly turned a solemn face to her guests. It took every jot of her acting abilities to hide her joy.

So, Lilly, will you stay here now that your husband is gone?

She straightened her thin shoulders, trying to remember who she was speaking to.

I have nowhere else to go. Until the will is read, I have no idea what my circumstances are. For all I know, I'll be tied to this damned house for the rest of my life. And if Roger wrote his will as he threatened, even beyond.

I shall not mourn his loss, she added silently. *Not one single day.*

Chapter Thirty-Five

Leigh

Stunned silence befell the house.

Leigh shivered as the chill in the grand foyer deepened. She stepped away from Clark with her hands outstretched, peering into the dark.

Behind her, Clark flicked on his phone's flashlight and swept the beam around the entrance hall. The two lovers had completely disappeared, and there was nothing left of the bereft and sorrowful Constance. The house echoed as it had never had before. Gusts whipped mournfully around the eaves as if grieving the lost lovers.

Leigh paced within the empty space. Her heart was broken into so many pieces, she wasn't certain she'd ever find them again. "What just happened?" she whispered.

"Leigh—"

"How— why did you bring that— that man here?" Her voice rose with every word as she looked up at him. "Your ghost. Why didn't you tell me?"

He hung his head. "I didn't think you'd believe me."

"I was living with a ghost most of my life," she whispered hoarsely.

"I didn't know."

Leigh nodded and closed her eyes, her ears straining for some sound of laughter from the second floor. All was silent but for the wind.

She wrapped her arms about herself.

"Leigh," he said.

She could barely hear him, a visceral sorrow-- the sound of her own heart beating in her ears drowned out everything. To her utter mortification, she began to weep, huge, ugly, noisy sobs.

From the corner of her eye, she saw his hand reach out to her. "Darling, it was her time. It was their time. We helped them come together—"

Leigh shook her head. "I know that. I should be happy for them, but I didn't know— didn't expect her to leave so suddenly. I thought I'd get to say goodbye. Does that make any sense?"

Covering her mouth, she shook back her shoulders and tried to stop the tears. "I need a moment to process this. Gram only hinted about her lover and barely spoke of her husband. All that sorrow. I never knew this house was filled with so much sadness. I don't know if I can bear to live here anymore." Leigh huddled in on herself, shaking with cold and anguish.

Clark was at her side, arms outstretched. "Leigh, the house is dark. And it's storming. You'll be frozen in minutes. I'm here, and I love you. You aren't alone. You needn't ever be alone again."

She shook her head, aware only that his arms dropped instead of wrapping them around her. "I can't...I don't know what... Clark, I'm not sure..." she looked at him. "And you lost someone too."

373

He nodded. "Jerome and I have been together for ten years. Darling, I tried to tell you so many times but was afraid you'd think me crazy."

"I can't bear this," she replied.

Despite her heartache, she heard Clark sigh. "I'm not going to force you to talk about it tonight. I need to process it too. Tomorrow, when we're both calmer, we can talk."

"Clark, I…" She reached for him, but it was too late. She could hear Clark's footsteps as he crossed the marble foyer. She waited for the door to open and close. Instead, in the distance, she heard him talking. Was it yet another ghost? Did he think she was nuts? Of course not. He knew she wasn't crazy because she saw ghosts. He saw them too. And so did Berry, though she didn't live with one for half of her life.

Moments later, Clark was at her side, her coat and boots in his hands. "You can't stay here. Moe's out plowing and will be until the storm ends. He or his brother will stop by in the morning with an electrician to get the generator running if the power's not back by then. Berry's getting her guest room ready for you. I turned on the faucets to keep the pipes from freezing. It's the best we can do right now."

So, Clark didn't want her to stay with him. She couldn't bear to ask and be turned down.

"Berry has everything you need. The weather is getting worse, so she wants me to get you there as soon as possible. We'll be lucky for my car to make it in this weather."

"We'll take mine," she said, unable to argue. She didn't want to sleep in the silent mausoleum. In the hush, she heard only the unhappy echoes of her own sorrow, compounded by that of Gram's long, lonely life. She wasn't sure she ever wanted to live there again.

"Are you sure?"

She shrugged, unable to care. "It's big. And safe. You can—you can take it home if you don't want to... We'll straighten it out tomorrow. I can send someone over—"

He helped her into her coat silently and steadied her as she slipped on her boots. Leigh couldn't find it in herself to flinch when he buttoned her coat and slipped a hat on her head.

"Where are your keys?"

She pointed limply to a small table by the door, where her purse sat.

Clark jammed his fedora on his own head. She cringed. It was so similar to Jerome's. Clark's ghost. How could she not have known what that man was? How irrational to think Gram was the only ghost in the world. Clearly, she was far more foolish than she'd believed. In all things.

Clark left to get the car. At any other time, she would have smiled, wondering if he'd get it into first gear without instruction. Instead, she felt numb. Moments later, it rounded the driveway, and he got out in the driving snow to help her down the steps and into the warm interior.

"Nothing like a little fear for me to finally master a standard transmission," he muttered.

"Keep it in second gear down the drive. And downshift if you can figure it out when you start to slide," she said quietly.

"Right, downshift," he agreed as he rounded the hood of the car to get in beside her. "Good thing everything else is automatic, or we'd be sunk. Let's hope everyone else is staying off the roads. It's deadly out here tonight."

She sank deeper into her seat. Death wasn't such as bad thing. It would put her out of her misery. But heaven help her if she were to return as a ghost, tied to that house. She stared out the window, mesmerized as snowflakes careened into the windshield no matter which way they turned.

It took a silent hour to drive what would normally take fifteen minutes. There were few cars out, but the roads were lined with

375

deep drifts. Leigh sat quietly in the passenger seat. Her eyes were dry, yet there were sobs welling within that she fought to squash that prevented her from talking or asking him to stay with her. Clark didn't need the distraction. Instead, not a word passed between them.

Berry must have been watching from the kitchen window. She was on her back porch when they pulled into the driveway and came down the stairs to help Leigh out of the car. She shared a meaningful look with Clark. He shook his head. "It's best I go. I'm not sure I'll be much good for Leigh tonight. She's upset with me, as well she should be. I'll call you when I get there," he said, staring out the windshield. Not a word to Leigh. As soon as the kitchen door closed, he pulled out of the drive and slowly made his way down the street.

Through the kitchen window, Leigh watched her car move into the distance. Once the rear lights were no longer visible, she turned to Berry and fell into her friend's arms. A fresh wave of grief swamped her. Why had she let him go? He was suffering too.

"There, there," Berry soothed as she hugged Leigh tight and rubbed her back. "Come and sit. I've poured bourbon. Wine's too good to waste on grief. I thought we needed something that would burn on the way down."

Leigh took the tumbler and upended it, then held it out for another. She hadn't said goodbye to Gram. Nor had she said another word to Clark. Or he to her. "Why did Clark leave?"

With a raised brow, Berry poured another. She set hers down as Leigh disposed of the second the way she had of the first and then shivered from the effects of two quick drinks. With a skeptical eyebrow, Berry moved the bottle out of reach. "He didn't say. I think he's hurting and needs to be alone. My guess is he thinks you hate him right now. Maybe he's hating himself, too. Can I get you something to eat? I'm not going to let you drink anymore on an empty stomach."

376

Leigh reached for the bottle but missed. Berry rose and took the bourbon with her as she went to the fridge. "Cold roasted chicken coming right up. And then, we talk."

Mr. Finch, it's been brought to my attention that I'm not getting any younger. I want you to take what money I have left and place it in a trust. Besides your modest fee, of course, I want a monthly stipend to pay my rent, the occasional martini, and ultimately to bury me. I've got a plot already bought and paid for. All I need for you to do is to create a certain amount of hoopla when I'm laid to rest. You know, press release, bring mourners in, etc. I've had my obituary written. It's there in the file.

I know it's been decades, but somewhere, somehow, I know my Izzy is out there. When I'm gone, if she can be found, I want her to have this money. Invest it well. I want it to be a goodly amount as I plan to live to a hundred and want her later years to be comfortable. And if she's gone, then I want the whole of it to go to whoever solves the mystery of her disappearance.

And put in there that all my worldly possessions go to the university. Heard they're building a fancy new building to study movies. Boy howdy, imagine that. But let it be a surprise. Don't want them starting to nag me before I'm gone to get a hold of my stuff. Can't bear the thought of anyone looking through it while I'm still around.

When they find her, tell her, tell my Izzy that she's the only woman I ever loved. And that I'm sorry I broke her heart. Tell her mine was broken too. Tell her that for me, will you?

Chapter Thirty-Six

Clark

He slumped against his apartment door. The ride from Berry's had been harrowing. He'd had to detour past blocked streets and once nearly hit a lone pedestrian walking along the road. He'd called Berry from the elevator to let her know he'd made it. He

378

hoped she would convey the message to Leigh. He hoped even more that Leigh would care, and not only that her car was safely parked in his lot. All Berry would say about Leigh was that she'd had a drink and was huddled by the fire in the family room.

Driving the expensive car had been traumatic. After Leigh lost her beloved Gram, the last thing he wanted was to abandon her car to the mercies of the blizzard. There was little chance she'd forgotten tonight's fiasco or the role he'd played in it, but he'd hoped at least she'd be on speaking terms with him once the first wave of sorrow had passed. What if he'd said no to Jerome's accompanying him? What if they'd brought the two old lovers together carefully? But how could they? Clark bore the guilt of not telling Leigh about Jerry. He should have told her as soon as he found out about Lilly.

Clark forced himself upright. He looked down at the puddle beneath his feet as he carefully peeled off his wet gloves, then his coat, taking care to not rip the lining further. He kicked off his boots and managed to step in the cold puddle. He stumbled into the room, still wearing his dripping hat.

With a weary sigh, he took it from his head and flung it across the room, half expecting it to disappear the way Jerome's always had. No such luck. It hit a lamp, and the two crashed to the floor, the bang and tinkle making him droop further.

"Crap."

Clark sat, one foot wet and the other dry, then leaned back, curving his spine to miss the damned coil that always got him no matter how he twisted. Maybe it was time to get rid of the damned chair. Clark closed his eyes and imagined Jerome looking down at him with a sigh and shake of his head. "You'll never be suave, m'boy. But you're an original." He could almost hear the wry humor in his friend's voice. But when Clark opened his eyes, he was alone.

"You damned rascal," Clark whispered to the empty room. "Always breaking the rules. Always had to go your own way, didn't you, Jerry?" He pursed his lips. "But you got the girl in the end. I have to hand it to you—well done. Can't say I'm mad. I admire the hell out of your tenacity. And it paid off better than you ever expected, didn't it, old man? Your last scene sure was a doozy."

He sat forward, pushing his glasses to the top of his head, and rubbed the heels of his hands against his eyes. "I didn't expect it to be so— so sudden." With a half-gulped sigh, Clark sat back. "I kind of thought you'd go gradually. Find out what happened to your Izzy one day, fade into the sunset the next." He gave a hoarse laugh. "I didn't know I'd actually find her for you. You lucky dog. You got your girl, but it looks like I might've lost mine." He sighed. "I don't have a clue what Leigh's thinking, but she didn't say a peep when I left her. I wish she had. I wish for a lot of things that maybe aren't meant to be."

Clark wrenched the cold, wet sock from his foot. "So, what's next?" he asked the empty room.

He looked to the corner where he had Jerome's top hat and cane propped on a table. He smiled, thinking about how he'd smuggled them out of the library years before. To think he never knew the flesh and blood man, only his shade. It was remarkable. Or was it all a dream?

He straightened the papers on his desk. Lilly had promised access to her papers. Would Leigh honor that? He had enough evidence to make a solid case for having solved the mystery without them, but it would be a thin volume. Anything Leigh contributed would solidify that. And it was an easy guess to think he'd be granted tenure after another year or so. But did he still want it? Better to head elsewhere. Somewhere he wouldn't run into Leigh by accident. Not unless she wanted to, and he had no idea what she wanted, only that she didn't want his comfort that night and didn't seem able to offer him any.

A gust whistled around his building, and he stared into the darkness, imagining Jerome would make one final appearance.

Just one. It would be like him to have to have the last word. And the one thing Clark needed at that moment was one word of advice and encouragement.

But all he heard was the moaning of the wind. Because wherever he'd gone, Jerome was not going to leave his lady love to fix things for Clark. He was finally going to have to figure out how to do that on his own, and he hadn't a clue how.

Two days after the big storm, Clark's car was returned to him. The same driver picked Leigh's up and drove off with a few words, none of them telling.

Leigh had not called or texted. She hadn't returned his attempts to reach out to her. The texts went unanswered, and each time he called, it went straight to voicemail. He'd left one, every time, but she hadn't returned a one.

The following Monday, while school was still on break, the department admin called Clark in a panic. A half dozen boxes had been delivered to his office, and she didn't know what to do with them.

Clark rushed to the administrative building and found his small office blocked by the crates. He opened the sealed envelope on the box nearest him.

The Sprague Family Trust (The Trust) has agreed to loan the following materials (packing list enclosed) to Professor Clark Conrad. All materials may be photographed, scanned, and cataloged, but the originals must be returned to The Trust in the period of four months upon receipt. No materials can be given away or images distributed other than as part of the in-progress monograph about Isabel Standish/Lilly Manning Sprague without prior permission from The Trust.

It was signed by a Trustee and included a list of the contents as well as return instructions. His heart sank. There didn't appear to be anything from Leigh personally.

Clark opened the box closest to him and found it carefully packed with what appeared to be diaries and bundles of letters tied in ribbons.

"Good God!" he cried. "Brenda, do we have any grad students around? I need help sorting through all this. I'll pay them out of my own pocket if I have to."

The admin blinked hard. "Let me see what I can do, Professor. Does this— does this have to do with your research? Did you solve the mystery?"

Clark nodded. "Yes. And a very generous… ah… donor has aided me in a way I never expected." He turned to the woman. "I don't imagine you have any time to help me, do you?"

She grinned. "Given that everyone is away until the middle of January, I do. And if this means you'll share what you found with me, I'm all in."

His heart felt lighter than it had in days. "As long as you swear you won't breathe a word to anyone—"

Hands on hips, she looked at him over the rims of her half glasses. "Professor, you insult me."

"Well, what are you waiting for? Let's get these into the conference room. There's a scanner there, right? I need to devise a strategy to catalog and label these, and we'll get started. But first, I need to call Dr. Davis. And my agent."

"Wait, I almost forgot. Something else came for you last week." She handed him a thick manilla envelope.

Clark glanced at it. The return address was from California, the Estate of Delores Percy-Grover, Jerome's fourth wife. He carefully opened the packet and pulled out a pile of photocopied pages. He scanned the cover letter. "Oh my god," he whispered. "This says— this says there's a something from a private eye from back in the day. It's the missing report. The PI had found Isabel,

382

and Jerome's wife hid it from him. Do you know what this means?" He looked up to find the woman shaking her head.

"No, what?"

"It means there's corroborating evidence from two different sources about Isabel's true name and fate."

"Congratulations, Dr. Conrad. Now, let me get started. I have a box of archival gloves around here somewhere…" She bustled away. Clark closed his eyes and whispered a word of thanks. One to Jerome. Another to Lilly, and the last, most fervent to Leigh, for being a woman of her word.

He added one more—that perhaps there was hope for something more as well.

Padre, thanks for staying with me. I know I don't have much time left.

Rest my son. No need to speak. I'll stay with you.

I got one thing to ask.

Certainly, my son.

That fancy plot: have my guy sell it and add the money to Izzy's pot. All I need is a small headstone. Have 'em stick my ashes in a small urn. I want Izzy to have 'em. She can flush 'em if she wants. Toss 'em in the ocean or plant a tree. Want 'er to know she's been the keeper of my heart. Can't rest until I know she's okay.

Yes, certainly, Mr. Percy. Jerome? Jerome? Good heavens, he's gone. Let me go get the nurse.

Jerome blinked as he floated upward. The pain was gone, and he felt better than he had in years. He looked around in curiosity. Where had he fallen asleep this time? Hopefully, there wasn't a sixth Mrs. Percy lying in wait. *Whoa, Nelly. What the heck? Is that me lying there? Jeepers, I look like hell. Wait a minute. Holy smokes, where are they taking me? I'd better get a move on to find out what the heck's going on. Somebody around here must be able to tell me what's gonna happen next.*

Chapter Thirty-Seven

Clark

"Larry, for the last time, I'm wearing the bow tie."

"You look like a geeky professor," his brother said with something close to a sneer. In other words, nothing had changed since they were boys.

Clark shrugged and went back to work on the paisley silk. "I *am* a geeky professor," he said. "Besides, it's kind of my thing. I don't remember how to knot a regular tie."

"It looks contrived," Larry said.

Clark caught his younger brother's gaze in the scratched mirror over the bathroom vanity as Larry leaned against the door jamb. Two months gone, and Clark still missed Jerome, especially at times when he was getting ready for an event. It was nice having someone to talk to while he got ready, even if it was his derisive next-in-line brother who was in town for an interview in the university's linguistics department. The thought of having family nearby was welcome. He smiled at the thought of introducing Larry to Berry to see what match-making efforts she'd put out on his younger brother's behalf.

Larry cleared his throat, awaiting a reply.

Clark smiled. "It's supposed to be contrived. It makes me memorable." Like the way Leigh used to tug on it to get him to follow where she led, not that she had to work at that so hard. "Nothing wrong with trying to stand out, you know. Especially when you're looking to impress your prospective department head like you should be doing."

It was Larry's turn to shrug. "I'm thinking my dissertation and personal charm should do the trick."

"There's a good chance you'll meet some professors tonight. I've been drawing quite a crowd at the film series. I'll introduce you if you'd like so you can size them up before your meeting on Monday." He turned off the light and passed his brother as he headed into the hall. He eyed Larry's dark brown corduroys, scuffed loafers, and faded oxford shirt with the worn elbows, and "You look like you're still a grad student. Why not put on my sweater and hide that stain on the front of your shirt."

Larry looked down and swore softly. "Crap. You'd think by now I'd know how to eat a taco and not spill on myself."

Clark laughed as he scooped his keys off the small table by the door. He tossed them to his brother. "You drive. It's about time you learned to drive a standard. And don't strip my clutch. It was just rebuilt," after he stripped it himself, learning how to drive his

385

brand-new used car the month before. "Just in case you need to drive yourself home tonight."

Right, he thought to himself. *As if Leigh will finally show up, forgive me, and invite me home with her. Like that will happen.*

I hope.

Leigh

She stepped out of her big, silent house that winter evening. She'd been working all day, not looking out the window until darkness had fallen. Now on her back steps, she found the nighttime air held a hint of spring as sometimes happened during a February thaw. She could almost imagine the scent of lilacs and freshly cut grass, though those were still months away.

While getting ready, Leigh indulged in a single spritz of Gram's favorite perfume. She wrapped the indigo scarf Gram always exhorted her to wear around her neck and wore a touch of makeup. It's what Gram would have wanted. She could almost hear that dear voice still in her mind, an echo really. She clasped the memory into her heart and carried on.

Leigh drove to the university, watching the time carefully. There was a film she wanted very much to see, but she didn't want to run into Clark. Her plan was to slip into the theater after the lights were lowered and exit before they came up. He was showing a rare copy of Gram's last movie, and nothing was going to stop her from seeing it.

The past two months had been difficult. The merger had meant many changes. Her staff was larger and more scattered than ever before, and she was traveling around the country every other week to ensure that the transition ran smoothly, as well as attending as many girl-focused STEM conferences as she could fit in. The days had been long. She worked most nights and weekends and knew she needed a short break. She hoped the months to come would ease up. It helped to be busy, to keep her mind off Clark and what

386

happened. And what didn't. He'd ignored her texts and hadn't returned a single phone call.

Leigh arrived at the school and hurried across campus, looking left and right in the hopes of finding a fedora-wearing shadow accompanied by a woman in a cloche hat. Alas, there were none.

She bought her ticket and slipped into the theater. She found a seat in the middle of a back aisle as Clark gave his pre-screening overview. She looked around to see if Jerome happened to be sitting with the fair Isabel Standish by his side, but there was no one other than a few older men in the front who turned to her and nodded before turning their attention to the stage.

Leigh stared at Clark. He looked much the same, though he smiled less than she remembered. He looked winter-pale and thin.

It had been a monumental effort to pack up Gram's letters and other papers. She'd wanted to pour over every one of them but knew he needed them more. Each silk-ribbon wrapped bundle had held faint hints of Gram's scent. Leigh had told her mother and sister what Clark discovered, and they had been all for letting Clark have the papers, with no objections to telling the world the Lilly Sprague/Isabel Standish story and letting the old girl have one last day in the spotlight. The board didn't seem interested, so Leigh had packed them all with care and a sigh, then watched as they were carted out of the house. She was glad to leave on a week-long business trip after that, for the house seemed emptier than ever.

Clark carried himself well, she thought. He stood comfortably on stage, holding a mic, and dressed as he ever was in a tweed jacket with leather elbow patches and pressed slacks, though his shoes looked like they needed a shine, and his hair was longer than she'd seen it. She smiled at his slightly crooked bow tie. Oh, how she used to love to tweak it into place. Her fingers twitched, but that was but a memory. He hadn't sent a note nor called or texted her to thank her for the papers. His department secretary sent a thank-you note to the board, which they'd given her. It held all the right words of sincere gratitude but was impersonal. There was nothing just for her. Apparently, he hadn't seen her note, or hadn't cared about it. She thought of the first text she'd sent to him the day after the blizzard, the one he'd never responded to. Given the state of his phone, she'd sent ten more in the days that followed, but those too were ignored. Her heart heavy, she'd finally given up.

The spotlight dimmed, and Clark walked off stage. Her eyes strained to see if he would join someone in the audience, but instead of heading to a seat, he went backstage. She settled in and waited for the movie to begin.

Clark

After introducing the film, Clark headed for the wings. It was week six of the spring semester. Six films. Each time he scanned the audience for Leigh, and each time he was disappointed. He knew it was crazy. She hadn't answered his texts or calls. He had to start believing it was over, but each week he thought maybe that night would be different.

All the joy had gone out of the film series when they'd broken up. Seeing Jerome on the silver screen only brought sorrow. He missed his friend more than he thought possible. It wasn't lost on him that, unlike the mystery that kept Jerome and Izzy apart, he and Leigh knowingly resided in the same city. Their great love affair was doomed—probably even into the hereafter. Why hadn't the two of them learned from Izzy and Jerome not to let the small stuff destroy the love of a lifetime?

Yet this particular time, he'd hoped she would come. It had taken a huge number of promised favors to get a copy of Isabel's last movie. It would be the only time in the entire series he was showing a full-length feature that didn't contain a single frame of Jerome Percy. But if that was what it took to draw Leigh out, he would do it and be happy about it, too.

But it was apparently all for naught.

Still, the theater felt different. Maybe it was the unusual spring-like air creeping through a cracked-open door, or perhaps he was starting to emerge from the funk he'd been in since the start of the new year. He felt the urge to scan the audience one more time, but it would have been fruitless in the dark.

Anticipating the familiar disappointment, he stood on the side of the theater and looked out as the Keystone Kop short played. The bright beam from the projection room gave him a hint of an old thrill as the dust motes waltzed and pirouetted within. Above the recorded music, he imagined he could hear the tick-tick-ticking of the reels as they spun, feeding film out and taking up the slack.

The light reflected off the screen allowed him to see faces in the first few rows as they reacted to the images on screen. He narrowed his eyes, for there were a few older gentlemen who appeared to be— wait, were they? Was the light shining through them?

He took a step closer, and one of them turned to him and winked. No, it wasn't Jerome, but one of his card buddies. Great Scott, what was going on?

The old ghost beckoned, and Clark strode forward as if in a dream. He leaned closer to the phantom. "Not sure if you noticed, but you've got quite an audience tonight, sonny boy."

"I'd have preferred paying customers," Clark replied.

The ghost's eyes crinkled in laughter. "Well, we're not all here on your dime. There happens to be a very pretty chickadee who came in late, you know. The kind who used cash-money to buy her ticket."

Clark's head bobbed up. "What?"

The ghost laughed again. "Way in the back. Want me to get the fellas to corral her after the show? Damn, but it's good to see the old films again."

"I don't need your help—"

389

"That's not what Jerry said. He told us to keep an eye on you, but time sorta got away from us, didn't it, boys?"

The men in the row nodded, their eyes riveted to the screen.

"I don't—" Clark's eyes scanned the theater until he saw her. Leigh sat in the last row, and her gaze was on him every bit as much as his was on her, "—need your help."

The apparition nodded with a smirk. "Jer said you were an all-right sort of fella, but kinda shy 'n awkward with the ladies. Maybe you got it all under control. Don't make no difference to me. But I happen to have a mystery for you to solve, now that you've fixed things for old Jer."

Clark did a double take. "What? I don't even know who you are."

The man frowned. "I guess I shoulda expected that. Name's Mack. I did a bunch of work in the movies back then. Never a big star like ole' Jer, of course. Used t' open his fan mail, I did."

"What's your mystery?" Clark whispered.

"I wanna know what happened to my money. Studio stiffed me and a bunch of other guys."

Clark scrubbed his face with his hands. "I— uh, I'm not an expert at financial forensics, especially after so much time." He stifled his smile. "And I'm not sure what you'd do with the money if I were able to find it."

Mack shrugged. "You've got a point. Still, wish I knew what happened to it. Never was much good with figures. Anyway, if you can't do the money, maybe you could figure out how to expose the guy who killed me when I went looking for it?"

Clark's mouth dropped open. He pulled a small pad out of his pocket along with a pen "Who did you say you were again?"

"Maybe I'll drop by one of these days, and we can talk, huh? And if you need help with the dame, we'll be around if you do. Just say the word. Now, get outta my way. I want to see that Mable Normand. She sure was a beaut."

Clark stood straight, his eyes on Leigh. She'd never looked more beautiful in all the months he'd known her. And sitting beside her seemed to be a bevy of ghostly lovelies. Leigh seemed unaware of her neighbors' natural state as they tittered and pointed surreptitiously at her.

"Jerome, you sly dog," he muttered to himself and once again planted his backside against the wall where he could watch Leigh until the films were over. What he'd do then was anyone's guess.

Leigh

Coming out of a daze after watching Gram on the screen, Leigh realized the credits were rolling. She gathered her things and stood, wanting to make a fast break before the lights came up. Unfortunately, the women in her aisle seemed to be unnaturally obtuse about allowing anyone to exit. They kept turning their backs to chatter with their friends if she tried to head out left or right, and she finally resigned herself to sitting, keeping her head down so no one would see her face.

That's when the lights came up, and the ladies all settled down with their coats on their laps, staring at Clark as if they hadn't seen a handsome man in years. Which is when Leigh noticed that the women to her right and her left were all wearing some sort of old-fashioned hats, many with short net veils. And their stockings all had seams. "What the hell—" she whispered. The woman on her left turned as if to shush her but winked instead, with her finger at her lips. "That Isabel was a favorite of ours. Don't you want to know what that handsome young man is going to say?"

"Actually, I need to—"

But the woman had turned. And that was when Leigh noticed that she could see right through her companion. "Oh no, you're not—"

The ghost gave another wink. "You're the spitting image of your Granny, my dear. Such a lovely thing she was. We missed her so much after she left. I'm Juliet, by the way. We all hitched a ride with the film canister," she said before she turned to face the stage.

And that was when Leigh noticed Clark looking right at her. Her heart began to pound.

As he lifted the mic to his lips, her hands tightened on the straps of her purse. "Oh god," she whispered and closed her eyes.

"Ladies and Gentlemen, persons of all persuasions present, past, and future, thank you for your kind attention tonight."

"He knows," she muttered.

"As those of you who have been regulars of this film series might have noticed, tonight's feature was a departure, but it is also a celebration of sorts. While my focus for the better part of the past decade has been on the actor Jerome Percy, I've had a secondary motive—a mystery I promised to solve. I've mentioned it a time or two from this stage, and that was finding what became of Jerome Percy's long-lost love, Isabel Standish."

He paused and looked down as if composing his thoughts.

"I am happy to report that several months ago, with the help of some individuals who shall remain nameless, I was able to solve that hundred-year-old mystery."

A titter ran through the audience, and Leigh felt her skin begin to tingle.

"I won't regale you with all the details here," Clark went on to say. "You'll need to buy my book for that. And before you do that, I'll have to finish writing it, of course."

The audience laughed, and Leigh felt herself smile.

"—but suffice to say there is a distinctly local flavor to the story, which was filled with all manner of wonderful and unexpected coincidences. Along the way, I made the acquaintance of several memorable historical characters—through their papers, of course." He gave a bright smile.

"I only bring this up because one of Isabel's decedents happens to be sitting in this theater tonight. It was through her generosity I was able to finally prove my theory, and though she probably wishes I wouldn't, I would like to publicly thank her tonight. Leigh Mason, would you please stand up?" He tucked the microphone under his arm and began to applaud, as did the rest of the audience remaining, all turning to look at her.

Leigh felt her face light up like a firecracker. She stood, wobbling a bit, then gave a short wave and sat. "I'm going to kill him," she said under her breath. Beside her, Juliet laughed in delight.

She didn't hear much after that. There were a few questions about his research that Clark gently sidestepped. Others had to do with the remainder of the film series and if he'd be running it again the following school year. That had Leigh's ears perking up.

"Dean Davis and I have been discussing what I'll be doing come September." He gave a small shrug. "We haven't come to any decisions, but I can say that an offer has been made, and I'm considering it."

Her heart started beating wildly. Clark would still be there in the fall?

She felt his gaze on her. "I, uh, have a few personal matters I need to see to before I make a decision, but I can tell you that if I'm here, I expect to resume this classic film series. In fact, the student association and I have already started talking about what films they'd like to show."

He took a few more questions as Leigh sat, fixed to her seat. "I want to thank you again for supporting this film series. We have several more in the coming months, and I hope to see you there. Thank you, all once more, and good night." He clicked off the mic and handed it to a student before he jumped off the stage and ran up the aisle to Leigh.

The ghosts tittered around her. "You have to talk to him," and "Your Gram would have wanted it that way." "Don't disappoint her," and "The two of you make a striking pair. Just like Isabel and Jerome used to."

She looked at them and then at Clark standing there, looking hopeful and terrified. "I guess I owe it to Gram, don't I?" she said to herself as they finally allowed her to exit.

"Hi," Clark said.

"Hi," Leigh returned. "It's, uh, good to see you."

"You look well. I was wondering— since you're here if maybe we can go for coffee or something? If you don't have any place you need to be."

Leigh shook her head. "Nowhere I need to be. Just a big empty house."

Clark nodded. "Me too. Not so big. Just as empty." He scuffed a foot. "Mind if we go off campus?" He looked over his shoulder where a contingent of male ghosts were eyeing the female ghosts at Leigh's back. "Since texts and phone calls don't seem to be your favorite way to communicate, I, uh, was hoping we might have a chance to talk. Just the two of us."

"What?"

Clark pushed his glasses up his nose. "I texted you. Kind of a lot." He shoved his hands in his pockets. "Since you didn't respond, I felt I would be imposing if I kept trying."

"Clark, I never got your texts." She tried to swallow, but her throat was dry. "You didn't get mine either?"

He shook his head slowly. "You texted? My old phone… I never got it fixed." He looked chagrinned. "Berry never said a word."

Leigh frowned. "She wanted to. I asked her not to get involved. I didn't want to seem desperate."

He sighed. "And I avoided her too. For the same reason."

Leigh gave a small laugh. "Knowing Berry, that must have killed her to keep her nose out of our business."

They looked at each other, unhappy surprise on each of their faces. "I never knew…" she started.

"…just like Jerome and Lilly getting their signals crossed."

"I put a letter in a box with Gram's things…"

394

Clark hung his head. "I'll bet it's one a grad student unpacked. They probably scanned it along with everything else. I haven't had a chance to look at every image yet."

"Oh, Clark…"

He winged out an elbow. "It seems like we have a lot of catching up to do." He looked over his shoulder as she did hers. "Without an audience."

There was some grumbling, but Leigh took his elbow. "I'd like that."

"Let me text my brother. He's in town. I don't want him to wait on me. I can get a ride home later…"

"Or I can drive you," she said too quickly, then blinked at him as she felt her face heat up. "Or not," she said with a smile as she saw one returned in his eyes.

"I rather like the 'or not' option," Clark said as he took her hand in his and entwined their fingers. "I like that option most of all."

He leaned over and kissed her, his palm to her cheek. "I'm not going to apologize for that," he said. "For many other things, but not that." And then he kissed her again, and once more for good measure.

"I'm not going to ask you to," she said breathlessly. "Would you kiss me once more?"

His gaze met hers. "Leigh, my love, as soon as we get a few things straightened out, I want to kiss you for the rest of our lives. If you'd let me."

She squeezed his hand. "I like the sound of that, Clark. I like the sound of that so very much."

Dear Diary,

I cannot believe after all these years, I still write those words every day. I laugh at myself, but habit is a hard thing to break.

My great-granddaughters are staying in the house while their mother is away. My, how they brighten things up. The youngest, Lei Lei misses her mother something fierce. She asked me to bake cookies with her. Me— at my age. Why, I've rarely entered the kitchen, let alone used an oven.

She agreed to story time instead. We read book after book until my old eyes burned. Then she turned on the television. Who should be there in some old show but Tommy. My Tommy. Goodness, but it was a shock to see him, how old he was, but still so handsome. The announcer came on and said something about a retrospective of his work due to the anniversary of his death. Alas, we're never again to meet in this lifetime. I wish I believed in the afterlife so that we could once again look into each other's eyes. I fear it won't be long.

I could only bear that glimpse of him before I too fade from this earth. I both dread and look forward to what comes next. I wish... oh how I wish... but what are the wishes of an old woman such as me?

At least I have Lei-Lei and her sister to entertain me. It is so good to hear children laugh in this house after all these years.

It grows late, and I'm so very tired...

Chapter Thirty-Eight

Fifteen months later...

Clark

He stared at the screen after he read the last diary entry in Lilly's hand. Her writing was spidery and shaky from her final illness. He wished she'd known she'd be back until her unfinished business was resolved.

He closed the cover of his laptop. The original documents and photographs were back at the Sprague mansion where they belonged. He'd be moving in, in a week and would have regular access to them, if he wanted it.

Leigh'd had her staff do a bit of creative computer work in bringing images of Isabel and Jerome together in preparation for their big day. It was good having a technical wizard around when you needed one.

He rubbed his hands and pushed the glasses up his nose. Now wasn't the right time to be reading or researching, but he had a few minutes to kill before Moe picked him up to bring him to the Sprague House, all done up as a fancy wedding venue. He eyed the top hat and cane sitting in the corner and made the rash decision that today was the day to take them out for a spin.

Clark walked to the table and carefully lifted the hat off its stand. He blew a speck of dust from it and went to the hall mirror to try it on, setting it at a jaunty angle. "Yes," he whispered to himself. "Jerome would appreciate the gesture."

Arm in arm, they posed for the photographer, just as Jerome and Isabel had done in the photo that had been restored from the two halves they'd found. A projected image of the original was behind them.

Moments later, Clark held his wife in his arms as they danced to the waltz Jerome told him had played on the set when he and Izzy danced in *Sin* all those years ago. They whirled before a screen where a loop of those very same personages, dancing together and gazing into each other's eyes, much as Leigh was gazing into his.

"How did I get to be so lucky?" he asked before taking a kiss from her on the dance floor.

"It's not like I was going to let you get away," she said with a smile. "I love you, husband."

He kissed her again. "And I love you, my dear wife."

They glanced behind them to see if they were still in synch with the dancers from over one hundred years before, just as they had practiced at the dance studio.

To Clark's utter amazement, rather than repeat the same loop once more, the images on the screen stopped dancing before their final step, and wearing broad smiles, grasped champagne glasses from a passing waiter, holding them up to the camera.

That wasn't part of the original movie.

"Leigh," he whispered. "Do you see what I'm seeing?"

She stood beside him, dumbstruck as her Great-grandmother mouthed a toast to the newlyweds, grainy footage notwithstanding. "Oh, my goodness," she breathed. "How— did you have your students do that?"

Clark shrugged, dumbfounded. "I thought it was your CGI department."

"No, it's not," she whispered.

"Then it's somehow got to be Jerry and Isabel's doing, but how, I have no idea. I only hope someone's captured that on their phones. I'm going to want to see that over and over again. Every year for our anniversary, for as long as we both shall live."

Leigh grabbed two champagne glasses. Handing one to Clark, they lifted their own to the two images before them. The four smiled at one another, Isabel and Jerome arm in arm as Jerome gave a jaunty wink. Isabel kissed her hand and blew it at Leigh, who caught it and pressed it to her cheek as tears coursed down her smiling cheeks. Jerry saluted Clark, who pressed a hand to his heart.

A moment later, the placard "AND THEY LIVED HAPPILY EVER AFTER..." blinked onto the screen before fading out. Their guests all applauded…

Epilogue

"Leigh, sweetie, I think I'm done," Clark called from the den. "Would you mind reading the ending for me?"

She came in from her home office and stood behind his chair, her hands on his shoulders. "Are you sure?"

Clark nodded. "Yeah. If I look at it once more, I think I'll go crazy."

She laughed and pulled on his arm. "Let me sit then."

Clark rose, kissed her cheek, and went to pace as she read.

...And in conclusion, what is the price of a misunderstanding? Sometimes, it would seem, more than one can afford to pay.

In the case of Jerome Percy and Isabel Standish, it was stardom, a future, adoration of fans the world over, reputation, and in the end, the demise of happiness.

As postulated in my first book, Jerome Percy found fame, a certain amount of fortune, but he never found peace and certainly never achieved happiness, but he did retain his freedom, such as it was.

Isabel Standish found security, privilege, and creature comforts, but lost, almost for the rest of her life, any joy. She certainly never again found love. She gave up all her fame, her own fortune, and the adulation of strangers because of a misunderstanding. When she left Hollywood, she cried herself to sleep after reading months-old gossip magazines but never learned of Jerome's efforts to find her, nor the trials and travails of his equally broken heart.

Poor Isabel, once again known as Lilly, eventually also gave up on friendships, society, the company of people other than her husband's bitter mistress.

She hid in plain sight the rest of her life, in the small city in which she was born, bearing a daughter and three sons for a man who coveted her beauty and her charm, but never loved the charming and vivacious woman she'd once been. Isabel contented herself in raising her daughter and later found delight in her granddaughter—and briefly her great-granddaughters. She lived a long, lonely life within a grand home, wanting for nothing but a full heart.

If one were of a fanciful nature, one might hope, wish for in fact, that through research and these words, the spirits of these two luminaries may, at last, have found one another on some ghostly plain, and that they might spend their happily ever after in the hereafter as they were not able to do so in life.

On a more personal note, were it not for the spirits of these two fascinating beings, I would never have found the one true love of my life, the great-granddaughter of the inimitable Lilly Manning-Sprague. I thank fortune and coincidence not only that we found each other, but that our love allowed me to solve the mystery once and for all.

To the spirits of Jerome and Isabel: we wish you well forevermore.

Leigh turned to Clark. "That's so sweet. They would have loved it. I love it." She picked up the framed image of Jerome and Lilly with their champagne glasses from the wedding. "It seems like we all have our happily ever afters, now."

Clark hugged her from behind. "I know I've found my heart's desire, and despite all the pain, I'm glad we helped them find theirs, at long last."

"Hear, hear," Leigh agreed and set down the picture. She rose and went into her husband's open arms. Neither of them saw Jerome's jaunty wink as he, too, kissed the woman he loved.

The End

Dream a Little Dream of Me at One-Nineteen Chestnut Street

A 'Reminiscence' by Mrs. Florence Electra McGillicuddy,

F.Gm, O.o.C., L.VI, Emeritus

As told to Solange DewBerry

Prologue

Mami had already unbraided her hair and brushed it out, running her hands through the dark curls. "Let's take off your pretty new party dress, *bebe*, and get you ready for bed."

"Mami, can I wear it again tomorrow? You can take my picture in it at the fountain."

"We just did that today, you silly goose. Let's save the dress for special times like the next time we visit our friends. You looked so pretty tonight. Even your little boyfriend liked it."

She gave a full belly laugh. "Hank's not my boyfriend. He's old."

Mami winked, making her giggle again. "Old! Hardly. Maybe he's too young to be your boyfriend. But someday, you'll both grow up. The difference between three and seven isn't so much. He plays with you so gently. Even his Mami says so. And he's an active boy, always climbing on things. Except for you, he stays still."

"But we can go to the fountain? I want to dance like those ladies dance."

Mami smiled. "Yes, we will return to the fountain, and we shall dance. Now, let's get you ready for bed."

The big yellow flower buttons were slipped from their holes, and Mami had just started to lift the dress over her head, being careful not to catch it in her hair when there was a loud banging on the door, followed by yelling. The smile vanished from Mami's face. She knelt, tugging the dress back in place. "Remember what we practiced? The hiding? You must go. Now. No sounds. Do not come out until I say."

The child wanted to cry, but there was no time. Mami shoved her into the closet. "Hide, bebe," she said in a harsh whisper. "Hide until I tell you it's okay to come out." Mami pressed the door closed with that horrible squeak that meant she couldn't easily get out on her own.

There were things on the floor that tripped her, others hanging from the rack high above her head that brushed her hair as she burrowed into the shadows. There were boxes that scratched. There were spiders…

She crawled deep inside the closet. It was so dark, and she tripped on the shoes there. She fell and scraped her knee but held in her sobs as she heard Mami and a man shouting at each other. They spoke a language she hardly ever heard, only when Mami spoke to her own Mami on the phone. Then there was a thump and a cry, and the little girl burrowed in deeper, silently slipping between the stiff plastic containers, and lay down until she was almost flat.

The closet was dark and smelled funny. It was scary, but what was happening in the other room was much worse. Mami had always had her practice hiding, but never for this long. Until that night, she'd shuddered every time she saw the door that led into darkness. Mami had even unscrewed the closet lightbulb. *"Darkness is the best way to hide,"* she'd said. *"In the far corner. Under the bags. Don't make a sound."*

"Just in case," Mami said when they'd practiced the hiding. Mami had always had a catch in her throat that made the little girl cling to her mother's knees. *It's a game.* But it never felt like one. The door would stick. She wasn't strong enough to open it herself.

There was more arguing. She heard her name, and then Mami said, "You'll never get your hands on her." There was a loud thud as if someone had fallen.

"Where is she? Tell me."

Another thud and another cry. "No. NO! Don't!"

There was a short scream and then silence.

The child listened as hard as she could. There was movement outside. A man called her name softly. She could hear him moving about the apartment, opening doors and slamming them closed. He called to her again, angry this time, threatening her with a spanking when he found her and more if she didn't come out. But that made no sense. He couldn't punish her if he couldn't find her. No wonder Mami wanted her to hide from such a dumb man.

She covered her mouth to keep her whimper inside.

He opened the closet door, tugging it with a bad word she'd heard once, a word Mami told her never to repeat.

"Kid could never open this door. She's what, two? Marta musta stashed her with some friends. Damn it." He slammed the door hard, but it stuck, and a slit of bright light broke the darkness.

She ducked even lower.

I'm big girl three, not a baby two, she thought fiercely. *I know my letters and how to put on my own socks and shoes. I have a big girl bed.*

The man cursed again and then was silent.

The little girl crept out of her hiding space and found Mami lying on the floor, asleep. Her eyes were open, but she wasn't moving. She knelt beside Mami, then noticed there was red on her brand-new dress beside the bright orange flowers she'd been so proud of. "I didn't mean to get my new dress dirty," she sobbed as she cuddled next to Mami.

Then something else happened. It was very bright and hurt her eyes. But it was so hard to remember, and she was so very tired.

There was a commotion in the hall. More yelling and then footsteps running. A moment later, she peeked up to see Mr. Pedro poke his head into the room. The old man gasped and then crossed himself, muttering before he yelled for his wife to call the police. He retched and ran from the room.

The rest happened so fast, she could not understand it all. There were flashing lights through the windows. Big men dressed in blue came in with pointy things in their hands. They saw her and froze. They asked her questions in English and Spanish. She did her best to explain hiding, and Mami and the man yelling, and then she came out, and she couldn't remember what happened next or where the man went. They didn't seem to understand her.

They talked to one another while staring at her, and then there was a woman who came to her and wrapped her in a blanket. She spoke softly, but the little girl was tired and couldn't understand much of it.

She was hurried through the rainy night and strapped into a car seat and handed a teddy bear. There was no more talking as they drove away.

The little girl fell asleep to the rhythmic windshield wipers, awakened only when she was being taken from the car seat and handed to another woman.

She heard Mami's name mentioned and her own. She heard the name of the man Mami had screamed.

"Poor kid might have seen it all. She's not safe. Are you sure you can take her for tonight? I flashed my card but didn't tell anyone where I was taking her. No one followed me." The soft-voiced woman broke down in tears. "I know. It's unprofessional, and I might lose my job, but I can't help it. I have to keep her safe."

"I can protect her," a stern voice said.

"This kid is going to go through hell if they find her. Probably will go through hell anyway. If ever there was a kid who needed a Fairy Godmother, it's this one."

The stern woman's arms softened as she chuckled. "I guess you couldn't be any more plain spoken than that."

The little girl was hefted higher in her arms, and a gentle hand pressed her head onto a shoulder. "I'll take care of her. You know I will. I'll make sure nothing happens to this child. I know just the thing."

"We can't use her real name."

The older woman looked the child over. "Poppy. Like the flowers on her dress. We'll call her Poppy Jones." A kiss was pressed to her head. "Now, I need to wipe your memory," the stern woman said. "It won't hurt a bit."

The first woman drove off into the rainy darkness. Poppy was carried into a house, into the bathroom, where her dress was removed and whisked away. Before she knew it, there was a bubble bath waiting for her. She was scrubbed from head to toe. Moments later, she was wrapped in a towel as she sat on a stool while the woman cut her long curls until her hair was short. "We need to hide you in plain sight, Poppy Jones."

"Mami?" she asked.

"I'm sorry, child, no more Mami for you. But you have me. And there are other children here to play with."

Poppy stuck her thumb back in her mouth. Mami didn't like her to suck her thumb—that was for babies. But if Mami was no more, then Mami wouldn't mind.

She was stuffed into a soft nightgown and brought into a warm, bright kitchen, and given a glass of milk. While she drank it down dreamily, the old woman put her hands on Poppy's head and began to say words Poppy had never heard before. The room began to smell sweet, like the perfume Hank's Mami wore. The old woman stood and began to walk around the kitchen, singing a song with more strange words. She had a small stick she pulled from her scrawny bun, and everywhere the old woman pointed it, there were flowers and birds spouting from the windows and doors, bright, pretty colors that faded into the walls before she could really see them.

Moments later, Poppy was tucked into bed with another kiss to her forehead, and in the morning, she'd forgotten she'd ever lived anywhere else.

A Note from the Authoress

My Dear Reader, please forgive the rush and lack of pleasantries, and permit me to introduce myself. My name is Mrs. Florence Electra McGillicuddy. Please, allow me to give you my card:

The initials—you're sure to want to know what they mean. I know you won't believe me, at least not immediately. Trust me, I'm accustomed to that, but here goes.

FGM: Fairy Godmother.

OoC. Order of Cinderella.

L6. Level 6. That is the highest level ever achieved, and without bragging, I can honestly tell you, I am the only one of my kind to reach it.

And yes, Emeritus, as I am officially retired. Unofficially, I like to keep my hand in things. And by that, I mean I actively promote Romances to those deemed worthy of my time and talents.

I sense your doubt. You're thinking of those Fairy Godmothers you've read in Fairy Tales or seen in film and television... pure poppycock they are, with none of the depth of training my kind actually receives. We are not tiny, little magical creatures who fly around on gossamer wings. Nothing tiny about us, for one. And to the best of my knowledge, not a single one of us is winged.

Mind you, not all Fairy Godmothers follow the same path. We were once all generalists doing a little of this and a little of that to earn our keep. In recent years, and by that, I mean in the last two hundred, give or take, the world has changed so much that we've tended to specialize. I chose Romance as my life's work. Others chose caring for Wayward children. Or Medicine. Or (and I shudder to mention it) Politics. You get the picture… Each of us dedicates our lives and talents to our calling. At the end of our allotted time (and none of us know what that will be until the time comes), we will generally let one of our sisters-in-wands know that we are failing before we fade away. If we are lucky, we get to make our bequests.

It's a full life, and one that I treasure. Why, I'd no more give up my powers than… well, anything. And if I or any other magical being were to, let me just say legend has it, we would simply cease to be. That's the way it is.

And for the record, Humans could never become magical beings. Law of nature. You are what you are born to, we say.

My kind stays in touch, of course. We belong to The Fairy Godmother Guild and meet once a month at our local chapter houses. But that is neither here nor there, nor exactly pertinent to this story.

There have been a few of us, and I shudder to think about them, who simply disappeared without warning. Left their clients high and dry. Shameful that they ignored the signs and sad to think they go all alone. But I'm certain you don't wish me to bore you with the Guild's dirty laundry or sad stories.

I, on the other hand, am nowhere close to my time of fading away. My retirement— well, that's a long story I shan't bore you with right now, other than to say after a long and storied career, it was not Voluntary. However, every Cloud does have a Silver Lining. I now find myself as the Proprietress of a delightful home, a boarding house, if you will, where I accommodate Deserving Young Ladies of Reduced Means. I can house up to six at a time, all with private rooms and two shared baths. I'm comfortably set after all my years of Fairy Godmothering, so no longer need to charge for my services. Instead, I seek out young women down on their luck and invite them to live, for a nominal fee, in my home on the outskirts of our Fair City. I make it my business to stay out of their business, unless, of course, I'm invited in, and by that, I mean, if when one of them utters a heartfelt desire regarding Love and Romance, and of course, Marriage, in my presence. That's all the encouragement I need to Take Action. And by taking action, I mean that I will say a few (ahem) words, wave my wand (or a dessert fork if that's all I have handy), think a few pointed thoughts, and hey presto, we have a Charm, or a Spell, or a bit of Fairy Dust, in other words, a little of something that will encourage those already leaning toward love, to lean a little harder. You see, it doesn't work unless the parties involved are already inclined in that direction. No charm lasts more than a few months. Most Fairy Godmothers worth their salt can make one last a full year if they really put their minds to it. When the occasion warrants it, I have made one last for three, but I assure you, that is the absolute maximum you'd want an active charm. Magic lasting forever is simply a myth, so don't believe anyone who tells you otherwise. Magic is, well, magic. However perfect it is out of the gate (or the wand), you wouldn't want it to be permanent. Life changes, but alas, once cast, a charm is in no way malleable. So, from that perspective, it is a good thing they all have a short duration.

Of course, I exaggerate. It takes much more than a word or two, or speck of dust to make a meaningful relationship. Most of the work those of my ilk do is along the lines of oblique hints and gentle persuasion. Magic is always the choice of last resort. There are Rules about this. Very Pertinent Rules that were created for Very Good Reasons.

Any-who, it's a full life I lead, if not quite as busy as I once was. I do so love mentoring some of the younger Fairy Godmothers in the guild. Why, not even a week ago, one of them asked me to keep my eyes open to see if I could find her a property like my own, for she wants to start a boarding house of her own, built on the same model as mine. Lots of comfortable bedrooms, a spacious common area, and, of course, a small, private suite for herself and a room for her housekeeper, not to mention plenty of closet space. But there I go... drifting off-topic once again.

So, this story you hold in your hands... while I have been practicing my craft for eons and have put out a short story here and there, this is the first, full-length Written rendering of a Romance I curated. I do so hope there are many more to come.

Now, enough about me. You're here to read about the romance of Poppy and Hank, and a delightful tale it is. But I must remind you, the path of true love is never easy. Nor does it run in a straight path. There are always, how shall I put it, a few Obstacles to overcome, and in this instance, those obstacles are named Poppy. And Hank. In this story, there was one other of note, but I shudder to write his name too early.

Is what I do easy, you want to know? I am asked that so often. Let me ask you this, Dear Reader, if it were easy, why, anyone could concoct a romance out of thin air. And what fun would that be? In fact, I leave the easy ones to my less experienced Sisters-in-Wands. No, my dears, it takes years and years of experience to be able to formulate the perfect romance out of difficult situations that will lead to marriage and a happily-ever-after. In my case, I specialize in Particularly Happily-Ever-Afters. Guaranteed.

And so, with no further ado, let us begin to tell this tale about those two lovebirds. Let me say as we begin...

Once upon a time...

About the Author

Solange DewBerry (not her real name) would like you to believe she's a puzzle inside a conundrum inside an enigma. In reality, her mind is more like a junk drawer—a tangle of orphaned shoelaces, mysterious keys, dried up lint rollers and a slew of batteries, none of which is the size she's looking for. And an old roll of tape that she swears she threw away but keeps reappearing.

Solange lives in a small city on the eastern seaboard of North America, where she writes in a turreted room within her restored Victorian home, located on a shady, tree lined street. She shares the house with her handsome husband, two perfectly adorable and photogenic children, and a cat who has yet to appear in any of her stories.

Her superpowers are legendary and have only been enhanced since meeting her favorite Fairy Godmother, Mrs. Florence Electra McGillicuddy.

In reality, Berry Conrad, (also not her real name) lives an ordinary life in the 'burbs of central Connecticut, USA, along with her attractive husband. She has two grown children in nearby orbits, and the memory of cats and dogs and goldfish past. She writes from whichever room suits her at the moment, none of them turreted. Alas, she doesn't know any Fairy Godmothers, though if one is lurking, she'd be happy to make her acquaintance. As for the superpowers... not telling.

If you enjoyed Clark and Leigh's story, please take a moment to leave me a wonderful review, and tell all your friends what a great read it is. You can also contact me at SolangeDewBerry@gmail.com.

You're the One for Me

Berry Samuels lives a humdrum life, determined to avoid being noticed. It's easier that way. On the other hand. Berry's alter ego and writer of hot romances, Solange DewBerry, has the uncanny ability to make her characters come to life. That's rarely been a problem until she unexpectedly sets Trista and Brad, her just published hero and heroine, free. Despite her best efforts, Berry can't get her larger-than-life characters back in the pages of their book and can only watch as they traipse their way through the real world.

Maurice 'Moe' Conrad is a nice guy, eldest brother, and owner of Conrad Brothers Building. He plans to spend the next years' worth of weekends flitting a wrecked Victorian house when he meets a shy writer who sets his world on its heels. Berry may seem quiet and cute, but there's a sassy side to her he can't wait to see more of. The problem is she's got some ultra-beautiful but very weird friends who don't mind having their most intimate moments exposed for all to see. He's more than a little interested in Berry, but the last thing he wants is for everyone to know the details of his love life.

Can Berry corral the elusive Trista and Brad back into her book without Moe finding out their true nature? And just what would happen if he did?

https://www.amazon.com/Waitress-Doughnut-Shop-Solange-DewBerry-ebook/dp/B087C9BLVX/ref=sr_1_3?dchild=1&keywords=solange+dewberry&qid=1610401021&s=books&sr=1-3

Waitress in a Doughnut Shop

Here's the scoop:

Jenny Ellsworth works at The Sweet Shop, serving doughnuts and coffee. She's been in love with Joey Conrad for years. And Joey Conrad's been in love with Jenny Ellsworth for just as long. But Joey is dating someone else and can't bring himself to break up with her. It's one of his quirks that no one seems to understand but drives everyone crazy.

And then one day it seemed there was magic in the air. Or a really thick fog. Some days it's really hard to tell the difference. Into The Sweet Shop walked the most beautiful woman in the world, and just like that, Joey was dating Karma, or was he? Regardless, Jenny's heart was broken. It seemed the fog made it hard to tell truth from fiction because just days later, Jenny happened to meet Hank, a handsome knight in shining armor. He was more than willing to sweep Jenny off her feet, but she wasn't crazy for the man who was too good to be true.

And then Karma decided she wanted Hank while she waited for Joey to fall in love with her…

Needless to say, things got complicated. There were secrets, and revelations, and finally, well, you'll see.

Join Joey's sister-in-law, Berry Conrad, better known as the writer Solange DewBerry, as she tries to write her next novel, and help this fog-addled couple find true love.

https://www.amazon.com/Waitress-Doughnut-Shop-Solange-DewBerry-ebook/dp/B087C9BLVX/ref=sr_1_3?dchild=1&keywords=solange+dewberry&qid=1610401178&sr=8-3

Meetings in Moonlight

Pete Conrad is one of the good guys. A good looking man, he works hard, plays fair, wants to get married and settle down with the right woman. Except once he's found her, she changes her mind and tries to take him for everything he has.

Enter Ana.

She's the ethereally beautiful, soft spoken, innocent woman of his dreams. She's like someone right out of a novel and seems too good to be true. Which is exactly what she is.

Can true love flourish between a flesh and blood man, and the perfect woman from a nineteenth century love story?
Follow author Solange DewBerry as she tells the tale of how her brother-in-law searches for his happily-ever-after.

https://www.amazon.com/Meetings-Moonlight-Solange-DewBerry-ebook/dp/B08J2BRX4Y/ref=sr_1_1?dchild=1&keywords=solange+dewberry&qid=1610401144&sr=8-1

First We Kiss

Rhea Hansen-Chalmbers isn't having the best year of her life. She's working her tail off at her law firm, and no matter how many billable hours she has, it's not enough. She's deep in debt. Her father is in a nursing home. Now the firm is about to merge with another, far less reputable. And then she sprains her ankle at the gym.

Paul Conrad is overdue for a break. He's out of work since a run-in with a drunk driver left him with limited use of his arm. He's driving a junker, and as for women… he's staying away until he's fit or meets the right one who can come close to the one who got away.

A chance encounter at the gym reunites Rhea and Paul, childhood friends and unrequited high school crush. Things are going well until Rhea's firm demands she represents a drunk driver, the same one who nearly killed Paul.

What's more, Rhea's hiding a secret that will send Paul running from her as fast as he can.

https://www.amazon.com/First-We-Kiss-Solange-DewBerry/dp/173422763X/ref=sr_1_2?keywords=Solange+Dewberry&qid=1626306472&s=books&sr=1-2

423

No One Else Will Do

Sammy Conrad is the youngest of the Conrad brothers and has a lot to live up to. He's been in the shadows for too long, working by day and dreaming of playing music by night... when he's not dreaming of the woman who stole his heart years ago. She remains present but oh-so untouchable. Priya Kumar lives a lonely life. Her dreams were snatched away when her parents bought a Laundromat/Bar and told her she had to run it along with her wayward younger brother. She dreams of escape. Could Sammy, the handsome, hesitant man who has adored her from a distance, help? Dare she use him, or will she fall in love with him? And what will he think of her once he learns her secret?

Coming soon:

Short Stories

(Overcoming: A Short Story Anthology About Overcoming published by Mystic Canyon Publishing)

> Lady be Good at One-Nineteen Chestnut Street

www.ingramcontent.com/pod-product-compliance
Lightning Source LLC
Chambersburg PA
CBHW072254020726
47501CB00002B/265